Black Thorn, White Rose

Other Fairy Tale Anthologies
Edited by
Ellen Datlow and Terri Windling

SNOW WHITE, BLOOD RED

BLACK THORN, WHITE ROSE

EDITED ❖ BY

ELLEN DATLOW &
TERRI WINDLING

An AvoNova Book

William Morrow and Company, Inc.
New York

AVON BOOKS
A division of
The Hearst Corporation
1350 Avenue of the Americas
New York, New York 10019

Published by arrangement with the editors
Library of Congress Catalog Card Number: 94-6432
ISBN: 0-688-13713-X

Library of Congress Cataloging in Publication Data:

Black thorn, white rose / edited by Ellen Datlow and Terri Windling.
p. cm.
1. Fantastic fiction, American. 2. Fairy tales—Adaptations.
I. Datlow, Ellen. II. Windling, Terri.
PS648.F3B53 1994 94-6432
813'.0876608—dc20 CIP

First Morrow/AvoNova Printing: September 1994

Printed in the U.S.A.

ARC 10 9 8 7 6 5 4 3 2 1

To my "Segur Sisters": Ellen Steiber, Wendy Froud, Edwina Jaques, Nancy Fielder, and Barbara Warden.

T.W.

To my father, Nathan Datlow, who helped make my childhood a wonderful experience—and filmed it all—every holiday.

E.D.

Acknowledgments

We would like to thank John Douglas, Anne Groell, Merrilee Heifetz, Valerie Smith, Robert Killheffer, Tom Canty, Keith Ferrell, and Robert Gould.

Contents

Introduction

Terri Windling and Ellen Datlow

YOU HOLD IN YOUR HANDS A BOOK OF "FAIRY TALES for adults," yet you will find few fairies in these pages. The old, familiar stories handed down through the generations that have come to be known as "fairy tales" are, more accurately, tales of wonder or enchantment; they are *märchen,* to use the German term for which there is no satisfactory English equivalent. Or as J. R. R. Tolkien poetically expressed it,[1] they are stories *about* Fairy, that is *Faerie,* the realm or state in which fairies have their being.

"Faerie," continues Tolkien, "contains many things besides elves and fays, and besides dwarfs, witches, trolls, giants or dragons: it holds the sea, the sun, the moon, the sky; and the earth and all things in it: tree and bird, water and stone, wine and bread, and ourselves, mortal men, when we are enchanted."[1]

These tales, which we now think of as children's stories, were not meant in centuries past for children's ears only—or indeed, in some cases, for chil-

[1,1] In his essay "On Fairy Stories", reprinted in *Fantasists on Fantasy,* edited by Boyer and Zahorski, Avon Books, 1984.

dren's ears at all. Only in the last century have the complex, dark, sensual, or bawdy tales of the oral folk tradition been collected, edited, set down in print in the watered-down forms we are most familiar with today: filled with square-jawed princes and passive princesses and endings that are inevitably "happy ever after."

Most of us grew up with the story of Sleeping Beauty; but how many modern readers know that in the older versions of the tale the sleeping princess is awakened not by a chaste kiss but by the suckling of twin children she has given birth to, impregnated by a prince who has come and gone while she lay in "sleep as heavy as death"? How many readers know that Cinderella transformed her life of servitude not with the help of talking mice and fairy godmothers, but with the force of her anger, sharp cunning, and wits? How many know that it was Red Riding Hood's nearsighted granny who cried, "Oh my, oh my, what big teeth you have!" to the wolf, who quickly gobbled her up—and then finished off Red Riding Hood for dessert, with no convenient woodsman near to save her?

The power of *märchen,* and the reason they have endured in virtually every culture around the globe for centuries, is due to this ability to confront unflinchingly the darkness that lies outside the front door, and inside our own hearts. The old tales begin *Once upon a time* or *In a land far, far away . . . ,* yet they speak to us about our own lives here and now, using rich archetypal imagery and a language that is deceptively simple, a poetry distilled through the centuries and generations of storytellers.

To understand the transformation of the potent

older stories into the anaemic ones popular today and segregated to the children's shelves, we must look at the history of fairy tales in the last one hundred years. After the invention of the printing press gave rise to the production of novels aimed at the new middle classes, the ever-shifting pendulum of adult tastes swung toward the fashion of social realism. Magical tales, with their roots in oral narrative, became associated with the lower classes (in particular, lower-class women, hence the popular term "old wives' tales"). Yet wonder tales survived, in the nursery, the kitchen, the countryside, and other places where oral storytelling was still a valued art. The Victorians, with their romanticization of the idyll of childhood, were largely responsible for designating these "simple" tales of the "rural past" as the special province of children, women, and the childlike.

It was during the Victorian years that fairy tales began to be widely collected and published. The versions of the stories popularly known in the English language today largely come from these editions: selected, edited, and occasionally rewritten altogether by white, middle-class, Victorian men to suit the tastes of their day. Now admittedly, it is the nature of the storytelling process that each generation should leave its stamp, each storyteller add something of his or her own to flesh out the bones of the tale. But in that century this consisted all too often of pulling the teeth of the darker old tales—and in that process something of their heart and lifeblood was lost to us as well.

Sadly, the process of bowdlerization continues to this day. Contemporary readers who know only the Little Golden Books or Walt Disney musical versions of the stories now firmly associate fairy tales with childhood, to be left behind like toys outgrown on the path that leads to adult life. The late Joseph Campbell, in his brilliant works on comparative mythology, has helped us to see how seemingly archaic stories relate to and enrich a modern adult life, providing a centuries-old human heritage that we should not lose or ignore. Fairy tales, like myths, are a part of our cultural heritage passed from generation to generation, connecting us to the dreams and the fears of men and women who have gone before us.

It diminishes our culture to diminish this heritage; to replace the powerful old tales with lifeless, simplistic simulacra. Take the case of the film *Pretty Woman*, promoted with apparent sincerity as a modern day Cinderella. What makes *Pretty Woman* a fairy tale? To an audience weaned on the Disney version of the tale, it is that a poor but beautiful girl grows up to marry a wealthy and handsome prince. The "knight on the white charger" who swoops into our lives and relieves us of the need to determine our own fate is a far more pervasive ideal in our modern advertising culture than it is in traditional folktales. What has the prostitute heroine of *Pretty Woman* done to win her prince or transform her life? Precisely nothing—except to be beautiful, and to be in the right place at the right time.

That's no fairy tale. The old tales, as Gertrude Mueller Nelson has succinctly expressed it[2], are about "anguish and darkness."[2] They plunge hero-

[2,2] From *Here All Dwell Free* by Gertrude Mueller Nelson, Doubleday, 1991.

ines and heroes into the dark wood, into danger and despair and enchantment and deception, and only then offer them the tools to save themselves—tools that must be used wisely and well, for used foolishly, or ruthlessly, they will turn back on the wielder. The power in old fairy tales lies in such self-determined acts of transformation. Happy endings, where they exist, are hard won, and at a price.

In modern parlance, the term "fairy tale" is often used to mean a lie or a fanciful untruth. This describes the story of *Pretty Woman;* it lies to us by reducing our dreams to simplistic formulas that empower no one, neither those who wait for Happily Ever After to arrive on the back of a shining white horse, or those who seek it in a pretty face. By contrast, the old tales use simple language to tell stories that are not simple at all, and go to the very heart of the truth. Shakespeare understood this when he mined the ore of old tales to use in *Macbeth, The Tempest, A Midsummer Night's Dream.* Yeats and Tennyson understood this, as did Oscar Wilde, Christina Rossetti, Mark Twain, John Steinbeck, John Barth, Angela Carter, Margaret Atwood, A. S. Byatt, Gabriel García Márquez, and the many, many other diverse writers who have taken themes from the oral folk tradition and given them vivid new life.

The literary fairy tale, like the music of jazz, is an improvisation on a theme. It eschews our modern obsession with novelty, our insistence on plots that surprise on every page and ideas that have never been uttered before. Like jazz, it is best appreciated by those with an ear for the original melody on which it is based. The pleasure lies in savoring the writer's skill as she or he transforms a familiar story, bringing to it *their* own unique vision of the tale, and of the world around *them*.

The stories in this book, based on classic fairy tales, travel the world and the lands of Faerie on paths both dark and bright. As in the sister volume to this collection, *Snow White, Blood Red* (Avon Books, 1992), we've mixed stories of fantasy and horror with many more that live in the rich shadow realm that lies precisely between the two. Like the best old tales, these new stories mix light and dark in equal measure—with no guarantee which will triumph in the end and no promises of happy endings.

We begin the collection with a tale that speaks, appropriately enough, about the magic inherent in words themselves. We'll then journey from the lands of Once Upon a Time into familiar fields much closer to home. In our previous collection, we began the volume with a newly created story written in classic fairy-tale style; in this volume we will end with such a story, a bittersweet tale about transformation's price, a tale whose surface simplicity belies the archetypal complexity beneath.

Rumplestiltskin, Cinderella, Tattercoats, The Princess and the Pea . . . You'll find familiar old music here, played with skill, wit, and style by new musicians. We hope that you'll enjoy this second journey into the Wood.

—Terri Windling
Ellen Datlow

Words Like Pale Stones

Nancy Kress

We begin the anthology with a thought-provoking fairy tale about the magic of words and the power of knowledge. Here the familiar tale of "Rumplestiltskin" is re-created in a rich story that works (like the best fairy tales) on several levels: as an entertaining piece of dark fantasy and as an exploration of the nature of the creative process.

Nancy Kress is the author of six books to date, including a wonderfully quirky fantasy (her first novel) titled The Prince of Morning Bells. *She has won the Nebula Award twice, for her story "Out of All Them Bright Stars" and the novella "Beggars in Spain." Kress lives in Brockport, New York.*

Words Like Pale Stones

THE GREENWOOD GREW LESS GREEN AS WE TRAVeled west. Grasses lay flatter against the earth. Brush became skimpy. Trees withered, their bare branches like crippled arms against the sky. There were no flowers. My stolen horse, double-laden but both of us so light that the animal hardly noticed, picked his way more easily through the thinning forest. Once his hooves hit some half-buried stone and sparks struck, strange pale fire slow to die away, the light wavering over the ground as if alive. I shuddered and looked away.

But the baby watched the sparks intently, his fretful body for once still in the saddle. I could feel his sturdy little back pressed against me. He was silent, although he now has a score of words, "go" and "gimme" and "mine!" that ordinarily he uses all day long. I couldn't see his face, but I knew how his eyes would look: wide and blue and demanding, beautiful eyes under thick black lashes. His father's eyes, recognizing his great-great-grandfather's country.

It is terrible for a mother to know she is afraid of her infant son.

* * *

I could have stabbed the prince with the spindle from the spinning wheel. Not as sharp as a needle, perhaps, but it would have done. Once I had used just such a spindle on Jack Starling, the miller's son, who thought he could make free with me, the daughter of a village drunkard and a washerwoman whose boasting lies were as much a joke as her husband's nightly stagger. *I have the old blood in me. My father was a lord! My grandmother could fly to the moon!* And, finally, *My daughter Ludie is such a good spinster she can spin straw into gold!*

"Go ahead and spin me," Jack leered when he caught me alone in our hovel. His hands were hot and his breath foul. When he pushed both against my breasts, I stabbed him with the spindle, square in the belly, and he doubled over like scythed hay. The spindle revolved in a stone whorl; I bashed him over the head with that and he went down, crashing into the milk pail with a racket like the end of the world. His head wore a bloody patch, soft as pulp, for a month.

But there was no stone whorl, no milk bucket, no foul breath in the palace. Even the spinning was different. "See," he said to me, elegant in his velvets and silks, his clean teeth gleaming, and the beautiful blue eyes bright with avarice, "it's a spinning wheel. Have you ever seen one before?"

"No," I said, my voice sounding high and squeaky, not at all my own. Straw covered the floor, rose to the ceiling in bales, choked the air with chaff.

"They're new," he said. "From the east." He lounged against the door, and no straw clung to his doublet or knee breeches, slick with embroidery and jewels. "They spin much faster than the hand-held distaff and spindle."

"My spindle rested in a whorl. Not in my hand," I said, and somehow the words gave me courage. I looked at him straight, prince or no prince. "But, my lord, I'm afraid you've been misled. My mother . . . says things sometimes. I cannot spin straw into gold. No mortal could."

He only smiled, for of course he was not mortal. Not completely. The old blood ran somewhere in his veins, mixed but there. *Fevered and tainted,* some said. Only the glimmerings of magic were there, and glimmerings without mastery were what made the cruelty. So I had heard all my life, but I never believed it—people will, after all, say anything—until I stood with him in that windowless room, watching his smile as he lounged against the door, chaff rising like dusty gold around me.

"I think you are completely capable of spinning straw into gold," he said. "In fact, I expect you to have spun all the straw in this room into gold by morning."

"Then you expect the moon to wipe your ass!" I said, and immediately clapped my hand over my mouth. Always, *always* my mouth brings me trouble. But he only went on smiling, and it was then, for the first time, that I was afraid. Of that bright, blue-eyed smile.

"If you don't spin it all into gold," he said silkily, "I will have you killed. But if you do, I will marry you. There—that's a sweet inducement, is it not? A prince for a husband for a girl like you. And for me—a wife with a dowry of endless golden fingers."

I saw then, as if in a vision, his fingers endlessly

on *me*, and at the expression on my face his smile broadened.

"A slow death," he said, "and a painful one. But that won't happen, will it, my magical spinster? You won't let it happen?"

"I cannot spin straw into gold!" I shouted, in a perfect frenzy of loathing and fear, but he never heard me. A rat crept out from behind the bales and started across the floor. The prince's face went ashen. In a moment he was gone, whirling through the door and slamming it behind him before the rat could reach him. I heard the heavy iron bar drop into its latch on the other side, and I turned to look at the foreign spinning wheel, backed by bales to the rough beams of the ceiling.

My knees gave way and I sank down upon the straw.

There are so many slow and painful ways to die.

I don't know how long I shrank there, like some mewling and whimpering babe, visioning horrors no babe ever thought of. But when I came back to myself, the rat was still nosing at the door, trying to squeeze underneath. It should have fit; not even our village rats are so thin and mangy. On hands and knees, I scuttled to join the rat. Side by side we poked at the bottom of the door, the sides, the hinges.

It was all fast and tight. Not even a flea could have escaped.

Next I wormed behind the bales of straw, feeling every inch of the walls. They were stone, and there were no chinks, no spaces made rotten by damp or moss. This angered me. Why should the palace be the only sound stone dwelling in the entire damp-eaten village? Even Jack Starling's father's mill had weak stones, damn his crumbling grindstone and his scurrilous soul.

The ceiling beams were strong wood, holding up stronger, without cracks.

There were no windows, only light from candles in stone sconces.

The stone floor held no hidden trapdoors, nor any place to pry up the stone to make a tunnel.

I turned to the spinning wheel. Under other circumstances I might have found it a pretty thing, of polished wood. When I touched the wheel, it spun freely, revolving the spindle much faster than even I, the best spinster in the village, could have done. With such a thing, I could have spun thread seven times as fast. I could have become prosperous, bought a new thatch roof for our leaky cottage, a proper bed for my sodden father . . .

The rat still crouched by the door, watching me.

I fitted straw into the distaff. Who knew—the spinning wheel itself was from some foreign place. "From the east," he'd said. Maybe the magic of the Old Ones dwelt there, too, as well as in the west. Maybe the foreign wheel could spin straw. Maybe it could even spin the stuff into gold. How would I, the daughter of a drunkard and a lying braggart, know any different?

I pushed the polished wheel. It revolved the spindle, and the straw was pulled forward from the distaff, under my twisting fingers, toward the spindle. The straw, straw still, broke and fell to the floor in a powder of chaff.

I tried again. And again. The shining wheel became covered with sticky bits of straw, obscuring its brightness. The straw fell to the stone floor. It would not even wind once around the spindle.

I screamed and kicked the spinning wheel. It fell over, hard. There was the sound of splintering wood. "By God's blood," I shouted at the cursed thing, "damn you for a demon!"

"If it were demonic, it would do you more good," a voice said quietly.

I whirled around. By the door sat the rat. He was a rat no longer but a short, ratty-faced man, thin and starved-looking and very young, dressed in rags. I looked at his eyes, pale brown and filmy, like the floating colors in dreams, and I knew immediately that I was in the presence of one of the Old Ones.

Strangely, I felt no fear. He was so puny, and so pale. I could have broken his arm with one hand. He wasn't even as old as I was, despite the downy stubble on his chin—a boy, who had been a rat.

What danger could there be in magic that could not even free itself from a locked room?

"You're not afraid," he said in that same quiet voice, and if I *had* been, the fear would have left me then. He smiled, the saddest and most humble smile I have ever seen. It curved his skinny mouth, but it never touched the washed-out brown of his eyes. "You're a bold girl."

"Like my mam," I said bitterly, before I knew I was going to. "Bold in misfortune." Except, of course, that it wasn't *her* who would die a slow and painful death, the lying bitch.

"I think we can help each other," he said, and at that I laughed out loud. I shudder now, to remember it. I laughed aloud at one of the Old Ones! What stupidities we commit from ignorance!

He gave me again that pitiful wraith of a smile. "Do you know, Ludie, what happens when art progresses?"

I had no idea what we were talking about. Art? Did he mean magic arts? And how did he know my name? A little cold prickle started in my liver, and I knew I wouldn't laugh at him again.

"Yes, magic arts, too," he said in his quiet voice, "although I was referring to something else. Painting. Sculpture. Poetry. Even tapestry—everything made of words and colors. You don't weave tapestry, do you, Ludie?"

He knew I did not. Only ladies wove tapestries. I flushed, thinking he was mocking me.

"Art starts out simple. Pale. True to what is real. Like stone statues of the human body, or verse chanted by firelight. Pale, pale stone. Pale as straw. Simple words, that name what is true. Designs in natural wool, the color of rams' horns. Then, as time goes on, the design becomes more elaborate. The colors brighter. The story twisted to fit rhyme, or symbol, or somebody else's power. Finally, the designs are so elaborate, so twisted with motion, and the colors so feverish—look at me, Ludie—that the original, the real as it exists in nature, looks puny and withered. The original has lost all power to move us, replaced by a hectic simulacrum that bears only a tainted relation to what is real. The corruption is complete."

He leaned forward. "The magic arts are like that, too, Ludie. The Old Ones, our blood diluted by marriage with men, are like that now. Powerless in our bone-real paleness, our simple-real words."

I didn't have the faintest idea what he was talking

about. His skin was so pasty; maybe a brain pox lay upon him. Men didn't talk like that, nor boys either. Nor rats. But I wanted to say something to cheer him. He had made me forget for a few minutes what awaited me in the morning.

"A slow and painful death" . . . the rack? The red-hot pincers? The Iron Maiden? Suddenly dizzy, I put my head between my knees.

"All you have to do," the Old One said in his thin voice, "is get me out. Of this room, of the palace, of the courtyard gate."

I didn't answer. *A slow and painful death . . .*

"Just that," he said. "No more. We can no longer do it for ourselves. Not with all this hectic . . . all this bright . . ." I heard him move wearily across the floor, and then the spinning wheel being righted. After a long moment, it whirred.

I raised my head. The wheel was whole, with no break in the shining wood. The boy sat before it on a bale of straw, his ashen face sad as Good Friday. From under his fingers, winding around the spindle turning in its wheel-driven whorl, wound skein after skein of feverishly bright gold thread.

Toward morning, I slept, stretched out on the hard stone floor. I couldn't help it. Sleep took me like a drug. When I woke, there was not so much as a speck of chaff left in the room. The gold lay in tightly wound skeins, masses and masses of them, brighter than the sun. The boy's face was so ashen I thought he must surely faint. His arms and legs trembled. He crouched as far away from the gold as possible, and kept his eyes averted.

"There will be no place for me to hide," he said,

his voice as bone-pale as his face. "The first thing they will do is paw through the gold. And I . . . have not even corrupted power . . . left." With that, he fell over, and a skinny rat lay, insensible, on the stone floor.

I lifted it gingerly and hid it in my apron. On the other side of the door, the bar lifted. The great door swung slowly on its hinges. He stood there, in turquoise silk and garish yellow velvet, his bright blue eyes under their thick lashes wide with disbelief. The disbelief changed to greed, terrible to watch, like flesh that has been merely infected turning dark with gangrene. He looked at me, walked over to finger the gold, looked at me again.

He smiled.

I tried to run away before the wedding. I should have known it would be impossible. Even smuggling out the rat was so hard I first despaired of it. Leaving the room was easy enough, and even leaving the palace to walk in the walled garden set aside for princesses, but getting to the courtyard gate proved impossible. In the end I bribed a page to carry the rat in a cloth-wrapped bundle over the drawbridge and into the woods, and I know he did so, because the child returned with a frightened look and handed me a single stone, pale and simple as bone. There was no other message. There didn't need to be.

But when I tried to escape myself, I couldn't. There were guards, pages, ladies, even when I went to bed or answered the call of nature. God's blood, but the rich were poor in privacy!

Everywhere, everyone wore the brightest of colors

in the most luxurious of fabrics. Jade, scarlet, canary, flame, crimson. Silks, velvets, brocades. Diamonds and emeralds and rubies and bloodstones, lying like vivid wounds on necks brilliant with powder and rouge. And all the corridors of the palace twisted, crusted with carving in a thousand grotesque shapes of birds and animals and faces that never were.

I asked to see the prince alone, and I came at him with a bread knife, a ridiculous thing for bread, its hilt tortured with scrollwork and fevered with paint. He was fast for so big a man; I missed him and he easily disarmed me. I waited then for a beating or worse, but all he did was laugh lazily and wind his hands in my tangled hair, which I refused to have dyed or dressed.

"A little demon, are you? I could learn to like that . . ." He forced his lips on mine and I wasn't strong enough to break free. When he released me, I spat in his face.

"Let me leave here! I lied! I can't spin gold into straw—I never could! The Old Ones did it for me!"

"Certainly they did," he said, smiling, "they always help peasants with none of their blood." But a tiny line furrowed his forehead.

That afternoon a procession entered my room. The prince, his chancellor, two men carrying a spinning wheel, one carrying a bale of straw. My heart skittered in my chest.

"Now," he said. "Do it again. Here. Now."

The men thrust me toward the wheel, pushed me onto a footstool slick with canary silk. I looked at the spinning wheel.

There are so many different kinds of deaths. More than I had known just days ago.

I fitted the straw onto the distaff. I pushed the wheel. The spindle revolved in its whorl. Under my twisting fingers, the straw turned to gold.

" 'An Old One,' " mocked my bridegroom. "Yes, most certainly. An Old One spun it for you."

I had dropped the distaff as if it were on fire. "Yes," I gasped, "*yes* . . . I can't do this, I don't know how . . ."

The chancellor had eagerly scooped up the brief skein of gold. He fingered it, and his hot eyes grew hotter.

"Don't you even know," the prince said, still amused, disdaining to notice the actual gold now that he was assured of it, "that the Old Ones will do nothing for you unless you know the words of their true names? Or unless you have something they want. And how could *you*, as stinking when I found you as a pig trough, have anything they wanted? Or ever hope to know their true names?"

"Do you?" I shot back, because I thought it would hurt him, thought it would make him stop smiling. But it didn't, and I saw all at once that he did know their true names, and that it must have been this that gave his great-great-grandfather power over them for the first time. True names.

"I don't like 'Ludie,' " he said. "It's a peasant name. I think I shall call you 'Goldianna.' "

"Do it and I'll shove a poker up your ass!" I yelled. But he only smiled.

The morning of the wedding I refused to get out of bed, refused to put on the crimson-and-gold wedding dress, refused to speak at all. Let him try to marry me bedridden, naked, and dumb!

Three men came to hold me down. A woman

forced a liquid, warm and tasting of pungent herbs, down my throat. When I again came to myself, at nightfall, I was standing beside a bed vast as a cottage, crusted with carvings as a barnacled ship. I wore the crimson wedding gown, with bone stays that forced my breasts up, my waist in, my ass out, my neck high. Seventeen yards of jeweled cloth flowed around my feet. On my finger was a ring so heavy I could hardly lift my hand.

The prince smiled and reached for me, and he was still stronger, in his corrupted and feverish power, than I.

The night before my son was born, I had a dream. I lay again on the stone floor, chaff choking the air, and a figure bent over me. Spindly arms, long ratty face . . . the boy took me in his arms and raised my shift, and I half stirred and opened my legs. Afterward, I slept again to the whirring of the spinning wheel.

I woke to sharp pain in my belly. The pain traveled around to the small of my back, and there it stayed until I thought I should break in two. But I didn't shriek. I bit my tongue to keep from crying out, and when the pain had passed I called to the nearest of my ladies, asleep in my chamber, "Send for the midwife!"

She rose, rubbing her eyes, and her hand felt first for the ornate jewels in which she slept every night, for fear of their being stolen. Only when she found they were safe did she mutter sleepily, "Yes, Your Grace," and yawn hugely. The inside of her mouth was red as a wound.

The next pain struck.

All through that long morning, I was kept from screaming by my dream. It curled inside me, pale and wispy as woodland mist in the morning. If . . . maybe . . . God's blood, let it be true! Let the baby be born small, and thin, and wan as clean milk, let him look at me with eyes filmy as clouds . . .

Near the end, the prince came. He stood only inches inside the door, a handkerchief over his mouth against the stench of blood and sweat. The handkerchief was embroidered with gold and magenta threads. Above it his face gleamed brightly, flushed with hope and disgust.

I bit through my lip, and pushed, and the hairy head slid from between my legs. Another push, and he was out. The midwife lifted him, still attached to his bloody tether, and gave a cry of triumph. The prince nodded and hastily left, clutching his handkerchief. The midwife laid my son, wailing, on my belly.

He had a luxuriant head of thick bright hair, and lush black eyelashes. His fat cheeks were red, his eyes a brilliant, hectic blue.

I felt the dream slide away from me, insubstantial as smoke, and for the first time that morning I screamed—in fury, in despair, in the unwanted love I already felt for the vivid child wriggling on my belly, who had tethered me to the palace with cords as bloody and strong as the one that still held him between my legs.

I walked wearily down the palace corridor to the spinning room. My son toddled beside me. The chancellor met me outside the door, trailing his clerks and pages. "No spinning today, Your Grace."

"No spinning?" There was always spinning. The baby always came with me, playing with skeins of gold, tearing them into tiny bits, while I spun. Always.

The chancellor's eyes wouldn't meet mine. His stiff jeweled headdress towered two feet in the air, a miniature palace. "The Treasury has enough gold."

"Enough gold?" I sounded like a mocking-bird, with no words of my own. The chancellor stiffened and swept away, the train of his gown glittering behind. The others followed, except for one courtier, who seemed careful not to touch me or look at me.

"There . . . is a woman," he whispered.

"A woman? What woman?" I said, and then I recognized him. He had grown taller in three years, broader. But I had still the stone he gave me the day he carried the stricken rat beyond the courtyard gate.

"A peasant woman in the east. Who is said to be able to spin straw into diamonds."

He was gone, his rich velvets trembling. I thought of all the gold stacked in the palace—skeins and skeins of it, filling room after room, sewn into garment after garment, used for curtain pulls and fish nets and finally even to tie up the feet of the chickens for roasting. The gold thread emerged blackened and charred from the ovens, but there was always so much more. And more. And more.

Diamonds were very rare.

Carefully I took the hand of my son. The law was clear—he was the heir. And the raising of him was mine. As long as I lived. Or he did.

My son looked up at me. His name was Dirk, but I thought he had another name as well. A true name, that I had never been allowed to hear. I couldn't prove this.

"Come, Dirk," I said, as steadily as I could. "We'll go play in the garden."

He thrust out his lip. "Mama spin!"

"No, dearest, not today. No spinning today."

He threw himself full length on the floor. "Mama spin!"

One thing my mother, damn her lying soul, had never permitted was tantrums. *"No."*

The baby sprang up. His intense blue eyes glittered. With a wild yell he rushed at me, and too late I saw that his chubby fist clutched a miniature knife, garish with jewels, twisted with carving. He thrust it at my belly.

I gasped and pulled it free—there was not much blood, the aim of a two-year-old is not good. Dirk screamed and hit me with his little fists. His gold-shod feet kicked me. I tried to grab him, but it was like holding a wild thing. No one came—*no one,* although I am usually surrounded by so many bodies I can hardly breathe. Finally I caught his two arms in one hand and his two flailing legs in the other. He stopped screaming and glared at me with such intensity, such hatred in his bright blue eyes, that I staggered against the wall. A carved gargoyle pressed into my back. We stayed like that, both of us pinned.

"Dirk," I whispered, "what is your true name?"

They write things down. All of them, all things. Births, deaths, recipes, letters, battles, buyings and sellings, sizes, stories—none of them can remember anything without writing it down, maybe because all of it is so endlessly complicated. Or maybe because they take pride in their handwriting, which is also complicated: swooping dense curlicues traced in black or gold or scarlet. They write everything down, and sometimes the ladies embroider what has been written down on sleeves or doublets or arras. Then the stonemasons carve what has been embroidered into designs across a lintel or mantel or font. Even the cook pipes stylized letters in marzipan across cakes and candies. They fill their bellies with their frantic writing.

Somewhere in all this was Dirk's true name. I didn't know how much time I had. Around a turn of the privy stairs I had overheard two ladies whisper that the girl who could spin straw into diamonds had already been captured and was imprisoned in a caravan traveling toward the palace.

I couldn't read. But I could remember. Even shapes, even of curlicued letters. But which curlicues were important? There were so many, so much excess corrupting the true.

The day after the privy stairs, the prince came to me. His blue eyes were cold. "You are not raising Dirk properly. The law says you cannot be replaced as his mother . . . unless, of course, you should happen to die."

I kept my voice steady. "In what way have I failed Dirk?"

He didn't mention the screaming, the knives, the cruelty. Last week Dirk cut the finger off a peasant child. Dirk's father merely smiled. Instead, the prince said, "He has been seen playing with rats. Those are filthy animals; they carry disease."

My heart leaped. Rats. Sometimes, in the hour just

before dawn, I had the dream again. Even if it wasn't true, I was always glad to have it. The rat-boy bending over me, and the baby with pale, quiet eyes.

The prince said, "Don't let it happen again." He strode away, magnificent in gold-embroidered leather like a gilded cow.

I found Dirk and took him to the walled garden. Nothing. We searched my chambers, Dirk puzzled but not yet angry. Nothing. The nobility have always taken great care to exterminate rats.

But in the stable, where the groom lay drunk on his pallet, were holes in the wall, and droppings, and the thin sour smell of rodent.

For days I caught rats. I brought each to my room hidden in the ugly-rich folds of my gown, barred the door, and let the rat loose. There was no one to see us; since the rumors of the girl who can spin diamonds, I was very often left alone. Each rat sniffed the entire room, searching for a way out. There was none. Hours later, each rat was still a rat.

Dirk watched warily, his bright blue eyes darting and cold.

On the sixth day, I woke to find a pale, long-nosed girl sitting quietly on the floor. She watched me from unsurprised eyes that were the simplest and oldest things I'd ever seen.

I climbed down from my high bed, clutching my nightshift around me. I sat on the floor facing her, nose-to-nose. In his trundle Dirk whimpered.

"Listen to me, Old One. I know what you are, and what you need. I can get you out of the palace." For the first time, I wondered why they came into the palace at all. "No one will see you. But in return you must tell me two things. The true name of my son. And of one other: one like yourself, a boy who was here three years ago, who was carried out by a page because he taught a washerwoman's daughter to spin straw into gold."

"Your mother is dead," the rat-girl said calmly. "She died a fortnight ago, of fire in the belly."

"Good riddance," I said harshly. "Will you do as I ask? In exchange for your freedom?"

The rat-girl didn't change expression. "Your son's true name would do you no good. The blood is so hectic, so tainted"—she twitched her nose in contempt—"that it would give you no power over him. *They* keep the old names just for ritual."

Ritual. One more gaudy emptiness in place of the real thing. One more hope gone. "Then just tell me the name of the Old One who taught me to spin gold!"

"I would sooner die," she said.

And then I said it. Spare me, God, I said it, unthinking of anything but my own need: "Do it or you will die a slow and painful death."

The rat-girl didn't answer. She looked at me with bone-white understanding in her pale eyes.

I staggered to my feet and left the room.

It was as if I couldn't see; I stumbled blindly toward my husband's Council Chamber. This, then, was how it happened. You spun enough straw into gold, and the power to do that did not change you. But when that power was threatened, weakened by circumstance—*that* changed you. You turned cruel, to protect not what you had, but what you might not have.

For the first time, I understood why my mother lied.

The prince was at his desk, surrounded by his councillors. I swept in, the only one in the room whose clothes were not embroidered with threads of gold. He looked up coldly.

"This girl who can spin diamonds," I said. "When does she arrive?"

He scowled. The councillors all became very busy with papers and quills. "Escort the princess from the Council Chamber," my prince said. "She isn't feeling well."

Three guards sprang forward. Their armor cover was woven of gold thread.

I couldn't find the young page of three years ago, who at any rate was a page no longer. But in the stable I found the stablemaster's boy, a slim youth about my height, dressed in plain, warm clothing he probably thought was rags. "In my chamber, there is a rat. If you come with me I will give it to you wrapped in a cloth. You will take it through the courtyard gate and into the forest. I will watch you do this from the highest tower. When you're done, I'll give you doublet and hose and slippers all embroidered with skeins of gold."

His eyes shone with greed, and his color flushed high.

"If you kill the rat, I'll know. I have ways to know," I told him, lying.

"I wouldn't do that," he said, lying.

He didn't. I know because when he came to my chambers from the forest, he was shaken and almost pale. He handed me a stone, clean and smooth and light as a single word. He didn't look at me.

But nonetheless he took the gold-embroidered clothes.

That night, I woke from the old dream. It was just before dawn. The two pale stones lay side by side on my crimson-and-gold coverlet, and on each was writing, the letters not curlicued and ornate but simple straight lines that soothed the mind, eased it, like lying on warm rock in the elemental sunshine.

I couldn't read them. It didn't matter. I knew what they said. The words were in my mind, my breath, my bone, as if they had always been there. As they had: *rampel,* the real; *stillskin,* with quiet skin.

The forest disappeared, copse by copse, tree by tree. The ground rose, and Dirk and I rode over low hills covered with grass. I dismounted and touched some stalks. It was tough-fibered, low, dull green. The kind of grass you can scythe but never kill off, not even by burning.

Beyond the hills the forest resumed, the trees squat but thick-bodied, moss growing at their base, fungus on their sides. They looked as if they had been there forever. Sometimes pale fire moved over the ground, as no-colored as mist but with a dull glow, looking very old. I shuddered; fire should not be old. This was not a place for the daughter of a washerwoman. Dirk squirmed and fretted in front of me on the saddle.

"You're going to learn, Dirk," I said to him. "To be still. To know the power of quiet. To portion your words and your makings to what is real."

As my mother had not. Nor the prince, nor his councillors, nor anyone but the rat-boy and rat-girl, who, I now knew, crept back into the corrupted palace because the Old Ones didn't ever let go of what was theirs. Nor claim what was not. To do either would be to name the real as unreal.

Dirk couldn't have understood me, but he twisted to scowl at me. His dark brows rushed together. His vivid blue eyes under thick dark lashes blinked furiously.

"In the real, first design is the power, Dirk."

And when I finished those words he was there, sitting quietly on a gnarled root, his pale eyes steady. "No," he said. "We don't teach children with fevered and corrupted blood."

For just a second I clutched Dirk to me. I didn't want to give him up, not even to his own good. He was better off with me, I was his mother, I could hide him and teach him, work for him, cheat and steal and lie for him . . .

I couldn't save my son. I had no powers but the tiny, disposable ones, like turning straw into gold.

"This time you will teach such a child," I said.

"I will not." The Old One rose. Pale fire sprang around him, rising from the solid earth. Dirk whimpered.

"Yes, you will," I said, and closed my eyes against what I was about to do: Become less real myself. Less powerful. For Dirk. "I can force you to take him. *Rampel stillskin* is your name."

The Old One looked at me, sadness in his pale eyes. Then Dirk was no longer in my arms. He stood on the ground beside the boy, already quieter, his fidgeting gone. The pale fire moved up from the ground and onto my fingers, charring them to stumps. A vision burned in my head. I screamed, but only from pain: Dirk was saved, and I didn't care that I would never spin again, nor that every gold thread in the kingdom had suddenly become stone, pale, and smooth and ordinary as a true word.

Stronger Than Time

Patricia C. Wrede

Patricia C. Wrede has an enormous and devoted readership of both children and adults for her charming, magical fantasy novels including Raven's Wing, Mairelon the Magician, The Seven Towers, The Harp of Imach Thysell, Snow White and Rose Red *(based on the fairy tale of the same name), and many others.* Talking to Dragons *and the other books of her* Enchanted Forest Chronicles *are particular favorites with children across the country. Wrede lives in Minneapolis, Minnesota.*

In "Stronger Than Time" Wrede visits Sleeping Beauty's tower in a bittersweet tale of witchery and devotion, told in the simple timeless prose of the best old fairy tales.

Stronger Than Time

THE KEEP ROSE HIGH ABOVE THE RING OF BRUSH AND briars choking the once-clear lawn around its base. Even when the sun was high, the tower's shadow lay cold and dark on the twisted mass of thorns, and at dusk it stretched like a gnarled black finger across the forest and up the mountainside. Arven hated walking through that somber dimness, though it was the shortest way home. Whenever he could, he swung wide around the far side of the keep to stay clear of its shadow. Most people avoided the keep altogether, but Arven found its sunlit face fascinating. The light colored the stone according to the time of day and the shifting of the seasons, now milk white and shining, now tinged with autumn gold or rosy with reflected sunset, now a grim winter grey. The shadowed side was always black and ominous.

Once, when he was a young man and foolish (he had thought himself brave then, of course), Arven had dressed in his soft wool breeches and the fine linen shirt his mother had embroidered for him, and gone to the very edge of the briars. He had searched all along the sunlit side of the keep for an opening, a path, a place where the briars grew less thickly, but he had found nothing. Reluctantly, he had circled to the shadowed side. Looking back toward the light he had just quitted, he had seen white bones dangling inside the hedge, invisible from any other angle: human bones entwined with briars. There were more bones among the shadows, bones that shivered in the wind, and leaned toward him, frightening him until he ran away. He had never told anyone about it, not even Una, but he still had nightmares in which weather-bleached bones hung swaying in the wind. Ever since, he had avoided the shadow of the keep if he could.

Sometimes, however, he miscalculated the time it would take to fell and trim a tree, and then he had to take the short way or else arrive home long after the sun was down. He felt like a fool, hurrying through the shadows, glancing up now and again at the keep looming above him, and when he reached his cottage he was always in a bad temper. So he was not in the best of humors when, one autumn evening after such a trip, he found a young man in a voluminous cloak and a wide-brimmed hat sitting on his doorstep in the grey dusk, waiting.

"Who are you?" Arven growled, hefting his ax to show that his white hair was evidence of mere age and not infirmity.

"A traveler," the man said softly without moving. His voice was tired, bone tired, and Arven wondered suddenly whether he was older than he appeared. Twilight could be more than kind to a man or woman approaching middle age; Arven had known those who could pass, at twilight, for ten or fifteen fewer years than what the midwife attested to.

"Why are you here?" Arven demanded. "The road to Prenshow is six miles to the east. There's nothing to bring a traveler up on this mountain."

"Except the keep," said the man in the same soft tone.

Arven took an involuntary step backward, raising his ax as if to ward off a threat. "I have nothing to do with the keep. Go back where you came from. Leave honest men to their work and the keep to crumble."

The man climbed slowly to his feet. "Please," he said, his voice full of desperation. "Please, listen to me. Don't send me away. You're the only one left."

No, I was mistaken, Arven thought. *He's no more than twenty, whatever the shadows hint. Such intensity belongs only to the young.* "What do you mean?"

"No one else will talk about the keep. I need—I need to know more about it. You live on the mountain; the keep is less than half a mile away. Surely you can tell me something."

"I can only tell you to stay away from it, lad." Arven set his ax against the wall and looked at the youth, who was now a grey blur in the deepening shadows. "It's a cursed place."

"I know." The words were almost too faint to catch, even in the evening stillness. "I've . . . studied the subject. Someone has to break the curse, or it will go on and on and . . . Tell me about the keep. Please. You're the only one who might help me."

Arven shook his head. "I won't help you kill yourself. Didn't your studies teach you about the men who've died up there? The briars are full of bones. Don't add yours to the collection."

The youth raised his chin. "They all went alone,

didn't they? Alone, and in daylight, and so the thorns killed them. I know better than that."

"You want to go up to the keep at *night*?" A chill ran down Arven's spine, and he stared into the darkness, willing his eyes to penetrate it and show him the expression on the other's face.

"At night, with you. It's the only way left to break the curse."

"You're mad." But something stirred within Arven, a longing for adventure he had thought buried with Una and the worn-out rags of the embroidered linen shirt he had worn on their wedding day. The image of the keep, shining golden in the autumn sun, rose temptingly in his mind. He shook his head to drive away the memories, and pushed open the door of his cottage.

"Wait!" said the stranger. "I shouldn't have said that, I know, but at least let me explain."

Arven hesitated. There was no harm in listening, and perhaps he could talk the young fool out of his suicidal resolve. "Very well. Come in."

The young man held back. "I'd rather talk here."

"Indoors, or not at all," Arven growled, regretting his momentary sympathy. "I'm an old man, and I want my dinner and a fire and something warm to drink."

"An old man?" The other's voice was startled, and not a little dismayed. "You can't be! It didn't take that long—" He stepped forward and peered at Arven, and the outline of his shoulders sagged. "I've been a fool. I won't trouble you further, sir."

"My name is Arven." Now that the younger man was turning to go, he felt a perverse desire to keep him there. "It's a long walk down the mountain.

Come in and share my meal, and tell me your story. I like a good tale."

"I wouldn't call it a good one," the young man said, but he turned back and followed Arven into the cottage.

Inside, he stood uneasily beside the door while Arven lit the fire and got out the cider and some bread and cheese. Una had always had something warm ready when Arven came in from the mountain, a savory stew or thick soup when times were good, a vegetable pottage when things were lean, but since her death he had grown accustomed to a small, simple meal of an evening. The young man did not appear to notice or care until Arven set a second mug of warm cider rather too emphatically on the table and said, "Your story, scholar?"

The young man shivered like a sleepwalker awakened abruptly from his dreams. "I'm not a scholar."

"Then what are you?"

The man looked away. "Nothing, now. Once I was a prince."

That explained the world-weariness in his voice, Arven thought. He'd been raised to rule and then lost all chance of doing so before he'd even begun. Probably not long ago, either, or the boy would have begun to forget his despair and plan for a new life, instead of making foolish gestures like attempting the keep. Arven wondered whether it had been war or revolution that had cost the young prince his kingdom. In these perilous times, it could have been either; the result was the same.

"Sit down, then, Your Highness, and tell me your tale," Arven said in a gentler tone.

"My tale isn't important. It's the keep—"

"The keep's tale, then," Arven interrupted with a trace of impatience.

The prince only nodded, as if Arven's irritability could not touch him. "It's not so much the story of the keep as of the counts who lived there. They were stubborn men, all of them, and none so stubborn as the last. Well, it takes a stubborn man to insult a witch-woman—even if he was unaware, as some have claimed—and then refuse to apologize for the offense."

Without conscious thought, Arven's fingers curled into the sign against evil. "The count did that? No wonder the keep is cursed!"

The prince flinched. "Not the keep, but what is within it."

"What?" Arven frowned and rubbed the back of his neck. Trust a nobleman to make hash of things instead of telling a simple, straightforward tale. "Go on."

"You see, the count's meeting with the witch-woman occurred at his daughter's christening, and the infant suffered as much or more than the father from the witch-woman's spell of revenge. Before the assembled guests, the witch declared that the girl would be the last of the count's line, for he would get no more children and his daughter would die of the pricking of a spindle before she turned sixteen. When the guards ran up, the witch laughed at them and vanished before they could lay hands on her.

"The count made fun of the curse at first, until he found that half of it at least was true. His daughter was the only child he would ever have. Then he raged like a wild man, but it did him no good. So he became wary of the second half of the curse, more because he did not wish his line to end than out of love for the girl.

"He was too stubborn to take her away, where the witch's power might not have reached. For seven generations, his father's fathers had lived in the keep, and he would not be driven away from it, nor allow his daughter to be raised anywhere else. Instead, he swore to defeat the curse on his own ground. He ordered every spindle in the castle burnt and banished spinners and weavers from his lands. Then he forbade his daughter to wander more than a bow shot from the outer wall. He thought that he had beaten the witch, for how could his daughter die of the pricking of a spindle in a keep where there were none?

"The count's lady wife was not so sanguine. She knew something of magic, and she doubted that the count's precautions would save her child. So she set herself to unravel the doom the witch had woven, pitting her love for her daughter against the witch-woman's spite."

"Love against death," Arven murmured.

"What was that?" the prince asked, plainly startled.

"It's something my wife used to say," Arven answered. His eyes prickled and he looked away, half out of embarrassment at being so openly sentimental, half out of a desire to cherish Una's memory in private.

"Oh?" The prince's voice prodded gently.

"She said that time and death are the greatest enemies all of us must face, and the only weapon stronger than they are is love." Arven thought of the grave behind the cottage, with its carpet of daisies and the awkward wooden marker he had made himself. He had always meant to have the stonemason carve a proper headstone, but he had never done it. Wood and flowers were better, somehow. Una would have laughed at the crooked marker, and hugged him, and insisted on keeping it because he had made it for her, and the flowers—she had loved flowers. The shadows by the wall wavered and blurred, and Arven rubbed the back of his hand across his eyes. Love might be stronger than death or time, but it had won him neither peace nor acceptance, even after five long years.

"Your wife was a wise woman," the prince said softly.

"Yes." Arven did not trust his voice for more than the one short word. The prince seemed to understand, for he went on with his story without waiting for Arven to ask.

"The countess was not skilled enough to undo the witch's curse completely, but she found a way to alter it. Instead of death, the prick of the spindle would cast her daughter into an enchanted sleep, never changing. The witch's curse would turn outward, protecting the girl for one hundred years by killing anyone who sought to enter her resting place. One hundred years to the day after the onset of the spell, a man would come, a prince or knight of great nobility, who could pass through the magical barriers without harm. His kiss would break the spell forever, and the girl would awake as if she had slept but a single night instead of a hundred years."

"And meanwhile men would die trying to get to her," Arven said, thinking of bones among briars. "It was a cruel thing to do."

"I doubt that the countess was thinking of anything but her daughter," the prince said uncomfortably.

"Nobles seldom think beyond their own concerns," Arven said. The prince looked down. Arven took pity on him, and added, "Well, it's a fault that's common enough in poor folk, too. Go on."

"There isn't much more to the story," the prince said. "Somehow, on the eve of her sixteenth birthday, the girl found a spindle and pricked her finger, setting the curse in motion. That was over a hundred years ago, and ever since, men have been dying in the attempt to break it."

"*Over* a hundred years? You said the curse would last a hundred years to the day."

"That's why I need your help." The prince leaned forward earnestly. "The curse was only supposed to last for a hundred years, but the countess wasn't as skilled in magic as she thought she was, and mixing spells is a delicate business. She was too specific about the means of breaking the curse, and now there is no way I can do it alone."

"Too specific?"

"She tied the ending of the curse to a precise day and the coming of a particular man. It would have worked well enough, if the right prince had been a steadier sort, but he was . . . impetuous." The prince looked down once more. "He arrived a day too soon, and died in the thorns."

"And thus the curse goes on." *The young are so impatient,* Arven thought, *and it costs them so much.* "How do you know all this?"

"He was . . . a member of my family," the prince replied.

"Ah. And you feel you should put his error right?"

"I must." The prince raised his head, and even in the flickering firelight, naked longing was plain upon his face. "No one else can, and if the curse is not broken, more men will die and the countess's daughter will remain trapped in the spell, neither dead nor alive, while the castle crumbles around her."

"I thought the girl would come into it somewhere," Arven muttered, but the image touched him nonetheless. He and Una had never had a child, though they had wanted one. Sixteen—she would have been full of life and yearning for things she could not name. He had known children cut off at such an age by disease or accident, and he had grieved with their parents over the tragedy of their loss, but now even the cruelest of those deaths seemed clean and almost right compared to this unnatural suspension. He shuddered and took a long pull at his mug. The cider had gone cold. "How do you hope to break the curse, if the right time and the right man both have come and gone?"

"I've studied this spell for a long time," the prince replied. "Two men can succeed where one must fail."

"How?" Arven insisted.

"The curse is really two spells muddled together. A single man, if he knew enough of magic, might hold it back for a few hours, but he couldn't clear a path through the briars at the same time. Sooner or later, his spell would falter and the thorns would kill him. With two men—"

"One can work the spell and the other can clear the path," Arven finished. He gave the prince a long, steady look. "You didn't really come looking for me to get information about the keep."

"No." The prince returned the look, unashamed. "But you wouldn't have listened if I'd begun by saying I wanted you to help me get inside."

"True enough." Arven considered. "Why at night?"

"I can only work the spell then."

Arven glanced sharply at the prince's face. He knew the sound of a half-truth, and that had been one. Still, there had been truth in it, and if the prince had additional reasons for choosing night over day, they could only strengthen his argument. Arven realized with wry humor that it did not matter any longer. He had made up his mind; all that remained was to nerve himself to act. That being so, hesitation would be a meaningless waste of time. He looked down and saw with surprise that his plate was empty; he had finished the bread and cheese without noticing, as they talked. He drained his mug and set it aside, then rose. "We'd best be on our way. Half a mile is a far distance, in the dark and uphill."

The prince's eyes widened. He stared at Arven for a long moment, then bowed his head. "Thank you," he said, and though the words were soft, they held a world of meaning and intensity. Again Arven wondered why this was so important to the younger man, but it made no real difference now. Whether the prince was trying to make up for the loss of his kingdom, or had become infatuated with the sleeping girl of his imagination, or truly wanted to repair the harm his unnamed uncle or cousin had done, Arven had agreed to help him.

"You take the lantern," Arven said, turning to lift it down from the peg beside the door.

"No," the prince said. As Arven looked back in surprise, he added a little too quickly, "I need to . . . prepare my mind while we walk. For the spell."

"Thinking won't keep you from a fall," Arven said, irritated. "There's no moon tonight."

The prince only looked at him. After a moment, Arven gave up. He took the lantern down, filled and lit it, and carried it outside himself. He was half-inclined to tell the young prince to go on alone, but each time the words rose in his mouth he bit them back. He shifted the lantern to his left hand and picked up his ax, then glanced back toward the door. The prince was standing on the step.

Arven jerked his head to indicate the direction of the keep, then turned and set off without waiting to see whether the prince followed him or not. If the prince wanted a share of the lantern light, let him hurry; if not, it would only be justice if he tripped and rolled halfway down the mountain in the dark.

Thirty feet from the cottage, with the familiar breeze teasing the first fallen leaves and whispering among the beeches and the spruce, Arven's annoyance began to fade. It was not the prince's fault that he was young, nor that he was noble-born and therefore almost certainly unaware of the perils of a mountain forest at night. Arven paused and looked back, intending to wait or even go back a little way if necessary.

The prince was right behind him, a dim, indistinct figure against the darker shapes of the trees. Arven blinked in surprise, and his opinion of the young man rose. Prince or not, he could move like a cat in the woods. Arven nodded in recognition and acceptance of the other man's skill, and turned back to the trail. He was annoyed at having been inveigled into misjudging the prince, but at the same time he was grateful not to have to play the shepherd for an untutored companion.

The walk up to the keep seemed to take longer than usual. The prince stayed a few steps behind, moving so quietly that Arven glanced back more than once to assure himself that his companion was still there. Mindful of the prince's comment about preparation, Arven did not try to speak to him.

At the edge of the briars, Arven halted. Though the keep was all but invisible in the darkness, he could feel its presence, a massive pile of stone almost indistinguishable from the mountain peaks, save that it was nearer and more menacing. "What now?" he asked as the prince came up beside him.

"Put out the light."

With more than a little misgiving, Arven did so. In the dim starlight, the briars reminded him of a tangle of sleeping snakes. Frowning, he untied the thongs and stripped the leather cover from his ax, feeling foolish because he had not done so before he put out the light. A breath of wind went past, not strong enough to ripple the prince's cloak but more than enough to remind Arven of the clammy fear-sweat on the back of his neck. *I'm too old for this,* he thought.

"Hold out your ax," the prince said.

Again, Arven did as he was told. The prince extended his hands, one on either side of the blade, not quite touching the steel. He murmured something, and a crackle of blue lightning sprang from his hands and ran in a net of thin, bright, crooked lines across the ax blade.

Arven jumped backward, dropping the ax. The light vanished, leaving a blinding afterimage that hid the ax, the briars, and the prince completely. Arven muttered a curse and rubbed at his eyes. When the dazzle began to clear, he bent and felt carefully across the ground for his ax. When he found it, he picked it up and slid a slow finger along the flat of the ax head toward the cutting edge, brushing off leaves and checking for nicks. Only when he was sure the ax was in good order did he say, "Your Highness?"

"I'm sorry," the prince's voice said out of the night. "I should have warned you."

"Yes."

"It will help with the briars."

"It had better." Arven wiped one hand down his side, then transferred the ax to it and wiped the other. "What else do you have to do?"

"I will restrain the thorns so that they will not harm you while you cut a path through them. I must warn you; I can only affect a small area. Beyond that, the briars will remain . . . active. The sight may be disturbing."

"This whole venture is disturbing," Arven grumbled. "Very well, I'm warned."

"One other thing: do not look back until you reach the castle gate. Your concentration is as important as mine; if you are distracted, we may both be lost."

"You're a cheerful one." Arven paused. "Are you sure you want to do this? I'm an old man . . . " *And you are young, with a long life, perhaps, if you leave this lunacy undone,* he thought, but did not say, because it was the same advice his elders had given him when he was young. The prince would probably pay as much attention to it as Arven had, which was none at all.

"You're the only one who would come with me," the prince said, misinterpreting Arven's question and confirming his opinion at the same time.

"You've about as much tact as you have sense," Arven said under his breath. He twisted the ax handle between his hands, feeling the smooth wood slide against his palms, and his fear melted away. He had worked these woods all his life; he knew the moods of the mountain in all times and seasons, and the moods of the keep as well; he had cut every kind of tree and cleared every kind of brush the forest had to offer, over and over. This was no different, really. He turned to face the briars, and said over his shoulder, "Tell me when you are ready."

"Go," said the prince's voice softly, and Arven swung his ax high, stepped forward, and brought it down in a whistling arc to land with a dull, unerring thump an inch above the base of the first briar.

The stems were old and tough, and as thick as Arven's forearm. He struck again, and again, and then his muscles caught the familiar rhythm of the work. A wind rose as he hacked and chopped and tossed aside. A corner of his mind listened intently for the warning creak of a tree about to fall in his direction, but otherwise he ignored the growing tempest.

All around, the briars shifted and began to thrash as the wind ripped their ends from their customary tangle to strike at air, straining against their roots. Where Arven stood, and for thrice the length of his ax in all directions around him, the air was calm and the briars inert. The only motion within the charmed circle was the rise and fall of his arm and the shifting of the cut stems as he pushed them aside. The sounds of the wind and the thrashing briars were clear but faint, as if they came from outside the walls of a sturdy house. The thud of his ax, the rustle of the briars as he passed, and the crunch of his boots against the mountainside were, in contrast, clear and precise, like the sound of Una's singing in a quiet room. Dreamlike, Arven glided onward, moving surely despite the gloom. His ax, too, never missed a stroke, though as the keep drew nearer, the night thickened until the faint light of the stars no longer penetrated its blackness.

Arven had no idea how long he spent carving his path through the snarl of briars. His arms grew tired, but his strokes never lost their rhythm and his steps never faltered. Even when he came to the ditch that surrounded the castle, three man-heights deep and nearly as wide, and so steep-sided that a mountain goat might have had difficulty with the climb, his progress slowed only a little. The briars grew more sparsely in the thin soil that veiled the rocky sides of the ditch, and now and again Arven left a stem in place, to catch at his sleeves and the back of his coat and help keep him from slipping.

He reached the bottom of the ditch at last and paused to catch his breath. He could feel the keep looming above him and hear the rushing wind and the thrashing of the briars, though he could see none of them. He wondered what would happen if he lost his direction, and was suddenly glad of the ditch. It was a landmark that could not be mistaken, even in such blackness; if he climbed the wrong side, his mistake would be obvious as soon as he got to the top, and he would only have to retrace his steps.

"Go on," the prince's voice whispered in his ear.

Arven jumped, having all but forgotten the other's presence. There was exhaustion in that voice, a deeper exhaustion by far than the world-weary undertone it had had when Arven first heard it, and in his concern he almost turned to offer the prince his arm. Just in time, he remembered the prince's warning.

"Put your hand through my belt," Arven said, forgetting his own fatigue. "We've a climb ahead, and you'll keep up better if I tow you a way."

The prince did not answer. Arven waited, but he felt no tug at his belt. "Stubborn young fool," he muttered. Holding back the briars must be more tiring than the prince had expected. Arven tried not to think of what would happen if the prince's magic failed before they got to the keep. Well, if the prince was too proud to admit he needed help, Arven had better finish his part of the business as quickly as he could. He raised his ax and started forward once more.

Climbing out of the ditch took even longer than climbing into it had done. Arven's weariness had taken firm hold on him during the brief rest, and his arms were nearly too tired to swing his ax. His back ached and his legs felt as if his boots were weighted with lead. He let himself sink into a kind of daze, repeating the same movements over and over without thinking.

The jolt of his ax striking unyielding stone instead of wood brought Arven out of his trance. He cursed himself for a fool; that stroke had blunted the ax for certain. He probed for a moment with the flat of the blade and realized abruptly that this was no random protruding rock. He had arrived at the outer wall of the keep.

Arven felt along the wall a few feet in both directions, but found no sign of a gate or door. The briars grew only to within two feet of the wall, leaving a narrow path along the top of the ditch. Without looking back, he called an explanation to the prince, then turned left and started sunwise around the keep, one hand on the wall.

He had not gone far when the wall bulged outward. He followed the curve, and as he came around the far side he felt the ground smooth out beneath his feet. The wind that whipped the briars ceased as though a door had been shut on it, and silence fell with shocking suddenness. A moment later, the prince said, "This is the gate. We can rest here for a few minutes, if you like."

Arven looked over his shoulder. The night seemed less dense now; he could just make out the prince's silhouette, charcoal grey against midnight blackness. He stood squarely in the center of an arched opening through which Arven had passed without noticing. Though the prince's voice was more tired than ever, Arven could see no trace of weariness in his stance.

"What else must we face?" Arven asked, leaning against the crumbling wall.

"Only finding the count's daughter and waking her," the prince said. "Whatever is left in the keep is not dangerous, though it may be unpleasant."

"Then there's no point in lingering," Arven said.

"Light the lantern, and we'll start looking for the girl."

There was a long pause. "I didn't bring the lantern."

"Young idiot," Arven said without heat. He should have thought to mention it; he was old enough to know better than to rely on an untutored and romantically inclined youth to think of practical matters. He smiled. He was old enough to know better than to try and penetrate the briars around the keep, too, but here he was. "I suppose we could just wait for dawn."

"No!" The prince took a quick step, as if he would shove Arven on by main force. "I can't—I mean, I don't—"

Knowing that the prince could not see him, Arven let his smile grow broader. "Well enough," he said, trying to keep the smile from showing in his voice. "I can understand why you'd be eager to have this finished. But while we look for your girl, keep an eye out for a torch or a lamp or something. I've no mind to come this far just to break a leg on the stairs for lack of light."

"As you wish," the prince said. "Are you rested?"

Arven laughed. "As much as I'm likely to be." He pushed himself away from the wall and started off. He kept one hand on the stone as he walked, feeling the texture change as he passed under the supporting arches. Despite his care, he stumbled and nearly fell a moment later. When he felt for the obstruction that had tripped him, he found a well-rotted stump of wood leaning against a heavy iron bar—all that was left of the first door. With a shrug, he rose and entered the outer bailey.

As he did, something brushed his face. He jerked and swiped at it one-handed, and found himself holding a handful of leaves.

"Ivy," said the prince from behind him, and Arven jumped again. "It's not the climbing sort; it grows in the cracks between the stones above, and hangs down."

"I know the plant," Arven said shortly. He threw the leaves away and looked up. A few yards ahead, the curved sides of the inner gatehouse rose dizzily above him and flattened briefly into the inner wall before bulging out into the round corner towers. This close, the gatehouse blotted out the shapes of the mountains. Its dark surface was broken only by the darker slots of the arrow loops and a few irregular clumps of ivy, swaying gently.

Arven blinked and realized that the darkness was fading. He could see the stars behind the towers, and there was a faint, pale haze in the sky that hinted at the coming of dawn in an hour or two. Somewhere a bird chirped sleepily.

"We must hurry," the prince said. "Come." He started for the twin towers of the inner gatehouse, and Arven followed. His part in this adventure might be over, but he had earned the right to see the end of it.

"There is work for your ax here," the prince called from the tunnel that led between the towers to the inner part of the keep.

Arven snorted at himself and quickened his step. When he reached the prince's side, the difficulty was clear. The first portcullis was down, but closer examination showed that the iron bands had rusted and sprung apart and the wooden grate was all askew and rotten besides. A few careful ax strokes cleared the way with ease. The second portcullis, at the far end of the tunnellike entrance, had fallen and jammed partway. Arven ducked under the spikes and stepped out into the inner bailey.

Another bird chirped from somewhere on the wall above his head, and another. Arven had never understood why birds insisted on chattering at each other from the moment the night sky began to lighten. Surely dawn was early enough! He turned to point out the perversity of birds to the prince, and did not see him.

"Your Highness?"

"Here." The prince waved from the door of the gatehouse. "There are candles."

"Good." The door was half-ajar. Arven shoved it wide and peered in, then recoiled. Two skeletons lay sprawled across the table in the center of the room, white bones protruding from rotting shreds of livery. Arven looked reproachfully at the prince. "You might have warned me."

"I didn't think." The prince sounded as much worried as apologetic. "They are only dead, after all."

"Next time, get the candles yourself, then," Arven snapped. He went in and retrieved two fat, stubby candles and a rusty iron holder, fixed one of the candles in place, and lit it with some difficulty.

The prince was waiting for him in the bailey. "The count's daughter will be somewhere in the great hall, I think," he said, pointing. "I . . . expect there will be more such as those."

"Dead men, you mean."

The prince nodded. "The spell—the curse—should have protected the whole of the keep, but it has gone on too long. I doubt there is anyone living, except the girl."

"Let's find her, then, and leave this place to the ghosts."

The prince winced, then nodded again. "As you say. Lead on."

"I?"

"You have the light."

Arven shot a glare at the prince, though he knew the effect would be lost in the darkness. There was nothing he could say to such a reasonable request, however, so he did as the prince had suggested.

The door to the great hall was made of solid oak planks, a little weathered but still more than serviceable. It took most of Arven's remaining strength to wrestle it open. He threw another glare in the prince's direction; the man couldn't be any more tired than Arven, no matter how wearing magic was. The prince did not seem to notice.

Inside, the main room was eerily still. On the far side, the window glass had shattered, letting in starlight and the small noises of wind and birds. Closer by, long tables filled the center of the room and the candlelight struck glints from gold and silver plate. Around the tables, and sometimes over them, lay a collection of black, shapeless figures. A faint, sweetish odor of decay hung in the air, and Arven grimaced. He skirted the edge of the room, avoiding the tables and taking care to shield the candle so that he would not see the details of the anonymous forms.

"There will be stairs in the corner," the prince said.

Arven found them: a narrow stone spiral built into the wall of the keep itself. He started up, his shoulders brushing the wall on one side and the central pillar on the other. The steps were as steep as the rocks of the upper mountain, and the climb was awkward. More than once, Arven wished he could lean forward a few inches more and climb on all fours, as if he were going up a ladder or scaling a cliff. He wondered whether castle folk ever became accustomed to the tight, circular ascent. Did they think no more of it than Arven did of shinning up a tree to cut away an inconvenient branch that might affect its fall? The prince, at least, did not seem bothered.

Around and around they went, passing one door after another, until Arven lost track of how far they had come. At each door, Arven stopped to ask, "This one?" Each time, the prince shook his head and they went on. Finally, they reached the top of the stairs. This time, Arven pushed the door open without asking; there was, after all, no other place to go.

He found himself in a narrow hall. "The far end," the prince said, and Arven went on. He found a door and pushed it open, and stopped, staring.

The chamber was small and cluttered. Broken boards leaned against one wall, some carved, others plain. A stool with a broken leg was propped on a circular washtub; next to it was a chair with only one arm. A stack of table trestles filled one corner, and a pile of rolled-up rugs and tapestries took up another. Old rope hung in dusty loops from a peg beside the window, and the window ledge was full of dented pewter and cracked pottery.

The center of the room had been cleared in haste by someone unconcerned with niceties of order. In the middle of the open space stood a broken spinning wheel. One leg was missing and two of the spokes were broken; the treadle dangled on a bent wire and the driving cord was gone. Only the spindle shone bright and sharp and new. Beside the spinning wheel, a girl lay in a crumpled heap, one hand stretched out as if to catch herself and a tumbled mass of black hair hiding her face.

Arven set the candle holder on top of the stack of table trestles and bent over the girl. Gently, he slid an arm under her. His work-roughened fingers caught on the heavy, old-fashioned brocade of her dress as he lifted her and turned her shoulders so that he could see her face.

She was beautiful. He had expected that; noblemen's daughters were nearly always beautiful, protected as they were from the ravages of sun and illness and general hardship. But he had not expected to find such determination in the pointed pixy chin, or such character in the fine bones of her face. Arven tore his eyes away and turned to the prince.

The prince stood in the doorway, watching the girl with such love and longing that Arven almost averted his eyes to keep from intruding on what should be private. "Well?" Arven said gruffly.

"Kiss her," said the prince, and looked away.

Arven stared, astonished. "Do it yourself. That's why you came, surely."

"I can't." The prince's voice was hardly more than a whisper.

"Can't? What do you—" Arven broke off as the prince raised his hand and stretched it toward the candle. Suddenly the pieces came together and Arven knew, even before he saw the candle gleaming through the translucent flesh, even before he watched the prince's hand grasp the holder and pass through it without touching. *No wonder he would not carry the lantern,* Arven thought, *no wonder he could only work the spell at night,* and marveled that he could be so calm.

"Please, it's almost dawn," the prince said. He gestured toward the window. The sky beyond was visibly paler. "Kiss her and break the curse, so that I can see the end of this before I must go." His eyes were on the girl's face again, and this time Arven did look away.

"Please," the prince repeated after a moment.

Arven nodded without looking up. Awkwardly, he bent and kissed the girl full on the lips.

For a long moment, nothing seemed to happen. Then there was a grinding sound from somewhere below, and a loud crash, and the girl heaved a sigh. Her eyelids flickered, then opened. As she looked at Arven, an expression of puzzlement crossed her face. She sat up, and glanced around, and saw the prince. Their eyes locked, and she stiffened, and Arven knew that, somehow, she understood.

"Thank you," the girl said.

"Thank him," said the prince. "He broke the curse. I did nothing."

Arven made a gesture of protest that neither of them saw.

"You came back," the girl told the prince with calm certainty. "That is a great deal more than nothing."

The prince went still. "How did you know?"

"I know." She rose and brushed her skirts, then gave the prince a deep and graceful curtsey. The prince stretched out a protesting hand, and the girl smiled like sun on morning dew. "And I thank you for it."

"You should blame me. If I had done it right the first time, there would have been no need for these makeshifts."

"True." The girl's smile vanished and she looked at him gravely. "I think perhaps you owe me something after all, for that."

The prince gave her a bitter smile. "What is it you want of me, lady?"

"Wait for me."

The prince stared, uncomprehending, but Arven understood at once. It was what he had asked of Una, at the last. *Wait for me, if you can.*

"It won't be long," the girl continued. "I can feel it."

"You have a lifetime ahead of you!" the prince said.

"A lifetime can be two days long; it needs only a birth at the beginning and a death at the end." The girl smiled again, without bitterness. "By any usual reckoning, I have had more than my share of lifetimes."

"The spell . . ."

"Was unraveling. If you had not come, I should have slept another hundred years, or two, dying slowly with no company but dreams. I have learned a great deal from my dreams, but I prefer waking, if only for a week or a month."

"I see." The prince reached out as if to stroke her hair, but stopped his hand just short of its unattainable goal. Arven could see the curve of the girl's shoulder clearly through the prince's palm. He glanced at the window. The sky was lightening rapidly.

"Then, will you wait?" the girl asked again.

"I will try," said the prince. He was almost completely transparent by this time, and his voice was as faint as the distant breeze that rustled the trees outside the keep.

"Try hard," the girl said seriously.

Arven had to squint to see the prince nod, and then the sky was bright with dawn and the prince had vanished. The girl turned away, but not before Arven caught the glitter of tears in her eyes. He rose and picked up the candle, unsure of how to proceed.

"I have not thanked you, woodcutter," the girl said at last, turning. "Forgive me, and do believe I am grateful."

"It's no matter," Arven said. "I understand."

She smiled at him. "Then let us go down. It has been a long time since I have seen the dawn from the castle wall."

Somnus's Fair Maid

Ann Downer

Now we have a second, very different take on the Sleeping Beauty legend. Ann Downer's version of the classic tale mixes its familiar ingredients into a surprising new concoction—arch, mannered, and delightful in the best Regency tradition.

Although she admits to a strong penchant for Regency romances, Downer is best known as a children's book writer, the author of the novels The Spellkey, The Glass Salamander, *and* The Books of the Keepers. *She lives in Cambridge, Massachusetts.*

Somnus's Fair Maid

AT THE CRUCIAL MOMENT, THE ASSEMBLED WELL-wishers were admiring a coral-and-bells from the child's godmother and did not see the hired carriage pull up in the drive.

"My m-medical man has the most modern ideas," said Aunt Grimbledon, "and says a coral is *not* the thing for an infant, but I must say I have always thought it one of the nicest christening presents. When she is older the bells may be removed from the rattle and m-made up with the coral into a bracelet."

The new mother, Lady Pembroke, smiled and shook the rattle softly over the cradle, where little Persephone dreamed beneath a gauzy curtain. "It is a lovely present, cousin."

There was still time to hide inside the armoire and under the sofa, and avoid a great deal of future grief and inconvenience, but no one had seen the small, stooped form scuttle from the carriage into the house. Therefore, the idea of pretending to be out did not occur to them.

Without waiting to be announced, the newcomer

entered the morning room on a rustle of puce silk. On her hunched form her bonnet seemed incongruous, as though one had taken something from under a rock and dressed it in doll's clothes.

A horrified silence fell over the company. Catherine Pemberly rose to her feet, acutely aware of a terrible omission. One liked to forget Olympia Winceley, but one did so at great peril.

"Great-Aunt! But I—one thought—you always spend this month in Bath!"

Lady Olympia made straight for the gauze-draped cradle and drew aside the curtain to gaze upon the sleeping child. Her ancient visage was devoid of color and curiously unwrinkled; complex emotions quivered across its dead-white surface. Mrs. Grimbledon had an unwanted thought of blancmange.

"What have you named it?"

"Persephone Aurora Pemberly."

Lady Olympia picked up the coral-and-bells. "Charming. From my cousin Grimbledon, if I am not mistaken. Nor have I been remiss. Here is my gift: the year she is six the child shall live with me."

Since her Great-Aunt Winceley was nearly eighty, Lady Pembroke acquiesced with some relief, and saw no harm in offering the weary traveler some wine.

But Mrs. Grimbledon had glimpsed upon the surface of the blancmange an omen that took her appetite away. Declining refreshment, she sat and mused upon a Winceley family legend. When she was nine years old, the story went, Olympia had fed her infant brother a "currant" bun with a beetle in it. It seemed to Ella Grimbledon her relative was not much changed.

* * *

In the spring of 1818, when little Persephone was yet in leading strings, her mother was carried off while confined with a second child. Distracted with grief, Peregrine Pemberly, Lord Pembroke, took to lingering over the port, drifting from his club to gaming house and back. Over the course of the next five years he sank deeper and deeper in debt. To Mrs. Grimbledon's dismay, Pembroke allowed his financial distress to be eased by his late wife's great-aunt. And when Lady Olympia suggested her house in Wiltshire might provide a more seemly home for a young child, Pembroke could barely raise his head from the table to nod his assent.

Persephone had no sooner set foot in her new home when word came that her unfortunate parent had lost everything at roulette and, lost in a rosy fog of claret, had strayed into the Serpentine and drowned.

It is too bad, Mrs. Grimbledon confided in a letter to her godson. For it seems Pembroke recently altered his will, making my cousin Winceley the child's principal trustee. It is too, too unfortunate, but there it is. My own solicitor tells me there is nothing to be done.

The late Lady Pembroke had had some money of her own, and six-year-old Persephone was now an heiress with a tidy fortune of some ten thousand a year. But not a cent of it could be spent without the consent of the bank and the trustees. And the bank and the trustees agreed that the child should remain in the care of her Aunt Winceley in Wiltshire.

* * *

So dire was the aspect presented by Frome Orchy that local gossip claimed its owner kept strange rituals at night upon the Salisbury Plain. Lady Olympia was very rich, in part because she lived on next to nothing. She used only half a dozen rooms of the fifty-two in the house, kept the minimum of servants, did without a carriage, drank no wine, and ate only salt fish and potatoes, which had been good enough for her father, the Admiral. She lit no candles after dark and kept no fires between March and November. She kept no gardener, and as a result the shrubberies had grown into a maze so high in places it hid the house from view.

Upon Persephone's arrival, however, she had the morning room and library furniture uncovered and a fire lit and the Oval Bedroom aired out. A maid, Robbins, was employed for the child. A governess was also engaged, one of a string of unfortunates, few of whom stayed at Frome Orchy beyond a fortnight.

At first, young Persephone wrote to her Aunt Grimbledon to complain of her tedium and ask for books. As she received in reply neither letters nor books, at length she became discouraged and stopped writing. For her part, Mrs. Gimbledon received short letters saying how much Persephone adored the Wiltshire countryside around Frome Orchy, and that she was quite getting on with her French.

In truth, Persephone was not getting on with any of her studies. It seemed the only books in the house were memoirs of naval heroes and manuals on estate management that had belonged to Lady Olympia's father. There was, in addition, a twelve-volume set of the collected sermons of the Reverend Cuthbertson Snell, from which Persephone was required to read aloud every night after prayers.

When she could manage it, Persephone would slip away from the governess of the week to walk in the maze that had once been a knot garden, behind the house. When summer made the house unbearably close, the maze was cool and green and gave off a crushed spiciness underfoot. At its center was a broken fountain ringed by four stone seats. Here she could stretch out with the cool stone beneath her cheek, and retreat into sleep.

One day she fell asleep in the maze and slept straight through the evening meal (the vicar was coming so that, with the salt fish and potatoes, there were riced turnips and an arrowroot shape). While the butler and maids searched for her, Persephone slept on through prayers.

She awakened in the morning amazingly refreshed, and wandered into the house with the vague thought that the sun was not where it ought to have been, and with no idea that she had slept straight through to Wednesday. She was promptly pronounced impertinent, and locked in a boxroom in the old wing, a part of the house that dated to the time of Richard Lionheart.

Persephone discovered that the trunk in the boxroom had been lined with old newspapers, and by craning her neck she could read old reports of the war with France. After that, she arranged to sleep through prayers on a regular basis, though not so often that her aunt should suspect her of being ingenious. Through these punishments, Persephone managed to keep herself passing literate. As it was, she developed a view of the world in which poisonings and *crîmes passionelles* were disproportionately represented among the news of the day.

At night she lay in her narrow bed in the Oval Bedroom, imagining herself a tiny princess, asleep inside a goose egg. If she were no bigger than a mouse, she would fly away on the back of a dragonfly to the Serpentine, where her father was king of the swans.

And so the years passed, until she had been at Frome Orchy almost ten years.

A few days short of her sixteenth birthday, Persephone returned from the maze to discover that Aunt Winceley had requested her presence in the Bamboo Salon. A neat, grey woman in a neat, grey dress stood in the middle of the room. When Persephone entered, the woman curtsied.

Lady Olympia was perched upon a red-and-gold japanned chair. "This is Mrs. Hobson. She has come to make you some dresses."

Persephone's wardrobe consisted of two plain wool dresses for at-home and a bombazine best for church. Her eyes widened as Hobson spread out upon a table the most recent numbers of the ladies' magazines.

"Miss would look quite fetching, I think, in the lawn sprigged with violets."

Aunt Winceley scrutinized the color plates through the filmy lens of her lorgnette. "Let us have the best. She must appear—attractive."

Mrs. Hobson's cheek flushed a delicate pink.

"Then may I suggest Madam consider our finest Lyons silk."

Persephone felt as though, just beneath the surface of her skin, her whole body was made of fireflies. Her eyes and ears were on fire; she wanted to shout. Was she to have a London Season? Was she to see the swans on the Serpentine?

But she received no hint: Mrs. Hobson took her measurements and went away.

The next week Persephone's trusted Robbins was dismissed, and a French maid hired in her stead, on the rationale that she could dress hair. Persephone became uncomfortably familiar with new scents: damp, singed hair and French pomade.

Twice a week a dancing master came to teach her the waltz. Afterward, somewhat too lame to walk, he stayed to luncheon so Persephone might practice conversation. While this was sprinkled a little too liberally with anecdotes of London crimes, the dancing master did not seem to mind. Lady Persephone was testing her charms.

Bonnets, shawls, boots, and petticoats of every description began to rain on Frome Orchy in the form of parcels from assorted provincial merchants. As though its mistress were staging a play, new curtains and carpets appeared in the drawing and dining rooms, the crumbling plaster ceilings were restored, and a man came from London to tune the pianoforte and replace those parts of it damaged by mice.

Under these attentions, Frome Orchy began by degrees to take on the look of an abode of the living, and rumors began to be spread abroad that it housed a beauty.

Regulars at St. Ambrose-in-the-Mead in Little Devizes found they had to arrive twenty minutes early, before all the best pews were filled with dandies from London and pallid undergraduates from Oxford, who whispered behind their hymnbooks during the Doxology and cast a great many looks at Miss Pemberly.

One Corinthian was seated in a pew apart from the rest, beside an attractive matron in stylish widow's weeds.

"Ned, must you stare? You're as bad as they are. I declare I shall move my seat next Sunday."

Edward Fitzhugh, Earl of Knoyle, paid no attention to his sister. He was going to London in a month's time on extended business, and before he left he intended to acquaint himself better with his neighbors.

Mariah Robbins knocked at the front door of Number Seventy, Cheyne Walk, and stared down the butler who answered.

"I will wait in the hall," she said firmly. "I am to see Herself on private business."

Mrs. Grimbledon came downstairs swiftly for a woman of six and eighty.

"M-my good R-robbins," she said, when she had rung for refreshment and it had been brought. "Whatever has happened?"

"I have not met with Satisfaction, and have been sacked. She found me out, keeping an eye on Miss. So I thought I had better warn you, hadn't I, and not by post."

"Oh, dear." Ella Grimbledon sipped her claret and devoted some thought to the matter. At last she shook her head as if to clear her brain.

"Never mind, Robbins. You did just as you ought. It is a dreadful nuisance, but I will m-manage something. Were you given your one month's salary and references? No? Well, then, wait here, and I shall get them. And have another claret while you wait—those g-glasses are small."

Hippolyte Dunsmore was the Oxford-educated son of a Scotsman who had made an enormous fortune exporting rum from Jamaica. He was a fine-figured man of twenty-seven, elegantly if quietly turned out, his neck linen pinned with a small lapis scarab. Since leaving Balliol with a first in Greek in '24, Hippolyte had divided his year between Oxford and Egypt, where he pursued studies in the picture writing of the ancients. The ladies present at Amelia Whyte-Jones's party found something heroic in his warm complexion and dark curls; his smile, they thought, bespoke an acquaintance with the hareem.

Two gentlemen from his club found his naïve manners affected and his looks a bit too exotic to be entirely well bred. Glibb recalled some whispers about the elder Dunsmore's wife.

"Prostrated by the tropical heat, they say. Strongly advised not to have children. It's been suggested old man Dunsmore made more in Jamaica than his fortune."

Fordyce nodded, watching Hippolyte turn the pages of the eldest Miss Whyte-Jones's music. "That complexion ain't from Egypt."

To their chagrin, the usurper took Miss Whyte-Jones in to supper. They could only watch from the opposite end of the table as she became hypnotized by the brown eyes behind those damned spectacles, apparently oblivious of the danger she was in, of being abducted to a tent in Luxor by the natural son of a Scots rumrunner.

The hot weather had passed and Persephone began to detect in the Wiltshire nights a hint of tang, of autumn crispness. If she could only hurry the days, turn them like the pages of a book, then the Season, her Season, would arrive.

One morning the astonished cook took delivery from the no-less-astonished grocer of a haunch of veal, several small pullets, hothouse asparagus, pears, and champagne. That afternoon the French maid, Hortense, informed Persephone that *un gentilhomme* was coming to dine with them, and Mademoiselle was to be made *très belle, très jolie*.

Her nails were manicured, her hair dressed, and she was helped into a new gown. Persephone gave herself over to these unexpected ministrations, all the while afire with curiosity. Who was the mysterious gentleman? If it was not the vicar or her dancing master, she could not imagine who it could be, for her aunt entertained no other gentlemen except her solicitor, and Persephone suspected Mr. Halfwicket did not much care for Lady Olympia's company.

At last Hortense gave her a little, final shove toward the looking glass. Persephone glanced shyly, then stood transfixed. Before her was a fabulous creature—feminine, it seemed—dressed in a gown of cream taffeta and stiffened blond lace. The color set off her dark gold hair and grey eyes to perfection. The beret sleeves and Sévigné bodice (she had memorized the names from the copies of *Ackerman's*) drew the observer's eye from the tops of her bare shoulders and along her collarbone to what the dressmaker had modestly referred to as her *décolletage*. But most magnificent of all was her hair, a towering edifice called an Apollo knot into which Hortense had stuck tortoise combs adorned with cream silk peonies.

It could not be her. She jiggled a pinky finger; the reflection moved its finger in echo. She surreptitiously stuck out her tongue; the reflection did likewise.

"*Madame votre Grand-tante,* she wishes *Mademoiselle* to wear zeese." Hortense fastened a necklace of pearls around Persephone's throat, and matching earbobs upon her ears. Hortense spit upon her palm, coaxed one last curl into position, and sent her young mistress downstairs.

Persephone abandoned all hope as soon as she saw the visitor's back, which was vast and stooped, the back of his head ringed with a grey, greasy fringe. He held his hands behind his back in a formal, naval gesture, so before she saw his face she knew his hands—massive, gnarled, with misshapen nails.

His face, when he turned to her, was bloated and he had watery eyes, of a dark indeterminate color, like the leaden, oily sea. He had a small bow mouth, and dark liver-colored lips.

Lady Winceley stood by, glancing from her ward to her gentleman.

"Vice-Admiral Leechlow, my niece, Lady Persephone Pemberly. Lady Persephone, this is my late father's dear friend, Vice-Admiral Leechlow."

Persephone understood immediately from her aunt's look that there was to be no Season. She was to be married to the Vice-Admiral.

"Really, Fizzey, I must object. You have lured me from London on the pretext of an angling holiday in Scotland. Instead, I find myself in deepest Wiltshire, embroiled in some half-witted escapade out of a fairy story. I tell you, it's unconscionable."

Dunsmore and Edward Fitzhugh were making their way by coach to Switherlee, the ancestral home of the Earls of Knoyle. With the death of his father eighteen months previously, Fizzey had become the newest Earl of Knoyle. The two men had shared a staircase at Balliol.

"Dammit, Dunsmore, a damsel's in distress! The fish can keep. She is quite the loveliest creature I've ever laid eyes on, and the frightful old woman keeps her locked away in that stinking mausoleum of a house behind a twenty-foot hedge, as though she were the Crown Jewels."

"Haven't you found," his friend replied without removing his eyes from the book he was reading, "that the very act of making something inaccessible has the effect of doubling its market value?"

"How crassly you put it! Well, she ain't on the market quite yet. She's barely out of the schoolroom."

"Come now, Fizzey. I know from unimpeachable sources that you and two friends have a guinea wager on which of you can win this paragon."

Knoyle laughed. "Heard about that, did you? Well, for God's sake, don't let on. Unless you want in on it. Can't be a monk forever, eh?"

Dunsmore smiled and went back to his book. "It will be amusement enough to watch the three of you. Who are the others?"

"Don't think you know 'em—New College men, Fordyce and Glibb."

If Dunsmore stiffened slightly, Knoyle didn't seem to notice. "As it happens, I know them from club business. But I wonder what our hostess will think, when I arrive at her door attired for the trout stream?"

The mistress of Switherlee was Knoyle's widowed sister Helen, who welcomed them wanly from a sofa, complaining of earache.

"I've asked Mrs. Bird to put out some cold meat for you at eight. It's so beastly hot for September. But then, Mr. Dunsmore, it must make you feel quite at home. You must be used to baking like a brick."

"Yes, I suppose I am."

There was estate business requiring Knoyle's attention, so Hippolyte took his walking stick and one of the spaniels and went out with the thought of visiting some of the ancient monuments nearby.

He had crossed a stile and was making for a ring of granite plinths when he spied a figure reclining upon one of the toppled uprights. Hippolyte called the dog to heel and hurried forward.

In the shade of the great stone slabs lay a girl, ash gold curls falling from beneath her bonnet. Realizing the dog was hardly a sufficient chaperone, Hippolyte cleared his throat.

She had not been asleep after all; he saw her foot

was propped upon a rolled-up shawl. Her eyes were a curious shade of grey-green that reminded him of something, if only he could remember what. But they were eyes without light, without life.

He bowed. "I was afraid you might be in distress. I am happy to see I was mistaken."

She did not return his smile, but stared ruefully at one slippered foot. "I have wrenched my ankle in a rabbit hole. My maid and I were out walking—she has gone to fetch the carriage, and should return any moment."

"Are you in pain?"

"Yes, a bit. I shall have to soak it when I get home."

Hippolyte looked at her furrowed brow and considered the situation. There was nothing he could do for her, and it was not entirely proper for him to remain. Still, he could hardly leave her alone.

"Will you allow me to leave Nero with you? He is quite gentle and will take good care of you."

"How kind!" She cautiously stroked one of the beast's ears. "But how shall I restore him to you?"

"With your kind permission, I shall send his master for him. He is your neighbor—Lord Knoyle."

"You are Mr. Dunsmore, then. I thought you must be." For the first time her eyes lit up, and he realized what their color had reminded him of: a peculiar stone the Egyptians favored for making scarabs.

"You have the advantage of me, madam."

"I am Lady Olympia's ward, Persephone Pemberly. We live at Frome Orchy. My aunt has such a small acquaintance, I know my neighbors' visitors secondhand." She looked down at her ankle, frowning.

"The Earl has told you about me, has he? Then you must think me an incorrigible rogue, who made the life of the Balliol porter a misery."

"Oh, nothing like that."

"You are too politic by far. You would be well advised, Lady Persephone, not to believe everything the Earl tells you. And now I must take my leave, or else your maid shall overtake us, and I shall not have an excuse to call on you."

The Earl lit a cheroot and stretched his legs toward the fire. Hippolyte was reading a thin volume of Latin lyrics.

"By the way, Fiz, I've lent your spaniel to a young lady I met out walking."

"What, Nero? Dammit, Dunsmore, what nonsense are you talking? Lent him? He's my prize water dog."

"I met a young lady in distress out upon the Plain. She required a protector, so I lent her Nero. You may retrieve him anytime. He is only over at your neighbor's. I forget the name. Frilly Orchid?"

"Frome Orchy? You've lent Nero to Persephone Pemberly? Dunsmore, you are a genius. I quite take back what I said about you during our game of whist last night."

Hippolyte smiled and shut his book. "It's late, and I have a letter to write. Good night."

In his room he opened his writing case and dipped his pen. He wrote for five minutes steadily, read the letter over, and blotted it.

Switherlee
Little Devizes
Wiltshire

7 September 1830

Dearest Aunt Nell,

Thank you for your last letter, which reached me before I set off. I am safely ensconced at Fizzey's and am carrying out your assignment to the letter.

I am glad to hear my parcel arrived safely and that the pattern has met with your approval. You are sure to be the only woman in the Pump Room (in Bath itself, for that matter) attired in muslin from a Cairo bazaar. Your own birthday gift was very much appreciated. I like Catullus above all other poets.

I hope the waters are proving all your physician hoped and that you are not too much provoked by Mrs. Galpers.

Your affectionate godson,
Hippo

Nero was retrieved the next day, and Lady Olympia felt impelled to invite the gentlemen to remain for luncheon.

"I never take luncheon myself, except for some fish soup, but a midday meal is always prepared for the child."

The child looked at her feet, where Nero was gazing up at her with adoring eyes. "I believe it is cress soup and cold veal."

The Earl practically trod on his friend's foot to be the first to offer Lady Persephone his arm, so he might lead her in to luncheon. But this victory, however sweet, was short-lived.

"Lady Persephone," said Hippolyte over the cheese, "if your ankle can bear it, will you take me for a brief turn through the grounds? It has been some time since I have been able to enjoy an English garden."

Persephone replied that exercise in moderation would probably do her ankle no end of good.

Lady Olympia could think of no way to refuse the request, and the Earl, to his chagrin, was left at her elbow, discussing the relative merits of various methods of soil drainage. Persephone led Hippolyte into the unkempt tangle that passed at Frome Orchy for a garden.

"Shrubbery is somehow too mild a word," she observed as they entered the maze. In the maze, she was a different person, her speech more natural, her voice and step light, her brow and gaze less troubled. "They have rather outgrown the category. But tell me, Mr. Dunsmore, about Egypt. Or are you sick to death of being asked? Shall I narrow my question and ask whether you prefer Egypt to Jamaica?"

"Oh, Egypt. I prefer my heat dry to swampy and, if I have to pick my plague, I will take flies over mosquitoes."

She smiled. "I shall never complain of Wiltshire's plagues again."

"Do you never escape the heat, Lady Persephone? Does your Aunt take you to Bath or Cornwall?"

"Oh, no. We never desert Frome Orchy."

"Not even for London?"

"Oh, no. We do not keep a carriage, you see. When

my aunt has some business in town she hires a post chaise."

"Does she leave you in the care of a governess?"

"When we have one. We seem always to be between governesses, somehow. Unimpeded by knowledge of the conjugation of irregular French verbs, I have been able to devote myself to my watercolors."

"And what subjects do you favor?"

"Insects, for the most part. I find flowers somewhat insipid, but a wasp is lovely, if only you drug it with enough honey to make it sit still." She glanced at him in sudden alarm. "Mr. Dunsmore, are you ill?"

"You must pardon me, Lady Persephone. The maze has overwhelmed me." His head was spinning. Hippolyte suffered from claustrophobia, a fault he had taught himself to control in the tunnels of the pyramids. The greenery seemed to close in on them from all sides. He turned about in the dimness of the enclosing boxwood.

"I fear we are lost."

The sudden movement made her shift her weight to the injured foot, and in taking his arm to regain her balance, Persephone found herself inches from his shirtfront. She stood shyly where she was, enchanted to discover the pin she had taken for a scarab beetle was in fact a small lapis lazuli hippopotamus.

"No, not at all," she said. "I know the way."

When they returned, Lady Olympia and the Earl had been joined by a new visitor, Vice-Admiral Leechlow. One look told Hippolyte all he needed to know.

* * *

As they rode home, Lord Knoyle was in a sulk.

"What's wrong, Fizzey? Did the veal knuckles disagree with you?"

"That was a dirty trick, spiriting her off like that and saddling me with the old aunt to talk about drains. And all the while you were—" Fizzey broke off angrily.

"—off in the maze making love to her? Hardly. As you well know, I have scruples about such things, and besides, she is shy and young and artless."

"You were gone for three-quarters of an hour. What on earth did you find to talk about?"

"The most recent poisoning case in London, and her watercolors. She likes to paint insects from life. She has promised to show me her praying mantis and her luna moth. She collects them from the hedgerows in bottles, then puts a little ether on some cotton wool—"

The Earl gave a slight shrug of disgust. "Stop! I take your meaning. Well, what about the Vice-Admiral?"

"The aunt plainly intends to marry her off to him, for reasons I find obscure."

"Thought that too, did you? Well, something must be done about it!"

Hippolyte smiled. "Wouldn't it be a little ill mannered to toss a coin for her?"

Here Knoyle lost control of his temper briefly. "Dammit, Dunsmore, what nonsense are you talking! All I want to know is, are you going to offer for her or am I?"

"My work is my life," said Hippolyte decidedly, "and my work is in Egypt. And if that does not convince you, I have booked passage to Alexandria by way of Lisbon and Naples. The tickets are in my money case, if you don't believe me."

Knoyle relaxed against the seat back and looked out the window in silence. His face wore a sheepish, silly grin.

Dunsmore looked out his own window. *Offer for her*. How could he, when he had nothing to offer her, not fortune, not title, not even respectability? He knew perfectly well what men like Fordyce and Glibb said about him when his back was turned. Knoyle could give her the life, the position, the happiness she deserved. What manner of love would it be that would stand in her way?

Persephone lay on the floor of the uppermost boxroom and wept. He had thought her young and unschooled and slight. He had gone away without even saying good-bye, and now the Vice-Admiral was coming to dinner and Aunt had said she must wear the gown with the French bodice and she knew that he was going to speak to her aunt and her life would end before ever it had begun.

And she could not even run to the maze, because now it was no longer a refuge, but a reminder of him.

At last she dried her eyes and went down to her room and let herself be dressed. Hortense curled her hair too tightly and put on the pendant pearls that hurt her ears, and made her blot her lips with rouge. Persephone did not care. Nothing, no indignity mattered, could ever matter.

She went down to dinner and there, his hand on the pianoforte as though he should collapse without it, stood Lord Knoyle, looking flushed and bright of eye and a little sick. Lady Olympia sat nearby, her features set in a sour scowl.

Persephone suddenly understood everything, and the relief passed over her like a wave.

"Lord Knoyle," she said in a clear voice, extending her hand. "I am happier to see you than I can properly express."

The room was narrow and small, but its high ceiling gave it an illusion of spaciousness. The only window had elaborately carved shutters that opened on a Cairo street scoured white-hot by the sun. In this room Hippolyte Dunsmore was baking like a brick in a kiln. He had just finished his lunch: a peppery mutton dish the color of dried blood, and cold lentils.

The post had brought a letter. It had arrived before lunch and all through the meal Hippolyte had kept it propped in the center of the table against the salt. Now the envelope bore a water ring that partly obliterated the return address. Hippolyte wiped his table knife on a napkin and opened the letter with it.

Switherlee
Little Devizes
Wiltshire

12 October 1830

My dear Dunsmore,

Persephone is going to write to you herself but I wanted to be the first to tell you it's official: She has accepted me. Helen is being quite grand about it and plans to sponsor her coming out at Almack's this winter.

You will never guess about old Leechlow. It has all come out that he was blackmailing Lady Olympia about her father. It seems the old Admiral did a little smuggling for the Jacobites in '45. Leechlow was going to give her the damning letters in exchange for Persephone's hand. When she told him Persephone was engaged he threatened to go to the newspapers with them. The shock has quite cowed her: the doctor says she has burst a blood vessel in her brain.

Hippolyte set the letter down without finishing it. She was safe, then; everything had turned out as arranged. He put some coffee on his brazier to brew and returned to his translation of a particularly troublesome passage of Demotic Greek.

But his imagination plagued him with pictures of Persephone, her ash gold hair falling in wisps from a matron's cap, an infant in her arms and one on her knee. And, beside her, twin boys in leading strings, two gawky schoolroom girls, a tall girl in riding dress, and a son in Regimental colors.

"Poor Beauty," he thought, "shall you slumber on after all?"

He thought of life in darkest Wiltshire. He did not think there would be much to awaken her there.

And what did it matter, he said to himself angrily, what became of her? She was pretty and charming, unschooled and naïve. She would make Knoyle the perfect wife.

Six months went by, and a parcel arrived from a colleague in England, the curator of Near Eastern antiquities at the British Museum. It contained six plaster reference copies of some small funerary objects of interest to Hippolyte in his studies. These had been swaddled for their journey in cheesecloth and newspaper, a *London Gazette* from October 17, 1831.

In his current circumstances, the newspaper was by far the rarest artifact. With tender care he smoothed the crumpled sheets flat on his worktable and weighted the corners down, scanning the columns eagerly for news. Thus unprepared he blundered upon a brief item in the social column.

> Lord and Lady Wigginshins lately hosted a small dinner party at their London home in Pelham Crescent. Among the guests were Lord Knoyle and his young Countess, the charming Lady Knoyle . . .

He stared at the lines of print, as though they might re-form into a new sentence if he sat and stared at them long enough. At last he crumpled the sheet of newspaper and fed it to the brazier.

That night he tossed restlessly beneath the mosquito netting, troubled by a dream. He was lost in a green maze. Every turning led him out of its cool confines, when all he wanted was to find its center. In the morning he woke unrefreshed, as though he had not slept at all. Too much coffee, no doubt, or coffee too strong. But he called for a fresh pot of it.

From Cairo the pursuit of his studies took him to Alexandria, and from there to Tunis, Athens, and Constantinople. Persephone's letter, if she sent it, never found him.

* * *

Hippolyte Dunsmore did not return to England for five years, and then as an invalid. He had contracted a river fever; the physician pronounced it to be sleeping sickness. His finances, Hippolyte discovered, had fared no better than his health. He was obliged to accept his godmother's offer to stay in Number Seventy, Cheyne Walk.

"I rattle around in this house by myself. I would quite like a gentleman's companionship. I have had Mr. Grimbledon's old rooms made up for you. You will be quite comfortable."

So he came to her, ill and all but penniless, to begin a long recovery.

For a great time all he could do was sleep. He was very weak, and so helpless his chief struggle was against self-disgust: He could not lift his head to read for more than a quarter of an hour, and had to be fed all his meals with a spoon. When she was not feeding her patient beef tea or bread-and-milk, Mrs. Grimbledon read to him. But he grew too sick even to listen to Ovid, so she read to him from the society pages.

". . . at the dinner party of Mrs. Smythe-Jones were the Earl and Countess of Knoyle, Mr. Anthony Glibb, and Mr. George Fordyce . . ."

One day he was a little better, propped up in a chair by the bed for a change of view. She glanced up from a description of a dinner party to see him staring intently at a watercolor of a rhododendron upon the wall.

"Did you notice the beetle? Remarkably lifelike, don't you think?"

"Yes. That is Lady Persephone's work, is it not?" He could not bring himself to use her married name.

"Yes, it is. Fancy you remembering her, after all this time. Though, since you knew her, she is much changed."

"Yes, I imagine she is."

He experienced a sudden reversal and returned to bed with a dropsy fever. The physician summoned from Harley Street shook his head and prescribed bitter powders to be taken with wine. The thought occurred to Hippolyte, one night when his fever was upon him, that London might yet kill him, something Egypt had curiously failed to do.

One afternoon he was listening to his godmother read, the thin March sunshine falling upon his pillow, when Mrs. Grimbledon cleared her throat, coughing.

"Excuse me—(ahem!)—I m-must get a glass of water."

He heard her rise from the chair and set down the book. Her steps receded from the room. He wondered sleepily why she did not use the carafe by his bed, but perhaps she did not wish to drink from it because of his fever. Still, he thought, she might have rung for it. It was odd that she hadn't. He hated the way his sick brain would take a thought the way a dog takes a rag in its teeth, to worry it to death.

There was faint movement of air and a rustle of fabric, like a woman's skirts. Curtains—she must have opened a window.

Suddenly a voice began to read where Mrs. Grimbledon had left off, but it was not her voice. Confused, Hippolyte opened his eyes.

In Mrs. Grimbledon's chair sat a young woman, her ash blonde head bent over the page. She looked up and gazed at him with frank eyes that were a curious color, now grey, now green.

"Were you sleeping? Shall I turn back a page and begin again?"

He struggled to raise himself upon one elbow. In confusion, he called her by her old name. "Lady Persephone . . ."

"Please, lie back. Your nurse is a tyrant; she will have my head if she thinks I have agitated her patient." Persephone rose from the chair and drew near to smooth the coverlet and rearrange his pillows.

"But you are no longer Persephone Pemberly . . ."

"No? And who do you think I should be?" she said, smiling at him.

"Lady Knoyle."

"Ned and I discovered we did not suit—Do lie back! Let me put this pillow behind your shoulder."

"But the newspaper—"

"Oh, Ned did marry: the former Miss Smythe-Jones, who can sit a horse and does not have my morbid taste in watercolor subjects. Oh, my dear, I do not mean to tease you. You are quite right: I am no longer Persephone Pemberly, no longer the meek dormouse you knew. Aunt Grimbledon has given me a little advance upon my inheritance, to further my studies in drawing and languages."

"You read it beautifully."

She bent her golden head over his, her eyes brimming with tender feeling. "I am most uncommonly devoted to my Greek. Shall I read on?"

He laced his fingers in hers and weakly squeezed her hand. "Not now. There will be time enough tomorrow." A terrible thought occurred to him. "You will come tomorrow?" he enquired anxiously.

She smiled. "Let them try and prevent me."

"My sweet Percy . . ." he murmured, pressing her hand to his lips.

She brushed the hair from his brow with an air of triumphant possession.

"My own Hippo!"

Mrs. Grimbledon observed this tender scene discreetly from the hallway with no little satisfaction. It had for some time been her advised opinion that there was nothing wrong with her godson that could not be made right by a kiss.

"S-sleeping sickness! N-nonsense!"

The Frog King, or Iron Henry

Daniel Quinn

Daniel Quinn, who has been described as a planetary philosopher, a futurist, "just an author," and "possibly a saint," is best known as the author of Ishmael, *the novel that won the $500,000 Turner Tomorrow Award in 1991. A previous novel,* Dreamer, *was published as horror. His short fiction has appeared in* The Quarterly, Asylum, Magic Realism, The Lone Star Quarterly, *and elsewhere. Among the projects he's working on in his home in Austin, Texas, is a novel provisionally titled,* Nightfall: The Grimms' Last Tale.

Herein lies a tale in which amnesia might be a blessing and there is no happily ever after. . . .

The Frog King, or Iron Henry

WHAT IS TO BE REMEMBERED, I SUPPOSE I REMEMBER; everything else dissolves and vanishes: breath on an icy mirror.

I am alone now. There is no one. A rectangle of moonlight blazes on the floor like a shield—this is all that's left of my visitor.

Nevertheless, without any real feeling of hope, I call out into the darkness: "Iron Henry?"

His departure is something I feel in my blood, now dry as dust in my veins. Beside the window, a shadow stirs in the darkness, and it is he, slipping away into the night.

"Iron Henry," I whisper, knowing that, for all that he loves me, he will not stop for my sake: "Please."

He hesitates and mutters, "I may not."

"Speak to me more."

"It will soon be dawn," he says, "and the queen will be sighing in her bed."

"That hardly matters, Iron Henry; what little I haven't actually forgotten has become meaningless to me."

His face in the moonlight is dreadfully furrowed

and scarred; it looks like a battlefield that has been preserved as a reminder of the cruelty of war.

"You have forgotten nothing," Iron Henry says.

"I've forgotten every word, I swear it."

"I'll not tell it again, that's final."

"It's like an enchantment, Iron Henry: another enchantment, hidden beneath the first. I can't find the end to it."

"The story is held in your soul," he tells me, "and the soul has no need to remember."

He nods, as if egging me on, and I seem to see a summery gleam of yellow in his eyes; until now they have been as cold and black as the ice of a glacier.

"The golden ball," I whisper.

"You see? You haven't forgotten."

I am astonished by my own powers of recollection. "The golden ball!"

He laughs harshly and then stretches out his hands in a trembling, pathetic gesture, as if imploring me to give him something; it's a long moment before I understand what he's trying to show me.

"There was . . . a little girl?"

"A princess, my lord; start there."

"Please," I groan.

"You know the story."

"I can't hold it in my head, Iron Henry, I don't know why. Tell it to me once more, just once more, please."

Iron Henry sighs and says, "You must somehow learn to tell the story to yourself, my boy."

"My God, I swear it's gone, utterly gone!"

"Come, come," he says gently, "it has only been a moment since you yourself recounted what the princess did for you."

"What the princess did for me?"

"Think, my boy—think of what the princess did for you."

"Help me, Iron Henry!"

"The princess, my boy."

"Someone was with me, Iron Henry, that's all I remember. A young girl . . . I wasn't alone—is that it?"

"Yes, yes, go on, my boy, go on."

"Wait, I remember something else now. I was lying on the floor . . ."

"And then . . . ?"

"Yes, yes—I remember this clearly—I was lying crushed at the foot of a wall!"

"Crushed . . . ?"

"I'd been flung, crushed . . . My God, Iron Henry, I remember now—it was I, it was I, *I myself* that was flung!"

"Think now, think carefully and remember: What *actually* was flung against the wall?"

"What?"

"What thing, what *object*, was flung against the wall?"

"Against the wall . . ."

"That's right, the princess flung *something* against the wall."

"Wait—the princess was . . . angry?"

"The princess was angry and . . . what? Come, come, my boy, this is the whole point of the story."

"I swear I haven't the slightest idea what you're getting at, Iron Henry."

"You never remember this part." His voice grates with bitter exasperation. "You never remember being a frog."

"A frog? What on earth are you talking about?"

"A miserable, stinking, odious little frog, my boy. That's what you were until she finally refused to put up with it any longer. You wanted to be her pathetic and helpless little pet, hopelessly unworthy of her, a creature far, far beneath her, a creature that she was continually obliged to lift up to her level—to the chair, to the table, to the bed—a creature that was ultimately just too pitiful and paltry to be the companion of a princess."

"I'm sorry, Iron Henry. I swear to God I don't remember it."

"You wanted to become her pet. You yourself insisted on it. It was what you demanded in exchange for fetching the princess's golden ball from the bottom of the well. Don't you remember? You were asking for a reward."

"Yes, I vaguely remember . . . asking for something."

"Yes. Anything else?"

"Dark. I remember that. The water was like ice. Yes, it comes back to me now."

"You're not far off, my boy; it was a well, a deep, deep well."

"In the end, I have only a very hazy recollection of it. A shaft of emptiness—yet not empty, full."

"I understand."

"It's very shadowy, I'm afraid."

"Go on."

"What more can I say? It's an emptiness, yet I have an impression of something full. Something full . . . something else. Wait." I close my eyes for a moment. "That's right, that's it—something near the castle."

"Very well, something else . . . something nearby?"

"No, that's not it; it's something else entirely."

"Perhaps this is what you're groping for, my boy: When she became your queen and left her home for yours, the princess left behind all her playthings, including the golden ball—an object notably full and empty at the same time."

"Good Lord, Iron Henry, you've lost me entirely."

"Didn't you ever wonder what happened to this precious object, this object you went to so much trouble to retrieve?"

"No, I'm afraid I didn't."

With difficulty, he suppresses yet another impatient sigh and says, "Well, try this: it was the golden ball that started the whole thing; you must have noticed that."

"For Christ's sake, Iron Henry, give me something simple and concrete to hold on to!"

"Believe me, my boy, I've given you all there is."

"There's still something missing, Iron Henry, something I can't put my finger on. What is it, for the love of God, what is it?"

"It's nothing so important, my boy."

"What is it, Iron Henry—tell me!"

"Only a sound."

"A sound . . . ? Wait! Wait! Yes, yes—I can no longer exactly hear it, but I remember it now, I remember it clearly: a terrible sound."

"The cracking of iron bands around my heart—the bands that kept it from breaking during the long years of your enchantment. It was the end of grief, my lord."

"That's it!" I cry, clapping my hands to my ears in astonished recollection.

"It was after the wedding, and we were riding in the coach."

"Was it after the wedding? Yes, I suppose so, but, for Christ's sake, what exactly were we doing?"

"You remember, my lord: we were returning to the castle. I'd brought the coach to carry you and your bride home. It's all there. You remember it, my lord, don't upset yourself."

"Some terrible sound . . . An end to enchantment . . . An end and a new beginning—for the love of God, help me, Iron Henry, it's slipping away again! An end to enchantment . . . Some terrible sound . . ."

"You remember it, my lord, don't upset yourself. It's all there. I'd brought the coach to carry you and your bride home. You remember, my lord: we were returning to the castle."

"Yes, I suppose so, but, for Christ's sake, what exactly were we doing? Was it after the wedding?"

"It was after the wedding, and we were riding in the coach."

"That's it!" I cry, clapping my hands to my ears in astonished recollection.

"It was the end of grief, my lord. The cracking of iron bands around my heart—the bands that kept it from breaking during the long years of your enchantment."

"Yes, yes—I can no longer exactly hear it, but I remember it now, I remember it clearly: a terrible sound. Wait! Wait! A sound . . . ?"

"Only a sound."

"What is it, Iron Henry—tell me!"

"It's nothing so important, my boy."

"What is it, for the love of God, what is it? There's still something missing, Iron Henry, something I can't put my finger on."

"Believe me, my boy, I've given you all there is."

"For Christ's sake, Iron Henry, give me something simple and concrete to hold on to!"

With difficulty, he suppresses yet another impatient sigh and says, "Well, try this: it was the golden ball that started the whole thing; you must have noticed that."

"No, I'm afraid I didn't."

"Didn't you ever wonder what happened to this precious object, this object you went to so much trouble to retrieve?"

"Good Lord, Iron Henry, you've lost me entirely."

"Perhaps this is what you're groping for, my boy: When she became your queen and left her home for yours, the princess left behind all her playthings, including the golden ball—an object notably full and empty at the same time."

"No, that's not it; it's something else entirely."

"Very well, something else . . . something nearby?"

"That's right, that's it—something near the castle." I close my eyes for a moment. "Wait. Something full . . . something else. It's an emptiness, yet I have an impression of something full. What more can I say?"

"Go on."

"It's very shadowy, I'm afraid."

"I understand."

"A shaft of emptiness—yet not empty, full. In the end, I have only a very hazy recollection of it."

"You're not far off, my boy; it was a well, a deep, deep well."

"Yes, it comes back to me now. The water was like ice. I remember that. Dark."

"Yes. Anything else?"

"Yes, I vaguely remember . . . asking for something."

"You were asking for a reward. Don't you remember? It was what you demanded in exchange for fetching the princess's golden ball from the bottom of the well. You yourself insisted on it. You wanted to become her pet."

"I swear to God I don't remember it. I'm sorry, Iron Henry."

"You wanted to be her pathetic and helpless little pet, hopelessly unworthy of her, a creature far, far beneath her, a creature that she was continually obliged to lift up to her level—to the chair, to the table, to the bed—a creature that was ultimately just too pitiful and paltry to be the companion of a princess. That's what you were until she finally refused to put up with it any longer. A miserable, stinking, odious little frog, my boy."

"What on earth are you talking about? A frog?"

"You never remember being a frog." His voice grates with bitter exasperation. "You never remember this part."

"I swear I haven't the slightest idea what you're getting at, Iron Henry."

"Come, come, my boy, this is the whole point of the story. The princess was angry and . . . what?"

"Wait—the princess was . . . angry?"

"That's right, the princess flung *something* against the wall."

"Against the wall . . ."

"What thing, what *object*, was flung against the wall?"

"What?"

"Think now, think carefully and remember: What *actually* was flung against the wall?"

"My God, Iron Henry, I remember now—it was I, it was I, *I myself* that was flung! I'd been flung, crushed . . ."

"Crushed . . . ?"

"Yes, yes—I remember this clearly—I was lying crushed at the foot of a wall!"

"And then . . . ?"

"I was lying on the floor . . . Wait, I remember something else now."

"Yes, yes, go on, my boy, go on."

"I wasn't alone—is that it? A young girl . . . Someone was with me, Iron Henry, that's all I remember."

"The princess, my boy."

"Help me, Iron Henry!"

"Think, my boy—think of what the princess did for you."

"What the princess did for me?"

"Come, come," he says gently, "it has only been a moment since you yourself recounted what the princess did for you."

"My God, I swear it's gone, utterly gone!"

Iron Henry sighs and says, "You must somehow learn to tell the story to yourself, my boy."

"Tell it to me once more, just once more, please. I can't hold it in my head, Iron Henry, I don't know why."

"You know the story."

"Please," I groan.

"A princess, my lord; start there."

"There was . . . a little girl?"

He laughs harshly and then stretches out his hands in a trembling, pathetic gesture, as if imploring me to give him something; it's a long moment before I understand what he's trying to show me.

"The golden ball!" I am astonished by my own powers of recollection.

"You haven't forgotten. You see?"

"The golden ball," I whisper.

He nods, as if egging me on, and I seem to see a summery gleam of yellow in his eyes; until now they have been as cold and black as the ice of a glacier.

"The story is held in your soul," he tells me, "and the soul has no need to remember."

"I can't find the end to it. It's like an enchantment, Iron Henry: another enchantment, hidden beneath the first."

"I'll not tell it again, that's final."

"I've forgotten every word, I swear it."

"You have forgotten nothing," Iron Henry says.

His face in the moonlight is dreadfully furrowed and scarred; it looks like a battlefield that has been preserved as a reminder of the cruelty of war.

"That hardly matters, Iron Henry; what little I haven't actually forgotten has become meaningless to me."

"It will soon be dawn," he says, "and the queen will be sighing in her bed."

"Speak to me more."

He hesitates and mutters, "I may not."

"Iron Henry," I whisper, knowing that, for all that he loves me, he will not stop for my sake: "Please."

Beside the window, a shadow stirs in the darkness, and it is he, slipping away into the night. His departure is something I feel in my blood, now dry as dust in my veins.

Nevertheless, without any real feeling of hope, I call out into the darkness: "Iron Henry?"

A rectangle of moonlight blazes on the floor like a shield—this is all that's left of my visitor. There is no one. I am alone now.

What is to be remembered, I suppose I remember; everything else dissolves and vanishes: breath on an icy mirror.

Near-Beauty

M. E. Beckett

M. E. Beckett was born in 1942. He has been writing science fiction since 1991. The second of several planned virtual reality novels with Smith Flanary is under way. He is an amateur astronomer.

Here is another, lighter tale of transformation, featuring one "sleeping beauty" and one amphibian. "Near-Beauty" is science fiction.

Near-Beauty

SHE WATCHED GRISWOLD MUNCHING FOR A MOment and wondered why she still bothered to come home with him. Or to stay. Or to shower here, rather than run home to wash him off in water of her own.

"There's a three-foot frog in your shower." The only thing she liked about the man this morning was his spacious shower, where she could dance in the falling water that sprayed from two separate sources if she wished.

"Cane toad." His mouth was full of breakfast, and it came out "Caym thoeb." She looked at him, waiting. He was just as offhand, as cold, really, as when he was talking about sex. Or love.

"Cane toad," he repeated. "Don't squeeze its neck, at least not at the back of it. Poisonous. Australian."

"Okay."

Amanda Weeks was not incurious, but she asked for no explanation. Griswold, the World Traveler, understood the specimens he collected as deeply as he did people; that is to say, not at all.

"I can shower, then?"

"Yuh. Sokay."

She did, gingerly, and the creature, which she no longer saw as loathsome, she told herself—just different—watched.

And watched. She became uneasy, at last, not because it was watching, but because it looked *intent*; if that stare had come from a human, she'd have called him horny.

She walked back into the corridor, and asked, "Could it be horny?"

"They've overrun Australia; s'pose they must be," answered Griswold, wiping his mouth with the back of his hand.

"Name?" Amanda asked.

"Killer Kane of the Forbidden Planet." He didn't even crack a smile. Griswold had obviously missed the reference when he'd heard it the first time.

"Okay," she told him, turning back toward the shower. " 'Scuse me, Kane, got to finish washing." And she stepped over the beast.

"S'awright."

She stopped washing herself and looked down at the toad, which assumed the aspect of an ordinary amphibian, to the point of flicking its tongue languidly at a fly on the wall of the shower.

Amanda was a worldly girl. She did not react in any conventional way to anything.

"What's all right?"

"You."

The gentle voice was low, but not bass. Bass-baritone? It was definitely a singer's voice, and she looked with new interest at the guest, because the voice sounded *amused*, too.

"Singer?"

"Opera, mostly, but some of everything."

It began to sing. It sang the song of the Phantom, the "Softly" one, and sang it most beautifully. As it sang, it was not "it"; became "he," and someone, and she knew the day was not a total loss after all. Besides, he knew a good woman when he saw one.

She was, in fact, nearly beautiful, and had a string of past lovers to show for it, and little else. All her homely friends were married with kids, and she wondered sometimes . . .

Here she would laugh. True, sometimes she wondered, but not for long, and not too often.

She had been a skier and a dancer, then a professional photographer for a while, but had lost the urge, for now, at least, at the beginning of the War of the Moment.

She'd begun by being enthusiastic, and almost was hired by a Name paper for the duration, but had lost all interest when she realized a) she might be killed, and b) the things she would have to report on in pictures were the things her granny had told her Florence Nightingale had seen, and worked on.

"Florence Nightingale was a saintly ascetic. Who needs that shit?" was her response after painful reexamination of her basic motivation to do the work, and now she only took pictures for fun.

Still, the world was good to a nearly beautiful raven-haired woman of twenty-four, if she didn't want a conventional life.

"You're not a friend of Griswold's, then?" she asked when he was done singing.

"The stud?" He sounded horrified. "He doesn't even know I can talk."

They looked at each other for a while, and both knew that Griswold was past tense for her now.

She rolled over in bed, and phoned Griswold's home. She hadn't seen Kane since yesterday, and her interest was piqued, and peaking.

The toad answered, instead of the guy. "Good morning."

"Need to see you," she mumbled. "Lunch? Here?"

"Okay," said Kane, and hung up.

She lay back in bed, drifting a little, and wondered idly how he would negotiate the trip without a human bearer. She hadn't said to come alone, but . . . she started awake, sat up in horror, almost covering her naked body in reaction. He wouldn't bring Griswold, would he?

"Nah. Too evolved." She dozed luxuriously until the doorbell rang, then answered it as she was, certain that he was alone.

Alone, and with flowers. Again, she didn't question the mechanics of it, but it must have been more difficult than it would be for a member of the same species as the taxi driver.

"Do you speak French?" she asked, a bit alarmed at the thought of anybody this different surviving in Montreal without the language of the powerful.

"No."

"Then how did you . . . ?"

"Sang to him," and the toad chuckled. Some chuckles are expressive, some are musical, and some are just plain nervous and unpleasant.

This one was quite beautiful. Had it belonged to a human male, she'd have swooned, she told herself, and turned to tell him so.

And found him looking at her again. This time, she blushed just a little. She was, after all, only twenty-four, and had little experience of nonhuman ogling.

"So you know," he said, in a flat voice she hadn't thought he could do.

"?"

"I'm a mammal." His voice was surprised now, as if he were telling her something he *knew* she knew.

"I guess I knew."

"I'm all equipped, heat regulation, but no vestigial nipples. Penis, too. Look."

She looked where he was holding his skin away from his lower belly, and sure enough, there it was.

"Shouldn't belong to a three-footer," was all she could think of to say.

"We're different species, of course, but we speak the same body language."

He was serious, and she searched his face for some explanation, then felt foolish.

He looked up, and the sides of his mouth pulled away from the sharp teeth a little, and he sort of jerked them upward at the end of the motion. She searched her suddenly limited vocabulary for a body language translation, but could only find *rictus*, and *snarl*. Oh, and *smile*.

He smiled again, and she smiled back. Then, feeling a little more uneasy now that she had common ground with him, she asked, "Why did you come here, Kane?"

For he couldn't be *from* here, could he?

"Looking for a chick," he said, flat-voiced, and a bit like Bogart.

Come to think of it, he looked a little like Bogey,

deadpan, of course, but kind of craggy, too, and maybe a little lost.

And so she said, "Do you remember Paris?"

He looked a bit surprised, and then he said, "Of all the *braaftz* joints in all the worlds, you had to come into mine."

"Only *braaftz* joint in town, love," she said. The nontoad smiled again, and asked her to sit with him for a little, as he had something to say to her.

"I was looking for a chick, I said, and you didn't react. Is that a reaction? Should I look elsewhere, my dear?"

Now he was more like Sydney Greenstreet.

And she panicked, a little.

If Kane went away, who knew how long it would be before she met another interesting mammal? Certainly the types she knew, like Griswold, were palling, and appallingly stupid, or sometimes wicked, and treated her with far less politeness and care for her than this ugly, and oddly moving man of the world. Or worlds.

She had a friendly feeling with him. He'd share a toothbrush, at least, and likely wouldn't want her for her body.

Better check that. "Sure you don't just want to get into my pants?"

"What pants?" His right eye swiveled, and extended a bit, in the direction of her crotch.

She felt no urge to move, or hide, just to laugh.

He added, "Wrong species, anyway, Amanda. We'll have to be just friends."

And she missed his slight hesitation, the reflexive shrinking of his nonhuman body just a trifle more, and believed him.

"Then what's with the eye-waving?"

She was teasing, but he was serious. "Bug-eyed monster," he said, sadly. "Part of the image."

And she asked the question. She'd been afraid to, and was still, but she asked, "What do you want me for, Kane?"

"Carnival. We need people, and I looked for somebody like you."

She felt a little cold, and hesitated. He noticed, and waited, looking, for once, out the window, across the city, and across the river, lovely in the fog-clothes of late winter, with the ice just breaking up, a constant renewal of the mist rising from the few dark, calm open patches.

"For what, the freak show, or the girlies?"

She knew it sounded like a judgment of him, and she tried to keep the bitterness out of her voice. When you are nearly beautiful, you get handled like a very desirable mating-thing that can be treated any old way at all, because you obviously didn't make it as a model-actress, and, if you're not powerful, you must be desperate, or at least vulnerable and usable.

But he laughed.

"No, love. Pilot. We're *all* freaks to each other."

"And how will you teach me how; sleep-training?"

He was a bit cynical, now, but kind.

"No, hard work. The sleep shit is good for teaching mating skills to about seven of our species, but we need reflexes and brains for Pilot."

So she went, and became a Pilot, and now she works her way across the galaxy from star to star. Of course, she'll never see the other side, but she'll see a hell of a lot, Kane says.

She believed him. And kept on believing for two years, until they were old friends, and easy with each other, and she could ask, without fear of threatening him, and without fear at all of her own, why some of the others could mate-for-fun, and they couldn't. And then, when he'd stammered some answer in his worst Bogart, asked why he had hesitated so long in telling her. (How could she know that he, too, was almost-beautiful, and almost used-up?)

They could mate, of course, and do, now. It's a good marriage.

They joke a little about frogs and princes and nearly beautiful maidens-in-distress, and he talks about sleeping beauties.

And she always says "near-beauties," and he shuts up. She wouldn't believe him, and so he shuts up.

But he's sure she's not really nearly beautiful anymore. She left the "nearly" at home, he thinks. The crew think that, too.

And she is their Lady and their Pilot.

Ogre

Michael Kandel

Michael Kandel lives on Long Island and works as an editor in New York City. He has translated several books by Stanislaw Lem (two of them were nominated for a National Book Award). His first novel was Strange Invasion. *His second,* In Between Dragons. *His most recent science fiction novel is* Captain Jack Zodiac. *Kandel was a finalist in 1991 for the John W. Campbell Award as Best New Writer. He is at work on an extremely odd quest-fantasy entitled* In the Key of Celery.

Kandel is an expert at hilariously depicting trauma's intrusion into everyday life during which the characters remain oblivious. This deadpan tale, purportedly based on "The Yellow Dwarf," showcases Kandel's unique talent.

Ogre

"WAIT A MINUTE," I SAID—I'LL NEVER FORGET this—"are you eating *human flesh*?"

He put down the sandwich. He looked at me but didn't look at me, embarrassed. Big jaw. Big pores. Pasty complexion, always a film of sweat. Dull brown eyes always slightly out of focus.

"Well, yeah," he said. And tried to shrug.

What a pathetic Mack Truck of a guy. Will do anything to please, but hopeless to work with. Terrible coordination, for one thing. Two left feet, bull in a china shop.

I took him by his huge arm and pulled him off to a corner, so the other actors couldn't hear. No point in humiliating him. Some directors take pleasure in humiliating. Sadism. Gestapo commandants slowly grinding cigarettes into open palms while the moon glints in their soulless monocles.

Connie's like that sometimes. No, not sometimes, a lot.

"Dennis," I said, explaining, "you can't eat human flesh at a rehearsal. Let alone before a performance.

It gives you bad breath, Dennis. It's like eating, well, raw garlic, or excrement.

"I mean," I said, explaining further, as to one retarded, "suppose you say your line to the Queen, that line, 'Your only daughter, All-Fair, I am in the power of her charms.' "

"Your only daughter, All-Fair," Dennis repeated, nodding, in his cast-iron pan of a voice, which always came out too loud, with a clang, no matter what you did. At least he had no problem carrying. "I am in the power of her charms."

"And the Queen, what happens to the Queen? Staggered, Dennis. If not knocked on her royal ass." I illustrated by expelling a stream of air on power. Phhower.

"Sorry," said Dennis, and he put his sandwich (hocks? rump? tongue? I didn't want to think about it) back into the bag.

Wistfully.

His mother had probably packed it for him.

The fact is, for casts, we have to make do. So few try out, these days. No one's turned away. Even our leads—they're fine people, all of them, they work hard, but let's face it, they don't have a lot of talent. Connie can put on all the airs she likes, her grande dame British accent and her sweeping arms and tinkly Nairobi bracelets, but the fact is, we're about as amateur here as amateur gets.

With the exception of Lou, the lighting-and-sets man, who comes from the City and has actually worked on big-time musicals. God knows what he's doing in this cultural hole. Hiding from creditors? Lou says little.

"All right," I called to everyone, "break over. Back to the salt mines."

They grunted, groaned, got to their feet. We'd been at it since eight that morning. And the air-conditioning, for all its industrious chug-chug-chug, wasn't working, probably out of Freon. And the soda machine still wasn't fixed, though I'd called the company a week ago.

We took it, once again, from where the Desert Fairy appears at the nuptials shaking her crutch. Once again, feeling like a broken record, I told the townspeople, suitors, and ladies of the court: Please, fellas, listen to the other lines, don't just stand there waiting for your own.

"Listen, think, react," I said, which was Connie's refrain, but I didn't use her rigid finger-stabbing one-two-three. I realized—it hit me for the first time—that I was getting fed up with Connie. Did this mean time to quit?

"Listen, think, react, every moment you're on stage. Dave, hands out of your pockets. Into character, into character. Jane, Pam, Dennis. Where's Pam?"

A needless question. Where was Pam always, when you turned your back? Up in the costumes room trying on grandmother dresses, Gay Nineties stuff—dust, bows, flounces—and masturbating.

"Mary, could you go up and get Pam?"

We're all misfits, I guess, in the theater. Otherwise we wouldn't be here. We'd be out building things, selling things, making money, writing letters to the editor, and paying our taxes with the long form. And on that long form all the numbers in all the columns would add up right.

"Look," I told them. "This is the last week. The last week. Some of you are still shaky. Shaky, that's putting it politely. What are we going to do, team? Stay until ten? Eleven? Twelve? Carter, remember, you enter on ''Tis a Spanish cat he rides.' We changed it."

"'Tis a Spanish cat he rides."

Carter nodded, made a scribble in his script, and everyone took their positions.

They were exhausted. I was exhausted. It was hot and stuffy, and the mildew-metal smell from the air conditioner that wasn't working made you wheeze. But Connie would be back tomorrow and ready to belch scorn and sarcasm into our wincing ears.

It's interesting: when Connie really gets going with her scorn and sarcasm, her grande dame British accent disappears completely. Close your eyes, and you can see her with a kerchief on her head and cursing from a back porch in a suburb of Detroit.

The dress rehearsal was, as usual, a nightmare. The spot didn't work, it kept overheating; some gels were missing; nobody could find the basket of millet, sugar candy, and crocodile's eggs the Queen brings to get past the two hungry lions; and Dennis, for no reason, bit off Jane's hand at the wrist. A fountain of blood spurted on three of the nymphs from the stump, which Jane hysterically waved around like a flag before she fell unconscious. The nymphs screamed their fool heads off, which didn't help. Dr. Davis had to sedate them. Nice girls, but not what you'd call troupers.

And Augusta, who was supposed to understudy

for Jane, didn't know any of the Mermaid's lines. Augusta, God bless her, is not exactly a genius.

From somewhere in the darkness of the auditorium, Connie said in her drawn-out, ice-cold monotone, "Correct me if I'm wrong. This is a fairy tale we're doing, isn't it? A fairy tale, yes? Not one of those avant-garde absurdist Marat-Sade *dégringolades* with frontal nudity? Correct me if I'm wrong. This is not Beckett or Artaud or Grotowski but family entertainment we're doing, yes? Hector, you haven't pulled a fast one on me while I was away? You're not getting gonzo artsy-fartsy on me again, are you, Hector dear?"

I hate it when she uses words like *dégringolade* to be witty. I hate it when she calls me Hector dear.

"Connie," I began.

"In all my thirty years in the theater," Connie continued, and her voice now started heating up, on its long careful climb to white-hot. An old routine, that climb to white-hot. And more than half the unpleasantness is in its step-by-step premeditation.

Silently, under my breath, I sighed.

"In all my thirty years in the theater," Connie said, now that she had made the dark auditorium her stage and the bright stage her audience, "I have never, ever, seen such a pathetic, such a pathetic comedy of errors."

And so on.

Comedy of errors. Did you ever know a dress rehearsal that *wasn't* a comedy of errors? I've always thought: the greater the despair and chaos during the dress rehearsal (we can't go on, no way, tomorrow, we need another month), the better the opening night. Nine times out of ten. Yes, the director's supposed to get a little exasperated, a little disgusted. But Connie. She's so personal, so toxic. Singles out people. Makes them cry, blush, turn pale. Makes them clench their fists and tremble, under the bright lights, in front of everyone.

She had Augusta gasping.

It's awful to watch.

Like seeing a branding iron put and held, ssss, inside a person's private self.

Really, there's no call for this. We're not professionals. Augusta—she joined us the way everyone joins us, the few that do: with that shy, awed, isn't-acting-wonderful glow in the eyes. I remember her first day, when she came with Clara. She was so excited. She kept looking around and brushing back her hair.

Secretaries, teachers, museum guards, students, sign painters, housewives—all ages, sizes, and types—they come, when they come, because in the gray grind of their lives they want a touch, a thrill of something special. They come to rub shoulders with color and fame and art and temperament. They come to live for a brief, sweet hour or two in fantasy.

So Bert says all his lines like a frog-throated taxi driver. So Jimmie camps hyperqueer no matter what his part, rolling his eyes and mincing even when he's a giant vomiting fire. And Scott chews gum even when there's nothing in his mouth. And Augusta looks like a dumb bimbo even in powdered hair and dowager lace. So? We try, we work together, we do our best.

It was Dennis's turn. Dennis, the biggest and most vulnerable target among us coming under the gun of Connie now. And he was a mess already, after that bitten-off hand business.

"I'm—I'm sorry," the pitiful Mack Truck of a bastard stammered to the vast, empty auditorium.

Connie, unseen in the darkness, began turning her Gestapo screws. "If you have a *problem*, Dennis," she said, "perhaps you belong in a therapy group and not a theater group. Or perhaps"—sotto voce, but not so sotto voce, no, that we couldn't all hear it clearly—"you belong in a cage." Then cleverly modulating to a frank, businesslike tone. "We're not social workers here, Dennis. We're trying—God knows *I'm* trying—to put on a play. That's all, just a play. And this play, Dennis, already *has* a monster."

And so on.

I took him aside afterward, but it was hard to talk to him, he was so distraught. His hands shook. The sweat on his forehead glistened. His big mouth moved, as if trying to speak, to mutter, but unable. And his tormented big dull brown eyes couldn't rest on anything. You would have said, if you didn't know Dennis, that this was gross overacting.

"Look," I said, putting a hand on his shoulder, "don't take it personally."

But withdrew my hand. Remembering Jane's stump, the way it spurted like a fountain. Who knows—Dennis seemed barely in control of himself now—he might suddenly have one of his fits, go off the deep end, do a little of the rampaging that was in his nature. He was at least as strong as a gorilla. If not two or three gorillas. By the time the police came running with gas and tranquilizer dart guns, I might be half-eaten. Unrecognizable. Bits of body pulled out of the clothes, like chocolate too impatiently from its wrapper. A mangled mess on a butcher's table, all red.

I shuddered.

This was nonsense. I steeled myself, put my hand back on his shoulder. He needed a little humanity.

Yes, Dennis was ugly and he smelled and I didn't really like him. But there's just too much putting down, excluding, and rejecting nowadays. Too much feeling superior to and lording over.

People probably had been laughing at Dennis all his life. In the playground, the children must have pointed their fingers and taunted, "Ogre, ogre!"

Hell of a way to grow up.

"Come on," I said, "pull yourself together."

"I'm not a monster," he said, tight-lipped, white-lipped.

"Of course you're not. Hey, look. You know Connie. Connie does this all the time. It's the way she is. You really shouldn't take it personally."

To myself I thought: time to leave. Greener pastures. No more of this.

The Yellow Dwarf, opening night, was a fantastic success. Not an empty seat in the place. The audience loved it. Laughed when they were supposed to laugh, like when the King of the Golden Mines sees the griffin feet of the beautiful lady who is really the Desert Fairy in disguise. Or when the Princess tries but can't remove the ring of red hair from her finger after she finally agrees to choose a husband. And they applauded—minutes, whole minutes of loud, enthusiastic applause—when the Mermaid with the looking glass frees the King from the enchanted island and takes him to the Steel Castle. Cathy did her speech perfectly, not having any problem, not the slightest hitch, with the line "Fear not, this is no snare laid for you!"

And when the lovers died in each other's arms and were changed into two palm trees, their trunks intertwined, you could hear noses being blown all over the auditorium.

Even the elementary schoolers were rapt. Not a peep out of them, no shuffling of feet or rustling of programs. Their eyes were glued on the stage; their mouths hung open.

The electricity in the air—I've seen this magic take place many times—entered every actor's spine, and straightened him, and filled his lungs, and made him better by twice than he'd ever been. An incredibly new and finer and more vibrant soul. Pam? I could hear almost every word she said, when I listened standing at one of the exits in the back. Carter? It was as if he'd never been ashamed of his height or the color of his skin. Jimmie's camping was barely noticeable, almost subtle. Augusta—well, she didn't look matronly, maybe, but then she didn't look like a bimbo either. And Dennis, poor hulking Dennis, somehow, by some miracle, acquired a panache, a finesse I never would have dreamed he had in him.

His cast-iron–pan voice took on a positively noble ring when he rebuked the evil fairies for having built the mausoleum of porphyry, jasper, agate, marble, and brass.

Say what you like, there is something wonderful about live theater—about any kind of live theater. Professional or amateur, city or boondocks, it makes no difference. The theater turns us into better people, at least for a moment, each time the curtain rises and the houselights dim.

Connie called me into her office, which was next to the dressing room, where the nymphs, damsels, and sphinxes were chattering and elbowing each other away from the mirror as they took off their makeup with cold cream. She didn't ask me to close the door.

"Hector, dear"—in a confidential tone but loud enough for everyone to hear, so I knew this wouldn't be Congratulations you did a good job.

"Yes, Connie," I said.

She fingered her Nairobi bracelet and became mournful and so British, you could cut it with a knife. "Hector, dear, I think." She lifted her eyes to the ceiling, knotted her brow. "I think you are not happy with us."

Jesus, she was firing me.

Beating me to the draw, damn her black heart.

I stood breathless. Felt sick in my stomach. A little numb, too.

I always get breathless and sick and a little numb when I'm being fired. I can't help it. It probably goes back to childhood. Getting smacked in the crib.

"You are ambitious, my dear," she said. "I know. Believe me, I know. You are young. Your eyes are fixed on higher artistic ground. Parnassus. Melpomene. Mime in black tights. We do our best here, of course, but we are, after all, Hector, only a modest, local theater group. I need hardly tell you that this is not the City."

And so on.

I gulped a lot. I said nothing very clever. Nothing that could be remembered later with satisfaction. I think I said I didn't mind working there at all. Nice people, nice group. And with her. There was a lot to learn. Challenges. If I was doing anything she didn't like, she should tell me and I would certainly try my best, et cetera.

Connie informed me with the crispness of a British biscuit that she had hired a young woman: delightfully down-to-earth, got along well with people, and had all kinds of experience and the best recommendations.

Wonderful. I nodded. I understood.

On my way out, one of the sphinxes, cold cream on her cheeks, stopped me, embraced me awkwardly but tightly, and said in a tearful voice that she was so sorry.

It was Paula. I gave her a kiss on her forehead and said, "Hey, I'm sorry too. I'll miss you."

I would miss all of them.

And then—I'll never forget this—a big, big face loomed before me. A face with an oversized frown of concern and sympathy, an oversized smile of support. The usual film of sweat.

Dennis.

He shook my hand, gave me a long look, slightly out of focus, and said, "Thank you, Hector."

It wasn't a thank you.

It was a thhank you.

And he must have just had lunch or dinner or a snack—hocks, rump? tongue?—that his mother packed for him. Pieces of it probably still between his big teeth.

Somehow—don't ask me how—I said, "Nothing to thank me for, Dennis." And somehow managed not to flinch, and somehow managed not to pass out.

I gave him a light punch in the arm, and called him a son of a gun, and said he was great, just great, on the stage today, and I smiled.

Yes, I actually smiled.

Can't Catch Me

Michael Cadnum

Michael Cadnum lives in Northern California. He is an award-winning poet and the author of Nightlight, Sleepwalker, Calling Home, Saint Peter's Wolf, Ghostwright, *and* The Horses of the Night. *His next book of poetry will be* The Cities We Will Never See *(Singular Speech Press). His short stories have been published in* Antioch Review, Beloit Fiction Journal, *and over a dozen other quarterlies.*

"Can't Catch Me," Cadnum's first short fiction foray into fantasy, retells the tale of the "Gingerbread Man," who here is a very hip little guy.

Can't Catch Me

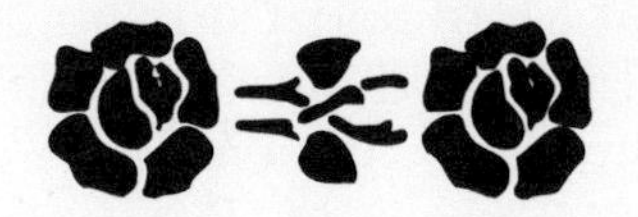

WHAT IT WAS WAS HOT.

Hot is fine if you want to get from being so much goop, and turn into something with a little structural integrity, but when you have what it takes you don't need hot anymore.

People say, Hey, Hot is sacred. And I say sure, you give Hot its due. I don't go around writing my name on ovens with Day-Glo paint, and I don't think you should encourage people to say Hot is nothing. But if you honestly expect me to spend any time at all visiting stoves and ovens and kitchens because some people think that the whole world would be nothing without a stove in the first place, I say you can forget all of that sanctimonious stove cant. I have no use for it.

So, I get out of the stove and the first thing you notice is: it's not hot.

Nobody talks about this. Parents, all they think about is the wood, the ashes, the ventilator; all they think about is keeping the heat. They never think to let you know what it's going to be like. They want you in the stove. That's what they want. You'd burn up in there, sure, but parents want you in the stove. "Keep him in the box," they think, "and we'll know where he is at night." It could kill you, but they know where you are.

So I'm out. I'm cold.

It was a shock, I can tell you, and I think I might have been a little bit more prepared, but I know everyone says that Mom and Dad should have done a better job, and I get tired of people blaming someone else for their problems. It's cheap, it's easy. I found out it was cold, I survived. But I could have been given a hint or two or a few clues. I could have been taken out for a little bit now and then to see what it was like. Because the truth is that when I got out it was on the run. I had been in there way too long. I was fast because I knew they wanted me hot so long I'd have ashes for britches. Parents do that. "So what he's a charcoal-colored crisp, he's my boy." I ran.

And you wouldn't believe the noise. You'd think nobody had ever run in the history of kitchen. My mother wailing, "My boy is running." And then she couldn't even finish the thought, practically gagging on the words. "My boy is running—" and she coughed out the word "away!" Tears, moaning, grabbing at her heart. I was cold, I was running. My father is after me, and you know how old guys are. They like to prove they're in shape and they like old guys who can wrestle a hog or toss a stack of hay down to another guy who really ought to be up there forking the load so the old guy won't die of a heart attack. But old guys like to show they aren't old and end up slipping on a great swath of goose guano, which is what my father did.

I wasn't all that happy to hear him go down, and

I even looked back to see if he was at least not going to need one of those devices you see on really messed up old guys, those things made out of straps, like a cage for the knee. But then I see my father is up, not because he's in physical condition for this kind of thing, but because the goose guano is a little thick around the puddles and he has some on his face. And he's hollering. He can't run but he can holler. He has a holler that scares roosters. So I really start to run, and then I see the neighbors.

We all have neighbors. I don't care who you are, you have neighbors. Maybe far away and you never see them except when their house floats down the river with one of them stuck on it yelling but you know them when you see them. Those are mine, you think. My neighbors. Well, here come the neighbors. Now you have put up with Mom and Dad. You know they are pathetic but if they are so totally dead-bone thoroughly pathetic that doesn't make you look so good, either. So you allow that maybe your parents, at one time, and maybe still for maybe one second a month, have a little dignity or sense, or at least know how to tell a fry pan from a cowpie, if it's not too dark. But you don't have to extend such broad-mindedness to neighbors, and let me say that these people would have taken a great deal of liberal open-mindedness and allowances for all kinds of foibles and defects and still come up wanting, because these neighbors were barbarians—big, slow, mean, and hairy. Except one was bald. And they weren't even that slow.

These guys don't care about me. My mother is a demented maniac but at least she had a set of assumptions about where I was and where I was going to be that make you at least understand why she's upset. And my dad, having green stuff on his face and practically in his mouth, you can really understand he's got a lot of responsibility and pride and self-image on the line right there and then if he doesn't pick those feet up and put them down pretty successfully. But the neighbors, they basically just want to tear into me.

That's the only way I can put it. They would just take a big chunk right out of me, and swallow it whole. They never heard of me, practically, until that very minute, but they start baying after me just like they had every right in the world. And one of the neighbors could run. As fast as I was, I decided that my best bet was to play a little psychology and find one of those high places you see in roads, where the ruts have made a little mountain, sometimes so high it scrapes an axle. And I stand up there and I say that famous line.

Don't make me repeat it, it was all I could think of at the time. I'll say it once here, for just the sake of accuracy and not because I think it was the most brilliant thing ever said or anything like that, but let me tell you it was easily a match for anything coming out of the faces of my dad or the neighbors. I said the famous run and run line, as fast as you can, and then I decided I will adopt a little sobriquet, give myself a *nom de run*, as it were, and I said "I'm the Gingerbread Man," but I really said it more or less to myself. I didn't think anyone was listening. It was just one of those things you end up being famous for and it's on T-shirts and people say did you really and you have to admit to it: that's what I said. And then one of the neighbors, a really big one, and hairy, was really running. This guy was a fast farmer.

He had a pitchfork, and where I come from these are by no consideration petite. These are big wagon load–size wooden fences attached to a pole, except it's not a fence it's a row of big wooden spikes. And this guy is getting ready to throw this fork, so if he forgets how to move his feet in the next second or two, which is pretty possible judging from the look in his eye—which is, to be charitable, stupid—then the fork will arc through the air and nail me where I am and that will be the end of me.

Which is how I looked at it. I took this very personally. When someone is about to turn me into so much flour and spice I don't think about his uneven education or how his brothers probably are as bad off as he is and he doesn't know any better. I saw this big projectile, this birchwood pitchfork, leave this guy's arm and soar up high, and reach its apex, and what did I do?

Some people think that there is pride, and then over here, at the red end of the spectrum, you've got hubris. Pride is a problem, but we have to have it. Otherwise, we'd all go around looking like our neighbors. No pride equals no personal upkeep. But hubris is when you really ask for it. When you really think that nothing bad can ever happen to you because Stove made you especially for a key purpose and nothing can ever hurt you.

What I did wasn't quite that bad, but it was close, I admit. With the big, knobby fork glittering in the light and coming down with an ugly quiet noise, not a whoosh, more of a whistle, I stopped. I put my hands on my hips. And I gave my speech a second time.

It was this version, when I had it all made up already, that I think was the one they heard and remembered. This was the speech that got to be famous. It was the very same one as the first one I ever said, no matter what some people might say. Let me admit here that I was scared. I was sure I was about to be crushed by a tine as big as a wagon tongue.

And let me add, to be frank, when that fork landed in advance of where I stood, and where I would have been standing if I hadn't stopped and delivered what some people eventually called my Taunt; well, maybe I did give just a passing thought to the idea that maybe Stove was looking after me for just that instant. So then I really ran, and not just the sprint that I had already mastered, but a new method of transport altogether, more of a bounding than running, and I needed it because the pitchfork neighbor was bearing down on me for no reason at all except that he had forgotten the rest of the world existed and forgotten who he was and where he lived. As far as he knew he had always been running after me and there was nothing more to life than me and him and pretty soon there would be only him.

Many people are like that. Just knowing there is someone else running along makes them want to start throwing things. So I turned my head in the middle of my bounds and there was Pitchfork Neighbor, developing a little bound of his own, and getting closer, too. And so what did I do?

Well, I gave the speech again. I got off my speech, and it went pretty well, a little breathy and under-projected but not too bad under the circumstances. And the Pitchfork Neighbor had me. There was riparian mud underfoot, the black stuff, and bounding was a distinctly poor choice because directly in front of me was water. The river here is not much. The current is slow and you might see a flood once every four or five years, otherwise this is not the sort of river to inspire song. Pitchfork Neighbor is not one to flinch at a little mud: he dived, he had me in his right hand, and he was squeezing.

By now I had been through some experience, and I was able to reflect upon the nature of the nuclear family, the way it loves you until it kills you, and then the nature of the rest of the world, how it just goes right ahead and kills you without bothering with any sort of emotional bonding. I see how relatively puny I am, being a construct of flour and sugar, and how both malleable and detachable my body parts are.

I left a finger in each one of Pitchfork Neighbor's eyes, debarked his grip without a further recitation of my speech, and ran up the river through reeds and algae, in great danger of losing my structural format altogether, when what should come slinking along the reeds but an unattractive creature, one of our river foxes, a smart but demoralized breed of animal, overly trained in one of those professions that fade but never quite go away. You hear a lot of bad things about river foxes, but they are still an animal you want to emulate if you want to be a liar.

The late morning sun glittered on the river. The sky was empty blue. There were footsteps, and cries, reeds snapping, mud slopping. A voice bellowed, "There he is!"

The fox regarded me.

The fox and I worked out an arrangement whereby he would carry me on his back across the river, at a point which, inconveniently, the river was at its widest. It was all he could do to keep from drowning. He splashed, struggled, so out of shape he could hardly enunciate words without shipping water into his snout, plus I think we had a substance abuse problem here. This was a sad circumstance, a fox lacking pride. Anyway, by now everyone knows how he got me on his head, and then on his snout, and then how he ate me with a snap.

This is true. I got eaten.

Everybody loves this part of the story. Youthful insouciance gets a hard and terminal lesson in hubris. But ginger and foxes don't agree. It happens. Try giving aspirin to a cat. It kills them. So I have some digestive juice to contend with. At least it's not an oven. It's not heat. Compared with the family hearth and home, fox vomit is nothing. And by the time the fox is heaving on the other shore, what's left of me is enough to run faster than ever.

Well, sort of run. And my career begins. Nothing special, but you've heard of me. I stay out of the water, and out of the kitchen.

It's not the winners who write history, it's the neighbors.

Journeybread Recipe

Lawrence Schimel

Lawrence Schimel is twenty-two and has sold his poetry to anthologies such as Xanadu 3, Excalibur *and to various periodicals including the* Wall Street Journal, Asimov's Science Fiction Magazine, *the* Writer *and the* Saturday Evening Post. *His numerous short stories have been published in* Grails: Visitations of the Night, Weird Tales from Shakespeare, Cat Fantastic III, *and* Young Blood.

It seems natural to go from a story about a tasty bit of gingerbread to a dish one might not actually choose to eat if it actually existed. Still, it's fun to read about.

Journeybread Recipe

Even in the electric kitchen there was
the smell of a journey.

—ANNE SEXTON,
"LITTLE RED RIDING HOOD"[1]

1. In a tupperware wood, mix child and hood. Stir slowly. Add wolf.
2. Turn out onto a lightly floured path, and begin the walk home from school.
3. Sweeten the journey with candied petals: velvet tongues of violet, a posy of roses. Soon you will crave more.

---

[1]Quoted from *Transformations* by Anne Sexton (Boston: Houghton Mifflin, 1971). Permission granted by Houghton Mifflin Company and Sterling Lord Literistic, Inc.

4. Knead the flowers through the dough as wolf and child converse, tasting of each other's flesh, a mingling of scents.

5. Now crack the wolf and separate the whites—the large eyes, the long teeth—from the yolks.

6. Fold in the yeasty souls, fermented while none were watching. You are too young to hang out in bars.

7. Cover, and, warm and moist, let the bloated belly rise nine months.

8. Shape into a pudgy child, a dough boy, lumpy but sweet. Bake half an hour.

9. Just before the time is up—the end in sight, the water broken—split the top with a hunting knife, bone-handled and sharp.

10. Serve swaddled in a wolfskin throw, cradled in a basket and left on a grandmother's doorstep.

11. Go to your room. You have homework to be done. You are too young to be in the kitchen, cooking.

The Brown Bear of Norway

Isabel Cole

The Brown Bear of Norway is a classic Scandinavian tale in the "animal bridegroom" folklore tradition. Isabel Cole's poetic treatment of the fairy tale brings the wintry magic of Norway to the streets of modern New York City . . . and then back again to northern Europe. In "The Brown Bear of Norway" the author implies that the sorcery of shapeshifting *is not so very different from the magic all young men and women must perform in the transformation from adolescence to adulthood.*

Isabel Cole is a young writer whose fiction has been published in various magazines. She lives in New York City.

The Brown Bear of Norway

ALTHOUGH I WAS FIFTEEN AND HAD ALMOST FORgotten my childhood's cold hazy Finger Lakes, the sound of the vast breathing of the forest, New York was still a foreign city to me. It was a place of mysterious connections, spies, spells, deals, travelers, foreigners, nets cast between times and places; a shore, a pier, a beautiful terminal like Grand Central, where I watched people rush in and out with the sound of the sea. It was not a city anyone could know for certain, and that made me happy and free. Once you knew something, you were stuck with it, you were old and confined to reality. In the blindness and bewilderment of the city's lights I felt I was about to part the glittering buildings easily with my hands, like curtains.

In five years I failed to make close friends or to really know anyone because I only had eyes for glamorous mysteries—love, the city, danger, flight. Loneliness was a weakness which I did not like to admit to. Sometimes I realized too vividly that I could not imagine what a woman felt when she was kissed. On screen a woman's luminous white skin was fluid as a spill of light. She was free; she flowed, fluttered easily through the shadows. She was kissed. A flickering spot of light knew more than I. I wanted to have connections and know mysteries.

Perhaps I only loved New York because there were so many people there from somewhere else. This year there was a Norwegian boy at my school. Whenever I looked at him it seemed possible to cross the Atlantic, to set foot on the land beyond, and to know someone from far away. Though he often looked at me and sometimes smiled, I was too shy to speak to him until the day before he left. He was standing sadly outside school, surrounded by over-friendly girls I disliked, and I thought I might as well walk past and go home. But instead I waited for the crowd to disperse and, as cynically as an autograph hound, offered him my yearbook to sign. I wanted to say something cruel and biting, because my longing had turned to bitter envy; he was about to fly away where I could not go. But I was quiet, ashamed of myself, and, to my surprise, he looked up from his earnest ink-stained fingers and offered me the address of a friend who wanted a pen pal in America. I nodded, and there was the address on the page, Norse-lettered like a string of runes. I felt shy again, and fled; when I looked back he turned abruptly to sign another yearbook. I was suddenly as tall as the buildings; I could not fit into the subway, and I had to walk all the way home.

A letter came a week later, before I thought of writing. It was heavy in my hand; I felt a moment of vertigo as if I had moved out of one body and into another. The mass of foreign paper was so thick that it began to split the open envelope. The stranger told me about the sea and rocks and roads of Norway, passionately, as if the force of his voice would make Norway open and swallow me. He told me about himself, a dozen different stories in one letter: he was a fish in the waves, a crow on a wire, a handsome troll in an underground palace, a beast wandering Oslo alone at night, a bear. He asked me to love him sight unseen.

The letter was signed *the Brown Bear of Norway*. I had to laugh; he must have read the same grim fairy tales as I. But I did not know how to reply to this extravagant story; I was not used to honesty and passion. Taking pen and paper, I wrote a long letter to the Brown Bear of Norway. I was moved, or at least my mind was, its surface ruffling, dazzling. At last there was someone to tell my fantastic visions of New York.

For a year, twice a week, the Brown Bear told me how he escaped and changed his form, climbing up the cliffs through steep fissures, padding across lichens, standing in the midst of an icy current to swallow the cold blood of a fish. Then he had to return home to his little room, but he would not tell me about that, only about his fierce wandering, which he did for my sake, in my name. His love for me made possible every step, every shedding of his skin. He said this many times.

I never said that I loved him. Several times I got to the point of saying it but my hand felt heavy and uncertain until I took a light jump aside and ran freely on. I was vaguely ashamed that I did not write with his directness, but I told myself that my elaborate turns of phrase were as good as his brave broken English. It only occurred to me later, when it was too late, that he had been stumbling over my words, thumbing through a dictionary, searching in vain for a shy short sentence he could understand.

To satisfy my parents and friends I invented mundane details about my Norwegian friend—a vacuous phantom teenage boy invoked for them at the dinner table. I never called up the ghost for myself or imagined any face for him.

But one day a letter came with something in it, a short accidental curve lying across the words, an alien object: a fine brown hair. It seemed to burn a thin welt in my palm, open a fissure; it had never occurred to me that he had hair, eyes, that a mouth whispered the words as a hand wrote them out. On my hands all these months I had carried the cells of his fingertips, his eyelashes, dust, salt, his prints in smears of ink. I touched the soft dry paper as if it were the delicate skin of a face, but it was flat and blank, and I did not know how another's face would feel under my hands. I held the envelope close to my face, smelling the paper and the sour ink of the address, and I kissed it. The strip of glue parted reluctantly from my lips.

In bed I held the harsh sweetness in my mouth like Juliet lying down with the sleeping draught, but I was more and more awake. I dozed restlessly and ached. The taste of the letter made my mouth burn—it was as I had imagined, in disgust, a French kiss must be, but I could not sleep for fear I would lose its sour taste. Why was I so hot? I could not get enough air, I was encumbered, my limbs could not move freely, because there was a body in bed with me. I wanted to know this body—was it my own, or someone else's? I wanted my thoughts to be clear, so that I would remember, but I could not tell what hands touched me, and what limbs were his.

I heard nothing but breathing and a clear voice that spoke deep in my ear. "Don't look at me," he said. "Don't turn on the light." I was glad; without his warning the magic would not be sealed, the secret would not be kept. Lights from the street darted through the darkness but showed nothing. His body lost its form in my incandescence; I could not tell what shape the Brown Bear of Norway had now. We seemed to lie in a chamber of invisible resplendence, and if I turned on the light, it would be gone. I fell asleep there, peacefully; I never thought then of disobeying, of risking the new half of my doubled world.

In the morning only sunlight lay next to me in bed, and I could not move; I was dry, shrunken, bitter. But when I went haltingly outside I remembered his touch, the heat of my skin. The embrace was like a brief rain in the middle of the night, gone by morning but exhaled by the streets, the ground, the trees. He came to me every night, when shapes became invisible and free and changed at will, even my shy one.

Once I had been all eyes, silently capturing the image of boys I passed and silently trying to speak to them. Now their faces and strange vexing shapes were beautifully invisible. I forgot even the face of the Norwegian boy whom I had shyly watched and who had given me the address of his shapeshifting friend. I was free; my form was newly carnate, and everything, everyone else was ghostly, transparent in a luminous haze or the evening blue. There was nothing unexpected, everything touched me delicately, slowly, gracefully.

His body would rest on mine no more heavily than the soft sheets or the breezes, the gentle wings of the air. The Bear, ashamed of its coarseness, stripped itself down to its core, to shapes without weight, as tender as leaves, rain. One night marble; another, warm wood; he was the smoky ink of Rackham elf kings and the shadow and silver of Cocteau's Beast; I felt the base of wings that opened across the room in the dark above me, beating slowly and brushing the windows. He smelled of old books and theaters, roses, the trees below my window. As long as I could not see him, he was everything; I held the whole weightless world in my arms.

I was still silent at night when he said that he loved me, though I knew from the way he quickly spoke of other things that he was hurt. I did not know if I could say it. If he were a real companion, I could say that love was his face, his voice, a joke we had, a place we always walked. But his face was invisible, his voice as false as my inner voice imitating a memory, and we went nowhere together but within me and my shadow.

After my evening ballet classes I walked home past quiet brownstones, and he stepped out near me whenever I walked in thick shadow. Once when I slipped in the snow he reached down and helped me up, and discovered that my coat was open, that the snow was melting on my neck. "I'm not cold—" I began, but he came close to wrap my scarf around my neck, then drew back abruptly, dropping it. My heart quickened; I had almost seen him, his hand, a human fearful face. Now he had vanished without a word. For a moment I was angry at him for turning away and leaving me alone in the cold, though I knew I had no right to be, when I was silent every night to his melancholy voice.

After my bare glimpse of him I began to see the faces of boys on the street. Their clumsy hands and inarticulate mouths stayed in my mind; they all laughed too loudly, they were shifty-eyed, they slouched. When I lay down in the dark and turned to the Brown Bear I imagined those faces there, too clear, too real, and fumbling, painful hands.

One night I lay on my side and looked into his shadows. I was ashamed but could not help wondering why he asked me not to look at him unless he mistrusted his own form. Quietly I turned on the lamp by the bed and caught him.

His shape was no more than shadows barring light with ribs, dappling it with crescent hollows of muscles, clothing space in solid limbs, soft skin. He was more beautiful than a real boy, as an artist's illusion is more beautiful than the model and contains more selves. This rippling, glowing water of shape was his freedom, which he wanted to keep secret from me.

He opened his eyes and shrank away like a wild caged animal. "What are you doing?" he asked miserably to the wall.

"I thought I would lose you," I whispered.

"You have now," he whispered back. "If you want to see me again, you must travel a long way." His back, the small sharp wings of his shoulder blades, told me I was already invisible and far behind him. He turned back, holding the covers to him, averting his face from me, and reached across me to turn off the light. I saw his body over mine for a moment, and then the light was out. Then I glimpsed him in the window, the fear on his face exquisitely clear, as if he, too, were glass, translucent to the shifting lights of the street. I could not move, and there was a hush, as if I had killed something very small.

I tried all the next day in agonized silence to recapture the few minutes of vision the lamp had cast, but his form was quick to flee. Even its shadow in my mind was gone too far for me to find except on the distant road of a dream. When I looked at his letters again, I realized that we had stopped writing since we had begun to meet at night. Now they might as well have been blank, a blank he turned to me instead of his face when I dreamed about him. I kept the dry, light corpses of the letters under my pillow, pleaded with him in the dark with the covers pressed to my mouth, and I dreamed of faceless things, darkness, a heavy flood of evening, the mocking caress of invisible hands on a bright dream-street.

I dreamed like that every night for months, perhaps as many months as he had come to my room, the nightmares canceling the memories one by one. I had earned my dreams; I was alone now, unable to find him even in my dreams and memory, because I had been alone all along. When we both lay in bed I was the only one there, listening only to my own breathing, feeling only my own stirring, hearing only a likeness of my own voice when he spoke. I had glimpsed a tremble of his hand and felt a tenderness and longing to know him, but I had turned on the light out of revulsion and suspicion. If I had found what I had feared, an imperfect living boy, I might have been the one to turn out the light, turn away, leaving him to an ugly pain which I would not want to know.

I had lost nothing, then. For awhile I thought it was over and I was free, and I went on numbly with my life. But after a time something returned in my sleep: a wary flash of eyes, a quick drawing back of a thin hand, the bending away of a narrow back. I still held his fear, his only truth, the only real one of his many shifting skins that had touched me. I patiently nursed the memory of his fear until it became a ghost which was always before me, melancholy and challenging. Now I knew someday I would follow the shadow to its source, and hold his fear and comfort it. I would never again see the liquid form I had seen under the lamp; I was growing too old. I had thought it was his core, his secret, but it was only another skin and disguise. I wanted what it covered, what I had never seen: a real person. I had never known him, but I loved him.

For two years I studied Norwegian. Gradually I was able to look at the old letters again and found that they were not meaningless, but binding pacts. I was glad to be bound; I was glad that words could bind me to someone instead of setting me free inside myself. People remarked that I looked much happier; I smiled, and in three years I had a ticket to Oslo for the Easter-time. I had never traveled before except in my parents' car, sleepy, blinking at the bright, sharp-smelling gas stations where we stopped briefly in the night on the way to my grandparents. For awhile, exhausted and lonely on the plane, I wished that I were going back there, that there was a grandmother, a warm kitchen waiting for me.

When the force of the takeoff thrust me back in my seat, I felt as if he were resisting me. When I sat in the train and saw the sea and the cliffs and the steep valleys lost in rain, the wild vastness he marked with his claws, I sensed his defiance, but I was as proud as he; I would follow him up onto the cliffs too.

His grey gaunt house stood apart from the town, close by the rocky shore. The fierce waves rushed to wash it away before I could reach it. I hurried up the muddy path and rang the bell. In a panic I almost began to laugh as I wondered what to say. There was no answer anyway. I went around the house through the tall grass, looking through the windows into the dark rooms. Everything was covered with dust covers, and the loneliness of my dreams returned, the terror when he turned his face to me covered or swept blank. The wind carried a cry to me, and when I turned around I saw a fair-haired boy waving at me from the beach. He scrambled up the undercut bluff and stood in front of me, squinting his bright blue eyes. He looked about fourteen, and scrawny.

"They went to France for the holidays," he said, worrying a tangle in his straw blond hair. "Who're you looking for?"

"A boy," I said, as I turned back down the path.

He let me go a dozen steps, then followed me, beginning to grin. "Hey," he said, "are you the Brown Bear's girl?" I stopped. I had forgotten my revulsion at boys' faces, but he brought it back. My old choking anger at the Brown Bear rose up stronger than ever now that I was in his domain.

"His girl," I said. "Why didn't he get a girl in Norway?"

"Too close," he said reflectively. "Also," he added, hurrying after me, "what would he do in the white nights? She had to be in a place where the nights are always dark, he said. That's all." He shrugged. I walked faster, and the boy stood with his hands in his pockets, grinning after me. My fury blinded me so completely that I could hardly remember who had hurt me. I tried to seize upon something the Brown Bear had said or done to focus my hatred on, but there was only the blankness of my anger, feeding on itself. When I was almost out of earshot, he shouted, "The Brown Bear didn't go to France." At the name a frightened face turned to me for one instant within my memory, and I stood still, unnerved with wonder. "He went to his grandmother in Stockholm yesterday. Want to know her address?"

I waited overnight in the station for a morning train to Stockholm. I was not hungry, and I felt a childish defiance as if I were willfully delaying a task forced on me. All I wanted was sleep, which came easily, and the stationmaster woke me up when the train pulled in, wishing me luck and breathing pipe smoke in my face.

The streets of Stockholm were invisible to me as I automatically made my way through them. The single flash of memory was gone, and I was not sure now if that was really the face I had seen three years ago. I did not know now what I was doing, why I was walking. My self of three years ago, more beautiful and more alive than I, stood behind me and moved my limbs forward with pitiless eagerness.

The address was a small town house on an empty street, like my brownstone streets where I had met him in patches of shadow.

I lifted the latch of the gate and hesitated, until I saw a hollow near a bush in the tiny garden: a great clawed print softened and filled up with the fine rain. He meant to leave it there, I thought, to warn me away, to flaunt his otherness and the places where he could go, that he could prowl Stockholm unseen. I went through the gate and up the short path, by the line of clawed hollows. At the top of the steps I rang impatiently.

A tall, fine, white-haired woman looked me over in the lamplight that spilled out through the rain. "Come in, please, young lady," she said in English, and I followed her into the house. There was no one else there, but in the light of her lonely pearls and diamonds and gilt-mirrored lamps I had no strength to confront her. She sat me on a plush couch, and I stared into the fire behind the grate while she brought coffee on a tray. When I did not take any she clucked her tongue, warmed my stiff hand in hers, and curled my fingers around the eggshell cup. "He's not here," I said.

"No." She sighed shortly, almost inaudibly. "Will you look for him further?" Her back was so straight, her eyes so sharp, I was afraid of her.

"Maybe he has another girl now," I said. "After all, it only matters that her nights are dark."

She laughed scornfully. "Who told you that?" I caught the fierce smile in her eyes and I smiled back with the ridiculous but absolute certainty which had flamed up often in the times when I counted hours to evening: the faith in an invisible brilliance, the belief that my hands could take anything out of the air. My anger and willfulness seemed childish when I was with this woman, who loved him and nonetheless kept her pride better than I. We ate roast duck and spoke English, until I fell asleep.

When I woke I saw a few brown hairs on the pillow, and realized that he had once sat by the fire in my place, drunk coffee from the same cup, climbed the stairs, slept in the bed with his face where mine lay, and I should have searched last night for these ghosts of him. Now, in the light, they would not venture out, but all around me I felt their breaths of longing, unease. I was hollow and angry at his cowardice as I went down the wide staircase. "You've been very kind," I said to the Brown Bear's grandmother, "but I can't look for him anymore."

She stopped rocking, and in her stillness, the line of her neck, I saw surprise and bitter despair. "He needs you," she said at last, her voice soft as if it hurt her own pride to say it.

"Why does a bear need anyone?"

"Oh," she said, turning, "not anymore. He is not a bear anymore." She rose as quickly as a young girl, took me lightly by the hand, and led me into a dim library. "This was once his favorite room," she said, lighting a lamp.

Chairs had been knocked over, books spilled, and a mass of fur lay twisted on the carpet, huge, formless. I could not see in the shadows, or breathe, or stand. She turned over an edge of the pelt with the poker and I saw the bloody underside and the thick blood on the carpet, the streaks and gouges on the wallpaper.

"Now don't be alarmed, child," she ordered with

a firm grip on my arm as I leaned against her. But it was half his own fear, reeking in the dim room, that made me weak. "It's only the skin. He was here yesterday, and he spoke of you. He said you had waited for him three years. I told him he would have to give something himself, then," she said sharply, "so, he tore the skin off."

What I saw was not the inside of the bearskin but of the last transformation it contained, the inside of the shape which had been all soft golden light when it slept, the shape I had thought was his core. He had torn it off too, but the weightless form had not come off easily, like the shedding of light or water; the skin, stiff with its blood, still had rough shreds of flesh on it.

"He can't have gone far without his skin," said his grandmother. "Please, you will go bring him back now?"

I shook off her hand. Why should I go farther? I had found him, I had found what I had loved—the skin, the bloody weight freed of him, his fear. "I'll go home," I said, "and take this thing as a keepsake."

"Do as you please," she said, opening a drawer and counting out a bundle of Finnmarks for me, "but he often stays with a friend in Helsinki."

So I left the skin behind and tracked his fear easily, the wounded shape, the Grendel with its trail of blood, half-human. In Helsinki I felt his human nearness in the dark, the pale shadow of his turned-away form no longer vanishing, but growing more distinct as I approached. He stood at every next crossing, by the snow-wet streets that glittered and rippled like rivers, in the light of a chocolatier's window. He vanished in the trees of a narrow park, and I fell in the dark tree roots by the snow-mantled statue which I had mistaken for him.

I was so tired I wanted to lean against the base of the statue and close my eyes, but an old man in an overcoat was staring at me. I stood, shaking, and then remembered the address I was looking for. "Mielikki Street?" I asked hesitantly. He stared at me even more sharply, nodded, and hurried away. I went out onto the street that edged the park, and knocked the snow off the street sign with a branch: Mielikki Street. I crossed the empty street against the light; the building was right there, cast iron and stone gleaming in the blue evening snow, and warm windows. I saw people moving behind the windows, children playing, men drawing curtains; there was a flicker of televisions and a smell of dinner. One window was dark; his, I guessed, since it was on the right floor, but I went up the stairway.

The door was half-open and banging in a draft. I closed it carefully behind me. At my feet was a dark, tangled mass. I knelt by it, my heart pounding. It was a discarded coat. In the darkness I felt the stiffened patches of the lining, and I held the coat closer to comfort it, the discarded, wounded shape. In the next room, under the window and its dim crystalline light, I glimpsed a pale back, thin shoulders. I looked away—if I left now and let the coat fall again, he would not know that I had seen him.

I went quietly about the room, picking up the clothing he had torn off. They were stiff with the blood of the bear's death, and I wanted to get rid of them. I took them into the bathroom and covered them with water, expecting the dark stains to be as fast as birthmarks. But I had no sooner held them under the water than the blood rose in clear red blooms and sank away entirely down the drain. I hung them over the radiator and hesitated for a long time as they steamed gently. The stench of fear drifted away. At last I went back into the dark room.

He lay still, breathing softly. He did not stir when I turned on the lamp and shut out the evening with my bright reflection. For a moment it was as if he were still dappled with the startled light and dark of change, as if he had just turned away from me angrily in my bed, hiding his face. But he was not the same. The light on him was harsh, his form no longer liquid, but heavy, certain. His skin no longer had the budding softness of a new, soon-fled form; it had some blemishes and already the slight weariness of something he would wear until he died. I seemed for a moment to recognize someone from long ago, from my years of curious watching, someone I had silently and wistfully watched.

I should have been tired of looking at his back, but it was touching and intimate now to see something of him that he could not see himself. There was blood only in the shadow of his shoulder blades and on the nape of his neck. He had washed, but there were spots on his back he could not reach, places of invulnerability unknown to him. I took a warm washcloth and wiped the blood from his shoulders and worked it out of the hair at the nape of his neck. The wetted blood gave off a sharp, wild, metallic smell, and he stirred, shrank away. Startled, I drew back.

He turned over and froze when he saw me. I saw

his face full of fear, as it had been three years ago. Numbly I waited for him to curse me, call me a traitor, flee again.

"Who are you?" he demanded.

I had been wrong: it was not the fear of betrayal, it was the fear of a stranger. I should have known that with his clothes like new, his skin washed, he would not be able to remember anything. I had erased all the traces of our love, and freed him.

"I love you," I said, my throat closing over the words in fear and bitterness. He only stared at me; I had spoken in English. I turned away, ran, tripping over the coat, eager to wash myself away as I had freed him of everything else. I left the apartment, passed the other doors and sounds of people, and went out into the street.

I felt light and dizzy. All the neat, bright stores were closed; I passed dimly illuminated windows of books, penknives, a blazing display of sleek lamps. This was no place to be alone at night. In New York I could be in brilliant company and tumult. Here I was the only one in the void of deep blue, black branches, lamps, heavy soft snow. It was potent; it warmed me.

Running steps spoiled my loneliness. I slowed down and waited for them to cease somewhere in the distant streets, but they approached me breathlessly. I recognized the Norwegian boy from school.

"I know you," he said in English. "You are the American girl who was writing me once. I thought we didn't write anymore." He smiled apologetically. "I'm sorry, I was stupid. But why didn't you say you would come?" I could not take my eyes from that uncertainty of his, the awkwardness of his hands, which had once been so sure and graceful.

He began to blush under my scrutiny, and looked away. "I couldn't recognize you," he said, "you looked so different in your school." He laughed. "Stupid, wasn't it . . . 'a friend.' I'm sorry." He shook his head ruefully. "You guessed before? You were angry at me, that's why we stopped writing?"

"No," I lied. "I guessed from the start."

His face brightened, and he said "Thanks," softly. We were walking now, and the vast night had shrunk; it ended just at the rooftops and the spheres of the lamps, enclosing the street. The snow fell from no farther than the tree's branches. At the corner we stopped for one sleepy, bright-eyed car. I noticed suddenly that at the nape of his neck was a patch of darker, coarser hair. He fingered it, perplexed, and dropped his hand self-consciously.

"You will be cold," he said, seeing my open coat, my dangling scarf gathering snow. He wrapped my scarf carefully around my neck, watching me curiously.

"I'm not cold," I protested. Melting snow trickled through my hair, down my face, from my eyes.

The Goose Girl

Tim Wynne-Jones

Tim Wynne-Jones has written three novels of suspense, eleven children's books, and a dozen radio plays for the Canadian Broadcast Corporation including a science fiction musical. He has also written many short stories. He lives with his wife, Amanda Lewis, and their three children in the woods of eastern Ontario.

Wynne-Jones's rendition of "The Goose Girl" tells the story from a surprisingly different point of view than the original.

The Goose Girl

THE CHILDREN ARE MAKING A SNAKE IN THE WATER. They wave, call up to me to watch. I watch. Two princelings, one princess: a snake, slim ankled, slim wristed, bone white, curving this way and that. Now the snake comes undone, knocked apart by a wave. Such a fragile snake. I clap, but the children cannot hear me. They go on to another game. Their servants stand with big rough towels at the water's edge, each waiting for his little bit of snake finally to succumb, blue lipped, to the chill of the ocean. Not even under the blazing late summer sun will the bay warm up. It was cold when my father brought me here to swim and my solitary servant waited for me on the shore. All I remember was the cold. But then I was an only child. My father believed in such torture. I pass the torture on. Such are the duties of kingship.

The queen is not present. Family outings tire her. Besides, she has her lover to contend with. He is a jealous attendant, demanding more and more of her time, lately. Frankly, he is a headache. It was not long after our marriage that she acquired this haughty admirer. Ah, you are thinking, are these snake children mine, truly heirs to the throne? But I am making a riddle. Her lover really is a headache. I am cuckolded by a headache! That there are children at all is a miracle of matter over mind, for the queen had no mind for it. She was a determined enough bride, as you shall soon see, but a chilling one once the doors of the bridal suite closed off the music of the marriage feast. The bride Father chose for me. Father figures prominently in this story.

There is a stirring in my groin. Not a frequent occurrence these days; no one to celebrate it with. I have got myself thinking of the false bride again. The bride Father would have none of, though I daresay the idea robbed him of more than one night's sleep.

I dig from my pocket three spikes. I always have them near at hand. I hold them up until they turn hot in my palm. This is what is left of her: this heat, this sharp longing. They are my unholy relics. Blood has stained the tips of these nails, rust. I pried them, myself, when no one was looking, from the barrel which was her coffin.

"The Goose Girl." Perchance you have heard some of this story? The minstrels made much of it some years back. It circulated the kingdom's public houses, where maidservants picked it up along with whatever else they could pick up on a night off. If the story exists at all any longer it is probably belowstairs, where those maids recount the lost days of their own longing or in the nursery, where they dress the story up in sweet, confounding mystery to distract fractious children. "The Goose Girl." I first heard it myself from the lips of a crone. Some court wag hoping to ingratiate himself to me when I was newly crowned dragged her in for my amusement.

Frightened for her life—and no Scheherazade—the story came out utterly garbled. But it did make me smile. For I had heard the story from other fuller lips, in the sweet dark, the words of it deposited in my ear in whispers. The retelling, confused as it was, stirred old coals. Perhaps it is time to tell *that* story, that of the false bride. Yes, and the false prince, for that matter. Time to confess, while the children play catch with the servants on the strand and the true bride, the queen, my wife, lies as still as death under the weight of her dull escort.

She was to come to me to be married. The betrothal arrangements had been hammered out by *her* father, since deceased, and my own father. Father and I had never seen the princess, which is where the confusion came in—but, I am getting ahead of myself. Her old mother was something of a fool, as near as I can tell. She loaded up her daughter with the agreed-upon dowry. Or, to be more precise, loaded up the chambermaid who was to accompany the princess safely into my keeping, with the dowry and the food and the changes of clothing and the night gear and the rain gear, et cetera, et cetera, as befits a princess traveling a great distance to be married. The princess had but one item weighing her down on that voyage (other than, I'm sure, an incipient headache) and that was a handkerchief which she kept tucked in her bosom, such as it was: she was a very young bride to be. Not so the chambermaid. The chambermaid—what brilliant devilry brought her to the batty old queen's attention? For she was ripe with womanhood, rude with it. Her charge, the princess, found her companion distracting to say the least.

Well, the truth of it is, the old queen was overly hasty. Her daughter had not even come into womanhood. But affairs of state demanded a wedding between our two kingdoms and so off she sent her portion of the bargain. Perhaps she was hoping that a long ride on horseback might just bring on the girl's flow. Or perhaps she was hoping that the handkerchief would do the trick. The queen, following an old wives' tactic, had pricked herself and let three drops of her queenly blood soil the handkerchief. The three drops of blood pressed near to the girl's heart were meant to speak to the princess's blood: "Bleed, child, bleed, for there is an impatient prince at the end of this journey." That, more or less, is what the old wives had in mind. Or so the chambermaid told me. In the popular version of the story, the blood is supposed to help the princess on her journey. But in her moment of need and in answer to her heartfelt cry for help the handkerchief only simpers: "Ah, if your mother knew, her heart would break in two!" Some help.

The crone, blubbering, wetting herself, had it that the princess and her chambermaid stopped their horses by a brook where the princess demanded a drink of water; to be fetched, no less, in a gold cup. The chambermaid's reply: "If you're thirsty, get down yourself. Just lie down by the water and drink. I'm not going to be your servant."

Taken aback, the princess in the crone's story dismounted and drank, humbly, from the brook, which is when the bloody handkerchief first sympathized with her: "Ah, if your mother knew, et cetera."

But the chambermaid told me the story in more leisurely fashion and in more vivid detail. There were willows and rushes beside the brook and dragonflies and watercress—the flesh of a story is always easier to swallow than the bones. Yes, they stopped, hot and thirsty, for it was this very time of the year, this time of the day, with the sun high over head. There was a glade and no one about. Within moments the chambermaid had stripped off her blouse and, in nothing but her skirts, waded out into the water. Indeed, the princess was alarmed! She knelt on the bank dipping her bloodied handkerchief into the water and dabbing ineffectually at her forearms and neck, which were not cooled by the action but only grew hotter, her pulse quicker. For her eyes betrayed her. She tried not to look but wherever she turned her gaze her eyes came in contact with her half-naked companion. And the child princess had never seen such rosy and abundant flesh distributed in such distracting proportions. Nor had she experienced such a wanton display of sheer pleasure. It quite made her swoon. I can only imagine what her mother's blood said to her at that moment!

After a moment the princess went to get a cup to drink from and when she returned the chambermaid was nowhere to be seen. Then suddenly, even as she leaned over the water, the woman jumped out at her from the rushes. In her hands, clutched to her breast, she held a fat bullfrog. The princess screamed. I'm sure she did. And fell over too. Then the chambermaid fell to her knees beside her on the wet bank and thrust the bullfrog's face up to the poor girl's eyes.

"Pretty, isn't it," she said, with a huge grin on her face, and stroking the bullfrog's throat with her finger. "Do you think the prince's will be so large?"

The princess had not until that moment even considered the idea that her betrothed might keep frogs. She had imagined he might have a dog. The thought of froggy pets occupied her mind for many miles before she got up the courage to further question her companion about it. The chambermaid only laughed and the subject did not come up again though it undoubtedly plagued the young girl's sleep.

I have corroboration on the chambermaid's version of these events. The princess's horse, Falada, assured me it happened in more or less this way. I have not told you about Falada yet. Falada could talk. We became close, Falada and I, but, unfortunately, not until after I had him beheaded. It was at the chambermaid's behest. I was, at that moment, I must now admit, completely in her thrall. But again I am leaping headlong and deep into the story; it is better to wade in slowly for the tides are treacherous.

The cup of water business came up again: another secluded pond at the end of another hot day's ride. But on this second occasion things happened quite differently. The princess was prepared. She had, in fact, been up half the night, half fearing and half hoping that just such an event might reoccur. The chance to see the chambermaid naked again toyed and fingered with her imagination terribly. It is hardly surprising, under the circumstances, that the chambermaid was able to convince the virgin to take the plunge herself. Oh, there was some maidenly timidity but the chambermaid soon overcame that. She had no time for caution.

Falada watched the episode over his feed bag: the sly chambermaid having trouble with the strings of her shift. "My fingers are too fat and stupid to untie these knots. Untie me, princess, with your slim fingers. Your soft, supple fingers . . ."

What with one thing and another the princess was soon frolicking in the cool springwater herself. Now I have dwelt on this vision often in my reveries. The chambermaid swore the princess frolicked. Falada swore she frolicked. If it is true, then it must have been the last time my queen ever did so. And that thought leads me to another: perhaps she has lost more than I have in this whole treacherous affair.

In any case, it was while she was engaged in this sport that her mother's hanky floated away. Dear Lord. "Ah, if your mother knew, her heart would break in two!"

There was no frog this time. Only the two of them, a dappled pond, a secret.

Upon leaving the place they struck on the idea of the switch. Oh, in the crone's tale and, undoubtedly, in the nursery version, the switch is all brought about at the authoritative demand of the wicked chambermaid—Heaven help us. Actually, it was all meant as a lark.

Still wet from her swim, the princess, giggling, clambered into the chambermaid's garb. She had never felt so utterly liberated in her life and I speak here of her habiliment. For the chambermaid's simple clothing was loose on this slip of a girl. She felt gloriously unfettered. It was in that cotton blouse and raw linen kirtle, in those scratchy knickers and on the back of the chambermaid's pony-gaited nag—for the switch was to be complete in every way—that her menses arrived. All in all a busy day.

As for the chambermaid, how proudly the princess's rigging propped up and displayed her lavish figure. How tightly. And with what spirit she spurred Falada on.

A lark, perhaps, but not an innocent one. The chambermaid had spied the castle from a rise above the pond. The princess, on the other hand, had no idea how near or far it might be. So it was quite soon thereafter that the two travelers arrived at their destination. Me. My father and I were there to meet them, he in the courtyard and I on the terrace. The regally dressed traveler arrived first, not surprisingly, for she rode a great, powerfully chested steed. My God, what a joyful leaping there was in my heart to see her, her hair dark and wild, her face flushed and radiant, her ample bosom heaving with the exuberance of the ride. My bride! My knees gave way underneath me and I had to grab the parapet wall to keep from falling over and tumbling down the stairs to greet her.

A good length behind her came her serving girl, looking awfully drained and riding the most sorry of piebald creatures. Is it any wonder that the masquerade worked so successfully?

"Come," I said to the false bride, having regained something like princely composure. "Let me show you around."

She slid unceremoniously off her horse and took my hand.

"You're making a big mistake." I heard the words clearly but could not identify the source. I looked around. The false bride, seeing my confusion, put me straight. "It was just the horse," she said. We laughed merrily and went our way.

I think my father knew.

I think I knew.

I had met enough princesses, God knows. Though I was young, I cannot claim naivity. I let the moment steal me away. The false bride and I went directly to the royal suite, leaving my father behind, perplexed. We laughed most of the way. We held hands. I'm not sure who pulled whom the hardest. I left my father down in the courtyard to deal with the victim of the chambermaid's clever deceit.

The next bit is tricky. I'm not quite sure how it came to pass. The whole thing was like an idle, adolescent dream. Sixteen hours of it—Bed, I mean. I expected at any minute the royal guard to come charging in and drag us both off to a cell—as long as it was the same cell I didn't care. Oh, my false bride was fed and feted. Musicians played for us and jesters joked, the bawdier the better for her tastes. Fine viands and fruits and flagons of our honest, hard wine were brought in on trays the size of doors. And then the scraps were taken away and the entertainment was booted out and my bride to be and I were left to get to know each other. Again and again. If this delectable creature was not to be my queen—and it seemed too good to be true—then I was going to delay for as long as possible the end of the dizzy-making illusion.

It is late now. The children are asleep. It is the time of year when hot days give way to cool evenings. The first frost is not far off. There are fires all over the castle. Strolling about earlier, I espied the queen. She was up, seemed in good spirits. She had two ladies-in-waiting with her playing spite and malice at a card table pulled up near to the fire. They were drinking. The new girl in my wife's entourage was quite tiddly.

I have retired to my study with a hot toddy to put this down. Why? I think not so much to record it as to rid myself of it. It will be a night of surgery with rum as the anaesthetic.

Early in the evening on the second day of my bride's arrival at the castle, my youthful ardor thoroughly slaked, I at last wandered out to confront the old king. I left my raw beauty sleeping in a tangle of sheets, which exposed provocative glimpses of her ruddy skin. I stood by the door for quite some moments connecting with my eyes those visible bits of her until she was complete again in my mind. She was snoring. I wondered if princesses snored. As I walked out to my fate I found myself recalling a story my old nursemaid had told me of a princess who showed up at a castle in rags but whose royalty was proved unequivocally when she could not sleep with any comfort because of a pea placed under her mattress. My bride could sleep on rocks, I thought. Make love on rocks! I couldn't help considering, what kind of a lover the tender creature of "The Princess and the Pea" would make.

Father was, not surprisingly, in quite a state, which manifest itself in icy silence. We walked out onto the ramparts. I waited for the blast to come. Finally, he stopped. From the battlement he pointed to where the geese were being driven home for the night from the western fields.

"I have put her to work with young Conrad," my father said.

I could see that a young woman tagged along at

a distance behind the goose boy, who turned—to taunt her, as near as I could figure—every few minutes. I could not see her features, but she walked, stumbled, as one unaccustomed to rough terrain. And even at a distance I could see that her hair was got up in an extraordinary fashion.

"This has been a most egregious connivance," said my father in a voice so low and solemn he might have been declaring war. The choice of words was, I'm quite certain, not spontaneous. But I responded passionately. "Then why did you not stop it!" I blurted out. He turned to me and looked me squarely in the eye. "Because," he said, "you will be king someday."

My father could say things in such a way that the words were like a door slamming in your face. He walked off and, though I meant to shout something after him, he was closed to me. Locked. I turned and watched the ragged, waddling procession approaching the gate below me. Conrad herded the gaggle in a desultory manner with a stick. As they passed through the gate the goose girl looked up at me. It is a glare I have learned to live with.

Why did she not state her identity in a forthright manner? Was she waiting, like the princess in my nursery story, to be tested? Were we to sneak around putting peas under her mattress, posing riddles only a blue-blooded true heart could answer. I have never broached the subject with her. As a matter of fact, we have not once spoken of any aspect of the "egregious connivance." Not in ten years.

In the crone's story the princess is forced to swear to the chambermaid "under open skies" that she will tell no one at court of her trick. But no oath was necessary to keep the princess's lips sealed. I could go on wanting to believe whatever I chose to, but there was no denying who was the true bride. In the crone's story it is the princess's fine features, her delicacy, her humility which convince the old king that she is the intended. It was her imperiousness which got to me.

Another night passed in the arms of my false bride. Well, part of it anyway—she had drunk heavily all evening, thrown up, made quite a mess of things. I spent some considerable time on the floor. Again I left her snoring, but this time I left her at sunlight. Shivering in the early morning chill I stood in the castle's shadow and watched Conrad and the goose girl take the geese out to pasture. Conrad poked at the girl, trying to tug at her hair. It was a still morning and I heard snippets of what the boy had to say to his new helper: suggestions, they were; in one such remark he mentioned somewhere she might like to sit a little later on.

Meanwhile, poor Falada had been knackered at my command. I came upon his head quite by accident the following day, when, for the third morning in a row, I came to observe the geese being led out to the fields. Surreptitiously I followed in the footsteps of the keepers of the noisy gaggle, out of sight, hoping to hear I know not what—that the goose girl was, in fact, nothing but a common wench? Hah! The disdain with which she treated Conrad's salacious jibes had all the earmarks of courtly upbringing. She carried a slim volume of poetry with her out to the fields to complete the impression.

The stinking alley through which they had to pass would have been otherwise a most unlikely place for a princess to find herself—or a prince in his right mind. Indeed, that is exactly what Falada said when he saw me. "What are you doing here?" he asked. Swinging around, I found myself face-to-snout with the noble head of the beast which had only a few days earlier carried the false bride into my life. He sniffed, whickered; perhaps he smelled her on me.

"You talk," I said.

"Even now," he answered. With a shock I stepped backward a pace or two, only then realizing that he was now nothing but a head and neck tacked securely to the wall.

Our goose girl, it seemed, had promised the knacker a gold coin if he would render her a small service. She wanted him to nail Falada's head on the wall under the dark gateway, where she could always see it on her way out to the fields and upon returning.

"She stops and speaks to me," Falada said. "We have a little routine. She says, 'Oh, poor Falada, I see you hanging there.' To which I respond, 'Dear Queen, is that you really there?' And such like. It's for the goose boy's benefit, I suppose. She expects him to run and tell someone that she is the true bride."

"Or," said I, upon digesting this startling piece of news, "perhaps it is for my benefit."

"In any case," Falada continued. "He's getting nowhere with her. I don't suppose it will be long before she drives him clear out of his meager mind."

We talked for some time. It was not easy, the problem being that Falada did not speak very loudly. Even before he had lost his head, this had been the case, he told me. He spoke in a thin dry whisper.

Not an unpleasant voice, and always polite. I apologized for having had him killed, to which Falada said that it was nothing really, hardly mattered to him, one way or the other. A most accommodating animal. Finally the stench of the alley got to me and I was about to leave when something occurred to me. Why hadn't the goose girl persuaded the knacker to disobey my command and hide her gifted horse? If the man believed she could get him a gold coin, then he could as easily be made to believe in two or three gold coins in payment for a slightly larger service.

Falada laughed. "After I had deserted her?" he said. "How little you know my little princess." And he continued to laugh. His thin, dry voice followed me out of the alley, where it was lost in the bustle of the waking castle.

But what he said stayed with me. I pondered my situation all day long and for the first day in three I stayed well away from the object of my desire in order to get my thoughts in order. They were, as you might well imagine, in a fine disarray. Reason has no image: one cannot picture it. But breasts and lips and hair . . . With a monumental effort I forced myself to look at the big picture. I knew by the day's end that there would be no stopping the goose girl, short of taking her life. I daresay, had my false bride suggested as much, I might even have considered it. I was, as I have said, completely in her thrall. It was then with great surprise that I arrived back at the royal suite to find her of quite a different turn of mind.

"How much longer can this go on?" she said as I walked into the room. I could tell that she had been drinking, but she was not drunk. She was terrifyingly lucid.

"What do you mean?" I asked her, expecting a confession. But no. She accused me of deserting her for the goose girl. Nothing could have been farther from the truth, I tried to assure her. But I blubbered quite badly. She would hear none of it. I asked her if my father had been talking to her. She said he had not.

"No one has visited me all the livelong day!" she raged.

Looking around I saw that she had kept herself busy in her boredom. There were plates of half-finished food here and there, portfolios of drawings from the gallery, and games I recognized from my childhood, brought to her from the nursery. Petulantly, she tipped a half-finished puzzle of a rocky coast onto the floor.

"Is this how I am to be treated!" she demanded. "The future queen!" She swung upon me as she said this and must have seen something in my eye: surprise? horror? Whatever it was, she seemed to swell with the intensity of her wrath. I must have cowered or winced because the next instant she convulsed with laughter. And then she fell on my chest, her arms about my neck hitting me and caressing me, her lips nibbling at me, her tongue, her tongue . . .

We made love. It was, I recall, a steely performance. We were by now quite clever: craftsman and craftswoman. We lay afterward, each swaddled in our separate thoughts though perhaps they were along the same line. I imagined keeping her, the way one keeps pets, pampered but under lock and key. I doubt if she was a woman who liked to chat. Ride, maybe? Gaming, certainly. Dinners of state? She must have read my thoughts. "This is our kingdom," she said patting the bed. "Here we will reign forever." Then she rolled into my arm and coiled up to my ear into which she spilled the whole extraordinary story of the voyage to me. The flesh of it complete with willows and rushes and dragonflies and watercress. I could taste it. Watercress has been for me ever since the peppery taste of Truth.

Then there was a knock on the door and a messenger to invite us formally to dine with the king at nine. There was no chance that this invitation could be disregarded. I wondered as I bathed whether she had caught wind of this unexpected banquet while I had been roaming about the castle coming to terms with my wretched predicament.

It was just before we left the room that she suddenly became very quiet. She had been banging around as was her way. (A hairbrush was not put down on a dresser but that the dresser knew about it.) I'm sure she was as nervous as was I but suddenly she came all over tamed, gentle if not truly genteel. She leaned her forehead on my chest. I was touched.

"I am pregnant," she whispered.

I knew little of such matters but in desperation I grabbed at straws. "How could you know that?" I demanded. She smiled with a sweetness I shall never forget. "It's alright," she said. "I know what I must do."

If there is any drama in the crone's telling of my story, it is saved for the banquet scene. Banquets, after all, make for a rich backdrop. The drama began the moment we stepped into the hall for there was the goose girl—I recognized her hair first of all—on the arm of my father. She was dressed to kill.

Conrad had got to the king, it turned out, claimed he could no longer work with the girl, who was a torment and a weird sister; he was hoping, perhaps, to see her burnt at the stake as one. The king had finally followed up on his suspicions and interviewed the girl. There is a curious bit in the tale here for, having sworn not to tell her tale under penalty of death, she would not satisfy the king's curiosity despite his keenest effort. At this point he is supposed to have said, "If you don't want to tell me anything then let the iron stove over there listen to your sorrows." I remember, at this juncture, stopping the crone for I could make nothing of this. I pressed a coin into her hand to reassure her. "Have no fear," I told her, "but tell me the story plain without prevarication."

She could only reiterate the stove nonsense. I turned to the wag who had dragged her in. "What is this stove she speaks of?"

He shrugged his shoulders. "The womb?" he suggested. "These folktales are crawling with such symbols. Nothing is what it seems but some dark, eternal verity." He seemed surprised that I expressed any interest in the story at all; the only thing that amused him was the crone's discomfort. Insolent fellow. I posted him to a distant and plague-ridden outpost at my earliest convenience.

But whatever the stove was, womb, confessional—the princess, according to the tale, finally decided to spill her story. And my father was there with a bowl and sponge to soak up every droplet of the outrage.

And here she was at court. She looked none the worse for her ordeal. It had, actually, been less than a week. In truth, there was some color in her cheeks and she did look dazzling and altogether at home. It was to be her greatest moment and her eyes sparkled like jewels on a crown.

Quite the contrary was the case for my unfortunate false bride. A duck out of water, she was. Of glorious plumage, but nonetheless a duck. The banquet must have been an unbearable ordeal for her, though she performed better than I might have expected. Admittedly, she drank too much and too quickly. But she acted her part well enough, standing up even to the old king's evil eye. I might add, his eye was only evil when it engaged in eye-to-eye combat with the perfidious wench on my arm. I did, at one point, however, observe him staring at her magnificent bottom and he was lost in respect. Then he caught my eye and something passed between us that defies the efforts of my pen to give shape to it. There was pain in it, at what was to come, I suppose, and longing, at what had been gone for too long for him, a widower of many years.

It was late and in the very heart of the revelry when Father proceeded to set his trap. He told a tale that was nothing less than the tale of the wicked chambermaid and the humble princess—"The Goose Girl." He addressed the story, as will a clever storyteller, to the entire assembly and yet to one listener particularly.

"Can you imagine!" my father said, as he finished his tale. "How does one punish such a she-devil?"

"Why she should be forced to live with the prince," suggested a droll friend of the court, winking at me as he said it. This sparked several other witty remarks, which the king took in good humor. But I could see by the set of his jaw that he had not set this trap for it to be sprung by a stick. The princess took a drink at this point. She had not touched a drop all evening to that point. Now she clutched her goblet and dared not look up. I contemplated a disruption: flipping over a table, picking a fight with one of the courtiers, hurling a torch at one of the tapestries, yelling "Fire! Fire!" and clearing the place. It was then, perhaps as a response to the fire in my eyes, that the false bride glanced at me. Cool. Full of herself.

"She deserves nothing better," she said, "than to be stripped completely naked and put inside a barrel studded with sharp nails. Then two white horses should be harnessed to the barrel and made to drag her through the streets until she's dead."

And here the crone's story heaves quite close to the truth of the thing, missing only in one critical detail, a glance in my direction from my false beauty. For me that glance corresponds to the eighth station of the cross of our dear Lord's march to Calvary: "He tells the women of Jerusalem not to weep for him." Her glance was to warn me that she knew what was happening—that I must not interfere nor must I weep.

The true princess choked on her wine at this moment and had to be slapped firmly on the back. That is not recorded in the popular telling. Nor is the voice of the false bride as she related what was to be her own death sentence. Unbelievably seductive. I think there was not a man in the room who didn't imagine for one horrible moment that he might share such a barrel with this virago.

"You're the woman," said the king, "and you've pronounced your own sentence."

But my father did not look at the impostor when he spoke. He looked only at me.

I hear noises out in the hall. I recognize the youthful titter of the queen's newest lady-in-waiting. She is, by the sounds of it, quite drunk. There is another voice, a patient, coaxing voice. The game of spite and malice is over for the night. I leave my desk and peep through the door. It is the queen who supports her beautiful young attendant in her arms, cooing to her, leading her gently on. The girl is falling out of her bodice. The queen will attend to that. She will attend to her attendant. There is something good to be said about this: it is not done for my benefit.

After the white horses had done their worst, the barrel was rolled off the top of a steep cliff not far from where I take the children swimming. By royal decree no one was to go near the chambermaid's final resting place. But for the next few weeks, while the castle prepared for my wedding day, I defied my father and went to her. The barrel had smashed open in its brief flight: an egg tipped from the nest. It had lodged itself between two jagged rocks. I stole my last glance at her brave and shattered body. I stole three nails.

Day by day I watched the sun and the tide and the sea gulls steal her away. I think I waited with some vain idea that the erosion of her flesh would eventually reveal the child she carried: an homunculus of me. But one day when I arrived at the jagged rocks there was nothing there. The tides had dragged off the last of her.

And then I was married. My wife's first act as the new queen was to have Conrad, the goose boy, put to death. The uncomfortable hiatus in her royal life was now thoroughly expunged.

I lay my pen down. I light my pipe from the lamp on my desk. It almost gutters in the draft. I replace the glass and walk over to close the shutters. On the distant horizon dawn will soon break. There is nothing left of summer in the wind.

"Have you written it?"

I close the shutters, turn. The voice comes from the bleached white horse's skull on my mantel.

"Yes," I say, after a moment.

"Is it good?"

"How should I know, Falada," I say. "Why does one attempt these things? Revive these memories? Put words into the mouths of the dead? It seems a hapless notion."

"Oh, I don't know," says the horse's skull in a thin, dry whisper. "It's good to talk."

Tattercoats

Midori Snyder

Midori Snyder's father is a French poet; her mother is an American scholar of Asian languages; her brother is Indian; and she herself was raised in the U.S. and Africa. This multicultural background fuels the rich storytelling skills evidenced in Snyder's six novels to date, including Soul String, New Moon, The Flight of Michael McBridge, *and* Hannah's Garden. *Snyder lives in Milwaukee, Wisconsin.*

"Tattercoats" is a thoroughly adult, romantic tale based on a story found in variations throughout the world. The test of love is a classic fairy tale motif, and the bold resourcefulness of the heroine is typical of the older, unbowdlerized tales.

Tattercoats

In the deep night Lilian lay awake staring up into the damask bed curtains. The morning would mark the seventh anniversary of her marriage to her husband, Edward; the seventh year of lying in this same bed with this same man. Lilian listened to Edward's soft snoring, felt the heat of his back as he lay curled beside her in the bed. She ought to have been happy, she thought, pursing her lips. She had married a decent man, one who worked hard for his family and the villagers under his care. She ought to have been content; she was the lady of the manor and mother to two beautiful children. But it wasn't contentment she was feeling at that moment, rather an irritable boredom. Lilian turned on her side and laid her palms against her husband's back. His skin was smooth and inviting in its warmth. She edged closer and allowed her body to follow closely the curves of his sleeping form. Her breasts pressed against either side of his ridged spine and the hollow of her hips cupped his buttocks. She wrapped her arm over his waist and held him tight, hoping that by his nearness, she might allay her feelings of discontentment. His heart beat slow and steady, his skin smelled spicy. Lilian closed her eyes, and sighed.

And then Edward twitched, his shoulders seeming to shrug off her embrace. He straightened his knees, and pulled away from her arm, mumbling in his sleep. He sprawled flat on the bed, arms and legs outstretched, giving her no room and no way in which to hold him.

Lilian curled herself into an angry knot on the edge of the bed. Her eyes were wide open and her mouth a taut line. Seven years ago he would not have pushed her away. Seven years ago she would not have lain awake in her marriage bed so angry.

On the night before Lilian was to be married, her mother, the Queen, had come to see her in her chambers. Lilian remembered how she lay on the bed then, her palms stroking the smooth silk counterpane. She had smiled, imagining Edward's face gazing down at her from the patterned damask of the curtains. He would be above her tomorrow, and she would smile into his face like this and feel the silky smoothness of his skin beneath her palms. Her hands had gripped the counterpane with excitement.

"May I enter?" the Queen asked at the door.

Lilian's face had pinked with embarrassment at the sight of the Queen. "Yes, please come in," she had replied and moved to let the Queen sit on the bed.

Lilian could still see her mother as she entered the room that night. Despite children and the years, her figure was slender, her walk slow and graceful. She wore a blue shift stitched about the bodice with seed pearls that gleamed softly in the candlelight. Her loosened hair rippled in grey waves over her shoulders. She sat on the bed, and laid a hand to Lilian's flushed cheek.

"Just so," the Queen had murmured. "I was like you on the eve of my wedding night."

"It's hard to sleep."

"And it'll be harder still tomorrow, but for different reasons," the Queen had answered with a light chuckle.

The heat of new blush had stained Lilian's throat.

"Would that marriage could be always like that first night; filled with celebration and the newness of one's partner," the Queen said softly. Then her expression became bittersweet. "But marriage that begins as a clear broth thickens quickly into a roux."

Lilian had laughed at the remark. "It was because of soup that you won the King's heart."

"And because of these," the Queen said. The Queen opened her hand to reveal three walnuts, their brown sides hinged with tiny gold clasps. "When I was a servant in the King's kitchen I placed these magic tokens in a bowl of soup that the King might come to know of me." She opened the first walnut and took out a golden thimble, a spindle, and a tiny gold ring. "And with these did I show the King that I was not a servant by birth." From the second walnut the Queen withdrew three gowns, each more stunning than the last, which she laid across the bed. The first was a gown that shone like the radiant sun, the second was silvery as the moon, and the third sparkled with the brightness of winter stars.

Lilian's eyes were dazzled at the sight of the expensive gowns.

"But of all the three," the Queen continued, "this was the best."

Lilian held her breath in anticipation of the last beautiful gift to be retrieved from the third walnut. What could be more precious than these rich and glittering treasures now spread over her counterpane?

The Queen opened the last walnut and withdrew a cloak of dark fur. She stood up and shook out the cloak, dust and ashes swirling away from the pelt. As it unfolded, Lilian could see that it was made of no single animal fur, but tiny patches of different furs stitched together. The room had been filled with the heady scent of the forest mingled with woodsmoke and the pungent musk of animals. The look of anticipation on Lilian's face had folded into disappointment.

But the Queen seeing it, had laughed. She ran her slender hand down the length of the fur and clutched it tight to her body. "By those fine and beautiful things did the King come to know me. But by this humble tattercoat, did I come to know myself." With slow reluctance the Queen had folded the tattercoat and returned it to the walnut.

She smiled at Lilian and stroked her long golden hair. "I give you these gifts on your wedding night, my daughter. Well may they serve you as they once did me." The Queen cupped Lilian's face and gave her a light kiss on the forehead. "I wish you well my dear."

After the Queen was gone, Lilian had examined the beautiful gifts. She had turned over in her palm the gold tokens, thrilled by the exquisite details carefully worked into each tiny piece. She had laid the beautiful gowns across her bed, her fingers stroking the fine fabrics that shone golden as the sun, silvery as the moon, and sparkled like starlight. But the dark and musty tattercoat she left folded in its walnut shell.

Since that night the years had passed as swiftly as the hare before the hounds. Lilian had learned that the Queen was right; the clear broth had indeed thickened into a roux. The responsibilities of married life and children had all come together like butter and flour into the broth and made of a single wedding night a marriage. Angrily curled on the edge of the bed, Lilian wondered at the changes in herself and Edward since that night. If she was discontent, was Edward not also feeling the same? Had she seen a restlessness in his eyes? Two nights ago she had watched Edward as he, in turn, watched a young serving girl moving about the table with the dinner plates. He had smiled at her and thanked her warmly when a plate of food was set before him. But to Lilian he had spoken in a flat and weary voice of this affair and that affair that either he must see to, or she must arrange. It was not a conversation, but statements of obligation and duty.

Lilian got out of bed, shivering as her bare feet touched the cold stone floor. She was a good wife. She had given everything that had been expected of her in marriage. She had managed the affairs of the manor with skill, her table was always well set, the beds dressed in clean linen, and the floors strewn with green rushes. She had borne children, a son, Arthur and a daughter, Rose, both of good demeanor and straight limbs. True, her body had changed, matured with each birth, but she was still shapely, though no longer as willowy as the serving girl. Lilian sat at her dressing table and from the top drawer pulled out a walnut hinged with a gold clasp. She weighed it in her palm as she thought. Her discontent, she decided, was but a reflection of Edward's restlessness. Did she love him still? Yes, came the answer, though it seemed hard now to know how to express it. Perhaps she could rekindle his affection by dazzling him, by turning his eye away from the narrow waist of the serving girl and back to herself. She opened the walnut just enough to see the radiant fabric of the golden dress and then shut it again. She returned to the bed and, giving Edward's sprawling limbs a shove, claimed a place for herself in the bed. Lying on her back she smiled up at the curtains. *I will seduce him,* she thought, *before he thinks to seduce another.*

The next evening the manor held a midsummer ball. The Great Hall gleamed with the golden light of a thousand candles. The serving girls fluttered like moths around the candelabras and wall sconces, trimming the wicks and replacing those that had burned too low with fresh candles. Along one wall tables groaned beneath epic weights of prepared food. Three cooked pheasants, with their brown crackling skin and jeweled feathered heads, were placed on their silver platters as if they meant to take flight. A roasted pig appeared to eat apples while from his gored side spilled victuals shaped from sausages, carved turnips, carrots, and wild morels. Skinless, exposing its pink flesh, a salmon drifted gently in a cream-colored sauce, its glassy eyes flickering with the reflection of candlelight. There were fruit compotes of apples, pears, and hard plums, white asparagus with tart green sorrel, crème brûlée and little tarts, some filled with bilberries and some with raspberries. And the wine flowed blood red from the clear crystal glasses to the stained lips of the guests.

The musicians, their faces sheened with sweat from the effort of playing, began another set of dances. Partners quickly gathered, as women and men pulled themselves from the edges of the crowded room and paired off into neat squares. The musicians had played no more than the introduction when the room was silenced by Lilian's entrance. The flute faltered and the guitarist, looking up from the neck of his instrument, lost the pattern of notes, his bewildered fingers dampening the strings.

In the dress that shone like the sun, Lilian blazed with more radiance than the thousand candles in the room. Her golden hair flowed like amber down her back. Her cheeks were burnished a pale peach by the rich light of the gown. The dancers parted before her with a sigh and the men averted their eyes as if the sight of her was too painful to behold. Only Edward faced her, his gaze holding hers steadily as his lips parted in a puzzled smile. He took her hand and with measured confidence led her through the intricate steps of the dance. Others were not so fortunate for Lilian's radiant presence addled them and she laughed softly to herself to see them stumble as they led their partners in the wrong direction.

Lilian's heart soared with pleasure, believing that she had recaptured Edward's attention. Until she saw his head tilt ever so slightly and his gaze fall away beyond the rim of her face. As he turned her in the dance, she saw that he stared at a serving girl caught in the glow of candlelight. Her hands were clutching a nearly spent candle as she tried to coax it out of its holder. The wax was warm and slippery and her hand slid unsuccessfully at first until her grip had tightened enough to wrench the candle free. The cream-colored wax splattered over her hand. Lilian frowned, anger pricking her heart. The girl was not beautiful, not even pretty. But Edward had found something captivating in the hands that clutched the candle. And Lilian felt the sun's radiance of her beauty eclipsed.

Edward left the following day to travel with his husbandman to a horse fair. And in the days of his absence, Lilian paced the neat paths of the garden, thinking. Outwardly Edward had done nothing to betray their marriage vows. But he had drifted from her and, except for matters of the manor life that concerned them both, he kept a silent counsel. Lilian crushed the petals of a fragrant rose, its perfume sweet in her hands. And what of her own counsel? Had not she too fallen silent beneath the necessary conversation? Where to begin to say that life had grown tedious and without the surprise of joy?

On the eve of his expected return, Lilian sat at her dressing table and opened the walnut with the tattercoat. She shook it out, her nose crinkling at its fusty smell. She tried to put her arms in its sleeves and found that with her dress on as well, it was too tight. So she took off her silk dress and, standing naked, slipped her arms easily into the sleeves of the tattercoat. The tattercoat clung to her like fur and though it had no buttons, no clasps to hold it together, it nonetheless covered her completely. She pulled up the hood and tucked away her golden hair. She glanced at herself in the mirror and was startled by her reflection.

Not a noblewoman any more, not even a serving girl. But an exotic creature, separate and distinct from the rest of her kind. She had no beauty to speak of, the mottled and dusty fur gave no hint as to her form hidden within. Without her mantle of golden hair her face appeared longer, her red lips fuller over teeth that gleamed animal white. Her eyes were shaded, the mauve lids and long black lashes concealing her startled glance. Inside the tattercoat, the tanned hide was soft as velvet against her skin and when she scurried down the manor corridors and out the front doors, it stroked her thighs like a gloved hand.

The moon rose full and squandered its light over the tops of the trees. Lilian had followed the road away from the manor and through the forest. She walked barefooted over the earth and felt the last heat of the summer sun drift up from the dry dirt. Cool mist settled around her shoulders, leaving tiny dewdrops sparkling in the fur of the tattercoat. She heard the night sounds of animals but felt no fear of them. A fox trotting across the road raised a curious snout in her direction and then, giving a yip of welcome, turned off the road into the bushes. A line of deer broke through the low shrubs and never stopped in their grazing as she wound her way through them. Lilian smiled and felt the freedom of the night gather in her breast.

At an old wooden bridge that marked the boundary of the village road and the manor road, Lilian waited on the banks of the stream for Edward. He would come this way alone, the others having turned their mounts toward the village road. As she sat in the grass she listened to the sweet babbling of the stream and dug her fingers into the wet earth of the bank. The moon broke into shards over the rocks and drifted into ribbons of light on the rushing water. At the sound of a bridle clinking Lilian scrambled up the side of the bank and onto the bridge.

Edward's horse shied at the sudden sight of the furred creature standing at the end of the bridge. Edward pulled the reins in tightly and tried to calm the beast. He squinted into the moonlight.

"Who goes there?" he called out, annoyed.

"Tattercoats," she answered, surprised by the boldness in her voice.

"Move off the bridge, or my horse may injure you as I pass."

"Come down and move me yourself."

"How say you?" The annoyance had deepened to irritation.

"Come to me yourself."

Edward kicked his horse lightly in the flanks but the animal refused to move one step closer in the direction of Tattercoats. It rolled its eyes and flattened its ears and settled onto its back haunches.

"What manner of creature are you?" Edward shouted angrily.

"Come and see for yourself," she replied.

Slowly Edward dismounted his horse and, leading it back to the road, looped the reins over a low branch that the animal might not frighten further and flee.

Lilian's heart beat rapidly as she watched him cross the bridge, his face in the moonlight stern and rugged. Carried on the breeze before him was the scent of horses and sweat. When he was near enough to see her clearly, she let fall open the front of the tattercoat. And as it parted, the light of the moon revealed the contours of her naked body within. A line of shadow marked the valley between her silvery breasts and farther down a second shadow formed a triangle beneath the white wedge of her rounded belly.

Edward stopped with a sharp intake of breath. He gazed intently at the partially visible shape of her body, appearing like the glimmering moon from between the clouds.

She opened the tattercoat wider, inviting him to come closer still. In the cool night air her nipples hardened into pearls on her silver breasts. Edward closed his eyes, struggling to tear himself away from the sight.

"Come to me," she said.

"No," he answered, but already his hand reached out to her, the fingertips grazing the coolness of her breast. His fingers slipped beneath the tattercoat, tracing the hidden curve until her whole breast rested firmly in his palm.

"Come," she whispered, "beneath the bridge."

"No," he said again but as she stepped back, his hand stretched forth to hold her anew. She waited and trembled as his hand slid to the small of her back and his fingers fanned over the rising curve of her buttocks. He lowered his head and with a groan clasped her gently around the waist and pulled her close to him. He hid his face along her neck and pressed his lips into the shallow well of her throat.

Lilian could scarcely find her breath as Edward's warm mouth fastened on the pearl nipples. His hands were kneading her flanks, her hips, as if he were creating her, shaping her outlines to suit his desire. When his hand parted her legs and planed smooth the length of her inner thigh, Lilian contracted with anger. She stepped away from him, her eyes blazing.

"What do you want?" he asked, his voice hoarse. She was just out of reach but he didn't venture closer.

"Beneath the bridge," she said, "and I will show you."

He nodded and approached her again. She took his hand and led him down the grassy bank of the stream until she found a spot beneath the bridge hidden from the bright moonlight. She lay down in the wet moss and ferns and pulled Edward down to lie beside her. She brought his hand to her lips and lay quietly for a moment, gathering in the sweet scent of the grass and the musk of the tattercoat.

"Take off your clothes," she whispered.

Edward did as she commanded and, once naked, stretched out on the bank beside her. Lilian ran her hands over his cool flesh, not so much to shape him for her purpose as to discover the shape that was him. Seven years had changed her and not until this moment had she realized it had changed him as well. There was more of him; the slim youth had thickened at the waist and shoulders. The once downy skin of his chest was shaded by dark curled hair. Her fingers traced an unknown scar on the top of his thigh and dimly she remembered the accident that had put it there. Lilian took her time, finding a renewed pleasure in this man who was at once familiar and strange as he lay in the wet grass beneath the bridge. The skin of his palms was dry and callused as she kissed them. But the skin of his lower belly was damp and her tongue lapped at the salty taste. And as she rubbed her cheek over the peak of his hipbone, and down again into the well of soft hair and even softer skin, it occurred to her that not since their wedding night had she made such a careful and loving journey of his body. It pleased her to do so now, just as it pleased her to hear his low cries. She set herself between his legs and laid her head on his thigh. With her arms around his hips, she held him tight, even as his haunches grew slick and he strained against her insistent mouth.

And when it was done, she laid herself beside Edward's slack body and felt the mist settle on their heated skins. In a stray shaft of moonlight, Edward's face was serene. He slept deeply, one arm circling her waist. Lilian looked up to the slatted boards of the bridge, the stars winking in the cracks, and breathed in the cool night air. She was of two minds. She wanted to rouse Edward and reveal herself to him. But a second thought kept her quiet. The tattercoat had given her a boldness and she was not yet ready to relinquish its power. From the pocket of the tattercoat Lilian took out the gold thimble. She put it in Edward's hand and, after kissing his sleeping face, she returned to the manor long before daybreak.

It was with a secret smile that Lilian passed the next few days. Edward arrived home in the morning, his expression troubled. He gave her vague excuses for being so late in returning and when she plucked a fiddlehead fern tangled in his hair, he blushed and turned away.

It was then she doubted the wisdom of her ruse, fearing that he would be sharp with her or turn his attention farther away from her, either from shame or lust for Tattercoats. But he surprised her by doing neither of those things. In the early evening, as the sun faded, he took her hand and walked her slowly through the garden. White roses sparkled in the twilight with an inner blue light and tall spikes of violet salvia reached to touch the first stars of night. Edward spoke easily to her, not about the manor, nor the stock, nor the hundred other affairs that dominated their lives. He spoke about himself as though he were a young man, his life a new sun breaking on the horizon and not a finished day. He spoke of the dreams he still harbored in his breast and the anguish of denying them in favor of the solid life he now had. Lilian listened, surprised and touched by the confidences he revealed to her. Yet she was also distracted by the memory of their night beneath the bridge. He wanted to talk but she wanted to touch her lips to his skin and be seized by passion.

Two nights later there was a dinner held at the manor in honor of the King and Queen. As Lilian sat at her dressing table and dragged the brush through her golden hair she made another decision. She opened the walnut and pulled forth the gown as silvery as the moon. She put it on and not even the pearls that wreathed her head, nor the opals dangling from her ears, shone with such a luminous glow. When she entered the hall, the assembled guests stood and bowed their heads and the King himself rose to salute his daughter's beauty. As she sat down next to Edward his hand closed over hers and she felt the surge of his pulse.

"You look lovely, my daughter," the Queen said softly, her cool grey eyes hinting at amusement. "My gifts seem to suit you."

"Indeed, I take pleasure in them," Lilian replied. Edward's hand was on her knee beneath the table, the warmth of his fingers bleeding through the gauzy fabric.

Throughout the meal Lilian watched the men eat. She couldn't help but notice that each man took to his food with a singular habit. One tore the wings from the breast of a squab, one sucked eagerly the marrow from the bones, and another plowed together a field of meat and side dishes until it was all one indistinct meal. But not Edward. Lilian noted the way he tugged gently at the leaves of an artichoke, pulling away the green veils that hid its downy heart. His teeth nipped lightly at the base of the leaves, and between his lips, the flesh yielded. He didn't hurry, but savored each course as it was set before him. At the close of the meal he gently cupped a golden pear in his palm and peeled it. The knife was sharp and the skin tore cleanly, revealing the glistening fruit. He sliced it and gave it to her with a small wedge of goat cheese. Lilian closed her eyes at the mingling of the sweet and faintly gamy flavor. The flesh of the pear was slippery on her tongue while the tart cheese coated the roof of her mouth.

Edward nudged her lightly and Lilian opened her eyes with a blush.

"I shall see your parents' carriage to the village road," he said.

Lilian sat very still at his words so as not to betray the sudden galloping of her heart.

"Are you well, my dear?" the Queen asked, seeing Lilian's face flush and tiny beads of sweat dot her upper lip.

"It is the wine," Lilian answered. "It has made me light-headed. I think I shall retire now."

"Yes, you must," the Queen said, kissing her daughter.

As Lilian passed through the doors of the Great Hall her steps moved faster and faster until she was no more than a streak of pale moonlight on the stairs. She reached her chambers and, trembling violently, threw off the gown of moonlight and reached for the tattercoat. She shrugged herself into its furred embrace and stopped only long enough to be certain that her golden hair was well hid in the folds of the hood.

Lilian was certain that Edward would be on the bridge looking for Tattercoats. And she was determined that Tattercoats would be there to greet him. It had rained recently and the ground was soft and muddy beneath her padding feet. She stopped at the bridge, a light mist wreathing her head as she panted from her run in the moist night air. The night was quiet, except for the gentle stirring of insects in the grass and the low throaty call of a wood dove. Lilian slipped down the grassy banks and quickly washed her feet in the rushing stream. The water was cold and she shivered at its unexpected sharpness. At the dull thudding sounds of a horse she returned to the road and stood on the bridge.

It was Edward and this time his horse did not shy at the strange scent of the tattercoat. It tossed its head nervously but humbled to a stop without a quarrel. Edward slid from its back and looped the reins over the branches to let it graze on the roadside grass. With long strides, he crossed the bridge and stood before Tattercoats.

"You have returned, my chance-met friend," she said.

"As have you."

"And have you come for more?"

"No, I intend to give more."

Tattercoats smiled, and the tip of her tongue wetted her upper lip.

Edward approached her, his eyes no longer averted, but raised shyly to hers. He touched her cheek and then stroked the smooth pelt of the tattercoat until he found where it opened in front. Tattercoats caught her breath as his hand slipped beneath the fur and cupped her naked breast. He kissed her, his mouth tasting of wine. The tattercoat crackled with static and in the dark night the fur bristled with a scattering of blue sparks. With Edward's arm around her, Tattercoats led him to the grassy bank beneath the bridge.

She settled her back against the damp ground and stared up at the dark halo that was his face. She couldn't see him clearly in the shadows of the bridge, but she could feel his hands moving slowly as he opened wide the tattercoat to reveal her white body. She heard him sigh and then bend to kiss the rounded wedge of her belly. She wove her fingers through his hair as his head lay against her hip and his hands stroked along the length of her thighs.

It was not the same as before. She had enjoyed him then, enjoyed hearing him cry out, knowing that it was her touch, her mouth, that had brought him to that state. But this time it was his touch and his mouth that made her sighs escape like butterflies released to the wind. Lilian thought she knew her body and yet, as Edward journeyed over her, she was surprised by the terrain he discovered. He showed her the hollow of her armpit, the soft curve of her waist, the small dimples above her buttocks, and the twin mounds of rounded flesh at the top of her inner thighs. And all the while his mouth tugged and nipped as though she were an artichoke until the leaves were parted and among the thistles he exposed the tender heart. Her fingers tore handfuls of wet grass and she contracted, curling like a cat around his head. Beneath her closed lids she glimpsed the whiteness of the moon as it shattered into blazing stars. And while she lay gasping in its light, he eased his body over hers and parted her thighs with his hips. He kissed her face and she caught the tangy scent of apricots on his lips and realized it was her own scent.

Afterward, they slept in the dew-covered grass beneath the bridge. Lilian woke first and, moving quietly, placed the second token, the golden spindle, in Edward's hand. She ran home and had barely enough time to wash the mud from her feet and hide the tattercoat before she heard the sound of Edward's horse, its hooves clattering over the stones of the courtyard. She pretended to be asleep when he came at last to bed and smiled to herself as she felt his hand settle on her haunch, and then his chest ease against her back. His warm breath drifted across the nape of her neck. She closed her eyes and slept within the comfort of his arms.

* * *

In the days that followed Lilian was perplexed by her happiness. Each task that came into her hands was done easily and with pleasure. She sat with the serving girls in the sewing rooms and was inspired to take her needle to a new piece of work. The silks were bright and gay as she stitched a vining leaf rich in gold fruit and deep green leaves. Lilian spent another day in the weaving rooms casting the shuttle from hand to hand and beating the wheat-colored linen threads into a smooth fabric, the steady thump of the treadles resounding in her pulse. She put on an apron and worked in the kitchens, counting sacks of grain, tasting the fruit brandy in the crocks, gathering eggs from broody hens and then rolling the dough for pastry brisée.

Lilian went into the garden and strolled through the stone paths, delighting in the scent of herbs. Bees ambled noisily through the clustered flowers of the thyme plants, and some, filled with the heady nectar, buzzed on the warm stones, too drunk to fly. Lilian picked a woody handful of thyme and then a sprig of olive-grey sage. She turned around in the garden until she found the silver-green leaves of the rosemary plants and then the delicate leaves of marjoram. She gathered them all into a bouquet and inhaled its dusty, sun-warmed perfume.

"Mama?" her daughter, Rose, called from the kitchen door.

Lilian looked at her child framed by the light of the sun and felt a burst of pride. The girl was lovely; her features delicate, her mouth a pale pink bud. Golden curls tumbled untidily down her back and she brushed wayward strands out of her blue eyes.

"Come and see what I have," Lilian said.

The girl stepped into the garden, her hands brushing the blooming flowers and dispersing the bees to the wind.

"What is it?" Rose asked eagerly, taking the little bouquet of herbs.

"Every good roux needs herbs to flavor it or it leaves the palate wanting more. These will go into a soup tonight and you will see what I mean."

As they walked back to the kitchens, the prickling scent of herbs following them, Lilian smiled at the unexpected wisdom of her remark.

That night she took out the third dress, which sparkled with the brilliance of stars, and put it on. She wore a necklace of black jet and her golden hair fanned her shoulders like the last rays of sunset. As she entered the Great Hall it was to dine with her husband and children. Her son, Arthur, sat beside the hearth tying on the fletch of an arrow. His profile was clean and sharp against the sooty stones of the hearth and when he looked up at her, his eyes open in mute astonishment, he resembled a young hawk startled at its perch. Rose left her place by the table and, opening wide her slender milk white arms, clasped Lilian around the waist.

"Mama, you are beautiful," she whispered, her face upturned and the starlight dress shining in her blue eyes.

Lilian stroked her daughter's head and smiled back. "You make me so," she said softly to the child.

Edward held the chair for her and as she sat, he brushed his lips lightly against the arch of her neck.

They sat together and the serving girls brought them a thick soup, its base made of a simple roux and broth. Mingled in the cream and stock were the first fruits of the harvest: tiny peas, carrots cut into shapes like flowers, yellow globed potatoes, and chunks of mutton. But beneath it all was a flavor not quite attributable to any one ingredient and yet indispensable to marrying together the whole soup.

Edward shook his head as he lifted another spoonful. "It's a common enough thing, this soup. So why does it taste so good?"

"It's the mutton," Arthur said stabbing at the meat. Soup splashed over the sides of his bowl in his eager hurry.

"No it isn't," blurted Rose, with a bright flush on her cheeks. "Mama said it was herbs that keep the soup from being plain."

Edward nodded, his eyes heavily lidded. "It's a gift to know how to turn a simple soup into a feast of surprises," he answered quietly.

When the meal was done and the children scuttled off to the upper rooms of the manor, Edward and Lilian sat beside the hearth and engaged in a lively conversation. They argued in a friendly fashion over the fate of a recalcitrant bull that Edward had purchased and about the upcoming harvest. Lilian teased Edward about the two fields beside the bridge that he had allowed to lie fallow. It was a crossroads, he replied, where laborers met to dance and sometimes take themselves into the fields for other sports. He didn't want the grain crushed by an ardent coupling. Lilian spoke about wanting to add new windows to the weaving rooms and about her plan to sell bolts of linen for the glass panes. Edward offered to speak to the masons for her. Into the late evening they talked, their thoughts and visions unfurling between them like a blanket stitched with bright threads. They were yoked to the tasks of marriage, but it seemed to Lilian at that moment that there was joy to be found amid the work of meeting those obligations. Edward's face, ruddy with the light of the fire, shone with an eager good humor.

Later they grew quiet, and sat peacefully before the fire. Abruptly, Edward stood and touched her lightly on the shoulder as she stared sleepily into the fire. Above her she heard him say that he was going to ride out and check the traps the huntsmen had set earlier in the day.

"But Edward, it's late," she protested.

"The better to catch the hare," he said softly and took his leave of her.

Lilian sat by the fire until she heard the sound of his horse's hooves clattering over the courtyard stones. Her pulse was rapping as her thoughts scurried before her. Unable to contain herself, Lilian leapt out of her chair and bolted toward her chambers.

She took off the gown of stars and put on the tattercoat. As she ran through the dark night to the bridge, the long wet grass of late summer snatched at her ankles. She reached the bridge just as Edward's horse pranced on the wooden planks, its clapping gait boldly announcing their arrival.

Edward swung down from his horse without even bothering to picket the creature to the bushes. He leaned forward, his body inclined toward her like a salmon cleaving the stream's driving current.

There were no words spoken, but they crashed into each other and, falling on the side of the road, rolled down the wet green banks of the stream, legs and arms entangled. As they clung to each other,

Edward struggled out of the confines of his clothes, the linen tearing with an urgent sound. At last, skin to skin and supple as a pair of mating otters, they wound about each other, their embrace fluid yet inseparable. The ferns were crushed and the mud thickened beneath their turnings. Edward's hands gripped her shoulders and with one keen thrust planted her into the softened earth. Tattercoats wrapped her legs around his waist, her muddied heels digging into the white skin of his buttocks. And as she held him tight, meeting his thrusts with her own, she felt a bubble of laughter rise in her chest. On the crest of her climax she was seized by a wild joy and burst out with unexpected peals of laughter. Edward, caught by the abandoned gaiety of its sound, joined her, his guttural laughs interrupted at times by groans. The air was tart with the sweetness of the broken ferns and churned mud. The sounds of their ragged breathing and laughter echoed on the underside of the bridge. Exhausted by the effort of their intense lovemaking, Edward laid his head on her breasts, his lips kissing the streak of mud that tarnished her silvery skin.

They slept beneath the bridge and it was with difficulty that Lilian roused herself, and that only after hearing the lark's cry herald the coming day. Gently she pulled herself free of Edward's embrace and placed in his hand the last token, a golden ring. High curling clouds on the horizon blushed a rosy color with the dawn as she fled home.

Almost as soon as Lilian arrived at the manor, she heard Edward's horse returning. She managed to reach her bedroom and stuff the tattercoat beneath the bed. Though her legs were still mud streaked, she threw a nightgown over her head, got into bed, and feigned sleep. Edward came in and quietly undressed. As he lifted the sheet to get in beside her the strong scent of earth, wet grass, and the musk of the tattercoat wafted from beneath the linen sheets. Lilian scrunched herself into a tight ball, trying to cover her muddy legs with her nightgown. Edward lay down close to her, and Lilian noticed that the scent of the earth was strong on him and hoped that perhaps he wouldn't notice it on her.

Harvest time occupied Lilian's every waking thought in the days that followed their third meeting beneath the bridge. The oats and wheat had to be cut and threshed before the heavy rains of autumn flattened the slender stalks or rotted the fallen grain. The villagers had come to assist at the manor and in return Edward offered the use of the draft horses, the mill for grinding, and the kitchens of the manor to feed the crews that came. In the early morning, he would leave, Arthur by his side, scythe in hand, and join the villagers on their way to the fields. Lilian remained at the manor and in the huge outdoor ovens they baked bread and stewed meat for those who returned from the fields with a fierce hunger. Tuns of wine were opened and poured into flasks, beer was tapped into pewter pitchers, and the long tables set in the courtyard held a collection of plates and tankards. Each villager brought his own knife and fork to the meal and none went home hungry.

The gowns of a noblewoman hung in closets for the time being as Lilian donned the plain woolen shifts and aprons of a serving girl. Her golden hair was bound back and hidden beneath a soft bonnet of white linen. She tied up her skirts, so as not to drag them in the dirt as she went from table to table, filling the flasks and pitchers and setting out bread and soup. To a group of women threshers she brought water to wash the dust and chaff from their faces and necks, and when one needed to nurse her baby, Lilian took her place in the circle of women, lifting the winnowing baskets and tossing high the grain.

The golden sunlight of the late afternoon gilded the backs of the tired villagers as they returned from the fields to take their meal. As tired as she was, Lilian felt a sense of pride looking down the long tables and hearing people laugh and scrape their forks appreciatively as they ate everything set out before them. Edward came up behind her and clasped her round the waist. He smelled of sweat, sunlight, and dusty grain.

She looked up at him and he smiled warmly back. Beneath his dusty brow, his eyes were dark and sparkled a hint of teasing.

"I've something for you," he said. He pulled from the pocket of his shirt a gold ring.

Lilian recognized it as the token she had placed in his hand at their last meeting. *Does he know?* she asked herself, wondering how to receive the gift.

"It's lovely. Where did you get it?"

"I came across it in the fields."

"How unexpected," she murmured.

Edward slipped it on her finger and chuckled. "It is as if it was made for you," he added. Then he kissed her on the brow and, ignoring her perplexed face, wandered off to find a plate of food.

Into the evening Lilian stared at the ring on her

finger with a mixture of sadness and confusion. Edward had lied in giving it to her. *What did you expect,* she scolded herself, *he believes he's having a dalliance with a woman named Tattercoats. Why should he tell you the truth? Because I'm his wife,* she argued back. *But you're lying too,* she answered herself. Everything suddenly seemed unreasonably complicated.

As she sat by the hearth, staring down at the troubling ring, Edward came to her. He wore his riding cloak wrapped around him. Dimly Lilian thought he looked bulky and wondered at the heavy cloak.

"I'm going to walk the fields," he told her. "The bull is out."

"Not the reluctant one," she scoffed. "He'll find his way home soon enough without doing damage."

"I must be certain," Edward insisted. "Don't wait for me," he finished and, turning on his heel, left the Great Hall.

Lilian sat there a moment longer, anger welling up at the sight of the gold ring and the distant clatter of hooves. She rose slowly and decided that the time had come. She went to her chambers, thinking to put on the tattercoat for one last time. She would meet Edward at the bridge and as Tattercoats end their secret dalliance.

But though she searched her chambers she could not find the tattercoat anywhere. Its gold-hinged walnut was missing. She grew frantic, looking beneath the bed, trying to remember where she had last tossed it. But the time was passing and the tattercoat was clearly gone. It was then Lilian decided that she would go as herself and meet Edward at the bridge. She would tell him the truth.

Her step was heavy as she walked the dirt road to

the bridge. Edward would be angry at being deceived, she thought. He would not trust her and the joy that had been rekindled between them would fade. And deeper within her heart, Lilian knew she would miss the wildness of the tattercoat and the unexpected self that emerged out of it. The Queen had been right, Lilian decided; the gowns were lovely and had made her seem beautiful to others. But the tattercoat had taught about herself and she grieved the loss of that freedom.

At the bridge Lilian halted in her step. Someone was waiting at the far side, cloaked in a dark cape. She knew it must be Edward but she couldn't see him clearly. His horse was nowhere to be seen. The figure moved into a path of shining moonlight. Lilian's hands flew to her mouth as she recognized in the silvery light the ruffled pelt of the tattercoat. Edward was grinning at her astonished face. She spluttered with amazement and he threw back his head to the moon's face and laughed. As he did the tattercoat opened in front and Lilian glimpsed the white ribbon of his naked skin from his throat to his feet.

Her mouth twitched into a smile and she took a step closer.

"What manner of creature are you?" she asked.

"Come closer and see for yourself," he retorted.

She flew to him, her arms reaching to clasp him around the neck. As she collided with him the tattercoat slipped farther down, revealing his naked shoulders. She kissed the skin of his neck and chest, as Edward held her, still chuckling. And then, abruptly, she stepped back away from his arms, her fists balled on her hips.

"How long have you known?" she demanded tartly.

"From the first."

She grimaced in disbelief.

"Well, almost from the first," he relented more sheepishly. "When I first saw you I didn't know. But when I touched you beneath this cloak of fur and inhaled your breath I knew it was you. Lilian," he said gently, taking her hands from her hips to hold them in his. "There is no other with skin so soft nor with breath that smells as sweet as yours. I would know you even if I were blind."

"But you deceived me," she pouted.

"You were deceiving me!" he insisted. And then his face became more serious as he held her gaze. He gently brushed away a strand of hair from her forehead. "It seemed important to you."

"I feel foolish."

"No," he said sharply. "You aren't. Things have changed between us since you put on the tattercoat. Changed for the better. What we would not say to each other in words, we could in touch and deed beneath the bridge."

Lilian smiled and cocked her head to one side. "It looks better on me than you," she teased.

"I think you're right," Edward said. He took off the tattercoat and placed it over her shoulders. The bright moonlight spilled over his naked body and turned his skin a soft pewter. He nodded with his head toward the bank of the stream.

Lilian gave a shy smile that opened into laughter. Edward offered her his hand and she took it. Together they left the bridge and stood on the wet grassy banks of the stream. And as they slipped down beneath the dark shelter of the bridge, the sounds of Lilian's bright laughter were lost in the rushing current of water that tumbled over the rocky streambed.

Granny Rumple

Jane Yolen

Here we have another take on "Rumplestiltskin" by a writer who blends the literary and oral storytelling traditions into a thoroughly original rendition of the classic tale.

Jane Yolen is one of the most celebrated writers of modern fairy tales, with well over one hundred books in print including Tales of Wonder, Dreamweaver, The Hundredth Dove, The Girl Who Cried Flowers, *and* BriarRose *(an extraordinary adult novel based on the Sleeping Beauty legend, set in Poland during World War II). She has also published* Touch Magic, *an excellent book of essays about fairy tales; she is the editor of the Pantheon Folktale Library's* Favorite Folktales from Around the World; *and she edits the imprint "Jane Yolen Books" for Harcourt Brace & Co. Yolen lives in western Massachusetts and St. Andrews, Scotland.*

Granny Rumple

SHE WAS KNOWN AS GRANNY RUMPLE BECAUSE HER dress and face were masses of wrinkles, or at least that's what my father's father's mother used to say. Of course, the Yolens being notorious liars, it might not have been so. It might simply have been a bad translation from the Yiddish. Or jealousy, Granny Rumple having been a great beauty in her day.

Like my great-grandmother, Granny Rumple was a moneylender, one of the few jobs a Jew could have in the Ukraine that brought them into daily contact with the *goyim*. She could have had one of the many traditional women's roles—a matchmaker, perhaps, or an *opshprekherin* giving advice and remedies, or an herb vendor. But she was a moneylender because her husband had been one, and they had no children to take over his business. My great-grandmother, on the other hand, had learned her trade from her father and when he died and she was a widow with a single son to raise, she followed in her father's footsteps. *A sakh melokhes un veynik brokhes*: Many trades and little profit. It was a good choice for both of them.

If Granny Rumple's story sounds a bit like another you have heard, I am not surprised. My father's father used to entertain customers at his wife's inn with a rendition of Romeo and Juliet in Yiddish, passing it off as a story of his own invention. And what is folklore, after all, but the recounting of old tales? We Yolens have always borrowed from the best.

Great-grandmother's story of Granny Rumple was always told in an odd mixture of English and Yiddish, but I am of the generation of Jew who never learned the old tongue. Our parents were ashamed of it, the language of the ghetto. They used it sparingly, for punchlines of off-color jokes or to commiserate with one another at funerals. So my telling of Granny Rumple's odd history is necessarily my own. If I have left anything out, it is due neither to the censorship of commerce nor art, but the inability to get the whole thing straight from my aging relatives. As a Yolen ages, he or she remembers less and invents more. It is lucky none of us is an historian.

As a girl, Granny Rumple's name was Shana and she had been pursued by all the local boys. Even a Cossack or two had knocked loudly at her door of an evening. Such was her beauty, she managed to turn even them away with a smile. When she was finally led under the wedding canopy, the entire village was surprised, for she married neither the chief rabbi's son, a dark-eyed scholar named Lev, nor the local butcher, who was a fat, ribald widower, nor the half dozen others who had asked her. Instead she chose Shmuel Zvi Bar Michael, the moneychanger. No one was more surprised than he, for he was small, skinny, and extremely ugly, with his father's large nose spread liberally across his face. Like many ugly people, though, he was also gentle, kind, and intensely interested in the happiness of others.

"Why did you marry him?" my great-grandmother had wondered.

"Because he proposed to me without stuttering," Shana had replied, stuttering being the one common thread in the other suits. It was all the answer she was ever to give.

By all accounts, it was a love match and the expected children would have followed apace—with Shana's looks, her mother had prayed—but Shmuel was murdered within a year of the wedding.

It is the telling of that murder, ornamented by time, that my great-grandmother liked to tell. Distance lends a fascination to blood tales. It runs in our family. I read murder mysteries; my daughter is a detective.

There was, you see, a walled Jewish ghetto in the town of Ykaterinislav and beyond it, past the trenches where the soldiers practiced every spring, the larger Christian settlement. The separate Jewish quarters are no longer there, of course. It is a family joke: What the Cossacks and Hitler only began, Chernobyl finished.

Every day Shmuel Zvi Bar Michael would say his prayers in his little stone house, donning *tefillin* and giving thanks he was not a woman—but secretly giving thanks as well that he had a woman like Shana in his bed each night. He was not a man unmindful of his blessings and he only stuttered when addressing the Lord G-d.

Then he would make his way past the gates of the ghetto, past the trenches, and onto the twisting cobbled streets of Ykaterinislav proper. He secreted gold in various pockets of his black coat, and sewed extra coins and jewels into the linings of his vest. But of course everyone knew he had such monies on him. He was a changer, after all.

Now one Friday he was going along the High Street where the shops of the merchants leaned despondently on one another. Even in Christian Ykaterinislav recessions could not be ignored and the czar's coinage did not flow as freely there as it did in the great cities. As he turned one particular corner, he heard rather loud weeping coming from beside the mill house. When he stopped in—his profession and his extreme ugliness allowing him entrée other Jews did not have—he saw the miller's daughter sobbing messily into her apron. It was a white apron embroidered with gillyflowers on the hem; of such details legends are made real. Shmuel knew the girl, having met her once or twice when doing business with her father, for the miller was always buying on margin and needing extra gold. As a miller's wares are always in demand, Shmuel had no fear that he would not be repaid. *Gelt halt zikh nor in a grobn zak:* Money stays only in a thick sack. The miller's sack, Shmuel knew, was the thickest.

The girl's name was Tasha—Tana to her family—and as pretty as her blond head was, it was empty. If she thought something, she said it, true or not. And she agreed with her father in everything. She would have been beaten otherwise. She was not smart—but she was not *that* stupid.

"Na—na, Tana," Shmuel said, using her familiar name to comfort her. "What goes?"

In between the loud snuffles and rather muffled sobs, she offered up the explanation. Her father had boasted to the mayor of Ykaterinislav that Tana could spin miracles of flax and weave cloth as beautiful as the gold coats of the Burgundian seamstresses.

"And where is Burgundian anyway?" Tana asked, sniffling.

"A long way from here," replied Shmuel. It was little comfort.

"I am a poor spinner at best," Tana confessed. She whispered it for it was nothing to boast of. "And I cannot weave at all. But I *can* cook."

"Na—na, Tana," Shmuel said, "but what is the *real* problem?"

"The real problem?"

"Why are you *really* crying?"

"Oh!" She took a deep breath. "Unless I can spin and sew such a cloth, my father's boast will lose us both our heads."

"This sounds like a fairy tale to me," said Shmuel, though of course he did not use the word *fairy*, that being a French invention. He said "It sounds like a story of the *leshy*." But if I had said that, you would not have understood. And indeed, I did not either, until it was explained to me by an aunt.

"But it is *true!*" she wailed and would be neither comforted nor moved from her version of the facts.

"Then I shall lend you the money—and at no interest—to buy such a cloth and you can give that to your father, who can offer it to the mayor in place of your own poor work."

"*At no interest!*" Tana exclaimed, that in itself such a miraculous event as to seem a fairy story.

"In honor of a woman as dark as you are fair, but equally beautiful," Shmuel said.

"Who is that?" asked Tana, immediately suspecting sorcery.

"My new bride," Shmuel reported proudly.

At which point she knew it to be devil's work indeed, for where would such an ugly little man get a beautiful bride except through sorcery. But so great was her own perceived need, she crossed herself surreptitiously and accepted his loan.

Shmuel found her a gold coin in the right pocket of his coat and made a great show of its presentation. Then he had her sign her X on a paper, and left certain he had done the right thing.

Tana went right out to the market of a neighboring town, where she bought a piece of gold-embroidered cloth from a tinker. It was more intricate than anything either she or her father could have imagined, with the initials T and L cunningly intertwined beneath the body of a dancing bear.

The mayor of Ykaterinislav was suitably impressed, and he immediately introduced his son Leon to Tana. The twined initials were not lost upon them. The son, while not as smart as his father, was handsome, and he was heir to his father's fortune as well. Dreaming of another fortune to add to the family's wealth he proposed.

Good husband that he was, Shmuel reported all his dealings to Shana. He was extremely uxorious; nothing pleased him more than to relate the day's business to her.

"They would not have killed her for a story," she said. "Probably her father had wagered on it."

"Who knows what the *goyim* will do," he replied. "Trust me, Shana, I deal with them every day. They do not know story from history. It is all the same to them."

Shana shrugged and went back to her own work; but as she said the prayers over the Sabbath candles that evening, she added an extra prayer to keep her beloved husband safe.

Who says the Lord G-d has no sense of humor? Just a week went by and Shmuel once again passed along the High Street and heard the miller's daughter sobbing.

"Na—na, Tana," he said. "What goes this time?"

"I am to be married," she said.

"That is not an institution to be despised. I myself have a beautiful bride. Happiness is in the marriage bed."

This time she did not bother to hide her genuflection, but Shmuel was used to the ways of the *goy*.

"My father-in-law-to-be, the mayor, insists that I produce the wedding costume, and the costumes of my attending maidens besides."

"But of course," Shmuel agreed. "Even beyond the gates . . ."—and he gestured toward the ghetto walls—"even there the bride's family supplies . . ."

"Myself!" she cried. "I am to make each myself. And embroider them with my own hands. *And I cannot sew!*" She proceeded to weep again into her apron, this time so prodigiously, the gillyflowers would surely have grown from the watering had the Lord G-d been paying attention as in the days of old.

"A-ha!" Shmuel said, reaching into his pockets and jangling several coins together. "I understand. But my dear, I have the means to help you, only . . ."

"Only?" She looked up from the soggy apron.

"Only this time, as you have prospects of a rich marriage . . ."—for gossip travels through stone walls where people themselves cannot pass. It is one of the nine metaphysical wonders of the world—number three actually.

"Only?" To say the girl was two platters and a bottle short of a banquet is to do her honor.

"Only this time you must pay interest on the loan," Shmuel said. He was a businessman after all, not just a Samaritan. And Samaria—like Burgundy, was a long way from there.

Tana agreed at once and put her X to a paper she could not read, then gratefully pocketed three gold pieces. It would buy the services of many fine seamstresses with—she reckoned quickly—enough left over for a chain for her neck and a net for her hair. She could not read but, like most of the girls of Ykaterinislav, she *could* count.

"I do not like such dealings," Shana remarked that evening. "The men at least are honorable in their own way. But the women of the *goyim* . . ."

"I am a respected moneylender," Shmuel said, his voice sharp. Then afraid he might have been *too* sharp, he added, "Their women are nothing like ours; and *you* are a queen of the ghetto."

If she was appeased, she did not show it, but that night her prayers were even longer over the candles, as if she were having a stern talking to with the Lord G-d.

Ah—you think you know the tale now. And perhaps you are right. But, as Shmuel noted, some do not know story from history. Perhaps you are one of those. Story tells us that the little devil, the child stealer, the black imp was thwarted. Of such blood libels good rousing pogroms are made.

Still, history has two sides, not one. Here is the other.

Tana and her Leon were married, of course. Even without the cloth it was a good match. The miller's business was a thriving one; the mayor was rich on graft. It was a merger as well as a marriage. Properties were exchanged along with the wedding pledges. Within the first month Tana was with child. So she was cloistered there, in the lord mayor's fine house, while her own new house was being built, so she did not see Shmuel again.

And then the interest on the loan came due.

A week after Tana's child was delivered, she had a visitor.

It was not Shmuel, of course. He would never have been allowed into the woman's section of a Christian house, never allowed near the new infant.

It was Shana.

"Who are you?" asked Tana, afraid that in her long and difficult pregnancy her husband had taken a Jewish concubine, for such was not unheard of. The woman before her was extraordinarily beautiful.

"I am the wife of Shmuel Zvi Bar Michael."

"Who is that?" asked Tana. For her, one Jewish name was as unpronounceable as another.

"Shmuel Zvi Bar Michael," Shana explained, patiently, as to a child. "The moneylender. Who lent you money for your wedding."

"My father paid for my wedding," Tana said, making the sign of the cross as protection for herself and the child in her arms.

Shana did not even flinch. This puzzled Tana a great deal and frightened her as well. "What do you want?"

"Repayment of the loan," Shana said, adding under her breath in Yiddish: *"Vi men brokt zikh ayn di farfl, azoy est men zey oyf"* which means "The way your farfl is cut, that's how you'll eat it." In other words, *You made your bed, now you'll lie in it.* You don't want to ask about *farfl.*

"I borrowed nothing from you," Tana said.

Talking as if to an idiot or to one who does not understand the language, Shana said, "You borrowed it from my husband." She took a paper from her bosom and shoved it under Tana's nose.

Tana shrank from the paper and covered the child's face with a cloth as if the paper would contaminate it, poor thing. Then she began to scream: "Demon! Witch! Child stealer!" Her screams would have brought in the household if they had not all been about the business of the day.

But a Jew—any Jew—knows better than to stay where the charge of blood libel has been laid. Shana left at once, the paper still fluttering in her hand.

She went home but said nothing to her husband. When necessary, Shana could keep her own counsel.

Still, the damage had been done. Terrified she would have to admit her failures, Tana told her husband a fairy tale indeed, complete with a little, ugly black imp with an unpronounceable name who had sworn to take her child for unspeakable rites. And as it was springtime, and behind the ghetto walls the Jewish community of Ykaterinislav was preparing for Passover, Tana's accusations of blood libel were believed, though it took her a full night of complaining to convince Leon.

Who but a Jew, after all, was little and dark—never mind that half of the population both in front of and behind the walls were tall and blonde thanks to the Vikings who had settled their trade center in Kiev generations before. Who but a Jew had an unpronounceable name—never mind that the local goyish names did not have a sufficiency of vowels. Who but a Jew would steal a Christian child, slitting its throat and using the innocent blood in the making of matzoh—never mind that it was the Jews, not the gentiles, who had been on the blade end of the killing knife all along.

Besides, it had been years since the last pogrom. Blood calls for blood, even if it is just a story. Leon went to his friends, elaborating on Tana's tale.

What happened next was simple. Just as the *shammes* was going around the ghetto, rapping with his special hammer on the shutters of the houses and calling out "Arise, Jews, and serve the Lord! Arise and recite the psalms!" the local bullyboys were massing outside the ghetto walls.

In house after house, Jewish men rose and donned their *tefillin* and began their prayers; the women lit the fires in the stoves.

Then the wife of Gdalye the butcher—his new

wife—went out to pull water from the well and saw the angry men outside the gate. She raised the alarm, but by then it was too late. As they hammered down the gate, the cries went from the streets to Heaven, but if the Lord G-d was home and listening, there was no sign of it.

The rabble broke through the gates and roamed freely along the streets. They pulled Jews out of their houses and measured them against a piece of lumber with a blood red line drawn halfway up. Any man found below the line was beaten, no matter his age. And all the while the rabble chanted "Little black imp!" and "Stealer of children!"

By morning's end the count was this: two concussions, three broken arms, many bruises and blackened eyes, a dislocated jaw, the butcher's and baker's shops set afire, and one woman raped. She was an old woman. The only one they could find. By pogrom standards it was minor stuff and the Jews of Ykaterinislav were relieved. They knew, even if the *goyim* did not, that this sort of thing is easier done in the disguise of night.

One man only was missing—Shmuel Zvi Bar Michael, the moneylender. He was the shortest and the ugliest and the blackest little man the crowd of sinners could find.

Of course the rest of the Jews were too busy to look for him. The men were trying to save what they could of Gdalye the butcher's shop and Avreml the baker's house. The women were too busy binding up the heads of Reb Jakob and his son Lev, and the arms of the three men, one a ten-year-old boy, and the jaw of Moyshe the cobbler, and tending to the old woman. Besides Shana had been too guilt-ridden to press them into the search.

It was not until the next day that she found his body—or the half of it that remained—in the soldiers' trenches.

At the funeral she tore her face with her fingernails and wept until her eyes were permanently reddened. Her hair turned white during the week she sat *shiva*. And it was thus that Granny Rumple was born of sorrow, shame, and guilt. At least that was my great-grandmother's story. And while details in the middle of the tale had a tendency to change with each telling, the ending was always tragic.

But the story, you say, is too familiar for belief? *Belief!* Is it less difficult to believe that a man distributed food to thousands using only a few loaves and fishes? Is it less difficult to believe the Red Sea opened in the middle to let a tribe of wandering desert dwellers through? Is it less difficult to believe that Elvis is alive and well and shopping at Safeway?

Look at the story you know. Who is the moral center of it? Is it the miller who lies and his daughter who is complicitous in the lie? Is it the king who wants her for commercial purposes only? Or is it the dark, ugly little man with the unpronounceable name who promises to change flax into gold—and does exactly what he promises?

Stories are told one way, history another. But for the Jews—despite their long association with the Lord G-d—the endings have always been the same.

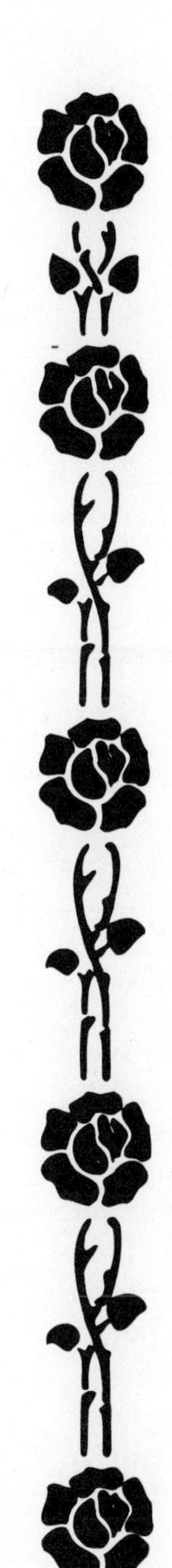

The Sawing Boys

Howard Waldrop

Howard Waldrop is from Mississippi but has lived in Austin for many years. He is the author of the novel Them Bones, *the novella* A Dozen Tough Jobs, *and in collaboration with Jake Saunders authored* The Texas-Israeli War: 1999. *Waldrop is best known for his extensive body of short fiction, having won the Nebula Award and World Fantasy Award for "The Ugly Chickens" in 1981. His short fiction has been collected in* Howard Who?, All About Strange Monsters of the Recent Past, *and* Night of the Cooters: More Neat Stories *(Ace). Cheap Street recently published his novelette "You* Could *Go Home Again." He is working on the novels* The Moon World *and* I, John Mandeville.

"The Sawing Boys" is based on "The Bremen Town Musicians," a classic fairy tale. Waldrop imbues it with his unique quirkiness by transporting it to the American South.

The Sawing Boys

For Arthur Hunnicutt and the late Sheldon Leonard.

THERE WAS A PLACE IN THE WOODS WHERE THREE paths came together and turned into one big path heading south.

A bearded man in a large straw hat and patched bib overalls came down one. Over his shoulder was a tow sack, and out of it stuck the handle of a saw. The man had a long wide face and large thin ears.

Down the path to his left came a short man in butternut pants and a red checkerboard shirt that said *Ralston-Purina Net Wt. 20 lbs.* on it. He had on a bright red cloth cap that stood up on the top of his head. Slung over his back was a leather strap; hanging from it was a big ripsaw.

On the third path were two people, one of whom wore a yellow-and-black-striped shirt, and had a mustache that stood straight out from the sides of his nose. The other man was dressed in a dark brown barn coat. He had a wrinkled face, and wore a brown Mackenzie cap down from which the earflaps hung, even though it was a warm morning. The man with the mustache carried a narrow folding ladder; the other carried a two-man bucksaw.

The first man stopped.

"Hi yew!" he said in the general direction of the other two paths.

"Howdee!" said the short man in the red cap.

"Well, well, well!" said the man with the floppy-eared hat, putting down his big saw.

"Weow!" said the man with the wiry mustache.

They looked each other over, keeping their distance, eyeing each others' clothing and saws.

"Well, I guess we know where we're all headed," said the man with the brown Mackenzie cap.

"I reckon," said the man in the straw hat. "I'm Luke Apuleus, from over Cornfield County way. I play the crosscut."

"I'm Rooster Joe Banty," said the second. "I'm a ripsaw bender myself."

"I'm Felix Horbliss," said the man in stripes with the ladder. "That thar's Cave Canem. We play this here big bucksaw."

They looked at each other some more.

"I'm to wonderin'," said Luke, bringing his toe sack around in front of him. "I'm wonderin' if'n we know the same tunes. Seems to me it'd be a shame to have to play agin' each other if'n we could help it."

"You-all know 'Trottin' Gertie Home'?" asked Felix.

Luke and Rooster Joe nodded.

"How about 'When the Shine comes Out'n the Dripper'?" asked Rooster Joe.

The others nodded.

"How are you on 'Snake Handler's Two-Step'?" asked Luke Apuleus.

More nods.

"Well, that's a start on it," said Cave Canem. "We can talk about it on the way there. I bet we'd sound right purty together."

So side by side by bucksaw and ladder, they set out down the big path south.

What we are doing is, we are walking down this unpaved road. How we have come to be walking down this unpaved road is a very long and tiresome story that I should not bore you with.

We are being Chris the Shoemaker, who is the brains of this operation, and a very known guy aback where we come from, which is south of Long Island, and Large Jake and Little Willie, who are being the brawn, and Miss Millie Dee Chantpie, who is Chris the Shoemaker's doll, and who is always dressed to the nines, and myself, Charlie Perro, whose job it is to remind everyone what their job is being.

"I am astounded as all get-out," says Little Willie, "that there are so many places with no persons in them nowise," looking around at the trees and bushes and such. "We have seen two toolsheds which looked as if they once housed families of fourteen, but of real-for-true homes, I am not seeing any."

"Use your glims for something besides keeping your nose from sliding into your eyebrows," says Chris the Shoemaker. "You will have seen the sign that said one of the toolcribs is the town of Podunk, and the other shed is the burg of Shtetl. I am believing the next one we will encounter is called Pratt Falls. I am assuming it contains some sort of trickle of fluid, a stunning and precipitous descent in elevation, established by someone with the aforementioned surname."

He is called Chris the Shoemaker because that is now his moniker, and he once hung around shoestores. At that time the cobbler shops was the place where the policy action was hot, and before you can be saying Hey Presto! there is Chris the Shoemaker in a new loud suit looking like a comet, and he is the middle guy between the shoemakers and the elves that rig the policy.

"Who would have thought it?" asked Little Willie, "both balonies on the rear blowing at the same time, and bending up the frammus, and all the push and pull running out? I mean, what are the chances?"

Little Willie is called that because he is the smaller of the two brothers. Large Jake is called that because, oh my goodness, is he large. He is so large that people have confused him for nightfall—they are standing on the corner shooting the breeze with some guys, and suddenly all the light goes away, and so do the other guys. There are all these cigarettes dropping to the pavement where guys used to be, and the person looks around and Whoa! it is not night at all, it is only Large Jake.

For two brothers they do not look a thing alike. Little Willie looks, you should excuse the expression, like something from the family Rodentia, whereas Large Jake is a very pleasant-looking individual, only the pleasant is spread across about three feet of mook.

Miss Millie Dee Chantpie is hubba-hubba stuff (only Chris the Shoemaker best not see you give her more than one Long Island peek) and the talk is she used to be a roving debutante. Chris has the goo-goo eyes for her, and she is just about a whiz at the new crossword puzzles, which always give Little Willie a headache when he tries to do one.

Where we are is somewhere in the state of Kentucky, which I had not been able to imagine had I not seen it yesterday from the train. Why we were here was for a meet with this known guy who runs a used furniture business on South Wabash Street in Chi City. The meet was to involve lots of known guys, and to be at some hunting lodge in these hills outside Frankfort, where we should not be bothered by prying eyes. Only first the train is late, and the jalopy we bought stalled on us in the dark, and there must have been this wrong turn somewhere, and the next thing you are knowing the balonies blow and we are playing in the ditch and gunk and goo are all over the place.

So here we are walking down this (pardon the expression) road, and we are looking for a phone and a mechanically inclined individual, and we are not having such a hot time of it.

"You will notice the absence of wires," said Chris the Shoemaker, "which leads me to believe we will not find no blower at this watery paradise of Pratt Falls."

"Christ Almighty, I'm gettin' hungry!" says Miss Millie Dee Chantpie of a sudden. She is in this real flapper outfit, with a bandeau top and fringes, and is wearing pearls that must have come out of oysters the size of freight trucks.

"If we do not soon find the object of our quest," says Chris the Shoemaker, "I shall have Large Jake blow you the head off a moose, or whatever they have in place of cows out here."

It being a meet, we are pretty well rodded up, all except for Chris, who had to put on his Fall Togs last year on Bargain Day at the courthouse and do a minute standing on his head, so of course he can no longer have an oscar anywhere within a block of his person, so Miss Millie Dee Chantpie carries his cannon in one of her enchanting little reticules.

Large Jake is under an even more stringent set of behavioral codes, but he just plain does not care, and I do not personally know any cops or even the Sammys who are so gauche as to try to frisk him without first calling out the militia. Large Jake usually carries a powder wagon—it is the kind of thing they use on mad elephants or to stop runaway locomotives only it is sawed off on both ends to be only about a foot long.

Little Willie usually carries a sissy rod, only it is a dumb gat so there is not much commotion when he uses it—just the sound of air coming out of it, and then the sound of air coming out of whomsoever he uses it on. Little Willie has had a date to Ride Old Sparky before, only he was let out on a technical. The technical was that the judge had not noticed the big shoe box full of geetas on the corner of his desk before he brought the gavel down.

I am packing my usual complement of calibers which (I am prouder than anything to say) I have never used. They are only there for the bulges for people to ogle at while Chris the Shoemaker is speaking.

Pratt Falls is another couple of broken boards and a sign saying Feed and Seed. There was this dry ditch with a hole with a couple of rocks in it.

"It was sure no Niagara," says Little Willie, "that's for certain."

At the end of the place was a sign, all weathered out except for the part that said 2 MILES.

We are making this two miles in something less than three-quarters of an hour because it is mostly uphill and our dogs are barking, and Miss Millie Dee Chantpie, who has left her high heels in the flivver, is falling off the sides of her flats very often.

We are looking down into what passes for a real live town in these parts.

"This is the kind of place," says Little Willie, "where when you are in the paper business, and you mess up your double sawbuck plates, and print a twenty-one-dollar bill, you bring it here and ask for change. And the guy at the store will look in the drawer and ask you if two nines and a three will do."

"Ah, but look, gentlemen and lady," says Chris the Shoemaker, "there are at least two wires coming down over the mountain into this metropolis, and my guess is that they are attached to civilization at the other end."

"I do not spy no filling station," I says. "But there does seem to be great activity for so early of a morning." I am counting houses. "More people are already in town than live here."

"Perhaps the large gaudy sign up ahead will explain it," says Little Willie. The sign is being at an angle where another larger dirt path comes into town. From all around on the mountains I can see people coming in in wagons and on horses and on foot.

We get to the sign. This is what it says, I kid you not:

BIG HARMONY CONTEST!
BRIMMYTOWN SQUARE SAT MAY 16
$50 FIRST PRIZE
Brought to you by Watkins Products
and CARDUI, Makers of BLACK DRAUGHT
Extra! Sacred Harp Singing
Rev. Shapenote and the Mt. Sinai Choir.

"Well, well," says Chris. "Looks like there'll be plenty of *étrangers* in this burg. We get in there, make the call on the meet, get someone to fix the jalopy, and be on our way. We should fit right in."

While Chris the Shoemaker is saying this, he is adjusting his orange-and-pink tie and shooting the cuffs on his purple-and-white pinstripe suit. Little Willie is straightening his pumpkin-colored, double-breasted suit and brushing the dust off his yellow spats. Large Jake is dressed in a pure white suit with a black shirt and white tie, and has on a white fedora with a thin black band. Miss Millie Dee Chantpie swirls her fringes and rearranges the ostrich feather in her cloche. I feel pretty much like a sparrow among peacocks.

"Yeah," I says, looking over the town, "they'll probably never notice we been here."

* * *

They made their way into town and went into a store. They bought themselves some items, and went out onto the long, columned verandah of the place, and sat down on some nail kegs, resting their saws and ladders against the porch railings.

Cave Canem had a big five-cent RC Cola and a bag of Tom's Nickel Peanuts. He took a long drink of the cola, tore the top off the celluloid bag, and poured the salted peanuts into the neck of the bottle. The liquid instantly turned to foam and overflowed the top, which Canem put into his mouth. When it settled down, he drank from the bottle and chewed on the peanuts that came up the neck.

Rooster Joe took off his red cap. He had a five-cent Moon Pie the size of a dinner plate and took bites off that.

Horbliss had a ten-cent can of King Oscar Sardines. The key attached to the bottom broke off at the wrong place. Rather than tearing his thumb up, he took out his pocketknife and cut the top of the can off and peeled the ragged edge back. He drank off the oil, smacking his lips, then took out the sardines between his thumb and the knife blade and ate them.

Luke had bought a two-foot length of sugarcane and was sucking on it, spitting out the fine slivers which came away in his mouth.

They ate in silence and watched the crowds go by, clumps of people breaking away and eddying into the stores and shops. At one end of town, farmers stopped their wagons and began selling the produce. From the other end, at the big open place where the courthouse would be if Brimmytown were the county seat, music started up.

They had rarely seen so many men in white shirts, even on Sunday, and women and kids in their finest clothes, even if they were only patched and faded coveralls, they were starched and clean.

Then a bunch of city flatlanders came by—the men all had on hats and bright suits and ties, and the woman—a goddess—was the first flapper they had ever seen—the eyes of the flatlanders were moving everywhere. Heads turned to watch them all along their route. They were moving toward the general mercantile, and they looked tired and dusty for all their fancy duds.

"Well, boys," said Luke. "That were a right smart breakfast. I reckon us-all better be gettin' on down towards the musical place and see what the otherns look like."

They gathered up their saws and ladders and walked toward the sweetest sounds this side of Big Bone Lick.

"So," says Little Willie to a citizen, "tell us where we can score a couple of motorman's gloves?"

The man is looking at him like he has just stepped off one of the outermost colder planets. This is fitting, for the citizen looks to us vice versa.

"What my friend of limited vocabulary means," says Chris the Shoemaker to the astounding and astounded individual, "is where might we purchase a mess of fried pork chops?"

The man keeps looking at us with his wide eyes the size of doorknobs.

"Eats?" I volunteers.

Nothing is happening.

Large Jake makes eating motions with his mitt and goozle.

Still nothing.

"Say, fellers," says this other resident, "you won't be gettin' nothing useful out'n him. He's one of the simpler folks hereabouts, what them Victorian painter fellers used to call 'naturals.' What you want's Ma Gooser's place, straight down this yere street."

"Much obliged," says Chris.

"It's about time, too," says Miss Millie Dee Chantpie. "I'm so hungry I could eat the ass off a pigeon through a park bench!"

I am still staring at the individual who has given us directions, who is knocking the ashes out of his corncob pipe against a rain barrel.

"Such a collection of spungs and feebs I personally have never seen," says Chris the Shoemaker, who is all the time looking at the wire that comes down the hill into town.

"I must admit you are right," says Little Willie. And indeed it seems every living thing for three counties is here—there are nags and wagons, preggo dolls with stair-step children born nine months and fifteen minutes apart, guys wearing only a hat and one blue garment, a couple of men with what's left of Great War uniforms with the dago dazzlers still pinned to the chests—yes indeedy, a motley and hilarity-making group.

The streets are being full of wagons with melons and the lesser legumes and things which for a fact I know grow in the ground. The indigenous peoples are selling everything what moves. And from far away you can hear the beginnings of music.

"I spy," says Chris the Shoemaker.
"Whazzat?" asks Little Willie.
"I spy the blacksmith shop, and I spy the general mercantile establishment to which the blower wire runs. Here is what we are doing. William and I will saunter over to the smithy and forge, where we will inquire of aid for the vehicle. Charlie Perro, you will go make the call which will tender our apologies as being late for the meet, and get some further instructions. Jacob, you will take the love of my life, Miss Millie, to this venerable Ma Gooser's eatatorium where we will soon join you in a prodigious repast."

The general mercantile is in the way of selling everything on god's green earth, and the aroma is very mouth-watering—it is a mixture of apple candy and nag tack, coal oil and licorice and flour, roasted coffee and big burlap sacks of nothing in particular. There is ladies' dresses and guy hats and weapons of all kinds.
There is one phone; it is on the back wall; it is the kind Alexander Graham Bell made himself.
"Good person," I says to the man behind the counter, who is wearing specs and a vest and has a tape measure draped over his shoulder, "might I use your telephonic equipment to make a collect long-distance call?"
"Everthin's long-distance from here," he opines. "Collect, you say?"
"That is being correct."
He goes to the wall and twists a crank and makes bell sounds. "Hello, Gertie. This is Spoon. How's things in Grinder Switch? . . . You don't say? Well, there's a city feller here needs to make a co-llect call.

Right. You fix him up." He hands me the long earpiece, and puts me in the fishwife care of this Gertie, and parks himself nearby and begins to count some bright glittery objects.

I tells Gertie the number I want. There are these sounds like the towers are falling. "And what's your name," asks this Gertie.

I gives her the name of this known newspaper guy who hangs out at Chases' and who writes about life in the Roaring Forties back in the Big City. The party on the other end will be wise that that is not who it is, but will know I know he knows.

I hear this voice and Gertie gives them my name and they say okay.

"Go ahead," says Gertie.

"We are missing the meet," I says.

"Bleaso!" says the voice. "Eetmay alledoffcay. Ammysays Iseway! Izzyoway and Oemay erehay."

Itshay I am thinking to myself. To him I says:

"Elltay usoway atwhay otay ooday?"

"Ogay Omehay!"

He gets off the blower.

"I used to have a cousin that could talk Mex," says Spoon at the counter. I thank him for the use of the phone. "Proud as a peach of it," he says, wiping at it with a cloth.

"Well, you should be," I tell him. Then I buy two cents worth of candy and put it in a couple of pockets, and then I ease on down this town's Great White Way.

This Ma Gooser's is some hopping joint. I don't think the griddle here's been allowed to cool off since the McKinley Administration. Large Jake and Miss Millie Dee Chantpie are already tucking in. The place is as busy as a chophouse on Chinese New Year.

There are these indistinguishable shapes on the platters.

A woman the size of Large Jake comes by with six full plates along each arm, headed towards a table of what looks like two oxdrivers in flannel shirts. These two oxdrivers are as alike as all get-out. The woman puts three plates in front of each guy and they fall into them mouth first.

The woman comes back. She has wild hair, and it does not look like she has breasts; it looks like she has a solid shelf across her chest under her work shirt. "Yeah?" she says, wiping sweat from her brow.

"I'd like a steak and some eggs," I says, "over easy on the eggs, steak well-done, some juice on the side."

"You'll get the breakfast, if'n you get anything," she says. "Same's everbody else." She follows my eyes back to the two giants at the next table. Large Jake can put away the groceries, but he is a piker next to these two. A couple of the plates in front of them are already shining clean and they are reaching for a pile of biscuits on the next table as they work on their third plates.

"Them's the Famous Singin' Eesup Twins, Bert and Mert," says Ma Gooser. "If'n everybody could pile it in like them, I'd be a rich woman." She turns to the kitchen.

"Hey, Jughead," she yells, "where's them six dozen biscuits?"

"Comin', Ma Gooser!" yells a voice from back in the hell there.

"More blackstrap 'lasses over here, Ma!" yells a corncob from another table.

"Hold your water!" yells Ma. "I only got six hands!" She runs back towards the kitchen.

Chris the Shoemaker and Little Willie comes in and settles down.

"Well, we are set in some departments. The blacksmith is gathering up the tools of his trade and Little William will accompany him in his wagon to the site of the vehicular happenstance. I will swear to you, he picks up his anvil and puts it into his wagon, just like that. The thing must have dropped the wagon bed two foot. What is it they are feeding the locals around here?" He looks down at the plates in front of Large Jake and Miss Millie. "What is *dat?*"

"I got no idea, sweetie," says Miss Millie, putting another forkful in, "but it sure is good!"

"And what's the news from our friends across the ways?"

"Zex," I says.

He looks at me. "*You* are telling *me* zex in this oomray full of oobrays?"

"No, Chris," I says, "the *word* is zex."

"Oh," he says, "and for why?"

"Izzy and Moe," I says.

"*Izzy* and *Moe?!* How did Izzy and Moe get wise to this deal?"

"How do Izzy and Moe get wise to anything," I says, keeping my voice low and not moving my goozle. "Hell, if someone could get *them* to come over, this umray unningray biz would be a snap. If they can dress like women shipwrecks and get picked up by runners' ships, they can get wind of a meet somewhere."

"So what are our options being?" asks Chris the Shoemaker.

"That is why we have all these round-trip tickets," I says.

He is quiet. Ma Gooser slaps down these plates in front of us, and coffee all round, and takes two more piles of biscuits over to the Famous Singing Eesup Twins.

"Well, that puts the damper on my portion of the Era of Coolidge Prosperity," says Chris the Shoemaker. "I am beginning to think this decade is going to be a more problematical thing than first imagined. In fact, I am getting in one rotten mood." He takes a drink of coffee. His beezer lights up. "Say, the flit in the *Knowledge Box* got *nothing* on this." He drains the cup dry. He digs at his plate, then wolfs it all down. "Suddenly my mood is changing. Sudden-like, I am in a working mood."

I drops my fork.

"Nix?" I asks nice, looking at him like I am a tired halibut.

"No, not no nix at all. It is of a sudden very clear why we have come to be in this place through these unlikely circumstances. I had just not realized it till now."

Large Jake has finished his second plate. He pushes it away and looks at Chris the Shoemaker.

"Later," says Chris. "Outside."

Jake nods.

Of a sudden-like, I am not enjoying Ma Gooser's groaning board as much as I should wish.

For when Chris is in a working mood, things happen.

They had drawn spot # 24 down at the judging stand. Each contestant could sing three songs, and the Black Draught people had a big gong they could ring if anyone was too bad.

"I don't know 'bout the ones from 'round here," said Cave Canem, "but they won't need that there gong for the people we know about. We came in third to some of 'em last year in Sweet Tater City."

"Me neither," said Rooster Joe. "The folks I seen can sure play and sing. Why even the Famous Eesup Twins, Bert and Mert, is here. You ever hear them do 'Land Where No Cabins Fall'?"

"Nope," said Luke, "but I have heard of 'em. It seems we'll just have to outplay them all."

They were under a tree pretty far away from the rest of the crowd, who were waiting for the contest to begin.

"Let's rosin up, boys," said Luke, taking his crosscut saw out of his tow sack.

Felix unfolded the ladder and climbed up. Cave pulled out a big willow bow strung with braided muletail hair.

Rooster Joe took out an eight-ounce ball peen hammer and sat back against a tree root.

Luke rosined up his fiddle bow.

"Okay, let's give 'er about two pounds o' press and bend."

He nodded his head. They bowed, Felix pressing down on the big bucksaw handle from above, Rooster Joe striking his ripsaw, Luke pulling at the back of his crosscut.

The same note, three octaves apart, floated on the air.

"Well, that's enough rehearsin'," said Luke. "Now all we got to do is stay in this shady spot and wait till our turn."

They put their instruments and ladder against the tree, and took naps.

When Chris the Shoemaker starts to working, usually someone ends up with cackle fruit on their mug.

When Little Willie and Chris first teamed up when they were oh so very young, they did all the usual grifts. They worked the cherry-colored cat and the old hydrophoby lay, and once or twice even pulled off the glim drop, which is a wonder since neither of them has a glass peeper. They quit the grift when it turns out that Little Willie is always off nugging when Chris needs him, or is piping some doll's stems when he should be laying zex. So they went into various other forms of getting the mazuma.

The ramadoola Chris has come up with is a simple one. We are to get the lizzie going, or barring that are to Hooverize another one; then we cut the lines of communication; immobilize the town clown, glom the loot, and give them the old razoo.

"But Chris," says I, "it is so simple and easy there must be something wrong with your brainstorm. And besides, it is what? Maybe a hundred simoleons in all? I have seen you lose that betting on which raindrop will run down a windowpane first."

"We have been placed here to do this thing," says Chris the Shoemaker. We are all standing on the porch of Ma Gooser's. "We cut the phone," says Chris, "no one can call out. Any other jalopies, Large Jake makes inoperable. That leaves horses, which even we can go faster than. We make the local yokel do a Brodie so there is no Cicero lightning or Illinois thunder. We are gone, and the news takes till next week to get over the ridge yonder."

Miss Millie Dee Chantpie has one of her shoes off and is rubbing her well-turned foot. "My corns is killing me," she says, "and Chris, I think this is the dumbest thing you have ever thought about!"

"I will note and file that," says Chris. "Meantimes, that is the plan. Little William here will start a rumor that will make our presence acceptable before he goes off with the man with the thews of iron. We will only bleaso this caper should the flivver not be fixable or we cannot kipe another one. So it is written. So it shall be done."

Ten minutes later, just before Little Willie leaves in the wagon, I hear two people talking close by, pointing to Miss Millie Dee Chantpie and swearing she is a famous chanteuse, and that Chris the Shoemaker is a talent scout from Okeh Records.

"The town clown," says Chris to me in a while, "will be no problem. He is that gent you see over there sucking on the yamsicle, with the tin star pinned to his long johns with the Civil War cannon tucked in his belt."

I nod.

"Charlie Perro," he says to me, "now let us make like we are mesmerized by this screeching and hollering that is beginning."

The contest is under way. It was like this carnival freak show had of a sudden gone into a production of *No, No Nanette* while you were trying to get a good peek at the India Rubber Woman.

I am not sure whether to be laughing or crying, so I just puts on the look a steer gets just after the hammer comes down, and pretends to watch. What I am really thinking, even I don't know.

There had been sister harmony groups, and guitar and mandolin ensembles, three guys on one big harmonica, a couple of twelve-year-olds playing ocarinas and washboards, a woman on gutbucket broom bass, a handbell choir from a church, three one-man bands, and a guy who could tear newspapers to the tune of "Hold That Tiger!"

Every eight acts or so, Reverend Shapenote and the Mt. Sinai Choir got up and sang sacred harp music, singing the notes only, with no words because their church believed you went straight to Hell if you sang words to a hymn; you could only lift your voice in song.

Luke lay with his hat over his eyes through two more acts. It was well into the afternoon. People were getting hot and cranky all over the town.

As the next act started, Luke sat up. He looked toward the stage. Two giants in coveralls and flannel shirts got up. Even from this far away, their voices carried clear and loud, not strained: deep bass and baritone.

The words of "Eight More Miles To Home" and then "You Are My Sunshine" came back, and for their last song, they went into the old hymn, "Absalom, Absalom":

Day-Vid The King—He-Wept—and Wept
Saying—Oh My Son—Oh my son . . .

and a chill went up Luke's back.

"That's them," said Rooster Joe, seeing Luke awake.

"Well," said Luke Apuleus, pulling his hat back down over his eyes as the crowd went crazy, "them is the ones we really have to beat. Call me when they gets to the Cowbell Quintet so we can be moseying up there."

I am being very relieved when Little Willie comes driving into town in the flivver; it is looking much the worse for wear but seems to be running fine. He parks it on Main Street at the far edge of the crowd and comes walking over to me and Chris the Shoemaker.

"How are you standing this?" he asks.

"Why do you not get up there, William," asks Chris. "I know for a fact you warbled for the cheese up at the River Academy, before they let you out on the technical."

"It was just to keep from driving an Irish buggy," says Little Willie. "The Lizzie will go wherever you want it to. Tires patched. Gassed and lubered up. Say the syllable."

Chris nods to Large Jake over at the edge of the crowd. Jake saunters back towards the only two trucks in town, besides the Cardui vehicle, which, being too gaudy even for us, Jake has already fixed while it is parked right in front of the stage, for Jake is a very clever fellow for someone with such big mitts.

"Charlie Perro," says Chris, reaching in Miss Millie Dee Chantpie's purse, "how's about taking these nippers here," handing me a pair of wire cutters, "and go see if that blower wire back of the general mercantile isn't too long by about six feet when I give you the nod. Then you should come back and help us." He also takes his howitzer out of Miss Millie's bag.

"Little William," he says, turning. "Take Miss Millie Dee Chantpie to the car and start it up. I shall go see what the Cardui Black Draught people are doing."

So it was we sets out to pull the biggest caper in the history of Brimmytown.

"That's them," said Rooster Joe. "The cowbells afore us."

"Well, boys," said Luke, "it's do-or-die time."

They gathered up their saws and sacks and ladder, and started for the stage.

Miss Millie Dee Chantpie is in the car, looking cool as a cucumber. Little Willie is at one side of the crowd, standing out like a sore thumb; he has his hand under his jacket on The Old Crowd Pleaser.

Large Jake is back, shading three or four people from the hot afternoon sun. I am at the corner of the general mercantile, one eye on Chris the Shoemaker and one on the wire coming down the back of the store.

The prize moolah is in this big glass cracker jar on the table with the judges so everybody can see it. It is in greenbacks.

I am seeing Large Jake move up behind the John Law figure, who is sucking at a jug of corn liquor—you would not think the Prohib was the rule of the land here.

I am seeing these guys climb onto the stage, and I

cannot believe my peepers, because they are pulling saws and ladders out of their backs. Are these carpenters or what? There is a guy in a straw hat, and one with a bristle mustache, and one with a red-checked shirt and red hat, and one with a cap with big floppy earflaps. One is climbing on a ladder. They are having tools everywhere. What the ding-dong is going on?

And they begin to play, a corny song, but it is high and sweet, and then I am thinking of birds and rivers and running water and so forth. So I shakes myself, and keeps my glims on Chris the Shoemaker.

The guys with the saws are finishing their song, and people are going ga-ga over them.

And then I see that Chris is in position.

"Thank yew, thank yew," said Luke. "We-all is the Sawing Boys and we are pleased as butter to be here. I got a cousin over to Cornfield County what has one uh them new cat-whisker crystal *raddio* devices, and you should hear the things that comes right over the air from it. Well, I learned a few of them, and me and the boys talked about them, and now we'll do a couple for yew. Here we're gonna do one by the Molokoi Hotel Royal Hawaiian Serenaders called 'Ule Uhi Umekoi Hwa Hwa.' Take it away, Sawing Boys!" He tapped his foot.

He bent his saw and bowed the first high, swelling notes, then Rooster Joe came down on the harmony rhythm on the ripsaw. Felix bent down on the ladder on the handle of the bucksaw, and Cave pulled the big willow bow and they were off into a fast, swinging song that was about lagoons and fish and food.

People were jumping and yelling all over town, and Luke, whose voice was nothing special, started singing:

> *"Ume hoi uli koi hwa hwa*
> *Wa haweaee omi oi lui lui . . ."*

And the applause began before Rooster Joe finished alone with a dying struck high note that held for ten or fifteen seconds. People were yelling and screaming and the Cardui people didn't know what to do with themselves.

"Thank yew, thank yew!" said Luke Apuleus, wiping his brow with his arm while holding his big straw hat in his hand. "Now, here's another one I heerd. We hope you-all like it. It's from the Abe Schwartz Orchestra and it's called 'Beym Rebn in Palestine.' Take it away, Sawing Boys."

They hit halting, fluttering notes, punctuated by Rooster Joe's hammered ripsaw, and then the bucksaw went rolling behind it, Felix pumping up and down on the handle, Cave Canem bowing away. It sounded like flutes and violins and clarinets and mandolins. It sounded a thousand years old, but not like moonshine mountain music; it was from another time and another land.

Something is wrong, for Chris is standing very still, like he is already in the old oak kimono, and I can see he is not going to be giving me the High Sign.

I see that Little Willie, who never does anything on his own, is motioning to me and Large Jake to come over. So over I trot, and the music really washes over me. I know it in my bones, for it is the music of the old neighborhood where all of us but Miss Millie grew up.

I am coming up on Chris the Shoemaker and I see he has turned on the waterworks. He is transfixed, for here, one thousand miles from home, he is being caught up in the mighty coils of memory and transfiguration.

I am hearing with his ears, and what the saws are making is not the Abe Schwartz Orchestra but Itzike Kramtweiss of Philadelphia, or perhaps Naftalie Brandwein, who used to play bar mitzvahs and weddings with his back to the audience so rival clarinet players couldn't see his hands and how he made those notes.

There is maybe ten thousand years behind that noise, and it is calling all the way across the Kentucky hills from the Land of Gaza.

And while they are still playing, we walk with Chris the Shoemaker back to the jalopy, and pile in around Miss Millie Dee Chantpie, who, when she sees Chris crying, begins herself, and I confess I, too, am a little blurry-eyed at the poignance of the moment.

And we pull out of Brimmytown, the saws still whining and screeching their jazzy ancient tune, and as it is fading and we are going up the hill, Chris the Shoemaker speaks for us all, and what he says is:

"God Damn. You cannot be going *anywhere* these days without you run into a bunch of half-assed *klezmorim.*"

Glossary to "The Sawing Boys"
by Howard Waldrop

Balonies—tires
Bargain Day—court time set aside for sentencing plea-bargain cases
Beezer—the face, sometimes especially the nose
Bleaso!—1. an interjection—Careful! You are being overheard! Some chump is wise to the deal! 2. verb—to forgo something, change plans, etc.
The Cherry-colored Cat—an old con game
Cicero Lightning and Illinois Thunder—the muzzle flashes from machine guns and the sound of hand grenades going off
Do a minute—thirty days
Dogs are barking—feet are hurting
Fall Togs—the suit you wear going into, and coming out of, jail
Flit—prison coffee, from its resemblance to the popular fly spray of the time
Flivver—a jalopy
Frammus—a thingamajig or doohickey
Geetas—money, of any kind or amount
Glim Drop—con game involving leaving a glass eye as security for an amount of money; *at least* one of the con men should have a glass eye . . .
Glims—eyes
Goozle—mouth
Hooverize—(pre-Depression)—Hoover had been Allied Food Commissioner during the Great War, and was responsible for people getting the most use out of whatever foods they had; the standard command from parents was "Hooverize that

plate!"; possibly a secondary reference to vacuum cleaners of the time

Irish buggy (also Irish surrey)—a wheelbarrow

Jalopy—a flivver

Lizzie—a flivver

Mazuma—money, of any kind or amount

Mook—face

Motorman's gloves—any especially large cut of meat

Nugging—porking

The Old Hydrophoby Lay—con game involving pretending to be bitten by someone's (possibly mad) dog

Piping Some Doll's Stems—looking at some woman's legs

Push and Pull—gas and oil

Sammys—the Feds

Zex—Quiet (as in bleaso), cut it out, jiggies! Beat it! laying zex—keeping lookout

Rules of pig Latin: initial consonants are moved to the end of the word and -ay is added to the consonant; initial vowels are moved to the end of the word and -way is added to the vowel

Godson

Roger Zelazny

Roger Zelazny, winner of both the Hugo and Nebula Awards, has earned a reputation as one of the leading writers of science fiction with such works as "A Rose for Ecclesiastes" and Lord of Light. *He is also the author of several notable works of fantasy, in particular the* Chronicles of Amber *series. "Godson" is a wickedly clever modern fairy tale that aptly demonstrates why Zelazny is considered a master of both the science fiction and fantasy forms. Zelazny lives in New Mexico.*

"Godson" is based on a German fairy tale found in the Brothers Grimm collections. We won't tell you the name of the original fairy tale, however. That would give too much away. . . .

Godson

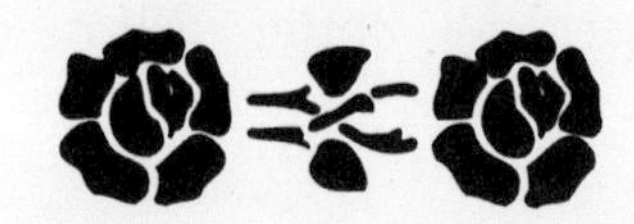

THE FIRST TIME I SAW MORRIS LEATHAM, AT THE baptismal font where he became my godfather, I was too small for the memory to stick. Thereafter he visited me every year on my birthday, and this year was no exception.

"Morrie," I said, knuckling my right eye and then my left. I opened them and stared through the predawn light of my bedroom to the chair beside the window with the dead geranium on the sill, where he sat, tall and thin, almost anorectic looking.

He rose, smiling, and crossed to the side of the bed. He extended a hand, drew me to my feet, and passed me my robe. "Put it on," he said, as he led me out of the room. My Aunt Rose and Uncle Matt were still asleep. Moments later, it seemed, Morrie and I were walking inside the local mall. It was dimly lit, and there was no one about.

"What are we doing here?" I asked.

"I'd like you to walk through, look around, and tell me what you'd like for a birthday present."

"I know right where it is," I said. "Come on."

I led him past the bench where the night watchman lay unmoving, a wet spot at the crotch of his uniform trousers. I stopped before a store window and pointed.

"Which one?" Morrie asked.

"The black one," I said.

He chuckled.

"One black bicycle for David," he said. "I'll get you one like that, only better. It'll be delivered later today."

"Thank you," I said, turning and hugging him. Then, "Don't you think we ought to wake that guard up? His boss might come by."

"He's been dead for some time, David. Myocardial infarct. Died in his sleep."

"Oh."

"That's how most people say they'd like to go, so he had it good," Morrie told me. "Just turned seventy-three last month. His boss thought he was younger. Name's William Strayleigh—'Bill,' to his friends."

"Gee, you know a lot of people."

"You meet everybody in my line of work."

I wasn't sure what Morrie's line of work was, exactly, but I nodded as if I were.

I woke up again later and cleaned up and dressed and went downstairs for breakfast. There was a birthday card beside my plate, and I opened it and read it and said, "Thanks, Aunt Rose."

"Just wanted you to know we hadn't forgotten," she said.

"My godfather Morrie remembered, too. He was by earlier, and he took me to the mall to pick out a present and—"

She glanced at the clock.

"The mall doesn't open for another half hour."

"I know," I said. "But he got me in anyway. Too bad about the night watchman, though. Died in his sleep on a bench. I'm getting a black ten-speed that'll be sent over this afternoon."

"Don't start on that business again, David. You know it bothers Uncle Matt."

"Just wanted you to know the bike was coming."

"Nobody's been here this morning. Nobody's been out and back in. You miss your folks. It's natural you have these dreams around your birthday."

"And I get presents."

"Hard for us to know, since you weren't with us last year."

"Well, it's true. Morrie always gives me something. Dad could have told you."

"Maybe," she said. "But it's strange that Morris has never gotten in touch with us."

"He travels a lot."

She turned away, began making French toast.

"Just don't mention him around Matt."

"Why not?"

"Because I asked you not to, okay?"

I nodded when she glanced my way.

The doorbell rang that afternoon, and when I opened the door it was there: a bike with a paint job so dark and shiny that it looked like a series of black mirrors. I couldn't find a manufacturer's name on it, just a silver-edged plate on the handlebar post in the shape of a small black heart. The note tied to the bar said, "Happy Birthday, David. His name is Dorel. Treat him well and he will serve you well. —M."

It was a long time before I knew exactly what that meant. But the first thing I did, of course—after removing the tag and handing it to Uncle Matt—was to take it down the steps, mount, and ride off.

"Dorel," I said softly. "He told me you're called Dorel." Was it my imagination, or did a brief vibration pass through that midnight frame just then?

Everything Morrie gave me had a special character to it—like the Magic Kit I had gotten last year, with the Indian Rope Trick I never used (I'm not a good climber) and the Five-Minute Time Warp which I never found any use for. I keep it in my pocket.

"My name's David," I continued. "You're beautiful and you're fast and you're easy to steer. I like you a lot."

It was as if I were going downhill all the way to the corner and back.

When I parked Dorel on the porch again, Uncle Matt was waiting right inside the door. "I just heard on the news," he said, "that the night watchman at the mall was found dead this morning, of a heart attack."

"I know," I said. "I told Aunt Rose about it earlier."

"How did you know about it?"

"I was over there, before the mall opened, with Morrie. He got us in, and I picked out the kind of bike I wanted."

"How did he get you in?"

"Uh, I don't really remember the details."

Uncle Matt scratched his chin through his beard and narrowed his gray eyes behind his thick glasses. They looked a lot like my eyes, and—I suddenly remembered—my dad's.

"What's he look like, anyway—your godfather?" he asked.

I shrugged. It was hard to remember just what he looked like. "Kind of thin. He has dark hair, I think. And a real nice voice. Makes you want to do whatever he says."

"That's all?"

"I guess so."

"Damn! That's no description, David. That could be almost anybody."

"I'm sorry."

He reached out and squeezed my shoulder as I began to draw back.

"I didn't mean to yell at you," he said. "It's just that the whole business is kind of—unusual. Not to speak ill of my own brother, but it's no secret that your father was a heavy drinker. Especially there at the end. It's why your mother left him. Probably what killed him, too."

I nodded. I'd heard—or overheard—all this before.

"He told a bizarre story of the way he met your godfather. Sounded like something a paranoid Trotskyite drunk might come up with, and I didn't believe a word of it. Still don't."

I stared at him. I knew what a paranoid was, also. And two out of three wasn't bad.

"I don't remember the story," I said, "if I ever knew."

Uncle Matt sighed, and told me the tale.

My father met Morrie at a crossroads, pursuant to a dream. He'd dreamed that a voice came to him out of a thundercloud limned with lightning, and it said, "I am God. You have alienated everyone close to you and I pity you. I shall stand for your son in my own church and make him happy in life." My father said,

"You give to the rich and leave the poor working stiffs to hunger. I do not want you for my son's godfather." And there was a clap of thunder and the cloud went away, and the earth split and a flame rose up out of the crack and a voice spoke from it, saying, "I am Satan. Have me. I will make him rich. I will see that he gets on well in the world." My father said, "You are the Prince of Bullshitters. I do not want you either, for I do not trust you." And the fire flared, and Satan was gone, also. Later then, as he was halfway to wakefulness, a shadowy figure passed near and told him, "When you awaken walk outside. Stop at the first crossroads you come to. I will meet you there." "Who are you?" my father asked. "I am he who makes all equal," came the reply, "in a most democratic fashion." And my father got up, dressed, went out into the darkness, and waited at the crossroads. There he met Morris, and he invited him to be my godfather, for he said that one who had him for a friend would lack nothing.

"Do you know what that means?" Uncle Matt asked me.

"Yeah. It's a good thing that he went to the crossroads, or I wouldn't have my bike."

He stared at me for several moments. "Rose and I weren't present at your christening. We'd had a disagreement with Sam earlier. So neither of us got to meet Morris."

"I know."

"The next time you see him, tell him it had nothing to do with him, or with you. Tell him we wish he'd stop by sometime."

"You will get to see him," I told him. "He says

everyone does. I'll ask him to name a date next time—"

"Never mind," he said, suddenly.

Later, that evening, after my birthday party, I went out on my new bike again. Lacking an address for a thank-you note, I resolved to go visit Morrie and say it aloud. In the past, when I'd wanted to see him between birthdays I would wander about trying to figure out how to do it and before long I always encountered him—most recently as part of the crowd at an auto accident, and once at the beach, where I was watching the guard give mouth-to-mouth resuscitation to a guy. This time, though, I'd go in style.

I pedaled hard till I got to the outskirts of town, coasted downhill to a wooded area, turned onto an old logging road now mainly used by hunters, fishermen, hikers, and kids from the high school following dances and movies. It was darker down here than it was up on the hill, and I bore to the left, coming onto a long, winding stretch under summer foliage.

"Dorel," I said, "I'm really happy with you, and I want to go and thank Morrie for such a great birthday present. I don't know where to find him but I've got a feeling you do. I'd like you to help me get to him—now."

A throbbing seemed to begin within the dark vehicle, and as we rounded the next corner a kind of stroboscopic effect began. At first it seemed that it might simply have been from the angle of the light and the trees' spacing. But after a while each period of darkness seemed more intense, lasted a little longer; and each time the light returned it came more dimly, came for a shorter bit of time.

Soon, I coasted down a dark tunnel—for I noted that I need no longer pedal but only steer in the direction of a distant light which now came into view. Dorel vibrated, and we picked up speed. After a time, the light grew brighter and I entered a gallery of stalactites and still pools. The place was a blaze of light, for there were candles everywhere I looked—on every ledge, in every niche, atop every flat surface. They varied in size, they burned with a still intensity. There were no drafts here, save for the rush of air from my own passage, and we were slowing, slowing. . . . I put my foot down, halted, and stared. I had never seen so many candles before in my life.

"Thanks, Dorel," I whispered.

I set the kickstand and walked about. There were tunnels leading off in all directions from the grotto, all of them blazing for as far as I could see with multitudes of candles. Every now and then a burnt-down candle stub would gutter and go out. Shadows darted about these like black butterflies as they died.

Wandering, I was suddenly concerned about finding my way back out. I halted and looked about for Dorel. Once I was back upon my bike, I was sure I could retrace my route.

A shadow glided around boulder, plinth, stalactite. It was my bike, with my godfather seated upon it and pedaling slowly, grinning. He wore what appeared to be a dark cloak. He waved and made his way in my direction.

"How good of you to come and visit," he called out.

"Wanted to say thanks for the present," I told him. "Dorel's really neat."

"Glad you like him." He drew up before me, braked, and dismounted, setting the stand.

"I never knew a bike to have a name before."

He ran a bony finger along the handlebars.

"He is something that owes me a great debt. He is paying it off in this fashion," he said. "Would you care for a cup of tea or hot chocolate?"

"I'd like a hot chocolate," I said.

He led me around a corner and into a niche where a slab of stone bore a red-and-white calico tablecloth. Two cups and saucers were laid upon it, along with napkins and spoons. Sounds of classical music were in the air, and I could not determine their source. We seated ourselves and he reached for a carafe which stood within a wire frame above one of the ubiquitous candles. Raising it, he filled our cups.

"What is that music?" I asked.

"Schubert's Quartet in D Minor, a favorite piece of mine," he said. "Marshmallow?"

"Yes, please."

He added marshmallows. It was hard to see his face, the way the shadows danced about him.

"Is this where you work, Morrie, or where you live?"

He handed me my cup, leaned back, and commenced cracking his knuckles, one by one, a talent I mightily envied him.

"I do a lot of my work in the field," he said. "But you might consider this my office, and I do keep an apartment here. Yes, it is both."

"I see," I said. "It's certainly well lit."

He chuckled. He gestured broadly, and the nearby flames flickered wildly.

"She'll think it a fainting spell," he remarked.

"Who?" I asked.

"The lady who belongs to that candle. Name's Luisa Trujillo. She's forty-eight years old and lives in New York City. She's got another twenty-eight years to go. *Bueno.*"

I lowered my cup, turned slowly, and regarded the immense cavern and all of the side chambers and tunnels.

"Yes," he said after a time. "All there, all of them. There's one for each of them."

"I read that there are several billion people in the world."

He nodded.

"Lot of wax," he observed.

"Good chocolate," I said.

"Thanks. The Big Ten's really come upon bad days."

"Huh?"

"Everything interesting's happening in the West," he said.

"Oh," I said. "Football. You're talking college football, aren't you?"

"Yes, but I like pro football, too. What about you?"

"I don't know enough about it," I said, "but I'd like to," and he commenced telling me.

Much later, we simply sat, watching the candles flicker. At length, he refilled our cups.

"You given any thought to what you want to be when you grow up?" he asked.

"Not really," I said.

"Consider being a physician. You'd have a knack for it. I'd see to that," he said. "Do you play chess?"

"No."

"Good game, too. You ought to learn. I've a mind to teach you."

"All right."

I don't know how long we sat there, using the squares on the tablecloth for our board. The pieces were of bone—the clean white of fresh, the almost-brown of aged, bone—which were quite elegant. As we played, I realized that I liked the game.

"A physician," I remarked after a time.

"Yes, think about it."

"I will," I agreed.

And so I did. It was good to have some sort of goal. I made it a point to study extra hard for math, chemistry, and biology classes. College wasn't particularly difficult, and while I worried as to where the money for med school would come from, a distant relative died at just the right time and left me enough to take care of it.

Even after I'd gone away to college I still rode Dorel—as sleek and shiny as ever—to Morrie's office every year on my birthday, where we drank hot chocolate, played chess, and talked football.

"You graduate in June," he remarked. "Then you do an internship and a residency."

"That's right."

"You've thought about the area in which you would like to specialize?"

"I was thinking of dermatology. I figure nobody will ever call me in the middle of the night with a dermatological emergency."

"Hm," Morrie said, stirring his chocolate with a delicate bone which served us as a spoon. "When I suggested the medical profession I had something a little more basic in mind. Internal medicine, perhaps."

A bat darted by, caught hold of Morrie's cloak, crawling inside, and hanging upside down from a seam. I took a sip of chocolate, moved my bishop.

"A lot of hard work there," I finally said. "Dermatologists make pretty good money."

"Bah!" Morrie said. He moved a knight. "Check," he added. "As an internist you will become the greatest consulting physician in the world."

"Really?" I asked, and I studied the chess pieces.

"Yes. You will manage some miraculous-seeming cures."

"Are you sure you've considered all the ramifications? If I get that good, I could be cutting into your business."

Morrie laughed. "There is a balance between life and death, and in this we play our parts. For mine, really, is the power over life, as yours will be the power over death. Think of it as a family business."

"All right. I'll give it a shot," I said. "By the way, I resign. You've got me in four moves."

"Three."

"Whatever you say. And thanks for the present, those diagnostic tools. I've never seen anything like them."

"I'm sure they'll come in handy. Happy Birthday," he said.

And so I went off to a big hospital in a big city in the Northwest, to do my time. I saw Morrie more than ever there. Usually, he'd stop by when I was on the night shift.

"Hi, Dave. That one in Number Seven. She'll be checking out at 3:12 A.M.," he said, seating himself beside me. "Too bad about the fellow in Number Sixteen."

"Ah, he was fading fast. We knew it was just a matter of time."

"You could have saved that one, Dave."

"We tried everything we knew."

He nodded. "Guess you're going to have to learn a few more things, then."

"If you're teaching, I'll take notes," I said.

"Not yet, but soon," he responded. He reached out and touched my cup of coffee, which had long ago gone cold. It began to steam again. He rose and faced the window. "About time," he said, and a moment later there came the blaring of a horn from the highway below, followed by the sound of a collision. "I'm needed," he said. "Good night." And he was gone.

He did not mention it again for a long while, and I almost thought he had forgotten. Then, one day the following spring—a sunny and deliciously balmy occasion—I went walking in the park. Suddenly, it seemed that I cast two shadows. Then one of them spoke to me:

"Lovely day, eh, Dave?"

I looked about. "Morrie, you're very quiet when you come up on a person."

"Indeed," he said.

"You're dressed awfully solemnly for such a fine, bright morning."

"Working clothes," he said.

"That's why you're carrying a long, sharp tool?"

"Right."

We walked in silence for a time, passing through a field and into a grove of trees. Abruptly, he dropped to his knees at the foot of a small rise, extended his hands amid grasses, and spread them. Two small flowering plants lay between his extended forefingers and thumbs. No, what had seemed a pair of plants could now be seen as but one. What had misled me was that it bore both blue and yellow flowers. I regarded the leaves. I recalled a botany class I had once taken. . . .

"Yes, study it," he said.

"I can't identify it," I told him.

"I would be most surprised if you could. It is quite rare, and the only sure way to know it and to find it when you need it is by means of introduction and by words of summoning, which I shall teach you."

"I see."

". . . And in your case it will be necessary to place samples under cultivation in your apartment. For you must learn its usages more deeply than any other who knows of it. Roots, leaves, stalks, flowers—each part has a separate virtue, and they can be made to work in a wide variety of combinations."

"I do not understand. I've spent all this time getting a first-rate medical education. Now you want me to become an herbalist?"

He laughed.

"No, of course not. You need your techniques as well as your credentials. I am not asking you to abandon the methods you have learned for helping people, but merely to add another for . . . special cases."

"Involving that little flower?"

"Exactly."

"What is it called?"

"Bleafage. You won't find it in any herbal or botany text. Come here and let me introduce you and teach you the words. Then you will remove it and take it to your home, to cultivate and become totally familiar with."

I ate, drank, and even slept with the bleafage. Morrie stopped by periodically and instructed me in its use. I learned to make tinctures, poultices, salves, plasters, pills, wines, oils, liniments, syrups, douches, enemas, electuaries, and fomentations of every part and combination of parts of the thing. I even learned how to smoke it. Finally, I began taking a little of it to work with me every now and then and tried it on a number of serious cases, always with remarkable results.

My next birthday, Morrie took me to a restaurant in town, and afterward an elevator in the parking garage seemed to keep descending, finally releasing us in his office.

"Neat trick, that," I said.

I followed him along a bright, winding tunnel, his invisible servants moving about us, lighting fresh candles and removing the remains of those which had expired. At one point, he stopped and removed a stump of a candle from a case, lit it from the guttering flame of one upon a ledge, and replaced the old one with the new one, just as the former went out.

"What did you just do, Morrie?" I asked. "I've never seen you replace one before."

"I don't do it often," he answered. "But that

woman you fed the bleafage to this afternoon—the one in 465—she's just rallied." He measured the candle stump between thumb and forefinger. "Six years, eight months, three days, seven hours, fourteen minutes, twenty-three seconds," he observed. "That's how much life you have bought her."

"Oh," I said, trying to study his face and failing, within the darting shadows.

"I'm not angry, if that's what you're looking for," he said. "You must try the bleafage out if you're to understand its power."

"Tell me," I said, "is it a power over life or a power over death that we are discussing?"

"That's droll," he said. "Is it one of those Zen things? I rather like it."

"No, it was a serious question."

"Well, mine is a power over life," he said, "and vice versa. We're sort of 'yin-yang' that way."

"But you're not restricted to your specialty, not when you have this bleafage business going for you, too."

"David, I can't use the herb. I can only teach you about it. I require a human master of bleafage to use it for me."

"Oh, I see."

"Not entirely, I'm certain. Go ahead and experiment. It may seem that the people you treat with it all come to you by chance, but this will not always be the case."

I nodded and studied the flowers.

"You have a question?" he asked.

"Yes. That candle stub you used for purposes of extending Mrs. Emerson, of Room 465, for six years, plus—How did it come to be snuffed out at just that point, rather than having burned itself all the way down? It's almost as if you'd—snuffed someone—prematurely."

"It is, isn't it?" he said, grinning broadly. "As I mentioned, death *is* a power over life. Let's have some coffee and our brandy now, shall we?"

I was more than a little puzzled by the way Morrie ran his business. But it was his show and he'd always been kind to me. He'd given me a whole new wardrobe for a birthday present, and when I completed my residency he gave me a new car. Dorel was still in fine fettle, but I needed a car once I began my practice. I moved Dorel to the rear of the garage and rode him only on the weekends. But I found myself going out there more and more, evenings, sitting on the high stool beside the workbench, popping the tab on a cold one and talking to my bike the way I had when I was a kid.

"Funny," I said, "that *he* should give me a wonder drug for saving lives. On the other hand," I reflected, "it's obvious that he did sort of push me into medicine. Could it be that he wants control over the life-*giving* half of the yin-yang? Not just letting someone live, but assuring quality time by removing causes of suffering?"

Dorel's frame creaked as he leaned slightly in my direction. His headlight blinked on, blinked off.

"Is that an affirmative?" I asked.

The blinking was repeated.

"Okay, I'll take that as 'yes,' " I said, "and two for 'no.' "

One blink followed.

"It would make a kind of sense," I said, "for two

reasons: First, back when I was still at the hospital, I gave a sample of bleafage to Dr. Kaufman, a biochemist, and asked him whether he could determine its major constituents. He died in the lab the next day, and a fire destroyed whatever he was working on. Later, I ran into Morrie in the morgue, and he told me that synthesizing bleafage was a no-no. He did not want it to become as common as aspirin or antibiotics. That would make it seem he only wanted certain persons to benefit.

"Second," I continued, "I believe this guess was confirmed by the instructions he gave me when I set up in private practice."

Morrie told me that I would get calls from all over for consultations. He never said where they'd get my name or number or why they'd want me, but he was right. They did start coming in. He told me to take my bleafage with me whenever I went, and my special diagnostic tools, but that the entire diagnosis and treatment—or lack of it—would be governed solely by a matter of personal perception. I can see Morrie when other people can't. He said that in those special cases where I'm called in to consult he would enter the room. If he were to stand at the head of the bed, I was to diagnose and treat, and the patient would live. But if he stood at the foot, I was to perform a few routine tests and pronounce it a hopeless case.

"It almost seems as if there were an agenda, as if he had a special deal with some of my patients or a plan into which they fit."

The light blinked once.

"Ah, you think so, too! Do you know what it is?"

It blinked twice, then a third time.

"Yes and no? You have some guesses, but you're not sure?"

It blinked once.

"Of course, no matter what the reasons, I'm helping a lot of people who wouldn't be helped otherwise."

A single blink.

"Morrie once said that you're working off a debt by being a bicycle."

A single blink.

"I didn't understand what he meant then, and I still don't. Is there a way you could tell me?"

Again, a single blink.

"Well, what is it?"

Abruptly, Dorel rolled across the garage, leaned against the wall, and grew still and lightless. I gathered that meant that I had to figure it out for myself. I tried, too, but was interrupted by a phone call. Emergency. Not at the hospital, but one of those special emergency cases.

"This is Dr. Puleo, Dan Puleo. We met at that ER seminar this spring."

"I remember," I said.

"Speaking of emergencies . . ."

"You got one?"

"There's a limousine on the way to pick you up."

"To take me where?"

"The governor's mansion."

"This involves Caisson himself?"

"Yes."

"How come he's not in the hospital?"

"He will be, but you're near and I think you can beat the ambulance."

"I think I can beat the limo, too," I said, "if I take the bike trail through the park."

I hung up, snatched my med kit, ran back to the garage.

"We've got to get to the governor's mansion fast," I said to Dorel as I wheeled him out and mounted.

What followed was a blur. I remember dismounting and making my way shakily to the door. Somehow I was inside then, shaking hands with Puleo and being escorted into a bedroom—as the doctor said something about a bad bout of flu recently, kidney stones last year, and no history of heart problems. No vital signs at the moment either.

I stared at the figure on the bed—Lou Caisson, a reform governor who was doing a great job on a number of fronts his predecessor had let slide, as well as maintaining the previous administration's gains. All that, and having an attractive, talented daughter like Elizabeth, as well. I had not seen her since we'd broken up back in school and headed for different parts of the country. As I moved forward to begin my examination, I felt a guilty pang. I had let Morrie break us up, with his insistence that I attend a West Coast med school after I'd been accepted at the one with the Eastern university she was to attend.

Speaking of Morrie . . .

A shadow slid forward and Morrie stood at the foot of the bed. He was shaking his head.

I checked for a carotid pulse. There was none. I raised an eyelid. . . .

Suddenly, I was mad. As I heard the sirens in the distance, I was swept by a wave of anger over every decision in my life that Morrie had influenced. In an instant, looking back, I saw just how manipulated I had been with all his little bribes and attentions. I opened my med kit and placed it on the bed.

"Are you going to treat him?" Puleo asked.

I leaned forward, slid my arms beneath Caisson, picked him up. I backed away then, walked around the foot of the bed behind Morrie, and laid him back down again, this time with Morrie standing at his head. I reached across and picked up my kit.

"I can't take any responsibility—" Puleo began.

I filled the long syringe.

"If I treat him right now, he'll live," I said. "If I don't, he'll die. It's as simple as that."

I unbuttoned Caisson's pajama top and opened it.

"David, don't do it!" Morrie said.

I did it—3 cc's of tincture of bleafage, intracardially. I heard the ambulance pull up out front.

When I straightened, Morrie was glaring at me. He turned away then and walked out of the room without even bothering to use the door. I heard Caisson gasp. When I checked his carotid again the pulse was present. A moment later he opened his eyes. I put my kit away and buttoned his shirt.

"You'll be all right," I said to him.

"What course of treatment is indicated now?" Puleo asked.

"Put him in the ICU and watch him for twenty-four hours. If he's okay after that, you can do whatever you want with him."

"What about continuing medication?"

"Negative," I said. "Excuse me. I have to go now."

When I turned away she was standing there.

"Hi, Betty," I said.

"David," she said, "is he going to be all right?"

"Yes." I paused, then, "How've you been?"

"Oh, pretty well."

I started toward the door, then stopped.

"Could we talk for a minute, in private?" I asked.

She led me to a little sitting room, where we sat.

"I wanted you to know I've been missing you for a long time," I said, "and I'm sorry about the way I broke up with you. I suppose you've got a boyfriend now?"

"I take it that means you're unencumbered yourself?"

"That's right."

"And if I am, too?"

"I'd like to go out with you again. Get to know you again. Is there any possibility? Might you be interested?"

"I could tell you that I'm going to have to think about it. But that wouldn't be true. I have thought about it, and the answer is yes, I will go out with you."

When I reached out and squeezed her hand, she returned the pressure. We sat and talked for the next two hours and made a date to go out the next night.

Riding back through the park, in the dark, I switched on Dorel's headlight and was reminded of our earlier "conversation."

"Talk! Damn you!" I said. "I want your opinion!"

"All right."

"What?"

"I said, 'All right.' What do you want to know?"

"How come you wouldn't talk to me earlier?"

"I could only talk if you ordered me to. This is the first time you have."

"What are you—really?"

"I was a physician he'd trained in early nineteenth-century Virginia. Name's Don Laurel. I did something he didn't like. Manufactured and sold a patent medicine—Laurel's Bleafage Tonic."

"Must have helped some people he didn't want helped."

"Aye, and maybe a few horses, too."

"I just saved someone he didn't want saved."

"I don't know what to tell you—except that I was arrogant and insolent when he confronted me concerning the medicine, and I wound up as transportation. You might want to try a different tack."

"Thanks," I said, plucking a quarter from under the headlight and flipping it. "Tails. I will."

Of course, Morrie came by later.

"Evening," I said. "Care for a cup of tea?"

"David, how could you?" he asked. "I've been good to you, haven't I? How could you go against my express wishes that way?"

"I'm sorry, Morrie," I said. "I did it because I felt sorry for the guy—starting off with such a great year in office, particularly those health care programs, putting all those fat-cat business interests in their place, and being taken out of the game so suddenly. And— Well, I used to date his daughter. I still like her, as a matter of fact, and I felt sorry for her, too. That's why I did it."

He put his hand on my shoulder and squeezed it.

"David, you're a good-hearted boy," he said. "It's hard to fault a man for compassion, but in my line of work it can be a liability. You're going to have to be ruled by your head, not your heart, when you're working my cases, you understand?"

"Yes, Morrie."

"Okay, let's have that cup of tea and talk football."

Three days later I was doing some work around the house when the phone rang. I recognized the governor's voice immediately.

"How are you feeling, sir?" I asked.

"Fine, and I know I owe you a lot, but that's not why I'm calling," he said.

I knew it. Before he said another word, I could feel it coming: Morrie's revenge. My test.

"Emergency?" I said.

"That's right. It's Betty, and from what Puleo told me about my seizure this sounds like the same thing. He didn't say anything about its being contagious."

"I'll be right over."

"Should I call an ambulance?"

"No."

I hung up, got my kit, went for Dorel. As we headed through the park, I told him what had happened.

"What are you going to do?" he asked.

"You know what I'm going to do."

"I was afraid of that."

And so, as I checked her over, Morrie entered the room and stood at the foot of the bed. I drew 3 cc's into the syringe, then I turned her around.

"David, I forbid it," he said.

"Sorry, Morrie," I told him, and I administered the injection.

When she opened her eyes, I leaned down and kissed her, at about the same time that I felt Morrie's hand upon my shoulder. This time his grip was icy.

"Me, too," he said.

. . . And then we were walking in total silence through a dim place of constantly shifting shadows.

I seem to recall moving amid pieces of my world, in monochrome, as well as the way into his, down under the ground, of caves, tunnels, still pools. I knew we were arrived when we entered a tunnel lined with candles and followed it to that bright and massive central grotto where we had played so long at chess and drunk so much chocolate.

Passing through that vast gallery I seemed to acquire solidity once more. My footfalls created echoes. I felt again that cold grip which steered me. Some of the shadows fell aside, like drawn curtains.

Morrie took me through the grotto, up a corridor, then down a small, chilly tunnel off to its left which I had never visited before. I was too proud to ask him where we were headed and so be the first to speak.

At length, we halted, and he released my arm and gestured.

Jamming my cold hands into my pockets, I followed the gesture but could not at first tell what he was indicating, as we stood in a fairly average area of his office, ledges and niches full of candles. Then I saw that one of them was much lower than all of the others and was flickering now, preparatory to guttering. Assuming it to be Betty's, I waited to see it replaced by the action of one of the invisible entities.

"It was worth it," I said. "I love her, you know."

He turned and stared at me. Then he chuckled.

"Oh, no," he said. "You think that that's her candle? No. You don't understand. She'll live. You've seen to that. Her candle is already in good shape. This is *your* candle. You started out kind of handicapped in that regard. Sorry."

I withdrew a hand from my pocket, reached out, touched it gently.

"You mean that's all I have? Maybe a few minutes? And you didn't mess with it because you're mad at me? That's *really* the way it is?"

"That's right," he said.

I licked my lips.

"Any—uh—chance of an—extension?" I asked.

"When you've crossed my will a second time, after I'd warned you?"

"I didn't do it lightly," I said. "I told you I'd known Betty years ago, and I cared about her then. I didn't realize how much until just recently, when it was almost too late. There was no real choice then. I had to save her. Perhaps such emotions are something you cannot quite understand—"

He laughed again.

"Of course I can understand caring about something," he said. "Why do you think I'd decided to take Governor Caisson right when I did? The son of a bitch's business policies had just cost the town a pro football franchise—for my favorite team. And I'd been angling to get them here for over a generation."

"So you *were* grabbing him off early?"

"You bet I was. Then you had to butt in for the first time in your life."

"I begin to understand. . . . Say, Morrie, you know it's not too late to transfer my flame to a fresh candle."

"True," he acknowledged, "and you *are* my godson. That still counts for something. . . ."

He stared a moment longer at the candle.

"Probably should," he said. "Shouldn't stay mad forever. Family counts for something," and he stooped and reached into an opened case back in a recess in the wall.

Drawing forth a candle, he stood and reached forward with his other hand toward my sputtering taper. He touched it, began to raise it. Then I saw it slip from his fingers and plunge groundwards.

"Shit!" I heard Morrie say as it fell. "Sorry, David—"

Lying on the floor, watching a tiny spark, feeling that something had worked properly, not recalling what. . . . And my cheekbone was sore where I'd hit it when I fell—

I lay amid countless lights. There were things I had to do, and do quickly. What were they?

I raised my head and looked about. Morrie was gone. . . .

Ah, yes. Morrie, my godfather. Gone. . . .

I placed my palms upon the floor and pushed myself up. Nobody there but me, a guttering candle, and a black bicycle. What was it I was supposed to remember? My mind felt heavy and slow.

"Get a candle out of the box, David! Hurry!" Dorel told me. "You've got to take the flame from the other before it dies again."

Dies again. . . .

Then I remembered and shuddered. That's what I had done—died. And I would do it again and for keeps if I didn't act quickly. Fearing the worst, I had been able to buy this brief recurrence of the light, finally finding a use for the Five-Minute Time Warp I kept in my pocket. But how long it would last, lying there, sputtering, upon the floor, I could not tell.

I moved with accelerated deliberation—that is to

say, as fast as I felt I could without disturbing the air to the point of ending the enterprise. It was just a piece of wick in an irregular puddle of wax now.

I groped in the carton, took out a candle, moved it to a position above the failing flame, held it there. For a second, the first one nearly died and my vision darkened and a numbness passed over me. But it caught, and these symptoms vanished. I turned it upright then and rose to my feet, groping once again in my pocket. I carried dried stems, flowers, roots, and leaves of bleafage wrapped in a handkerchief.

I placed the handkerchief on Dorel's seat and unfolded it.

"Good idea," he suggested as I began eating the specimens. "But as soon as you're finished I want to lead you to another tunnel where we can hide your candle amid many. We ought to hurry, though, in case he's still in the area."

I stuffed the last of the bleafage into my mouth and set off walking beside him, carrying my candle.

"Could you locate Betty's candle and hide it, too?" I asked.

"Given the time, the appropriate form, and the access," he said.

I followed him down another tunnel.

"I used to work here," he went on. "I was an invisible entity before he made me a bike. If I were an invisible entity here again I could keep moving your candle and Betty's so that he'd never know. I could correct any number of his petty abuses the way I used to. Might keep lighting you new ones, too, if you got into bleafage research."

"I could be persuaded," I said. "What would it take to make you an invisible entity again?"

"I'm not permitted to say."

"Even if I order you?"

"Even then. This is a different category of restriction. I can't think of a way to tell you how to get around this one."

We moved a little farther down the tunnel and he halted.

"To your left," he said, "in that low niche where several others are burning."

I dribbled a little wax to anchor it, set it upon that spot, held it in place till it was fixed.

"Mount," Dorel said then.

I climbed onto the seat, and we coasted through a series of chambers. Soon the stroboscopic effect began again.

"Back to where you were?" Dorel asked.

"Yes."

After a time, the upper world flashed into being for longer and longer intervals, as the underworld diminished.

Then we were slowing before the governor's mansion. Then we were halted there. I was dismounting. There was still some daylight, though the sun hovered just above the western horizon. As I was setting the kickstand, I heard the front door open.

"Dave!" she called.

I looked up, watched her approach down the stair. I realized again how lovely she was, how much I wanted to protect her. In a moment, she was in my arms.

"Dave, what happened? You just sort of faded away."

"My godfather, Morrie, took me. I'd done something he didn't like."

"Your godfather? You never mentioned him before. How could he do that?"

"He is a person of great power over life," I said, "who is responsible for whatever power I possess over death. Fortunately, he thinks I'm dead now. So I believe I'll have some reconstructive surgery, change the spelling of my name, grow a beard, move to another state, and run a small, low-key practice to cover the expense of my bleafage research. I love you. Will you marry me and come along?"

Dorel said, "I hate to tell you that you sound a little crazy, Dave, but you do."

She stared at my bike.

"Are you a ventriloquist, too?" she asked me.

"No, that was Dorel talking. He just saved my life. He's a rebel spirit doing time as a bicycle, and he's been with me since I was a kid. Saved my life a couple of times then, too." I reached out and patted his seat.

Descending the steps, she leaned forward and kissed the top of the handlebars.

"Thanks, Dorel," she said, "whatever you are."

Whatever he was, it was no longer a bicycle. He fell apart in the days-end light into a swirling collection of golden motes. I watched, fascinated, as the phenomenon resolved itself into a tower about six feet in height, narrowing as it grew.

I heard Betty draw in a long breath.

"What did I just set off?" she asked.

"Beats me," I said. "But since there was no frog I don't think you get a prince."

"Guess I'm stuck with you then," she said, and we watched the bright whirlwind assemble itself into a human shape—that of a tall, bewhiskered man in buckskins.

He bowed to Betty.

"Don Laurel," he said. "At your service, ma'am."

Then he turned and shook my hand.

"Sorry to deprive you of transportation, Dave," he said. "But I just got my enchantment broken."

"Calls for a celebration," I said.

He shook his head.

"Now that I'm unbiked I have to find a niche quick," he said, "or I'll fade to airy nothingness. So I'll be heading back below, and I'll take up residence in the caves. He'll never spot an extra invisible entity. And I'll keep moving both of your candles out of his way. Good luck with the bleafage work. I'll be in touch."

With that, he turned once more into a tower of light. The motes darted like fireflies and were gone.

"That's a relief," I said, moving once more to embrace her. "But I wish things had gone differently with Morrie. I like him. I'm going to miss him."

"He doesn't exactly sound like a nice guy," she observed.

"His line of work hardens him a bit," I explained. "He's actually quite sensitive."

"How can you tell?"

"He likes football and chess."

"They both represent violence—physical, and abstract."

". . . And hot chocolate. And Schubert's Quartet in D Minor. And he does care about the balance between life and death, most of the time."

She shook her head.

"I know he's family," she said. "But he scares me."

"Well, we're going incognito now. He shan't be a problem."

I was able to leave it at that for a long time. Betty and I were married, and I did change my name and move to a small town in the South—though I opted against cosmetic surgery. The beard and tinted glasses and a different hairstyle altered my appearance considerably, or so I thought. I built up a satisfactory practice, had a greenhouse full of bleafage, and set up a small home laboratory. For over a year I managed not to be present at life-and-death crises, and when visiting my patients in hospital I was able to avoid other patients at terminal moments which might have resulted in an undesired family reunion. You might say I was pathologically circumspect in this regard; even so, I did glimpse Morrie going around corners on a few occasions.

I kept wondering, though, given my line of work, when—not if—we would meet, and whether I would be able to carry the encounter with sufficient aplomb so as not to reveal that I possessed the ability to see him. When it did occur, of course, it was nowhere near the hospital, and I was not even thinking of these matters.

It was a Saturday evening in October and I heard the squeal of brakes followed by the sound of a heavy impact up the street from our home. I grabbed my bag and a flashlight and was out the door in moments. Betty followed me as I hurried to the corner where two cars had collided. Broken glass was everywhere and the smell of gasoline was strong.

Each vehicle had but a driver. One was obviously

dead, and the other—a younger man—was badly injured, but still breathing.

"Go call 911!" I shouted to Betty as I moved to succor the second man. He had been thrown from the car and lay upon the pavement, a massive, well-muscled individual with a bubbly pneumothorax, heavy arterial bleeding, numerous lesser lacerations, a possibly broken back, and fractured skull.

As I slapped a cover on the pneumothorax and moved to deal with the bleeding a familiar figure was suddenly beside me. I forgot to pretend to be unseeing. In the press of the moment, I simply nodded, and said, "Can't argue with you about this one. Take him if you must."

"No," he said. "Save him for me, Dave. Shoot him up with bleafage. You've got all the time you need."

"What's so special about him, Morrie? I haven't forgotten how you treated me when I wanted to make an exception."

"All right. I'll forgive and forget if you'll do the same—and save this guy. My power, as I've often said, is not over death."

"Then how's about you promise to let me save whom I can, and do whatever I would with the bleafage?"

"Looks like you're doing that, anyway. But all right, I'll make it formal."

"I wish you could have been at my wedding, Morrie."

"I was there."

"You were? I didn't see you."

"I was in the back. I wore bright colors so you wouldn't notice."

"That guy in the Hawaiian shirt?"

"Yes, that was me."

"I'll be damned."

"And I sent you the microwave oven."

"There was no card with it—"

"Well, we weren't talking."

"I did wonder about the Heat of Hell brand name. Good oven, though, I'll give you that. Thanks."

My patient moaned.

"About this guy, Morrie— Why are you so dead set against taking him?"

"You don't recognize him?"

"Too much blood on his face."

"That's the new quarterback for the Atlanta Falcons."

"No kidding. But what about the balance between life and death and all that?"

"They're really going to need him this season."

"I forgot you were a Falcons fan."

"The bleafage, boy, the bleafage."

And so . . . The Falcons are doing well this season, not the least because of their new quarterback. Not too many people die during Falcons' games, because Morrie comes by for beer and pizza and we watch them on the tube together. He collects with a vengeance afterward, though, if the Falcons don't do well. Read the obits.

Morrie hints strongly that he'd like to know what I did with the candles. But he can keep on wondering.

Don Laurel and I stay in touch. He comes by every Halloween for a glass of blood and we bring each other up to date on everything from bleafage to candles. And sometimes he changes into a bicycle for old times' sake, and we ride between the worlds.

This morning I walked back to the crossroads where the accident had occurred. Morrie was standing beside a lamppost petting a dead cat.

"Morning, Dave."

"Morning. You're up bright and early."

"Thought you might be coming by. When's she due?"

"In the spring."

"You really want me for godfather?"

"Can't think of anyone I'd rather have. Was that the same dream you sent my dad?"

"No. It's a remake. I updated it. Been watching some MTV."

"Kind of thought so. Care for a cup of coffee?"

"Don't mind if I do."

We walked home as the morning shadows fled. Whoever catches them may make himself a cloak of darkness.

Ashputtle

Peter Straub

Peter Straub is the author of the novels Marriages, Under Venus, Julia *(filmed as* The Haunting of Julia*)*, If You Could See Me Now, Ghost Story, Shadowland, Floating Dragon, The Talisman, *(with Stephen King)*, Koko, Mrs. God, Mystery, *and* The Throat, *as well as the collections* Wild Animals *and* Houses Without Doors *and two books of poetry,* Open Air *and* Leeson Park and Belsize Square.

We approached Peter Straub about writing a fairy tale because of his powerful retelling of "The Juniper Tree," in which he created a modern classic about child abuse and its consequences. In this chilling tour de force, based on "Ashputtle," Straub creates another memorable character in his gallery of the walking wounded.

Ashputtle

PEOPLE THINK THAT TEACHING LITTLE CHILDREN has something to do with helping other people, something to do with service. People think that if you teach little children, you must love them. People get what they need from thoughts like this.

People think that if you happen to be very fat and are a person who acts happy and cheerful all the time, you are probably pretending to be that way in order to make them forget how fat you are, or cause them to forgive you for being so fat. They make this assumption, thinking you are so stupid that you imagine that you're getting away with this charade. From this assumption, they get confidence in the superiority of their intelligence over yours, and they get to pity you, too.

Those figments, those stepsisters, came to me and said *Don't you know that we want to help you?* They came to me and said *Can you tell us what your life is like?*

These moronic questions they asked over and

over—*Are you all right? Is anything happening to you? Can you talk to us now, darling? Can you tell us about your life?*

I stared straight ahead, not looking at their pretty hair or pretty eyes or pretty mouths. I looked over their shoulders at the pattern on the wallpaper and tried not to blink until they stood up and went away.

What my *life* was like? What was *happening* to me?

Nothing was happening to me. I was *all right.*

They smiled briefly, like a twitch in their eyes and mouths, before they stood up and left me alone. I sat still on my chair and looked at the wallpaper while they talked to Zena.

The wallpaper was yellow, with white lines going up and down through it. The lines never touched—just when they were about to run into each other, they broke, and the fat thick yellow kept them apart.

I liked seeing the white lines hanging in the fat yellow, each one separate.

When the figments called me *darling,* ice and snow stormed into my mouth and went pushing down my throat into my stomach, freezing everything. They didn't know I was nothing, I would never be like them; they didn't know that the only part of me that was not nothing was a small hard stone right at the center of me.

That stone has a name. MOTHER.

If you are a female kindergarten teacher in her fifties who happens to be very fat, people imagine that you must be very dedicated to their children, because you cannot possibly have any sort of private life. If they are the parents of the children in your kindergarten class, they are almost grateful that you are so grotesque, because it means that you must really care about their children. After all, even though you couldn't possibly get any other sort of job, you can't be in it for the money, can you? Because what do people know about your salary? They know that garbagemen make more money than kindergarten teachers. So at least you didn't decide to take care of their delightful, wonderful, lovable little children just because you thought you'd get rich, no no.

Therefore, even though they disbelieve in all your smiles, all your pretty ways, even though they really do think of you with a mixture of pity and contempt, a little gratitude gets in there.

Sometimes when I meet with one of these parents, say a fluffy-haired young lawyer, say named Arnold Zoeller, Arnold and his wife Kathi, Kathi with an i, mind you, sometimes when I sit behind my desk and watch these two slim, handsome people struggle to keep the pity and contempt out of their well–cared-for faces, I catch that gratitude heating up behind their eyes.

Arnold and Kathi believe that a pathetic old lumpo like me must love their lovely little girl, a girl say named Tori, Tori with an i (for Victoria.) And I think I do rather love little Tori Zoeller, yes I think I do think I love that little girl. My mother would have loved her, too. And that's the God's truth.

I can see myself in the world, in the middle of the world.
I see that I am the same as all nature.

* * *

In our minds exists an awareness of perfection, but nothing on earth, nothing in all of nature, is perfectly conceived. Every response comes straight out of the person who is responding.

I have no responsibility to stimulate or satisfy your needs. All that was taken care of a long time ago. Even if you happen to be some kind of supposedly exalted person, like a lawyer. Even if your name is Arnold Zoeller, for example.

Once, briefly, there existed a golden time. In my mind existed an awareness of perfection, and all of nature echoed and repeated the awareness of perfection in my mind. My parents lived, and with them, I too was alive in the golden time. Our name was Asch, and in fact I am known now as Mrs. Asch, the Mrs. being entirely honorific, no husband having ever been in evidence, nor ever likely to be. (To some sixth-graders, those whom I did not beguile and enchant as kindergarteners, those before whose parents I did not squeeze myself into my desk chair and pronounce their dull, their dreary treasures delightful, wonderful, lovable, above all *intelligent*, I am known as Mrs. Fat-Asch. Of this I pretend to be ignorant.) Mr. and Mrs. Asch did dwell together in the golden time, and both mightily did love their girl-child. And then, whoops, the girl-child's Mommy upped and died. The girl-child's Daddy buried her in the estate's churchyard, with the minister and everything, in the coffin and everything, with hymns and talking and crying and the animals standing around, and Zena, I remember, Zena was already there, even then. So that was how things were, right from the start.

The figments came because of what I did later. They came from a long way away—the city, I think. You don't have to be religious to have inspirations. We never saw city dresses like that, out where we lived. We never saw city hair like that, either. And one of those ladies had a veil!

One winter morning during my first year teaching kindergarten here, I got into my car—I *shoved myself* into my car, I should explain, this is different for me than for you, I *rammed myself* between the seat and the steering wheel, and I drove forty miles east, through three different suburbs, until I got to the city, and thereupon I drove through the city to the slummiest section, where dirty people sit in their cars and drink right in the middle of the day. I went to the department store nobody goes to unless they're on welfare and have five or six kids all with different last names. I just parked on the street and sailed in the door. People like that, they never hurt people like me.

Down in the basement was where they sold the wallpaper, so I huffed and puffed down the stairs, smiling cute as a button whenever anybody stopped to look at me, and shoved myself through the aisles until I got to the back wall, where the samples stood in big books like the fairy-tale book we used to have. I grabbed about four of those books off the wall and heaved them over onto a table there in that section and perched myself onto a little tiny chair and started flipping the pages.

A scared-looking black kid in a cheap suit mumbled something about helping me, so I gave him my happiest, most pathetic smile and said, well, I was here to get wallpaper, wasn't I? What color did I want, did I know? Well, I was thinking about yellow, I said. Uh huh, he says, what kinda yellow you got in mind? Yellow with white lines in it. Uh huh, says he, and starts helping me look through those books with all those samples in them. They have about the ugliest wallpaper in the world in this place, wallpaper like sores on the wall, wallpaper that looks like it got rained on before you get it home. Even the black kid knows this crap is ugly, but he's trying his damndest not to show it.

I bestow smiles everywhere. I'm smiling like a queen riding through her kingdom in a carriage, like a little girl who just got a gold-and-silver dress from a turtledove up in a magic tree. I'm smiling as if Arnold Zoeller himself and of course his lovely wife are looking across my desk at me while I drown, suffocate, stifle, bury their *lovely, intelligent* little Tori in golden words.

I think we got some more yellow in this book here, he says, and fetches down another big fairy-tale book and plunks it between us on the table. His dirty-looking hands turn those big stiff pages. And just as I thought, just as I knew would happen, could happen, would probably happen, but only here in this filthy corner of a filthy department store, this ignorant but helpful lad opens the book to my mother's wallpaper pattern.

I see that fat yellow and those white lines that never touch anything, and I can't help myself, sweat breaks out all over my body, and I groan so horribly that the kid actually backs away from me, lucky for him, because in the next second I'm bending over and throwing up interesting-looking reddish goo all over the floor of the wallpaper department. O God, the kid says, O lady. I groan, and all the rest of the goo comes jumping out of me and splatters down on the carpet. Some older black guy in a clip-on bow tie rushes up toward us but stops short with his mouth hanging open as soon as he sees the mess on the floor. I take my hankie out of my bag and wipe off my mouth. I try to smile at the kid, but my eyes are too blurry. No, I say, I'm fine, I want to buy this wallpaper for my kitchen, this one right here. I turn over the page to see the name of my mother's wallpaper—Zena's wallpaper, too—and discover that this kind of wallpaper is called "The Thinking Reed."

You don't have to be religious to have inspirations.
An adventurous state of mind is like a great dwelling place.
To be lived truly, life must be apprehended with an adventurous state of mind.
But no one on earth can explain the lure of adventure.

Zena's example gave me two tricks that work in my classroom, and the reason they work is that they are not actually tricks!

The first of these comes into play when a particular child is disobedient or inattentive, which, as you can imagine, often occurs in a room full of kindergarten-age children. I deal with these infractions in this fashion. I command the child to come to my desk. (Sometimes, I command two children to come to my desk.) I stare at the child until it begins to squirm. Sometimes it blushes or trembles. I await the physical signs of shame or discomfort. Then I pronounce the child's name. "Tori," I say, if the child is Tori. Its little eyes invariably fasten upon mine at this instant. "Tori," I say, "you know that what you did is wrong, don't you?" Ninety-nine times out of a hundred, the child nods its head. "And you will never do that wrong thing again, will you?" Most often the child can speak to say *No*. "Well, you'd better not," I say, and then I lean forward until the little child can see nothing except my enormous, inflamed face. Then in a guttural, lethal, rumble-whisper, I utter, "OR ELSE." When I say, "OR ELSE," I am very emphatic. I am so very emphatic that I feel my eyes change shape. I am thinking of Zena and the time she told me that weeping on my mother's grave wouldn't make a glorious wonderful tree grow there, it would just drown my mother in mud.

The attractiveness of teaching is that it is adventurous, as adventurous as life.

My mother did not drown in mud. She died some other way. She fell down in the middle of the downstairs parlor, the parlor where Zena sat on her visits. Zena was just another lady then, and on her visits, her "social calls," she sat on the best antique chair and held her hands in her lap like the most modest, innocent little lady ever born. She was half-Chinese, Zena, and I knew she was just like bright sharp metal inside of her, metal that could slice you but good. Zena was very adventurous, but not as adventurous as me. Zena never got out of that town. Of course all that happened to Zena was that she got old, and everybody left her all alone because she wasn't pretty anymore, she was just an old yellow widow-lady, and then I heard that she died pulling up weeds in her garden. I heard this from two different people. You could say that Zena got drowned in mud, which proves that everything spoken on this earth contains a truth not always apparent at the time.

The other trick I learned from Zena that is not a trick is how to handle a whole class that has decided to act up. To keep life under control you must maintain an adventurous state of mind. These children come from parents who, thinking they know everything, in fact know less than nothing. These children will never see a classical manner demonstrated at home. You must respond in such a way that demonstrates your awareness of perfection. You must respond in a way that will bring this awareness to the unruly children, so that they too will possess it.

It can begin in a thousand different ways. Say I am in conference with a single student—say I am delivering the great OR ELSE. Say that my attention has wandered off for a moment, and that I am contemplating the myriad things I contemplate when my attention is wandering free. My mother's grave, watered by my tears. The women with city hair who desired to give me help, but could not, so left to be replaced by others, who in turn were replaced by yet others. How it felt to stand naked and besmeared with my own feces in the front yard, moveless as a statue, the same as all nature, classical. The gradual disappearance of my father, like that of a figure in a cartoon who grows increasingly transparent until total transparency is reached. Zena facedown in her garden, snuffling dirt up into her nostrils. The resemblance of the city women to certain wicked stepsisters in old tales. Also their resemblance to handsome princes in the same tales.

She who hears the tale makes the tale.

Say therefore that I am no longer quite anchored within the classroom, but that I float upward into one, several, or all of these realms. People get what they need from their own minds. Certain places, you can get in there and rest. The classical was a cool period. I am floating within my cool realms. At that moment, one child pulls another's hair. A third child hurls a spitball at the window. Another falls to the floor, emitting pathetic and mechanical cries. Instantly, what was order is misrule. Then I summon up the image of my ferocious female angels and am on my feet before the little beasts even notice that I have left my desk. In a flash, I am beside the light switch. The Toris and Tiffanys, the Joshuas and Jeremys, riot on. I slap down the switch, and the room goes dark.

Result? Silence. Inspired action is destiny.

The children freeze. Their pulses race—veins beat in not a few little blue temples. I say four words. I say, "Think what this means." They know what it means. I grow to twice my size with the meaning of these words. I loom over them, and darkness pours out of me. Then I switch the lights back on, and smile at them until they get what they need from my smiling face. These children will never call me Mrs. Fat-Asch, these children know that I am the same as all nature.

* * *

Once upon a time a dying queen sent for her daughter, and when her daughter came to her bedside the queen said, "I am leaving you, my darling. Say your prayers and be good to your father. Think of me always, and I will always be with you." Then she died. Every day the little girl watered her mother's grave with her tears. But her heart was dead. You cannot lie about a thing like this. Hatred is the inside part of love. And so her mother became a hard cold stone in her heart. And that was the meaning of the mother, for as long as the little girl lived.

Soon the king took another woman as his wife, and she was most beautiful, with skin the color of gold and eyes as black as jet. She was like a person pretending to be someone else inside another person pretending she couldn't pretend. She understood that reality was contextual. She understood about the condition of the observer.

One day when the king was going out to be among his people, he asked his wife, "What shall I bring you?"

"A diamond ring," said the queen. And the king could not tell who was speaking, the person inside pretending to be someone else, or the person outside who could not pretend.

"And you, my daughter," said the king, "what would you like?"

"A diamond ring," said the daughter.

The king smiled and shook his head.

"Then nothing," said the daughter. "Nothing at all."

When the king came home, he presented the queen with a diamond ring in a small blue box, and the queen opened the box and smiled at the ring and said, "It's a very small diamond, isn't it?" The king's daughter saw him stoop forward, his face whitening, as if he had just lost half his blood. "I like my small diamond," said the queen, and the king, straightened up, although he still looked white and shaken. He patted his daughter on the head on his way out of the room, but the girl merely looked forward and said nothing, in return for the nothing he had given her.

And that night, when the rest of the palace was asleep, the king's daughter crept to the kitchen and ate half of a loaf of bread and most of a quart of homemade peach ice cream. This was the most delicious food she had ever eaten in her whole entire life. The bread tasted like the sun on the wheatfields, and inside the taste of the sun was the taste of the bursting kernels of the wheat, even of the rich dark crumbly soil that surrounded the roots of the wheat, even of the lives of the bugs and animals that had scurried through the wheat, even of the droppings of those foxes, beetles, and mice. And the homemade peach ice cream tasted overwhelmingly of sugar, cream, and peaches, but also of the bark and meat of the peach tree and the pink feet of the birds that had landed on it, and the sharp, brittle voices of those birds, also of the effort of the hand crank, of the stained, whorly wood of its sides, and of the sweat of the man who had worked it so long. Every taste should be as complicated as possible, and every taste goes up and down at the same time: up past the turtledoves to the far reaches of the sky, so that one final taste in everything is *whiteness*, and down all the way to the mud at the bottom of graves, then to the mud beneath that mud, so that another final taste in everything, even in peach ice cream, is the taste of *blackness.*

From about this time, the king's daughter began to attract undue attention. From the night of the whiteness of turtledoves and the blackness of grave-mud to the final departure of the stepsisters was a period of something like six months. It was in this period, when nothing was happening to the king's daughter, when she was all right, that she learned what it was to live in the middle of the world and be the same as all nature.

I thought of myself as a work of art. I caused responses without being responsible for them. This is the great freedom of art.

They asked questions which enforced the terms of their own answers. *Don't you know we want to help you?* Such a question implies only two possible answers, 1: no, 2: yes. The stepsisters never understood the queen's daughter; therefore, the turtledoves pecked out their eyes, first on the one side, then on the other. The correct answer, 3: person to whom question is directed is not the one in need of help, cannot be given. Other correct answers, such as 4: help shall come from other sources, and 5: neither knowledge nor help mean what you imagine they mean, are also forbidden by the form of the question.

Assignment for tonight: make a list of proper but similarly forbidden answers to the question *What is happening to you?* Note: be sure to consider conditions imposed by use of word *happening.*

* * *

The stepsisters arrived from the city in grand state. They resembled peacocks. The stepsisters accepted Zena's tea, they admired the house, the paintings, the furniture, the entire estate, just as if admiring these things, which everybody admired, meant that they, too, should be admired. The stepsisters wished to remove the king's daughter from this setting, but their power was not so great. Zena would not permit it, nor would the ailing king. (At night, Zena placed her subtle mouth over his sleeping mouth and drew breath straight out of his body.) Zena said that the condition of the king's daughter would prove to be temporary. The child was eating well. She was loved. In time, she would return to herself.

When the figments asked, *What is happening to you?*, I could have answered, *Zena is happening to me.* This answer would not have been understood. Neither would the answer, *My mother is happening to me.*

Undue attention came about in the following fashion. Zena knew all about my midnight feasts, but was indifferent to them. Zena knew that each person must acquire what she needs. This is as true for a king's daughter as for any ordinary commoner. But she was ignorant of what I did in the name of art. Misery and anger made me a great artist, though now I am a much greater artist. I think I was twelve. (The age of an artist is of no importance.) Both my mother and Zena were happening to me, and I was happening to them, too. Such is the world of women. My mother, deep in her mud-grave, hated Zena. Zena, second in the king's affections, hated my mother. Speaking from the center of the stone at the center of me, my mother frequently advised me on how to deal with Zena. Silently, speaking with her eyes, Zena advised me on how to deal with my mother. I, who had to deal with both of them, hated them both.

And I possessed an adventurous mind.

The main feature of adventure is that it goes forward into unknown country.
Adventure is filled with a nameless joy.

Alone in my room in the middle of Saturday, on later occasions after my return from school, I removed my clothes and placed them neatly on my bed. (My *canopied* bed.) I had no feelings, apart from a sense of urgency, concerning the actions I was about to perform. Perhaps I experienced a nameless joy at this point. Later on, at the culmination of my self-display, I experienced a nameless joy. And later yet, I experienced the same nameless joy at the conclusions of my various adventures in art. In each of these adventures as in the first, I created responses not traceable within the artwork, but which derived from the conditions, etc., of the audience. Alone and unclothed now in my room, ready to create responses, I squatted on my heels and squeezed out onto the carpet a long cylinder of fecal matter, the residue of, dinner not included, an entire loaf of seven-grain bread, half a box of raisins, a can of peanuts, and a quarter pound of cervelat sausage, all consumed when everyone else was in bed and Zena was presumably leaning over the face of my sleeping father, greedily inhaling his life. I picked up the warm cylinder and felt it melt into my hands. I hastened this process by squeezing my palms together. Then I rubbed my hands over my body. What remained of the stinking cylinder I smeared along the walls of the bedroom. Then I wiped my hands on the carpet. (The *white* carpet.) My preparations concluded, I moved regally through the corridors until I reached the front door and let myself out.

I have worked as a certified grade school teacher in three states. My record is spotless. I never left a school except by my own choice. When tragedies came to my charges or their parents, I invariably sent sympathetic notes, joined volunteer groups to search for bodies, attended funerals, etc., etc. Every teacher eventually becomes familiar with these unfortunate duties.

Outside, there was all the world, at least all of the estate, from which to choose. Certain lines from Edna St. Vincent Millay describing the manner in which the world, no wider than the blissful heart, stands out on either side, best express my state of mind at this moment. I well remember the much-admired figure of Dave Garroway quoting the poet's lovely words on his Sunday afternoon television program, and I pass along Miss Millay's beautiful sentiment to each fresh class of kindergarteners. They must start somewhere, and at other moments in their year with me they will have the opportunity to learn that nature never gives you a chance to rest. Every animal on earth is hungry.

Turning my back on the fields of grazing cows and sheep, ignoring the hills beyond, hills seething with coyotes, wildcats, and mountain lions, I moved with stately tread through the military rows of fruit trees and, with papery apple and peach blossoms adhering to my bare feet, passed into the expanse of the grass meadow where grew the great hazel tree. Had the meadow been recently mown, long green stalks the width of a caterpillar leapt up from the ground to festoon my legs. (I often stretched out full length and rolled in the freshly mown grass meadow.) And then, at the crest of the hill that marked the end of the meadow, I arrived at my destination. Below me lay the road to the unknown towns and cities in which I hoped one day to find my complicated destiny. Above me stood the hazel tree.

I have always known that I could save myself by looking into my own mind.

I stood above the road on the crest of the hill and raised my arms. When I looked into my mind I saw two distinct and necessary states, one that of the white line, the other that of the female angels, akin to the turtledoves.

The white line existed in a calm rapture of separation, touching neither sky nor meadow but suspended in the space between. The white line was silence, isolation, classicism. This state is one-half of what is necessary in order to achieve the freedom of art, and it is called "The Thinking Reed."

The angels and turtledoves existed in a rapture of power, activity, and rage. They were absolute whiteness and absolute blackness, gratification and gratification's handmaiden, revenge. The angels and turtledoves came streaming up out of my body and soared from the tips of my fingers into the sky, and when they returned they brought golden and silver dresses, diamond rings and emerald tiaras.

I saw the figments slicing off their own toes, sawing off their heels, and stepping into shoes already slippery with blood. The figments were trying to smile, they were trying to stand up straight. They were like children before an angry teacher, a teacher transported by a righteous anger. Girls like the figments—much younger than my present age—never did understand that what they needed, they must get from their own minds. Lacking this understanding, they tottered along, pretending that they were not mutilated, pretending that blood did not pour from their shoes, back to their pretend houses and pretend princes. The nameless joy distinguished every part of this process.

Lately, within the past twenty-four hours, a child has been lost.

A lost child lies deep within the ashes, her hands and feet mutilated, her face destroyed by fire. She has partaken of the great adventure, and now she is the same as all nature.

At night, I see the handsome, distracted, still hopeful parents on our local news programs. Arnold and Kathi, he as handsome as a prince, she as lovely as one of the figments, still have no idea of what has actually happened to them—they lived their whole lives in utter abyssal ignorance—they think of hope as an essential component of the universe. They think that other people, the people paid to perform this function, will conspire to satisfy their needs.

A child has been lost. Now her photograph appears each day on the front page of our sturdy little tabloid-style newspaper, beaming out with luminous ignorance beside the columns of print describing a sudden disappearance after the weekly Sunday School class at St. Mary-in-the-Forest's Episcopal Church, the deepening fears of the concerned parents, the limitless charm of the girl herself, the searches of nearby video parlors and shopping malls, the draggings of two adjacent ponds, the slow, painstaking inspections of the neighboring woods, fields, farms, and outbuildings, the shock of the child's particularly well off and socially prominent relatives, godparents included.

A particular child has been lost. A certain combination of variously shaded blond hair and eyes the blue of early summer sky seen through a haze of stratocumulus clouds, of an endearingly puffy upper lip and a recurring smudge, like that left on Corrasable bond typing paper by an unclean eraser, on the left side of the mouth, of an unaffected shyness and an occasional brittle arrogance destined soon to overshadow more attractive traits, will never again be seen, not by parents, friends, teachers, or the passing strangers once given to spontaneous tributes to the child's beauty.

A child of her time has been lost. Of no interest to our local newspaper, unknown to the Sunday School classes at St. Mary's-in-the-Forest, were this moppet's obsession with dolls Exercise Barbie and Malibu Barbie, her fanatical attachment to My Pretty Ponies Glory and Applejacks, her insistence on introducing during classtime observations upon the cartoon family named Simpson, and her precocious fascination with the music television channel, especially the "videos" featuring the groups Kriss Kross and Boyz II Men. She was once observed holding hands with James Halliwell, a first-grade boy. Once, just before nap time, she turned upon a pudgy, unpopular girl of protosadistic tendencies named Deborah Monk and hissed, "Debbie, I hate to tell you this, but you *suck*."

A child of certain limitations has been lost. She could never learn to tie her cute but oddly blunt-looking size 1 running shoes, and eventually had to become resigned to the sort fastened with Velcro straps. When combing her multishaded blond hair with her fingers, she would invariably miss a cobwebby patch located two inches aft of her left ear. Her reading skills were somewhat, though not seriously, below average. She could recognize her name, when spelled out in separate capitals, with narcissistic glee; yet all other words, save *and* and *the*, turned beneath her impatient gaze into random, Sanskrit-like squiggles and uprights. (This would soon have corrected itself.) She could recite the alphabet all in a rush, by rote, but when questioned, was incapable of remembering if **O** came before or after **S**. I doubt that she would have been capable of mastering long division during the appropriate academic term.

Across the wide, filmy screen of her eyes would now and then cross a haze of indefinable confusion. In a child of more finely tuned sensibilities, this momentary slippage might have suggested a sudden sense of loss, even perhaps a premonition of the loss to come. In her case, I imagine the expression was due to the transition from the world of complete unconsciousness (Barbie and My Pretty Ponies) to a more fully socialized state (Kriss Kross). Introspection would have come only late in life, after long exposure to experiences of the kind from which her parents most wished to shelter her.

An irreplaceable child has been lost. What was once in the land of the Thinking Reed has been forever removed, like others before it, like all others in time, to turtledove territory. This fact is borne home on a daily basis. Should some informed anonymous observer report that the child is all right, that nothing is happening to her, the comforting message would be misunderstood as the prelude to a demand for ransom. The reason for this is that no human life can ever be truly substituted for another. The increasingly despairing parents cannot create or otherwise acquire a living replica, though they are certainly capable of reproducing again, should they stay married long enough to do so. The children in the lost one's class are reported to suffer nightmares and recurrent enuresis. In class, they exhibit lassitude, wariness, a new unwillingness to respond, like the unwillingness of the very old. At a schoolwide assembly where the little ones sat right up in front, nearly every one expressed the desire for the missing one to return. Letters and cards to the lost one now form two large, untidy stacks in the principal's office, and with parental appeals to the abductor or abductors broadcast every night, it is felt that the school will accumulate a third stack before these tributes are offered to the distraught parents.

Works of art generate responses not directly traceable to the work itself. Helplessness, grief, and sorrow may exist simultaneously alongside aggressiveness, hostility, anger, or even serenity and relief. The more profound and subtle the work, the more intense and long-lasting the responses it evokes.

Deep, deep in her muddy grave, the queen and mother felt the tears of her lost daughter. *All will pass.* In the form of a turtledove, she rose from grave-darkness and ascended into the great arms of a hazel tree. *All will change.* From the topmost branch, the turtledove sang out her everlasting message. *All is hers, who will seek what is true.* "What is true?" cried the daughter, looking dazzled up. *All will pass, all will change, all is yours,* sang the turtledove.

In private conference with the principal, I recently announced my decision to move to another section of the country after the semester's end.

The principal is a kindhearted, limited man still loyal, one might say rigidly loyal, to the values he absorbed from popular music at the end of the 1960s, and he has never been able quite to conceal the unease I arouse within him. Yet he is aware of the respect I command within every quarter of his school, and he has seen former kindergarteners of mine, now freshmen in our tri-suburban high school, return to my classroom and inform the awed children seated before them that Mrs. Asch placed them on the right path, that Mrs. Asch's lessons would be responsible for seeing them successfully through high school and on to college.

Virtually unable to contain the conflict of feelings my announcement brought to birth within him, the principal assured me that he would that very night compose a letter of recommendation certain to gain me a post at any elementary school, public or private, of my choosing.

After thanking him, I replied, "I do not request this kindness of you, but neither will I refuse it."

The principal leaned back in his chair and gazed at me, not unkindly, through his granny glasses. His right hand rose like a turtledove to caress his greying beard, but ceased halfway in its flight, and returned to his lap. Then he lifted both hands to the surface of his desk and intertwined the fingers, still gazing quizzically at me.

"Are you all right?" he enquired.

"Define your terms," I said. "If you mean, am I in reasonable health, enjoying physical and mental stability, satisfied with my work, then the answer is yes, I am all right."

"You've done a wonderful job dealing with Tori's disappearance," he said. "But I can't help but wonder if all of that has played a part in your decision."

"My decisions make themselves," I said. "All will pass, all will change. I am a serene person."

He promised to get the letter of recommendation to me by lunchtime the next day, and as I knew he would, he kept his promise. Despite my serious reservations about his methods, attitude, and ideology—despite my virtual certainty that he will be unceremoniously forced from his job within the next year—I cannot refrain from wishing the poor fellow well.

* * *

Author's Note: (Certain phrases and sentences here have been adapted from similar phrases and sentences in the writings of the painter Agnes Martin. There is no similarity at all between Mrs. Asch and Agnes Martin.)

Silver and Gold

Ellen Steiber

Ellen Steiber was for many years an editor of children's fiction for various New York publishing companies; she is now a full-time writer in the same field with several fantasy and mainstream novels in print, including the magical tales Sunblind *and* Moonspell. *She is currently at work on her first novel for adults, to be published next year by Tor Books. She lives in Tucson, Arizona.*

"Silver and Gold" is a poem that beautifully demonstrates how fairy tales can provide rich metaphors for the complex issues of adult life. Based on the "Red Riding Hood" story, it is about the paths we take and the wolves we face right here in the real world.

Silver and Gold

". . . Walk nicely and quietly,
and do not run off the path,
and when you go into your grandmother's house
do not forget to say, 'Good-morning,'
and don't peep into every corner before you do it."
Mother's instructions.
The thick-knit cloak without which
I never dared venture into the world.
Is it any wonder that when the wolf appeared,
coat of silver, eyes of gold
when the wolf sauntered toward me, kindly as you
please,
and showed me fields of lavender and jessamine,
hawkweed and flax—
purple and yellow and flame run wild,
blue stolen from the skies;
when he bade me shed the heavy woolen cloak
and hear the birds calling their young,
spinning the noon light on their song;
when he taught me to follow the sunbeams
dancing through the trees,

warming the pine needles till their scent filled the air
and led me far from the path;
when he told me there was no need to be so grave
when the wood was merry;
is it any wonder I went deeper and deeper into the green trees?

Now the doctor asks me
how it was I could not tell my own grandmother from a wolf.
The huntsman had no such problems, you see.
He strode right into that cottage, called out,
"Do I find you here, you old sinner! I have long sought you!"
He even guessed my grandmother was inside,
and was wise enough not to fire
but to take scissors
and cut open the stomach of the sleeping wolf.
A man who knows his enemies, hunts them down cleanly,
and disposes of them efficiently,
taking care not to harm
what good they may contain.

I was not nearly so clear.
The doctor asks me
whether I was not living among wolves from the start.
How could one confuse a grandmother with a wolf
unless the grandmother and wolf were kin all along?
It's complicated, I tell him,
thinking that in sunlight
my grandmother's hair is as silver as the wolf's pelt,
that at dusk her eyes have always glittered gold,

that always in the corners of her cottage
there have been small treasures waiting—
toys made from thimbles, ribbons for my hair.
Sometimes, I explain,
it's hard to tell the difference
between the ones who love you
and the ones who will eat you alive.
The explanation doesn't wash.
Open your eyes, child, he tells me.
Appearances may deceive.
Dangers seduce.
You must give thanks to the huntsman.
You needed an avenging angel,
a savior strong and unafraid,
a man to tear open the wolf's belly
and help you out.

I tell him I am grateful
that my grandmother still lives in her cottage
with gifts tucked in every corner;
grateful that I am alive,
that a stranger held out the hope
that from what nearly destroys you
love may emerge.
What I do not tell him is that
I will again leave the path
and wander into that fragrant green wood
and when I see
coat of silver, eyes of gold
I will follow.

Sweet Bruising Skin

Storm Constantine

Storm Constantine is a highly original English writer whose works, such as the Wraeththu Trilogy, *straddle the line between science fiction and fantasy and manage to combine both lyrical and "Techno-goth" sensibilities. Constantine lives in a household of musicians in Stafford, England.*

"Sweet Bruising Skin" takes the innocent story of "The Princess and the Pea" and combines it with several other classic fairy tales' tropes into a tale that is deliciously dark and disturbing.

Sweet Bruising Skin

MY CRITICS HAVE OFTEN SAID—THOUGH NEVER TO my face—that I overindulged my son Marquithi. Some people believe that because his poor father, the late king of Gordania, succumbed at a relatively young age to a morbid excitement of the brain, Marquithi is heir to an undesirable malfunction. Myself, I blame the premature thrusting of a responsible position on the boy for his witless behavior. It is certainly no fault of mine, for I have always maintained the highest standards of discipline, from the nursery to the exalted chambers. Still, it is easy for others to criticize. I would have liked to see them cope as efficiently as I did in such a crucial situation. In any case, madam, the night is young, your mead flagon full, and it is a propitious time for a story. It is my privilege to tell you all.

Everyone in the palace was still wearing mourning weeds and chewing the berries of grief-tarry-not when my late husband's chamberlain, Tartalan, came to me in my rooms of resiance. Although my husband had been removed from our marital quarters for some months prior to his demise, I had since been haunted by a restless ghost of sickness-stench and, for that reason, had ordered the place to be thoroughly fumigated by the perfume of burning stomach-mint and pine. Everyone moved like phantoms through the antiseptic fusc, and it did little to lift their spirits, which had understandably been rather low over the past obsequy-heavy days.

I myself felt less than joyous as, far from being allowed the limpid sighing and aimless preoccupation of a widow, I had been subject to callous antagonism from the king's councillors. They were impatient to inaugurate some inbred relative of my late husband's as regent until Marquithi reached his twentieth year, being blind to the fact that, despite my son's relatively coltish nature, he was more than capable of administering the land. I, as Queen Mother, was incomparably qualified to assist him in his new duties. For some reason, the Council objected to this. I suspect that financial inducements originating from the estates of my late husband's kin were responsible for this dreary obstinacy. However, following the king's funeral, I had efficiently lambasted all the Council's feeble propositions. Beneath the palace lies a vast catacomb—much of it flooded—which is stuffed with the rotting and moldering remains of the state archives. A thousand years of judicial silliness reposes there in corruption; laws which refute previous laws, labyrinthine edicts, and a host of contradictory narratives of Gordanian history. I had directed my personal staff to scour the archives for material that might serve to promote my cause. Being a foreigner, I was unfamiliar with the early history of this barbarous country, so it was with great rejoicing I learned that four centuries previously, some other king had been crowned at the age of twelve—a boy who had gone on to survive a productive if rather unmemorable reign. As Marquithi was eighteen years old, the Council's argument was effectively boggled. However, I was aware they would continue to obstruct me until the moment Marquithi took the crown. The fact that they had sent the obsequious Tartalan to interview me personally oppressed me with foreboding, but I received him courteously, nevertheless.

"Your Highness," Tartalan said, pausing to indulge in a sequence of rather outlandish bowing and scraping, "I regret there is a matter of some delicacy to be discussed."

I had never known the man to be capable of delicacy in any situation before but, because I am groomed for my role, I murmured some suitable response and bade him be seated. I myself remained standing, in order to peer down at him. He is a cadaverous yet handsome man of some forty years, but frightened of women, I think. His eyes were running because of the fumigation, a circumstance which he lost no time in employing to lend an emotive tone to his discourse.

"Prince Marquithi," he said, blinking rapidly.

I did not respond verbally, but raised an eyebrow. The chamberlain's goatish eyes slithered away from mine.

"The Council feel—*know*—that in order for the prince to assume the crown, the population of our country would be more comfortable with—would prefer him to be married."

I sighed. "My dear Tartalan, as you know, this is

a matter close to my own heart, one which I am currently intent on resolving. No one wishes more than I to see my son happily wed, but neither will I permit him to be persuaded into an alliance with which he feels uncomfortable."

"Of course, we all realize the industry you have applied to the subject," Tartalan gushed, "but, with regret, I must remind you that the waters of time trickle ever to drought . . . In short, Your Highness, we respectfully suggest that Prince Marquithi take advantage of the offer tendered by the House of Crooms, and accept the hand of Lady Selini."

I had to sit down abruptly. It was common knowledge that the Lady Selini was subject to fits and constant drooling; her father had despaired of ever marrying her off. "My Lord Chamberlain, I must *respectfully* disagree! As long as I live, I will not see my son wed to a woman with more than one chin! I beg you to remember his status. How would our people react to the proposition of such a homely queen?"

"With favor, I suggest! A homely queen is better than none!"

"I would agree, but you seem to have forgotten this realm already has a queen: myself. For this reason, I feel we can be lenient with Marquithi's desire to find a wife whom he finds both attractive and companionable."

Tartalan rubbed his face in apparent agitation. "We are rapidly coming to the conclusion such a woman cannot possibly exist!" he said. "Do you realize how long Council agents have now been scouring every known land for ladies of adequate breeding? Four years! And every girl—all of them eminently suitable as prospective brides—has been summarily rejected by the prince! In fact, I will confess that standards have lately been compromised in the hope of unearthing, in some desolate spot, a woman Marquithi will consent to wed!"

I closed my eyes for a moment and took a heavy, shuddering breath. "Can you not, for one moment, put yourself in my son's position? Not only has he recently lost his father, but is being harried by insensitive fools to deny himself the chance of love! I can assure you, Marquithi will not be persuaded into accepting the Crooms lump as a wife!"

"By his advisors and councillors maybe not," Tartalan agreed, "but I cannot imagine him countermanding the desires of his mother."

"You already know my views on the subject."

Tartalan nodded. "Indeed. However, it might interest you to know that I myself have been combing the judicial archives. I have discovered an ancient edict relevant to this situation. As I hope you know, my loyalty lies unfalteringly with you and the prince, Your Highness, which is why I feel compelled to warn you . . ."

"I am afraid you will have to remind me of the contents of this edict," I said. Of course, I knew there was treachery afoot, but what Tartalan related still dismayed me profoundly.

"In short it states that should an unmarried heir to the crown fail to wed within two months of the king's demise, the regency falls automatically to the next of kin, in this instance Lord Romolox of Brude."

"What!" So they had managed to raise the head of that moronic oaf again.

Tartalan raised his hands. "Believe me, it pains me

to inform you of this edict, and I am sure no one of this House would happily welcome the scion of Brude as king, but you know how some of the older councillors are sticklers for procedure. Therefore, I and my immediate colleagues beg your cooperation. After all, if memory serves me correctly, I recall there is little affection between your own family and Brude. I am not sure how effective the Council's influence would be should Romolox act imprudently and decide to remove you from the palace."

My first instinct was to strike the sly beast with the nearest sharp object, but, because I am queen, I collected myself. Anger would have to be vented later. Some years previously a cousin of mine, having been sold into a marriage alliance with Brude, which she bitterly resented, had, through deft application of toxins, reduced her husband's intelligence to something less than that enjoyed by a vegetable, and had also rendered all children of the family under the age of ten incurably insane, before escaping the Brudish demesne with her maid. Consequently, I had scant appetite to be under the control of that family. "Your words do indeed stimulate my thoughts," I said. "Perhaps you would be so kind as to deliver a message to my son, requesting his presence here immediately."

The chamberlain stood up and bowed. "I felt sure we could rely on you," he said.

Marquithi had always been a compliant and sensitive child: I had made sure of it. It is imprudent to let careless Fate have too strong a hand in the fortune of kings, so I had always ensured my son's temperament remained equable, through practical employment of certain philters. Likewise, I had made sure my late husband had lived a serene and tranquilized life. Therefore, I was discomforted by the tantrum Marquithi manifested once I informed him he should marry the daughter of Crooms.

"My darling, it is quite bad for the complexion to work yourself into such a rage," I said. "Remember that being royal precludes displays of a brutish nature."

"I don't want to marry such a sow! I won't marry her!" Marquithi declared, gesturing widely with stiff, angry arms. His slim, delicate frame was visibly shaking, his dark hair tumbling into disarray. I had to turn away. The sight of so much indiscretion alarmed me. Naturally, I shrank from explaining our predicament in too much detail. I had no wish to frighten him, his being such a dainty constitution.

"I fear I must order you to concede, my lamb," I said.

"No!"

"Oh, do you want to hurt your mama?" I appealed to him with open arms.

"I won't do it," he said, stepping back from me. "If I can be pushed around in this manner now, it hardly bodes well for my future as king. I know my youth is against me, Mother, and that many of this court would prefer to see another in my place. Therefore, I must remain steadfast over this matter. It is the only way to gain respect."

Poor deluded boy! Still, it was hardly gratifying for me to discover he had acquired a will from somewhere.

* * *

One thing I had learned from the women of my own family in far Loolania; as a lady of standing and therefore vulnerability to the spite and jealousy of other, less important, mortals, I should never be without recourse to a competent alchemist. In comparison to their Loolanian contemporaries, the alchemists of Gordania were grievously incompetent, and for most of my married life I had been forced to rely upon my own resources. However, the previous year my sister had sent me as a birthday gift a recently graduated student from the Alchemical Academy in Panossos. Anguin was a serpentine young man, with yellow eyes and an eerie fondness for bones, but who was nevertheless canny and discreet. I kept him in a suite of rooms, high above my own, and now consulted him regularly on matters of dire significance.

His apartment was approached by a narrow dusty stair, beyond three locked doors. Only Anguin and myself possessed keys to these doors. Coming up the last of the stairs, I emerged through the floor of Anguin's workroom. It was an arcane place, the ceiling strung with bizarre devices, some of which were astronomical, some decidedly necromantic. His worktables were littered with parchments, books, alembics, athames, roots, herbs, and brass dishes in which he burned his substances. The air reeked of the various fluids and powders he employed in his art; musty, half-pleasant, half-sour. An enormous open chest stood against the far wall, filled with a muddle of broken bones, all of which I knew to be human despite Anguin's claims to the contrary.

Anguin was so engrossed in his work, he did not hear me approach. The sound of my feet was quite drowned out by the angry hissing of a sparking substance he was holding in a small metal tray. I watched him for a moment or two; his faded yellow hair, tied at the neck, the sweet knobs of vertebrae pressing out against the tawny skin above the collar of his shirt. He had an iridescent pile of dismembered damselflies beside him, which he was dropping one by one into the blue sparks.

"Anguin, if I may disturb you?"

He turned and looked at me slyly over his shoulder. I had to repress a shudder. Sometimes he can look so menacing.

"Your Wondrousness, I am ever yours to disturb," he said. There is a slight hiss to Anguin's voice, which is not a lisp exactly, but something distinctly more reptilian. I had never had occasion to inspect his tongue minutely, but it would not have surprised me to find it forked.

I sat down upon the only chair that was not occupied by boxes, manuscripts, fusty animal pelts, or piles of thin, jointed metallic arms. "Anguin, I have a problem which I feel you may be disposed to solve for me. I need a wife for my son. Speedily."

Anguin was familiar with this subject, since I had previously consulted him about it. Knowing that the simpering females of aristocratic birth my late husband's sycophants had so far presented to Marquithi were all unsuitable to share his bed, never mind his throne, I had commissioned Anguin to concoct an elixir that would make all females unattractive to Marquithi's eyes. The only good wife was a wife chosen by a loving mother. Preferably, she should be a girl whose like mind would make her a reliable accomplice to the mother, well versed in the arcana natural to womankind. If such a female proved unobtainable, a cowering mouse should be procured; a girl who could be confidently ignored. Intelligence would only be tolerated in examples of the former. Under no circumstances should a son's wife be in love with him, because she might become prone to acting unwisely. Husbands, like horses or dogs, should be admired for their conformation and, when they have it, their kind nature. As with domestic beasts, they should be cared for with consideration and gentleness, but one should not become too attached to them because then they are likely to take advantage of the situation. Also, you never know when they might die unexpectedly.

"Do I detect a change of circumstances?" Anguin inquired.

I nodded. "Quite so. I want a girl who is beautiful but mindless, someone of royal birth, but without a royal family behind her. She must be controllable, yet charmingly capricious. She must be an accomplished courtesan, yet a virgin. She must be at our threshold within a few days."

Anguin stood up and cupped his chin, tapping his lips with long fingers. "Hmm, this is a challenging request."

"But not, I trust, beyond your capabilities."

He grinned, displaying his small, white teeth. "Certainly not. In fact, one of my final year projects at the Academy involved a similar difficulty, which I solved with honors."

"I am relieved to hear it. Will you require any special equipment for this task?"

He pondered for a moment. "There are one or two

items which might prove difficult to procure in this region. That is, at their proper value."

"I shall consult my personal treasurer immediately," I said. "Come to me when you have finalized your costings."

"Also, I shall require the prince's foreskin."

It was lucky that my late husband had allowed me to observe the custom of my native kingdom whereby all male infants are circumcised at birth. I had, of course, kept this scrap of skin as both a memento and insurance against any future filial intractability. It seemed my prudence had been justified.

I glided through the next few days with calm detachment, confident of my alchemist's art. I had discontinued the use of Anguin's elixir in Marquithi's food and had satisfied the subsequent gust of libido with a stream of catamites who were members of my personal staff and thus to be trusted. Women, I kept far from my son's apartment, in order to prime him for his bride-to-be.

One afternoon, the late summer balm turned sour in the sky, and heavy purple clouds bustled in from the west. From my window, I could see that the greenery in the garden glowed unnaturally lush beneath the murk, and the air was full of powerful scents; the loamy earth, voluptuous late flowers, recently cut hay beyond the palace grounds, putrid offal from the slaughterhouses. I had a slight headache. By dinnertime, the clouds had burst, and a wind had arisen to drive the rain into hard spears that came down at a slant over the gardens. The temperature dropped so dramatically, everyone was forced to don extra clothing in order to withstand the chill in the dining hall. Rain came down the great chimneys to drip upon the blackened tiles of the hearths. Dogs moaned and licked their paws beneath the tables. Marquithi, dressed in midnight blue, seemed feverish, his pale skin flushed along his cheekbones, his black hair strangely lank about his shoulders.

Thunder growled like the nightling shades that exist at the boundary between our world and the next. Crooked tridents of sulfurous lightning flashed beyond the windows, while nervous servants hurried wraithlike from the kitchens to load the table with rich viands and wine. The storm was uncommonly violent, indeed almost predatory in tone. Windows rattled, candelabra shook, the air was oppressively damp. One or two of the less-spirited courtiers were beginning to look greatly alarmed. I myself felt only a momentous thrill building up within me, similar to how I'd felt when the obsequy-horn had bleatingly announced my husband's death. Fate was turning a page in her Book of Delusions. I wondered whether my loyal Anguin, having slipped out through the lichened slates, was presently poised atop the palace roof, conjuring up these fierce elements of storm and light. Elaborating upon this fantasy, I imagined him naked, his wet body lissome as a river snake's, his genitals swinging heavy and fat between his thighs.

"Something amuses you, Your Highness?"

I was dragged from my pleasant revery by Tartalan's stiff, nasal voice beside me. "A private matter," I said, dabbing my mouth with a napkin. On my other side, Marquithi stared at me narrowly but did not speak. I forgave him his continuing unfriendliness. Soon, all the knots in our relationship would be cut away.

"Your Highness," Tartalan murmured, bending toward me. "If I might remind you of our conversation the other day . . ."

I raised my left hand a fraction and glanced significantly at Marquithi. "Being attended to," I whispered.

Tartalan opened his mouth to deliver further indiscretions but, at that precise moment, the thunder suddenly abated. Diners blinked at each other, dazed by the abrupt stillness as much as they had been deafened by the former noise. For a few long seconds, nobody so much as murmured. The only sound was that of the rain patting softly at the windows, like little fingers seeking ingress. Then, the great doors to the hall swung open and a solitary liveried steward, puny in the immensity of the storm's departure, minced hurriedly toward the high table. He went directly to Tartalan, and whispered in his ear. Everyone had stopped eating, and all eyes were directed toward the high table. It was as if they had all experienced some dire precognition and were waiting for terrible news.

"Well?" I said to Tartalan. "Has some catastrophe occurred to the fabric of the palace? Has someone been killed?" My voice, which was usually low and musical, sounded loud and harsh in my ears.

The chamberlain looked thoughtful and spoke with some reluctance. "No, Your Highness. It seems a stranger has presented herself at the gates, most insistent upon speaking to the prince."

"Oh? Who?"

"A *girl,* Your Highness. She says she is a princess."

* * *

At a brief inspection of the girl, it was hard to imagine why any of the palace staff had entertained her claim, and had not propelled her instantly back into the storm. From her apparel, our little visitor hardly resembled a princess. However, a longer glance at her face and hands revealed she was no gypsy scrap. I had expected some ploy of Anguin's to come into manifestation; therefore, I was less perplexed than the chamberlain by the news of this female's arrival. Indeed Tartalan was clearly astonished when I ordered the steward to accommodate the girl in one of the staff sitting rooms until I could interview her myself.

"Is this wise, Your Highness?" he inquired. "Doubtless we are host only to some wandering mooncalf."

I shook my head. "Instinct, my dear Chamberlain, speaks to me most emphatically at this time. I feel we should indulge the girl's request."

He shrugged. "As you wish."

Both Tartalan and Marquithi accompanied me to the staff quarters to interview the girl. Under normal circumstances, I'd have never set foot in the servants' domain, simply because many unprepossessing sights could greet the unwary there. I had little interest in the procedures that ensured a comfortable life in the higher apartments of the palace, because most of them were grossly repulsive. The servants' quarters were a hot dismal warren of steaming laundry, greasy smoke, and humpbacked scullions, and there seemed too many rooms dedicated to the disembowelling of carcasses for my liking. Marquithi berated me during our passage, declaring it was beneath our royal dignity even to view this unprecedented guest, never mind speak to her. I had been encouraged by the way he'd demanded to accompany me though. It was not a response I would have expected from him, and I suspected it might have been involuntary.

"Have a little faith, my lamb," I said. In truth, I was beginning to realize there were few lamblike qualities left in my son. Once this matter was resolved, I would have to direct Anguin to concoct a more potent philter to restore Marquithi's docility.

The girl had been accommodated in a small room dedicated to the maintenance of royal footware, and was seated in a high-backed chair, beside an open fire. She was surrounded by a tumble of boots and shoes, through which the steward made a path for us. The slim little storm-maiden, who did not look up as we entered the room, held my entire concentration. A sodden cloak hung along the back of her chair, and her hair drooped down over her face and chest in damp tendrils. Her gown was torn and muddied, her shoes split along the seams. As I approached her, I noticed that, despite her frail body and sodden condition, she did not shiver. Her body was surrounded by a fragrance of crushed, wet flowers, quite at odds with the odors of starch and cooking meat that predominated in this area.

"What is your name, girl?"

She looked up at me then. Her face was utterly white and her eyes seemed overly large within it. She had the most astounding eyes. I was reminded of black poppies. She squinted at me only slightly before she spoke. "I am Papavera," she said. "I am a princess."

"A princess of where?" demanded Tartalan, sidling up beside me. His voice was hardly friendly.

The girl screwed up her face. "I cannot remember," she said. "I am lost."

Tartalan glanced at me with a sneer, which I divined I was supposed to return. "Poor child," I said, pulling a sympathetic frown.

"If your memory has gone, it is astounding you can still remember your status," Tartalan said in a sarcastic tone.

The girl shrugged. "It is the truth. I am royal."

"Why have you come here?" the chamberlain snapped.

Again, a shrug. "The lights in the high towers drew me."

Tartalan sighed and leaned toward me. "Well, what are we to do?" he whispered. "I am loath to accept her claim simply because, having recently become familiar with all royal ladies of nearby kingdoms, I have not come across this girl before."

"I am from a far place," the girl murmured. She must have had extraordinarily acute hearing.

Tartalan visibly jumped and then fussily collected himself. "Tch! I say we send her to the local nunnery in the morning. They can care for her there, until the time some person comes to claim her as kin."

I was about to remonstrate with him when my son, with unprecedented conviction, spoke before me. "No, my Lord Chamberlain. Any person can see this poor girl is of noble birth. Look at her skin, listen to her voice! Are these the attributes of a drab? No doubt she has become estranged from traveling companions. Perhaps suffered some accident, which has addled her mind." I was astonished by his interest, even though I should have perhaps anticipated it. He turned to me. "Mother, I recommend we have our guest conveyed to the visitors' suites, where she may be attended in proper surroundings. Perhaps you would lend a couple of your women for the task?"

I raised my hands. "Well . . . if you wish, my son."

Spots of color bloomed along his cheekbones. He dropped his eyes. "I do. It is only polite."

Of course.

It will come as little surprise that Marquithi, beloved innocent, found himself the victim of an irresistible attraction to the so-called Princess Papavera. She, like a dark velvet bloom with an intoxicating scent, pervaded the palace with her alluring presence. She had a slow, halting gait, as if she had recently awoken from a daze. Her skin glowed pellucidly along the darker passages of the upper suites, where she roamed continually, one white hand held out from her side, touching the dusty drapes, the dimmed brass candelabra, the goblin carvings on the walls. Marquithi also took to haunting these upper apartments, dancing attendance on eager feet to the fey princess. I myself interviewed her several times during the following two days, subjecting her to a gentle yet relentless inquisition. She slumped blinking in a chair as I spoke, responding slowly but without displeasure. She could remember nothing about her origins, the only memories being those of waking on drenched ground into the fury of the storm, with the slim yet consistent conviction that she was a princess. Her name, she confessed, she only remembered at the time it was asked of her. Papavera came into her head, so she naturally assumed this must be the correct epithet. She was a lovely, misty creature, languid and graceful in all her movements. Her voice was soft as a dove's and her face ever reposed in a timorous smile. To my pleasure, she also appeared quite stupid.

Anguin proved annoyingly obtuse when I went to congratulate him on his success. All my questions concerning the origin of Papavera were met with grinning silence. "I have no proof that the lady you describe is actually attributable to my influence," he said eventually. "It might be coincidence."

"Then perhaps we shall end up with two winsome beauties in the palace!" I said. "And my dear Marquithi's will have a choice! Really, Anguin, I can't understand why you don't want to view the girl yourself. I am not averse to bringing her here. She is vague and largely witless."

Anguin shook his head. "No," he said. "It is not necessary. If the prince is enamored of her, it hardly matters who or what she is, does it?"

I shrugged. Perhaps he was right, but I felt uneasy.

The creatures of the court were naturally most inquisitive about the princess, and I had to fend them off from plaguing her with their boisterous company, claiming she was feeling ill and weak, and needed some time in which to recompose herself. Their pique at this response was further augmented by a reckless declaration Marquithi made at dinner one evening. We had finished our repast and were drinking port while supervising a few floggings of recalcitrant serfs between the tables. Marquithi looked flushed and excited. The last groaning carcass had barely been removed from the hall, when he suddenly stood up and commanded silence.

"Friends, lords and ladies of the court. I have great news!" he said, beaming. I noticed he was rather unsteady on his feet. "I have found the woman I wish to marry!"

The councillors all rose to their feet like a flock of aged birds and hooted in unison: "Who?"

Marquithi's face was positively glowing. "The Princess Papavera, of course!"

Well, I was hardly surprised, although a little concerned he had not voiced his conviction to me first. A low roar of grumbling voices greeted this announcement, as the councillors predictably objected to Marquithi's choice.

"It's infatuation!"

"Folly!"

"Totally inappropriate!"

"Grossly improper!"

No one knew who Papavera was, or even what she was. She could be an actress, a madwoman, a bastard daughter. She had no pedigree, and no dowry. She might be diseased, barren, or host to an hereditary peculiarity. I myself remained silent while the storm of voices raged above my head. In fact, I poured myself some more port and sat back to enjoy the proceedings. Still, I foresaw difficult days of persuasion ahead. Tartalan caught my eye and shook his head, sighing. At that moment, we were in total accord.

As soon as Marquithi and I had retired for the evening, the councillors scurried to Tartalan to persevere in their complaints. However, having anticipated this reaction, I had already sent the most intelligent of my servants—a dashingly attractive northern girl named Vienquil—down to the archives. Having supervision over a team of six others, she was instructed to scour the ancient documents for anything I could employ as artillery in my battle with the Council. "Bring me anything, however bizarre, that I might utilize in this instance," I had told her. "And, on no account contemplate returning from the catacombs until you have found something."

Despite the efficiency of my swift-fingered operatives, and the familiarity they had recently acquired with the archives, it still took them nearly two days to uncover something of use. This, my servant Vienquil brought to my apartment the next afternoon.

The poor creature looked exhausted—her clothes, her skin, even her lustrous, black hair fouled with reeking dust and cobwebs. In her hands, she held the friable remains of an ancient parchment, which she had soaked in oil in order to prevent its utter dissolution. "The search was hard, Your Highness," she said. "And I'm afraid this was all we could find." She did not sound at all confident I would be able to use it.

I took the parchment from her and carefully laid it out on a table. Together, we scanned the faded lines of text. "Hmm, I am having trouble convincing myself the Council will accept this," I said.

Vienquil shrugged. "We found nothing else down there remotely connected with your dilemma, Your Highness."

I sighed, and patted her arm. "Well, a law is a law,

however ancient or peculiar. Thank you. You have done well under troubling circumstances. Take this coin."

I carried the parchment to Anguin right away.

It took him some time to read the document and I was forced to wait impatiently as he did so. He grinned to himself as he perused the lines and then laughed openly when he had finished reading.

"I agree the content is amusing," I said, "but would value your opinion as to how I might successfully invoke this law."

Anguin narrowed his eyes at me. "Didn't I promise you a princess?" he said. "Simply follow the instructions in this document."

"It is preposterous!" I cried, and gestured at the parchment. "No one could be affected by that. Flesh bruised by a handful of dried peas beneath a score of mattresses? If I attempt this procedure, I will be laughed out of Gordania!"

"You must trust me, Your Highness."

"Trust you?" I paused to consider. "Well . . . obviously you will have to medicate the girl in some way."

"Oh, that won't be necessary!" he said.

I blinked at him in disbelief, on the verge of losing my temper. "I suspect you are being rather too flippant, Anguin! If this plan fails, which I am sure it is doomed to do, I will appear foolish, if not deranged, and Marquithi will lose his opportunity to marry."

"Have I failed you before?" Anguin asked. "Have a little faith in me, Your Highness." He handed me the parchment. "Prepare the bed as instructed."

* * *

Tartalan shook his head gloomily when I showed him the parchment. "A desperate measure," he said, "destined only for failure."

I patted his arm. "I think we shall both be surprised." It was strange how the chamberlain and I had become allies, albeit reluctantly. He had no love of Brude either and felt, as I did, that only by Marquithi's becoming king could the comfortable stability of the kingdom be ensured.

"I wonder what circumstances inspired this paper," he said. "Are there no historical records giving explanation?"

I shook my head. "Regrettably, no."

He frowned. "But it is so bizarre! Can a royal integument really be so sensitive?"

"We shall have to hope so."

"The Council will contest this action."

"Of course they will . . . until my experiment proves successful."

Tartalan sighed heavily. "I wish I had your confidence."

I smiled at him in encouragement, even though I still harbored the greatest of qualms myself. "Don't fret, Lord Tartalan. Convene the Council and have the scullions search the storerooms for the hardest dried peas they can find."

The bed in question was an enormous construction, whose canopy brushed the ceiling of our highest chamber. Onto this framework, I ordered a score of mattresses to be piled. The stuffing for these was varied; some were to be of horsehair, some of feathers, some of straw. The topmost mattress had to be filled with lavender and dried basil, in order to ensure the slumber of the person who lay within the bed. In the center of the base mattress, with due ceremony and before witnesses, I placed a handful of small, dried peas. Then, I stood back to supervise the placement of the subsequent mattresses. If the ancient text was accurate, after sleeping upon this bed for a single night, the royal flesh of Papavera would be bruised black and blue by the peas, because the skin of a *real* princess was so delicate, it was sensitive to the slightest pressures. It is hard to believe that such absurd trials must once have been conducted on a regular basis. I pondered the fate of those unfortunate princesses whose skins had proved unsatisfactorily resistant. The Council were naturally sceptical about the test, and demanded to inspect the bed themselves, thereby indicating they suspected deceit on my part. I happily allowed them their examination, after which they had to admit there was no sign of trickery at work.

"Do you agree," I inquired, "that if Papavera's sweet skin is indeed bruised after a night's repose upon this bed, you will accept her claims—and allow Marquithi to marry her? After all, the parchment was taken from your own archives. It is genuine."

"Madam," said the oldest of the councillors, eyeing the mountain of mattresses, "if the girl's skin is marked by the peas to the slightest degree, I will be forced to reevaluate my whole philosophy on life and creation. Assenting to her marriage to the prince will be a minor concern, in comparison."

"Well, that's settled then."

At sundown, the girl Papavera was escorted down from the guest's suite by a retinue of ladies, and taken to the main floor room in which the bed had been built. It was a cold, dark, and unfriendly chamber, whose windows faced an overgrown, neglected courtyard that was forever devoid of sunlight. I noticed that the upper walls were lividly stained by aged patches of mold. In these less than savory surroundings, Papavera was subjected to a minute examination by the wives of the councillors, who confirmed her skin was unmarked by blemishes of any kind. As the women poked and prodded at her body, the mysterious princess stood swaying, as if in a daze. Her expression reminded me of those found upon the countenances of marbled saints in the ruined cathedrals dotted around the kingdom; imbecilic yet uplifted. She had made no objection whatsoever to the outrageous test of the peas, and after the inspection, climbed the ladder propped up against the bed as if she were ascending an angels' stair to paradise.

The councillors' wives had arranged to keep a vigil over the girl as she slept, patently to prevent one of my staff slipping in halfway through the night in order to inflict bruises upon her.

The night passed without incident, although one or two of the invigilating ladies claimed Papavera sighed very deeply occasionally. In the morning, they all converged upon the bedroom in a bustling throng, myself among them. When Papavera descended the ladder, I was alarmed to see there were dark circles beneath her eyes, which were scarcely open. On the removal of her white nightgown, as she stood quivering and naked upon the hard, balding carpet, it was easy to see her soft skin was marked with the most appalling contusions all around her lower back and belly, even along the tops of her thighs. The councillor's wives were aghast at the injuries, as indeed I was myself. I hastened to cover the poor girl with a gown, keeping my arm around her shoulder. "I feel this is conclusive evidence," I said.

"It is unwholesome!" declared one lady.

"An abomination!" whinnied another.

"It is as the law decrees," I reminded them, and led the girl from their presence.

When examined by the physicks, Papavera repeated the same words, "There were stones in my bed. They made me sleep on stones." She was restless with discomfort in a strange, disquieting manner, rather like an animal who, suffering from some internal impairment, can find no position in which to assuage the hurt. Marquithi was at once furious that his beloved had been damaged and ecstatic that she appeared to have fulfilled the requirements of the law. He held her hand as they sat together in my rooms after the physicks had left, and while he crooned devotion into her ear, she ignored him and blinked dazedly at the floor. My approval of the girl increased immeasurably.

Papavera and Marquithi were married in the autumn, an event preceding their coronation by only five days. By this time, having become inured to the idea, the Council grudgingly allowed themselves to celebrate both occasions in the proper manner. All the guests, from every neighboring kingdom, complimented Marquithi on his choice of bride. Papavera floated throughout the proceedings like the phantom of an opiate dream, as if unaware of her surroundings, smiling at Marquithi occasionally. Being such a modest and winsome creature, she could not fail to glide her way into the hearts of all the court.

Following the coronation, she assumed her role in an appropriate manner. She worked with a deft hand upon tapestries with the other ladies, took protracted and aimless walks in the palace grounds, and attended executions without complaint. When we had foreign guests, she danced enchantingly every night until dawn. She smiled continually in the presence of others, nodded often, but spoke little herself. This made her a much sought after companion, and many ladies of the court considered her to be their confidante. She was trustworthy because she never repeated anything she was told. In the palace, this was a refreshing novelty.

Prudently, I had urged one of the catamites, Eluski, to continue visiting Marquithi, in order to discover how the marriage was progressing in his eyes. The knowledge I gleaned was intriguing. Typically, my son did not consider Papavera's silence and lack of female curiosity as unusual, although he was concerned about the delicacy of her skin. Once, he had pulled her toward him playfully, without violence of any sort, and her arm had bloomed purple to the shape of his demanding fingers. Yet as a lover she, in her silence, became a succubus. Marquithi was astounded by the intensity of her interest in the marriage duties, and confessed it was the only time she made much noise. However, driven to disclose further confidences by the vigilant Eluski, my son admitted to a certain distaste that his wife's body was so cold within. Sometimes—and he thought this might be connected with her female cycles—it felt as if his member was grabbed by cold, wet meat. Eluski faithfully reported all this to me. I began to wonder exactly how, and from where, Anguin had procured the girl. More to the point, *what* was she? Very soon, these questions became more urgent.

There was some fuss one afternoon, when Papavera was found lurching around the palace gardens, her garments in some disarray, her voice a moaning and relentless lament. Servants carrying her back into the building claimed she appeared extremely unwell, and that thick hanks of her hair had fallen out into their hands. Alarmed, I went to inspect her in her chambers, and the sight that greeted was far from appealing. Papavera lay virtually motionless upon the bed and her appearance reminded me horribly of some dreadful ghoul unearthed from a desecrated grave. Her normally translucent skin had turned a dull grey-white. Her gums and eyelids were unnaturally red, and her tongue, which reflexively licked her cracked white lips, was a strange bluish color. The odor she gave off was sweet yet corrupt. I fled to Anguin's rooms immediately, so unnerved I actually grabbed his arms and shook him wildly.

Shrugging off my assault, he appeared unconcerned about Papavera's condition. "Simply have her brought here," he said, fiddling with some equipment on his bench, "and I will do what I can to ameliorate her condition."

Normally, nobody but myself ever visited Anguin's residence, but on this occasion I was forced to secure the services of Vienquil and Eluski to carry the young queen up the stairs, because I was loath to touch the girl myself. Despite their unflinching loyalty to me, they still complained in the most forthright terms about the disagreeable odors and liquids emanating from the queen's body. At Anguin's direction, they laid Papavera on the largest table, which the alchemist had cleared of debris. I had to hold a kerchief to my nose, for the stench was indeed terrible, although Anguin hastened to assure me this was only because the poor girl had soiled herself. My servants and I were then asked to depart, which we did without question.

Back in my rooms, I poured us all a stiff tincture of narcoceine, which we drank in silence with shaking hands.

"Your Highness," Vienquil ventured. "If I may speak plainly, I feel there is something quite seriously amiss with the young queen."

"Something rather more than a simple illness," Eluski added.

"A deduction I share, my dears!" I said briskly. "However, I feel it is a subject we should not discuss at this point, at least until Anguin has reported back to me."

Both servants assumed a mulish expression, sensing my refusal to include them in my secrets. "Come now," I said in mild admonishment. "No need for hard faces! Vienquil, massage my shoulders, if you would. I feel quite shaken!"

As the girl's long, agile fingers plunged with shuddering accuracy into my muscles, I was beginning to question whether I had done the right thing in commissioning a bride for my son from the alchemist. Perhaps it would have been wiser to have asked him to concoct a philter whereby Marquithi would have become so senseless, he'd have married a sheep if I'd asked him to. Still, it was too late for regrets. We could only live with the results of my actions and trust that Anguin knew what he was doing.

At dinnertime, when Marquithi returned from a tour of the neighboring estates, he came rampaging into my rooms, demanding to know what I had done with his wife.

"Mother, Papavera's ladies claim you had Vienquil and Eluski carry her off this afternoon! They say my beloved was quite ill! Where are the physicks? Where the sickroom fumes? Where, indeed, is Papavera?"

"Calm yourself, my pet," I said. "The girl is in good hands."

"Those of your slithering wizard, no doubt!" he cried. "Take me to my wife at once!"

I regret that we fell into serious dispute at that point, resulting in my having physically to restrain Marquithi from barging to the secret stairway and breaking down the doors. I don't know what would have happened if, at the climax of our altercation, when the exchange of blows seemed imminent, the door to Anguin's stairway had not opened and Papavera herself walked into the room.

Marquithi let go of my hair and arms immediately and swept across the room to smother the girl in a fond embrace. "My love, my dear sweet love," he cooed. "What have they been doing to you?"

There was not the slightest trace of illness lingering about Papavera's body. Her pale skin had resumed its limpid translucency, her long, black hair its luster. She smelled so strongly of honeysuckle that the air in the room was drenched in perfume.

"Mother, what has transpired here?" Marquithi asked, his arm protectively clutching the slim shoulders of his wife. "There is nothing wrong with Papavera."

The girl caught my eyes with her own, and gently, imperceptibly, inclined her head. A weird intelligence, which I had not recalled seeing there before, sparkled in her gaze.

"Indeed not," I said, patting my hair, which had come quite adrift from its tressure in the struggle. "Happily, your illness seems to have been of a temporary kind, Papavera."

"I am quite well," she said softly.

An idiot light bloomed in my son's face. "A temporary sickness? Mother, call the physicks at once! Can it be my beloved is with child?"

I shuddered and turned away. Somehow, the prospect of that was distinctly gruesome.

Mercifully, Marquithi's blithe assumption proved incorrect. Physicks examined Papavera and could find no trace of sickness, but neither any trace of pregnancy. It was decided her condition had been caused by something she'd eaten, or else a twist of the gut from some female complaint. Whatever the cause, she now appeared to be in the best of health and as vibrant as she ever could be. However, I could not dismiss a feeling of unease. Anguin again manifested infuriating obstinacy when I attempted to question him about the girl.

"You saw her condition!" I said. "She appeared dead, indeed half-rotted! Yet, hours later, she trips into my chambers as lively as a doe! What was wrong with her, and what did you do about it? I demand to know, Anguin. Remember, I am your mistress!"

Anguin waved aside my outburst. "The puissance of my work is ensured only by its secrecy," he said. "Therefore, I regret I cannot comply with your requests."

"At one time you doubted you were responsible for Papavera's presence here at all," I reminded him.

He grinned, an expression one would expect to find upon the slack-jawed face of a slaughtered dog. "Did I? And you believed me?" He laughed. "Do you think a person who can induce an ancient parchment, as authentic as the hair on your head, to manifest spontaneously in the archives would encounter any difficulty conjuring up a princess?"

I narrowed my eyes at him. "What are you saying? The document was genuine. It bore an antique seal no one from Loolania could possibly have known about, but which the councillors vouched was official, if rather outdated. You could not have created it."

He shrugged. "True . . . perhaps. Anyway, you must smother your fears about the young queen, Your Highness. The lady Papavera has a very delicate constitution and is therefore prone to minor maladies. It is nothing beyond my adroitness to handle."

"You mean this might occur regularly?" I had to sit down. The prospect was not pleasant.

Anguin shrugged. "To preclude such inconvenience, it might be best if the young queen visits me regularly, so that I might attend to her needs."

"Did you foresee this, Anguin?" I demanded.

He turned away. "It is impossible to anticipate in full the outcome of any experiment," he said.

After her illness, the character of my daughter-in-law seemed subtly to change. There was less evidence of vacuity, although she remained as mute as ever. I perceived a calculating glint in her eyes as they gazed, downcast, at the floor. Her followers and sycophants seemed hysterical in their desire to ingratiate themselves into her favor, and she seemed to grow taller from their attentions, trailing them behind her like the hem of a sumptuous gown that is worn for effect, but has become quite invisible to the wearer through its utter familiarity. Marquithi, on the other hand, shrank before the eruption of his wife's dark glory. He locked his door upon Eluski's requests for entrance, and I could no longer glean any information as to his condition or thoughts. Every night was spent with Papavera, and all that Eluski could report was that upon pressing his ear to the king's bedroom door, he heard the sound of a woman's laughter and the moans of a man in ecstasy—or torment.

I never encountered Papavera in my rooms on those days when she went to visit Anguin, although I always knew when she had been through them, because the scent of honeysuckle hung heavily on the air. Anguin must have cut another set of keys for her, because she never had to request entrance from me. I gradually realized that the palace and its occupants had all become subject to Papavera's power. She had grown from a pathetic scrap of a girl into a creature of insidious strength. All were besotted by her. All, that is, but for myself and my immediate staff. One evening, I instructed Vienquil and Eluski to monitor the young queen's behavior, as I knew the time must be approaching when I would again encounter the flavor of honeysuckle lingering in my rooms. "Watch her with great care," I said, "and report."

Neither of them returned to my rooms that night, nor even in the morning. I believed them to be engaged upon some course of investigation, trusting that their intelligence and survival skills would ensure their safety. At noon, I was aroused from the contemplation of a book by a faint, high-pitched scream that emanated from some distant corner of the palace. Later, two of the postprandial guard came to my rooms and reported that my beautiful Vienquil and Eluski were dead. Vienquil had been found spread-eagled beneath the royal beehives, quite stung to death, her body unrecognizably swollen in the most hideous fashion. The beekeepers were aghast and could not imagine what had impelled the swarms to behave in such an uncharacteristically aggressive manner. Eluski, having met the Black Summoner in an even more grisly way, had been found dead in a well, his genitals and his eyes having been brutally torn from his body. Upon receiving these unwelcome tidings, my body went into spasm and two of my maids had to beat my chest fiercely to force my lungs to draw breath. Emotion overtook me and I succumbed to a fit of weeping. The sensation of it was curious, for I had never suffered it before. How vile to be subject to such uncontrollable convulsions on a regular basis! Eventually, however, after a large dose of narcoceine, the reaction abated, and I was able to examine the situation with a placid eye. It seemed obvious to me who was responsible for these repulsive crimes. Papavera was clearly of my particular female clan, yet she was far from an accomplice of mine. How dare she despatch my favorite retainers with such aplomb! I was in the process of formulating a suitable response, when the bitch preempted me. Even as I reposed in my bed fashioning a wax poppet, she swept, without knocking, into the room and posed, hands on hips, at my feet. The scent of honeysuckle was so strong, it almost made me gag.

"I can't recall inviting you here to see me," I said, covering the poppet with a corner of blanket. "Neither did I hear you knock."

Papavera ignored my remarks. "I take exception to the eyes of spies," she said. "Do not presume to have me watched again." I don't think I'd ever heard her speak so many words at once. She seemed like a towering column of evil vapor, as beautiful as she was wicked.

"Papavera," I said, attempting to sound tranquil. "Would I be correct in thinking you are attempting to lock horns with me in some way?"

She did not answer.

"Look," I continued, "if any of my staff *have* been observing you, it was simply through my concern for your welfare."

"Pah!" she spit. "I don't need your concern! I am quite capable of looking after myself."

I could see that, and it vexed me greatly. I attempted a rueful smile. "My dear, I do not wish us to become enemies. We are sisters, after all, in a way."

Papavera flexed her narrow shoulders, and pulled

her mouth down into a sneer. "Sisters? You attempt to amuse me, obviously. I am not your sister, I am your son's wife. I am the queen of Gordania, and you are the widow of a dead king. I have no intention of becoming your creature, like Marquithi is—*was*. I value my independence. All I have to say to you is this: leave me be, and I shall leave you be. This seems a sensible and workable arrangement."

"You have murdered the most valued of my people!" I cried.

She shook her head. "Indeed, I have not! Whatever gave you that idea? The beasts were punished in a just and fitting way, but not by me, I assure you."

"By whom then?"

Her face assumed a dreamy expression. "My kin are vigilant on my behalf," she said.

"Your kin?" A cold, dark shadow smothered my heart.

"Quite so," she replied with a crooked grin. "Now, no more pretty boys sent to my husband's room, no more spies, and I promise there'll be no more unfortunate accidents. Are you agreeable to this?"

My hand beneath the coverlet clutched convulsively around the wax poppet. I opened my mouth to speak, but Papavera interrupted me.

"And images of wax will certainly have no effect upon me," she said. "Of this you can be sure. Now, comply or suffer. It is your choice."

She mocked me. I had no choice.

The sinister turn events were taking would have to be dealt with immediately, I knew that. With Vienquil and Eluski gone, I realized how alone I was.

Marquithi was lost to me, a paralyzed insect in the web of the dark queen. Anguin, I felt I could no longer trust. In desperation, I appealed to the chamberlain. For all his faults, I had realized Tartalan was no fool. Surely, he, of all the court, could discern the malevolent aspect of the young queen? He came to my rooms at nightfall, obeying my furtive summons.

"Tartalan, there is something diabolical about Queen Papavera," I said. "She is dangerous and wicked, indeed possibly inhuman. It is imperative we do something about her."

Tartalan screwed up his nose in vexation. "Diabolical? Dangerous and wicked?" He shook his head. "Why should you think that?"

I took a few deep breaths to calm myself. There was no way I could convince Tartalan of the truth with an hysterical tremor in my voice. "My Lord Chamberlain, I beg you to listen to what I have to say. Every word is truth. Will you believe me?"

He studied me profoundly for a few moments, and then nodded. "Of course. I believe you to be many things, my lady, but a liar is not one of them."

"I am glad to hear it. Your credulity may indeed be stretched by what I have to relate."

Because I needed an ally so badly, I gambled with Fate and told the chamberlain everything, from the moment when I had approached Anguin with my dilemma. He listened in silence to my words, one finger pressed against his thin mouth. Near the end of my narrative, he was beginning to cast nervous glances over his shoulder. I have a gift for storytelling. Even I felt a little frightened.

Tartalan shook his head, and rubbed his face. "This is a startling tale," he said and then peered at me sideways. "Still, it could be said you have brought this misfortune on yourself."

I made an exasperated sound. "I know! Don't you think I haven't admonished myself severely for that? Anyone can make a mistake. I did it for the sake of Gordania, not just for myself."

He nodded vaguely, apparently deep in thought. Then he said, "I will need proof of Papavera's malignance before I dare approach the Council."

I gasped in horror. "Approach the Council? Are you mad? No, no! We must see to this abomination ourselves! But of course I respect your desire for tangible evidence . . ."

"So, what do you suggest?" he inquired, as if we were discussing some trivial issue of palace etiquette.

"We must observe what transpires in Anguin's chambers on those occasions when Papavera visits him for her . . . treatments," I said. "It is to be hoped we should gain the knowledge of how to deal with her."

Tartalan looked doubtful. "With respect, I have no desire to suffer the same fate as other members of this household who have observed Papavera's behavior," he said.

"Neither have I! But it seems to me that the young queen is at her least powerful when she needs Anguin's attentions. It is the obvious time to set about dealing with her."

"I hope you are right," said the chamberlain. It was a sentiment I shared.

Papavera now visited Anguin once a month. I was unsure whether this was because her descent into illness had begun to occur on a more regular basis or simply because Anguin had stepped up her treatments in order to avoid any serious relapse. I was distinctly nervous of interfering. Anguin had withdrawn from me and I no longer enjoyed visiting him in his workroom. I realized I had badly underestimated his personal strength and overestimated his loyalty to me. He had created his own queen. Who really wielded the power in this House?

As I counted the days to the dark of the moon, that time when the scent of honeysuckle invaded my rooms, I thought wistfully, even affectionately, of the doltish Lady Selini of Crooms. Perhaps there was still room for maneuver in that direction—should Queen Papavera be removed from Marquithi's life. This thought cheered me a little, as I wrought what sorcerous protection I could to provide Tartalan and myself with at least a measure of security.

On the evening in question, a chill midwinter night, Tartalan came to my chambers dressed in black. I myself donned the apparel of a man, so that I should be able to move quickly if the occasion merited it. Ever since my initial talk with the chamberlain concerning this night's venture, I had been considering how this might be the only chance I would get to rid myself of the presence of both Anguin and his creation. Consequently, I had armed myself with razor-edged metal crescents and topical poisons. Tartalan, as my witness, would be my only defense against any legal unpleasantness which might follow. We hid in one of the anterooms and waited for the scent to reach us. At the hour when evening turns to night, all the lamps in my apartment became weirdly dimmer, and the appointments took on a vigilant, breathless appearance. Power sizzled invisibly in the air, raising the hairs on my arms and neck. I glanced at Tartalan as we crouched among the curtains. "Do you feel it?" I asked him.

He nodded.

"She is coming," I said. "We will not see her, but she is coming."

A faint breeze that held the promise of snow lifted the golden fringes of the curtains, and I shrank back against the window casement. I was terrified that, at any moment, Papavera would swoop into the room and throw the curtain wide. She would stand there, tall as a tree, with her black hair whipping round her colorless face, and she would point a finger right at me, utter some fatal words . . . No, no, I must not direct my thoughts along such a fell avenue. I had charms aplenty around my neck, my skin had been anointed with an essence of protection. Papavera did not consider me a threat. As she glided through my rooms, she would not even give me a single thought. I pressed my hands against my mouth.

The scent came insidiously, trickling like smoke into the room. At first, I thought I was imagining it. Then, Tartalan said, "It smells like early summer." He began to stand up.

"She is here," I hissed, putting a restraining hand on Tartalan's arm. "Keep down."

"I feel ridiculous," Tartalan whispered back. "This is a child's prank!"

I shook my head. "No!" I clutched Tartalan's arm for several minutes, until the overpowering scent faded a little and I was sure the dark queen had entered the locked doors. My body felt hot and yet I could see my breath steaming on the chill air.

Stealthily, I led the chamberlain into the main

room. The fire was a dull, angry glow in the hearth and the lamplight looked weak and sick. The very air felt polluted. With shaking hands, I took the keys to Anguin's doors from my trouser pocket. For a moment, I considered abandoning this course of action, packing my bags and fleeing back to my parents' estate in Loolania that same night. Then, a shred of dignity reasserted itself. Had I not held sway in this kingdom for the last eighteen years? I had been a mere child, just past her first bud, when Marquithi's father had taken me to wed. And that child had been afraid of nothing. If she could have looked forward in time, she would have been ashamed to see the woman she was to become hesitating and shying like a skittish mare. Straightening my back, I strode toward the secret stairway, Tartalan padding along behind me.

The stairwell to Anguin's rooms was in darkness, and we could hear no sound. I had to remind myself to breathe as we advanced cautiously up the dusty treads. I pulled one of the crescents from a leather pouch fixed inside my shirt, and with my free hand unstoppered a phial of caustic bane. If there was trouble, I intended to attack immediately.

Anguin's workroom was lit by the flickering, yellow glow of a single candle. As I poked my head through the floor, I could see he was busy working on something on one of the tables. On a metal band around his brow he wore a refracting crystal, which directed beams of the guttering light onto whatever lay on the table. Because of the design of the room, it was impossible to enter it and hide without being seen, so with a last prayer to my grandmother's spirit, I walked over the wooden floor, straight toward my erstwhile alchemist. He looked up with alarm when he realized he was no longer alone, and I experienced a swift thrill of satisfaction to see the expression of shock on his face.

"Yes, it is I, your mistress," I said. "I have come to inspect your work."

I went to stand beside him. "My Lord Chamberlain," I said, without looking around. "If you would be so kind as to examine this . . . handiwork."

Papavera lay on the table, split open from breast to groin. Where one would expect to see entrails and blood was only a jumble of thick purplish juices. There was evidence of bone, but it was strangely jointed together with gnarled sticks and metal rods. Undulating bags of soaked cloth approximated the position of stomach and guts. As for her face, it was an eerie caricature of her normal beauty; the mouth hung open, the black tongue lolled, the clouded eyes stared at the ceiling. A more repulsive sight was hard to imagine; neither was the odor of this operation particularly benign. Anguin had not spoken at all. He looked distinctly sullen.

"Perhaps you can explain what it is you're doing," I said to him. Tartalan stood behind me, making small anguished noises of disgust, a kerchief held to his nose.

"Well, as you can see, I am working upon the queen," Anguin said lamely.

I folded my arms and nodded. "Indeed. Now, you will destroy the monster." I picked up a sharp tool from beside the body and began stirring one of the bags of fluid in Papavera's torso with it. "If you do not, Anguin, I shall rip this abomination apart myself!"

"My lady, I am most reluctant to do as you ask. There are certain implications of which you are unaware . . ."

"Such as?" I raised the dripping instrument and pointed it at his face. "Hurry, Anguin. Your explanation would indeed gratify me."

"Her kin," he said flatly. "I fashioned her body from whatever materials I could lay my hands on, but her soul was not created by my acts. It was quickened by nightling energy."

I blinked at him, aghast. It is no coincidence that, in some places, nightlings are called the Devourers. "Destroy it!" I hissed. "For the love of all things lit, Anguin, I will discount your insubordination and add my strength to yours against any eventuality, but destroy this creature now!"

His mouth opened and closed a few times. I think he would have complied with my wishes, but at that point, the sound of splintering wood and heavy feet came from below. Seconds later, the chamber was suddenly flooded with light and filled with palace guards, who were pouring through the floor brandishing weapons. Then, Marquithi himself leapt through the trapdoor. I don't think I'd ever been so pleased to see him. My pleasure, however, was short-lived.

Upon seeing my son, Tartalan jumped backward a few steps and raised his hand, pointing at Anguin and me. He waved the kerchief at us like a flag. "Arrest these traitors!" he cried.

Anguin and I exchanged a shocked glance. Angrily I turned to my son. "Marquithi, restrain the chamberlain. He has lost his wits!" Marquithi was staring at the table where the parts of his wife lay in disarray. His face was unreadable, but he would not look at me.

"Take them away!" he said to the guards and left the room.

You can imagine that the shock of Marquithi's action quite drove me senseless. I was utterly benumbed, mercifully, even to the point where I was unaware of my surroundings. I was incarcerated beneath the palace in a secure lodging best described as squalid, although that conveys little of the true horror of it. One of the councillors came to see me, to explain that I was to be put on trial for treason, along with Anguin and the young queen, whom Marquithi had demanded be reconstituted to meet her fate. Till that point, I had not enjoyed a warm relationship with the councillor, but I felt he sympathized with my position and perhaps felt uncomfortable with Marquithi's harsh treatment of me. They are sticklers for tradition, these Gordanians, and my blood, after all, was quite royal. I told him I'd acted in good faith, admitted I'd miscalculated, and he seemed to accept my explanation. However, it appeared Tartalan had reported everything I had told him to the king, and in a particularly venomous manner (how could I have misjudged him so!). Therefore, on the night when he and I had crept up to Anguin's room, Marquithi had already been alerted. It had been prearranged that the three of us should be caught *in flagrante.* My son knew everything: how I had kept him docile, how I had arranged for Papavera to be created, everything. I suppose in his position I too might have felt somewhat chagrined, but blood is thicker than water, as they say, so he really was going a little too far by persisting in keeping me in detention.

The hours passed interminably. To this day, I have no way of telling how long I spent in that abysmal hole. Sleep evaded me, and I could not eat. I realized that, should Marquithi stick to the letter of the law, I was finished. I only hoped the method of despatch would be painless, if it came to that. How ungrateful a son can be! Had I acted in any way but to spare him pain and bother? He did not even come to speak with me.

At some point, Queen Papavera was brought in to share my cell. She had indeed been restored, although her face was tight with some unnamed emotion. At first, she did not speak, while I, upon seeing her, desired only to execute the plan I'd had in Anguin's chamber, namely, tear her to pieces. We sat upon opposite sides of the small cell, glaring at one another. Eventually, because of my breeding and innate gentility, it was I who broke the silence.

"Look at me in that way if you wish," I said, "but the fact is we are both in error. I, for having Anguin conjure you in the first place, and you for becoming too ambitious. Together we could have lived in harmony for many years and, I might add, in rewarding control of this country!"

Papavera made a guttural, hissing sound. "Empty comfort!" she said in a harsh voice. "I anticipate an ignoble end to my reign."

Having made communication, my mind had begun to stir itself from torpor. I tapped my lips thoughtfully with my fingers. "Papavera, we are both in the direst of predicaments. Marquithi is a fool. However, if my memory serves me correctly, you at least have recourse to assistance."

She growled dismally. "Hardly! Once Anguin finished his ministrations upon me, Marquithi had the soldiers cut off his hands. I expect he is already dead."

"I did not mean Anguin," I said. "I was referring to your kin."

She looked up at me sharply. "Do not think I haven't tried to petition them," she said. "The fact is, they are contemptuous of my ineptitude at manipulating my circumstances. They believe I deserve to lose this human form and revert to my true state."

"Is that a sentiment you share?"

She looked thoughtful for a moment. "No," she said at last. "There are certain enjoyable aspects of this incarnation."

"In that case, it is obvious what we have to do," I told her.

"What?" I was gratified by the ignition of hope in her eyes.

"First, you must give me your most binding vow you will not desert me, betray me, or harm me in any way."

She nodded. "Excise me from this mess, and I shall shower you with devotion for eternity."

"Very well, we shall see to the solemnizing of that vow presently. First, I will tell you this. In order to attract the assistance of your kin, we must have something to offer them in return, for even though I am unacquainted with the customs of your people, I know there is no form of life in existence that does not respond to the prospect of gain."

"True enough," said the young queen. "But what do you suggest?"

I reached over and patted her clenched hands. "My dear, there is not one bumbling foreign nobleman who is not slave to your charm and beauty. Should we escape our distress, I am convinced we will find succor somewhere else beyond Gordania. It seems to me that your kin would welcome ingress into some area of human activity. Perhaps we could facilitate that."

Papavera smiled. "With your knowledge of the human condition and my access to nightling caprices, it does indeed seem a workable plan."

The trial was a farce, although I must admit it gave me some satisfaction to hear my crimes recited. Papavera was declared demonic and would be burned at the stake. I, as conspirator in diabolic practices and consequently a traitor to the crown, must also be executed but, because of my rank, I would be allowed to drink poison. Anguin, already half-dead and mutilated, would be thrown to the royal hounds and be devoured alive. Marquithi maintained a pale, cold distance while the fates of the women in his life were proclaimed. It was almost as if he'd never loved either of us. It was very strange, but I could not hate him. He simply could not understand our female ways, which seemed very ordinary to me. Still, it was a mistake to let a man witness the true nature of our power, and if anyone deserved to die that day, it was Tartalan.

As a formality, I was allowed to speak in my own defense, a procedure I knew would have no effect upon the outcome. I spoke plainly, remarking that, as I saw it, the only problem was a disagreement between Papavera and myself, and that I could not imagine why it had reached the grand court of Gordania. These comments caused a rumble from the spectators' gallery, where the dimwitted councillors' wives flapped themselves with fans and gorged their spirits on my humiliation. I refused to be penitent or cowed. At least Papavera gave me her support through her gentle smile across the court. She was allowed no defense, poor creature. At length, after all the talking was done, the judge donned his black cowl and named the time of our executions. Sunfall. Papavera held my eyes as she was taken from the room. I had to trust her; not just her intention, but her ability. I prayed for her success.

Papavera and Anguin were returned to the dungeons, whilst I was escorted to my former rooms to await the hour when the physicks would bring me the deadly cup. I sat in my favorite chair by the window, watching the shadows lengthen. No one came to tender their farewells. My servants were all gone. Only a couple of whiskered slaughterhouse women kept me company, and a brace of guards beside the door. I reflected how badly my life had gone awry, and yet, given the time again, would I have acted differently? It was difficult to tell. As the dusk stole quietly toward the windows, I heard their steps outside the door. My heart began to beat much faster. I saw the night-black shadow of an enormous wing across the sill.

So you see, that is my story, that is how I am here beside your fire, and my fellow travelers asleep in your hayloft. What? Oh do not be afraid; our unseen companions will not attack you, or your animals. Although I must admit the ferocity of their attack, when the mood takes them to indulge in violence, is quite incredible. Did I tell you how quickly it is possible to shred the bodies of two guards, two large women, and a brace of physicks? No? Well, perhaps I had better spare you the details. We had to bring Anguin with us, of course, in order for my dear companion to retain her physical splendor on a long-term basis. To date, he has been teaching me some measure of his skills, although—please don't tell him this—my lady and I are considering allowing him to build himself a pair of hands. He did so well with Papavera's bodily equipment after all, and, well, he is so tractable nowadays. Anyway, I've kept you awake long enough. So gracious of you to offer us accommodation. Now, I must sleep. Tomorrow, we have business with the squire of this parish. Madam, you are too kind, but I insist you accept my coin as payment. Are we not sisters, after all, sisters of a certain persuasion? Before bed, I would walk in your mandrake garden. So fortunate we saw you weeding it from the road as we were passing, so fortunate. I have longed to share my story with a woman of like mind. A night of blessings to you, madam, a night of blessings.

The Black Swan

Susan Wade

Susan Wade lives in Austin, Texas, and has sold fiction to the magazines New Pathways, Amazing Stories, Fantasy and Science Fiction, Weird Tales, *to the anthology* Snow White, Blood Red, *and Ellen Datlow's untitled cat horror anthology. Wade is working on a contemporary novel set in New Mexico called* Walking Rain. *It will be published by Bantam in 1995.*

Although she has been writing for only a relatively short time, Wade's stories are increasingly powerful and effective.

"The Black Swan" follows perfectly in the wake of "Sweet, Bruising Skin" in its pungent commentary on how far women will go to achieve a particular time's ideal of feminine beauty.

The Black Swan

I REMEMBER YLIANNA'S ARRIVAL AT THE PALACE PERfectly, because it coincided so nearly with my own, though she was a royal cousin and I no more than a raw country boy taking up my first post, Third Footman to the Under-Steward.

Truth be told, there was less difference between Ylianna and me than one would have thought, for she was a country girl herself, and, like me, from the wild rocky hills of the north. And we were much of an age; I in my thirteenth summer and she in her twelfth, a strapping girl as tall as I was—and I was not short, else I would never have gone for a footman, no matter what my uncle's influence in the servants' hall. Worse for Ylianna, she was ruddy-complected and deep-voiced, with hair brown as a mudlark. (That day, it was also as wild and tangled as a mudlark's nest.)

My uncle put me in for a place because he said I had a quick eye and a knack for aping my betters, which he thought best turned to use before it made trouble. And my uncle was right. From the scant experience of my six days in the palace, I knew as soon as I saw Ylianna that she was hopelessly out of fashion, for all the fine wool of her gown, for all the brilliance of her black eyes and flashing smile.

The Queen's six sons were blondly handsome, ranging in coloration from silver pale to glowing gold, with creamy fair complexions and bright blue eyes. She was a doting mother and a generous Queen, and it was only natural that the fashions of court would follow the fondness of her maternal eye. And the Queen herself, though a matron, was slim and graceful and daintily proportioned, and so that too was the fashion.

Ylianna was doomed—by her lineage and her dead father's wealth—to live with her royal aunt, under the unforgiving scrutiny of the court, compared ceaselessly to the impossible standard her cousins presented.

My own transition from the simple life of my plain north-country home to the rich complexities of the servants' hall had already proved exacting. Thus, my heart went out to Ylianna the instant I saw her stride into the main hall, her round face blotched from sun and her shapeless wool dress muddied and out at the hem. As the Queen's Steward moved languidly forward to make her welcome, Ylianna turned and called to her maid to hurry with the bags, saying she was famished and must change for dinner on the instant. Her voice rang from the grey stones of the entry hall like the tone of some huge deep bell, and the Fancies of the court—or, at the least, those who had drifted hence to observe this new addition to their Lady's brood—turned their faces away from her and laughed in their scented sleeves. For not only was this great hulking girl a disgraceful bumpkin, it was scarce six o'clock, and the Queen never dined before ten.

As I say, my heart went out to her in that moment. Living as I had for the past week with my own dread of saying or doing the wrong thing, I was devastated for her sake by this immediate—and likely irreparable—stumble.

The Queen entered the hall at that moment (it was a great condescension for her to leave her apartments to greet her young niece). But as I said, the Queen had a generous heart. So the cruel whispers and spiteful snickers of the court were silenced, at least for a time.

It was then that I silently vowed the Queen would not be the only ally Ylianna found in the palace.

At the first, my duties kept me more than occupied, and occupied far from the apartments of the royals. The Under-Steward had high standards for service, prime among them that good servants should be neither seen nor heard. It was many months before I was able to execute my duties with the degree of invisibility required of the household staff. So I was relegated to the ferrying of dirtied dishes from the serving station to the kitchens, of dirtied linens to the laundresses, and of dirtied chamber pots to the privies. But I would occasionally catch a glimpse of Ylianna as she tramped through the hall or gamed with her male cousins in the gardens—races and rough rounds of stickball and mock fencing matches. From a distance, she did not seem sad, and I grew hopeful that, even as I was beginning to know my way about and to understand what I must say when the Sous-Chef bade me to fetch him more carrots, so was Ylianna making her own small nest here amid the mazed confines of the palace walls.

But then, when I was returning from an errand to the kitchen garden (the Steward had entrusted me with a message to the head vegetable gardener regarding the availability of the white asparagus for which the Queen had developed a sudden craving), I came upon Ylianna and her eldest cousin, the heir, Prince Sigfried. He was sixteen at the time, beginning to outgrow the games his brothers played (and which he had long dominated), and was an altogether glorious youth. Sigfried was tall—taller even than Ylianna—and silvery fair, with lashes that lay like white-silk lace against his glowing golden skin, and eyes the blue of the glacier-fed lake in the mountain above the Summer Palace. Well-grown and well-spoken, with a certain noble masculine beauty, our Prince was a source of pride amongst all the citizens of the palace, above stairs and below.

Thus it did not amaze me to see the manner in which Ylianna gazed at him, when I came round a turn in the path to the kitchen garden that day, but it certainly smote my heart. For I knew—as who in the servants' hall did not?—that Prince Sigfried was betrothed from birth to the Princess Annaliesl, sole heiress to a certain neighboring principality on which the Queen had long had designs. And worse for Ylianna was the expression in the young Prince's eyes as they rested on her face, for he looked at her as though she were some nestling hatched by one of the kitchen hawks: He might be briefly entertained by its antics, but he would never dream of training it to his wrist.

Immediately I saw them, I concealed myself behind one of the stone columns that supported the grape arbor. The Under-Steward's lessons were carefully instilled in me by then. But invisibility does not convey deafness.

"—but *why* won't you award the fencing medals, Sigfried? I'm certain to win, for I've been practicing every morning for a month and I have the reach on Karl—"

"I told you, Cousin, I am otherwise engaged this afternoon."

"Doing what? Can't you change your schedule?"

The tone of his voice revealed that he was smiling, a slow and secret smile, without a doubt. "You wouldn't understand, Ylie. Have the fencing master award the medals. He's a better judge than I."

"Never!" she said, in her ringing voice, and he laughed at her. Chagrin and annoyance and a certain careless affection commingled in that laugh, and he said, "Foolish child." I did not know at that instant whether to despise him or sympathize with him over this hoydenish young cousin who was so embarrassing in her adoration.

And then they were beyond the curve of the path, and I slipped from my hiding place and away. But, though I carried the white asparagus straight to the Chef and reported its acquisition quite properly to the Steward—who deigned to be pleased with my efficiency—I carried also an aching weight, knowing how bitter was to be Ylianna's disappointment over her beloved Prince.

By my third year with the palace staff, I had risen to the rank of Second Footman—no small progress—and had earned the Under-Steward's trust in the discharge of my duties. Given signs of his favor, I broached the topic of a change in quarters—not, I hasten to add, a request for lodgings better than those normally allocated for staff of my rank, but simply a rearrangement that would permit me a greater degree of privacy and quiet. In short, I proposed to remove to the loft above the stables, which had once been occupied by the stable lads themselves, and were consequently equipped for such residence. (Our gracious Queen had since established separate quarters for the stablehands.)

The Under-Steward frowned at the silver urn that he was polishing, his long upper lip curling until it looked rather like a horse's. "Rather irregular," he said, and paused, giving the gleaming silver a judicious buff. "Are you, perhaps, homesick, my boy?"

"Not at all, sir," I replied. Suddenly the air of the butler's cabinet seemed very close. "It is merely that—without seeking to place myself above my station, sir—I feel my abilities to study and improve myself would benefit from privacy in the evenings. Sir."

"Study?" He actually looked up from the urn. "Do you mean that you can read, Eriksen?"

I stood very still. "Yes, sir. The village prefect taught me."

"Ah," he said. "Very good. By all means, remove your belongings to the stable loft this evening. I shall take it upon myself to mention it to the Steward and to the Stablemaster."

I thanked him and left. It was to be hoped that the removal would not reduce my assignment for special responsibilities—my distance might prove in some ways a disadvantage—but would achieve a certain separation between myself and the other footmen. Already, I had my eye on the post of Second Under-Steward, when old Gould was pensioned off in a year or so, and my uncle had long advised me that too much fellowship with one's colleagues could prove extremely awkward in the event of such an advancement.

Forgive my digression; I merely meant to explain how my association with the Lady Ylianna came about. For it was the move into the stable loft that precipitated our meeting, such that she later suffered me to be of some small assistance to her.

Now sixteen, the Lady Ylianna had grown even taller and more robust of limb, her skin ever more ruddy and her hair ever darker. In nowise did she fulfill the court's model of an aristocratic young beauty. No matter how the Queen's dresser gowned Ylianna—notwithstanding laces and silks and intricately fashioned and beribboned skirts—she could not be other than she was, a strapping great girl, unfashionably dark and tall, who was completely deficient in graceful bearing, modulation of voice, or even charm of manner.

And, sadly, the court—in its cruelty—never allowed Ylianna to forget her differences, nor her noble relations' disapprobation of them. She was mocked to her face and behind her back: ridiculed when she dared present herself at table, shunned at dances and cotillions, yet belittled when she failed to join her cousins' graceful golden formation. Ylianna had found her only—grudging—acceptance on the hunting field, and though the ladies of the court found much to criticize in her dress and her brashness in following the hounds, none could disparage her horsemanship.

It seemed to me, from my distant observations, that Ylianna had undergone some internal modification that allowed her to endure the snubs and slanders of the court with detachment. On taking up residence in the stables, I soon learned of my error.

It was early summer, when all hunting was canceled by order of the Queen, so that the hunted animals could raise families to be hunted in their turn. Stripped of the opportunity to apply her only viable social ability, Ylianna took lengthy rides alone, often retreating to the palace only after the torches were lit. One night she was so late returning that all the stable lads had gone and I had been excused from my duties at table—I had progressed to such responsibilities only that summer—and gone to my loft for the night.

She entered the stable yard at a canter, her huge black stallion blowing and badly frothed. I heard his hooves ring on the cobbles, and hastened down the ladder that served as my staircase, in hopes of catching a glimpse of her. I was astonished to find that she had not called for a lad, but had dismounted unaided, and was leading her exhausted mount into the stable herself.

I stepped forward and said, "Please, my lady, permit me."

She drew back, peering at me in the flickering light. "You're not one of the stableboys. You're the footman, the one who fetched my other slippers when I broke the strap of my shoe at Sigfried's birthday ball."

Much gratified, I bowed. "Please, permit me to be

of assistance, my lady. It is late, and the lads have gone to their rooms." I reached for the horse's bridle, but she did not relinquish it. The steamy smell of the horse mingled with the sweet hay scent of the stable, reminding me of my childhood.

"What are you doing here?" she demanded, and her voice was harsh. "Did Lady Mulken send you to spy on me, searching for further evidence of my ill behavior to carry to the Queen?"

"No, my lady," I said, shocked. "Never that! I have been permitted to take up residence in the old stable rooms of the loft. I was merely preparing for bed, as you see." I indicated my shirtsleeves.

She faltered, and put one hand to her head. Her hair had turned darker over the years since I had first seen her, and it was in a terrible tangle from the wind. After an instant, she shoved it impatiently back from her face and asked, "Why would you wish to live above the stables?" Her voice was hard and suspicious, and her gaze raked me insultingly. "You might get hay in your hair, and the horses won't be impressed by your elocution."

"I come from the north country," I said quietly. "I sleep better out here than inside the palace."

She was still watching me, but with a surprised expression. "I am from the north country as well," she said.

I bowed and took the stallion's bridle, and this time she did not offer resistance. Blown as he was, he offered none either, but followed docilely to the grooming box, where I removed the saddle and covered him with a blanket.

His mistress had followed as well. "What part of the country do you come from?"

"Bergen. A little village near the Bourne." I rubbed a cloth along the horse's neck, then brought him out of the box and began walking him.

"Do you miss it?" she asked, her voice a whisper filled with her own longing.

"At times," I said. "And you?"

"Always," she said, walking beside me. "This place is so—so *tame*. And with all these walls around me, I feel as though I can't breathe."

"It is quite different," I replied.

"How did you learn to speak as you do?" she asked, stopping suddenly in the stable corridor. Although I had grown several inches in the years since I came there, we were still of a height.

"Listening. Practicing," I said. "My uncle always said I was good at aping my betters."

"You are," Ylianna said. "You sound more like a noble than I do, and I am one. Or I'm supposed to be." And she began to cry, a harsh, broken weeping.

I stopped, instinctively reaching out a hand to her, but she remembered our respective places better than I. "No," she said, "I beg your—pardon."

I touched the stallion's withers. He was not cooling overfast under his blanket, so I turned him into his loose box and gave him some grain. When I came back, Ylianna was seated on a hay bale near the tack room, scrubbing at her face with a dirty handkerchief. With her swollen eyes and her red face, she looked like some rude milkmaid, fresh from the farm.

I bowed to her, and said, "My lady, perhaps I could be of some small assistance to you."

"No. There is nothing you or anyone else can do. I am ugly and ungainly and too tall, and my hair is all wrong—there is nothing for me to do but run away, back to Owen Hall, except that I could never repay my aunt's kindness in such a manner. Perhaps I should cast myself from the tower and be done with my misery."

"Never, my lady!" I knelt in the straw before her. "You must not! I believe there is much that could be achieved toward—rectifying—what you perceive as flaws in your person. With minor tutelage and some practice, you could be more graceful than any of the courtiers, for you are strong and athletic. And with simple alterations in your mode of dress, and the styling of your hair—"

"It's no use," she said. "I'm stout and misshapen and have a red, ugly face. Not even those absurd dandies will ever glance twice at me, much less—" She broke off, and I averted my eyes. Certain things were best left unspoken.

"I have effected great alterations in my own manner and appearance," I said. "My style of speech and attire, my bearing even. If you will but trust me a little, I believe the same could be accomplished on your behalf." I stopped then, fearful of having overstepped my bounds. But I longed to be of service to Ylianna, knowing I could never be more to her than a servant.

She looked at me, her dark eyes sad and uncertain. Then she sighed and said, "What would you have me do?"

We agreed that she would come to the stable each midnight, at which time my duties in the household were generally fulfilled. There, in that humble setting, we should remake her.

* * *

I should like to explain that there was never any hint of impropriety between myself and the Lady Ylianna, and I make this statement not in defense of my own actions, but to protect her good name. If I had been an old family retainer, would our association be looked upon as improper? Surely not. And though I was never employed on Lord Owen's estate, Ylianna and I shared a memory of the wild rocky hills of the north country, which—to my mind, at least—excuses her lapse in allowing me such minor familiarities as perhaps occurred.

I was reassured to discover that Ylianna was neither slow nor clumsy in her lessons, and I could not but wonder that the Queen had never provided tutelage for her niece. Perhaps having only sons, it had not occurred to her that young ladies require a certain sort of guidance. Whatever the case, Ylianna learned quickly to modulate her voice, and the low sweet tones that resulted were sufficiently enticing to give me pause in the endeavor.

But Ylianna was so delighted by the alteration that I hadn't the heart to protest. Deportment came more slowly; Ylianna was accustomed to striding about in riding boots, and took slowly to the notion of gliding along the floor, scarcely lifting her feet, head and shoulders unmoving. But that lesson too was learned.

I had a word with the Queen's dresser—a very careful word, considering her stature in the servants' hall—and contrived to help her realize that simple, fluid designs would be more becoming to Ylianna's tall figure than were gowns that looked like the Dessert Chef's latest confection.

Ylianna and I were working on table conversation

and dance party protocol, each night from midnight to the early morning hours. The late-night study left me with less energy for my daily duties, but I was accomplished enough at them by then to continue to acquit myself creditably even when tired. Ylianna began sleeping during the day, and, as a result, her complexion lost some of its blotchiness, though it was still too highly colored for fashion.

During this period, of perhaps two months, Ylianna had kept strictly to her own rooms on my advisement. To effect a metamorphosis of the court's opinion of Ylianna, a dramatic transformation would be far better than some incremental alteration that might pass almost unnoticed.

Still, my lady retained a somewhat stocky figure, and was very conscious of the fact. She essayed a reducing diet, to good effect. This new shapely strength she displayed was quite stunning. I had arranged (by the small subterfuge of intimating that it was necessary to my own toilette) for the transfer of an old full-length looking glass from the attics to my rooms in the stable loft. But even beautifully garbed in a sweep of midnight blue satin, skin clear, eyes brilliant, her tangles tamed into glossy ringlets—even this transformed vision of herself did not content Ylianna.

"It is no use," she said. "I am still a big hulking girl, and Sigfried will never think of me as anything else. To him I will always be his clumsy country cousin, instead of a woman."

I cleared my throat. "My lady—perhaps you are unaware of the prince's betrothal?"

She glanced at me and her black eyes flashed. "That old arrangement? The Queen will never insist upon it, if Sigfried's heart lies elsewhere. She has said as much, often and often." Then she turned back to the glass and gazed at her own reflection. "But how can I turn his heart, when I am ugly?"

"You are beautiful, my lady," I assured her, and it was true. She was striking, an astonishingly lovely woman. But she would not listen (and who could fault her for discounting the opinion of one like myself, so far beneath her in station?). I felt then, as now, that it was inequitable that Ylianna should be forced to turn to one such as I for companionship and aid.

"No," she said, still watching herself in the glass. "I'm too big. He will never love me while I look like this."

I tried to console her, but she grew wild in her despair, and, before I could stay her, raced her stallion out into the darkness, still clad in her satin gown. Over the following days, I feared for her reason, and became convinced that she would indeed cast herself from the tower if her love for Sigfried continued unrequited.

She insisted that she must be delicate, with the fragile, ethereal appearance the Queen had so successfully cultivated. I was of two minds, but Ylianna's desperation decided me. I made discreet inquiries, and discovered that certain remedies were commonly used in aid of feminine beauty. Purported to brighten the eyes, clarify the complexion, and attenuate the form, this medicament was taken in the form of a crystalline powder, derived from belladonna, and I confess to having procured it for my lady.

If I were free to choose again, would I persevere

in Ylianna's transformation, even by such dangerous means? In truth, I cannot say. For though I mourn at what we wrought of her, it is not in me to deny my lady her heart's desire.

At the time, I would have sworn that her eyes could be no brighter, but I was mistaken. After she began employing the white powder, Ylianna's eyes became black diamonds, they did glitter so, and her skin like milk in the moonlight. And it seemed to me that her hair grew darker, as black as a raven's wing, but that may have been no more than the contrast with her skin. Yes, the powder fulfilled all the promises made of its efficacy, and it was not so many weeks before Ylianna's form was as slender as that of the Queen. And with the new slimness, the contours of her face were planed to an unearthly perfection.

Ylianna was determined to make her grand reentry to court at the Harvest Cotillion, which fell at the autumnal equinox, also marking the beginning of the hunting season. I believe—though I cannot know—that she envisioned some glorious resurrection of every fond memory Sigfried had of the old Ylianna, roused in confluence with his introduction to the new, this stunning dark beauty that Ylianna and I had created together.

There were rumors in the servants' hall that the Cotillion was to mark some further occasion this year, as we were to prepare for double the usual number of guests. None but the Queen and the Steward himself were privy to certain of the arrangements.

I confess to feelings of uncertainty, to misgivings. It was such an immense undertaking, to transform

Ylianna in the eyes and minds of the court. All to rest on this one affair, Ylianna burdened with so much that she must recall—it was such an enormous strain to place upon one young girl. Yet it was she who decreed that every movement, every smile, every word she uttered must be perfect. I could not but fear the results of such . . . exertion.

But the wheels I had set in motion in early summer had turned, and brought us to this juncture. It seemed as though fate had borne us to this point. I cast aside my misgivings and helped Ylianna prepare for the ball.

She had determined that she would wear black, and commissioned her gown in secret. We discussed the timing of her entrance and her choice of accessories in exhaustive detail; we played for hours at what the Prince might say and how Ylianna might respond. And we practiced the dances night after night, until her every gesture, her every movement, her every breath, was as graceful as a leaf turning in the wind.

Her behavior became wilder as the date approached; she and her stallion disappearing on mad late-night gallops across the countryside; wild, insane rides that risked his legs and her neck at every turn, particularly when I knew her strength to be so much less than it had been. When I remonstrated with her, she merely looked at me, and said, "But I must breathe sometime, Eriksen, else I should die."

I worried myself near to collapse before the ball. She began consuming her powder in greater and greater quantities, in her drive toward that single elusive moment of perfection. Her beauty became even more eldritch, terrifying in its contrasts: silken white skin and raven hair; sleek, honed bones forming the fluid suppleness of her face and form; strength and fragility captured, frozen, in the instant of their embrace.

I confess that she frightened me. At odd moments, I found myself longing for the old Ylianna, the great glumping girl who had arrived at the palace and called for her supper in a voice that rang to the rafters.

I pleaded with her to moderate her use of the powder, even going so far as to imply that procuring more of the substance would be problematic. She merely laughed, her eyes as wild as the stallion's after one of their midnight gallops, and said, knowingly, that I should manage more if the need arose.

I was assigned to serve at the Cotillion, which was both fortunate and troublesome, as I found it near impossible to keep my gaze properly forward, instead of trained upon the tower staircase, by which Ylianna would enter the dance.

She came on the stroke of midnight, stepping into the hush that preceded the Naming Day Dance, and prolonging it. By the time she set her foot to the third step, every face in the room was turned toward her.

The gown was of black silk, with glittering crystalline beads sewn over the silk in a feathery pattern. In this dress, she looked like a slim black lily, her face white above the willowy stem. Her hair was drawn high, with gleaming black ringlets falling loose from the crown. She wore no necklet, nothing to obstruct the swanlike white sweep of her throat. Her only ornament was a gauze-thin whisper of silk that flowed from her wrists to the short train of her gown, and when she stood upon the lowermost step and reached out her arms to the Prince, that glitter-sewn, silken expanse lifted around her like shadowy wings.

Sigfried came to her, a man in a waking dream; bowing deep, and saluting her hand with a kiss that made widows blush. The musicians took their cue from her answering *révérance* and soared into their appointed song.

Not a breath was drawn in the hall as the two danced; I would swear to that. It was as if we watched the mating of the moon to the sun, or the night sky to the stars: a coming-together that was fated, inevitable, yet fraught with the peril of opposites. They moved like a pair of swans, one dark, one silver-fair, circling the floor in a perfect arc, though whether their dance was a preface to love or to death, I could not at that moment have told.

It was her moment, her single, luminous instant of perfection. And then the music ended, and the pair stood gazing at each other in the hushed reaches of the hall.

It was the Princess Annaliesl who broke the spell. She was a refined young woman, delicate and small, with golden hair and soft green eyes; and when she came up beside Sigfried and took his arm, the points of her dainty tiara came scarcely to his shoulder.

"Sigfried, I don't believe you have presented me to your cousin," the Princess said.

"Oh, of course," he replied. "This is my cousin, the Lady Ylianna, Princess. Ylianna, the Princess Annaliesl."

"His betrothed," the Princess added with a smile. "We were to announce it at midnight and seal our troth with a dance. The dance you have just stolen, my dear."

Ylianna spoke for the first time. "Is this true, Sigfried?" Her voice sent a shiver through me, though I stood at some small distance, and was accustomed to her low sweet tones. I cannot conceive of how it must have pierced the Prince. He held her hand, having never released it after the dance, and I saw him lift it, as if for another kiss.

The Queen approached them then, surrounded by the most influential personages of the court, and her gaze, as it rested upon Sigfried, did not express the fondness to which he was accustomed. "My son," she said, and there was steel in her voice, "you are neglecting our most honored guest. And at her own betrothal party! Do you leave your cousin to me now, and dance with your bride-to-be."

But the Prince did not release Ylianna's hand. "Mother," he said, "you have always sworn that should my heart alight on another suitable—"

The Queen's color was high, her lips firm. "The question is irrelevant at this moment, my dear. Go and have your dance with Annaliesl."

I could not breathe. Ylianna's face was calm, her faith in Sigfried—and in the Queen's old promise—unassailed. But I could read the Queen's ambition and pride in the set of her shoulders.

Sigfried faced her. "You have always said that I should be free to choose anyone I cared for, that the arrangement could be unmade." His voice was true and clear, his face at once sober and shining with love. "And I choose—"

Old Lady Mulken pressed forward, her face bright

with malice. "You cannot mean to choose a girl who holds liaisons in the stable. With a footman, no less!"

The Prince turned on her, his fist clenched. "You shall not say such a thing!"

"Ah, but I do say it," Lady Mulken replied, "and several of my staff will swear to it as well! They have witnessed her late-night visits to the stable to consort with him!" She flung out her arm and pointed to me. "His name is Eriksen, and he has taken rooms above the stable, no doubt to facilitate his illicit affair with her."

Sigfried dropped Ylianna's hand and stood as though stunned by a terrible blow.

"No!" Ylianna cried. "He is not my lover, Sigfried. He is not! He is only my friend. My only friend."

"Seize that footman," the Queen ordered. Two of the palace guards took rough holds on my arms. I should have come to Ylianna's defense then, but I was far too horrified by Lady Mulken's allegations to speak. To think that I should have brought this on my lady!

Ylianna spoke again, her voice trembling. "It's true I went to the stables. He was teaching me to be a lady, you see, how to walk properly, and speak properly, and make polite conversation. I wanted you to love me, Sigfried. I wanted to be beautiful enough for you." She stretched out her arms to him, offering herself, with all the love that had driven her to this self-transformation. "See what I have done for you?"

The nobility, it seems, are even less forgiving of perfection than of defect. Sigfried looked at her for one long moment, and I saw his hunger for her, even if she did not. But when he spoke, he said, "Cousin, all you have accomplished is to ruin yourself."

I shall never forget Ylianna's face, not so long as I live (which requirement should not overtax my mind, given the circumstances). The marble purity of her countenance became colorless, and she stared at the Prince in wounded horror. He buried his face in his hands, and turned away from her.

She fled up the stairs, racing toward the summit of the tower. I wrested free of the guards and followed her, with the guardsmen and much of the court at my heels. Up and up the spiraling stone steps I ran, hearing her footsteps ahead of mine, fleeting, unhindered.

She was always swift, Ylianna.

I burst onto the rooftop and hurled myself after her, trying to catch her and hold her. But she was strong, as strong as the old Ylianna, though far wilder. As if my struggles were nothing, my grip insignificant, she flung herself from the battlement.

The sky was bright above and dark below, the valley circled with smoke black clouds. But, as she fell, each stitched feather of her gown sparked in the scant moonlight like sketched lightning. As she passed from my sight, she cried out. Her cry was a mournful note that streamed across the night, and I am not ashamed to say that my own voice echoed that trumpeting call.

Suddenly, the only sound was that of the wind whipping my sleeves. Sick at heart, I clung to the stone battlement and listened for the crushing impact of her body against the paving stones below. The guardsmen and courtiers stood behind me in uneasy silence.

But the sound that reached me was not that of a frail body crushed on stone; no, it was the sound of great wings beating the night air in vast, powerful surges. I leaped for the battlement and stared downward; one of the guards grasped my coat and held me fast.

And then, in the coursing moon-cast shadows of the valley, far beneath us, I saw—we all saw—a darker shadow rising, with feathers gleaming black and a long slim neck that stretched forth from between immense inky wings. She rose, with mighty surges of those great wings, spiraling up from the dark ground, circling the tower, upward, until she gleamed beside me for a moment, then soared overhead in an enormous wash of wind.

The black swan trumpeted, her voice ringing like a huge deep bell, and, in that sound, I heard Ylianna's voice again, just as it had been on the day I first saw her.

I threw myself after her, but the guardsman held me fast, and all I could do was call her name.

She whirled in the sky above us with a mad flurry of feathers and wind and wings that stroked the sky, circling, as if waiting for me—a moment, two—and then she wheeled about. My last glimpse was of a gleaming shadow racing the wind; an untamed soul winging north, toward the wild, welcoming countryside of her home.

Ylianna learned well this trick of self-alteration. Far better than I; for, with it, she earned her freedom. As I write this, here in the dungeon where I await my own fate, I can only pray that in the wild fastness of the north country, there is one who remembers me with kindness.

Recommended Reading

Fiction and Poetry

Katie Crackernuts, by Katherine Briggs

A charming short novel retelling the Katie Crackernuts tale, by one of the world's foremost folklore authorities.

Beginning with O, by Olga Broumas

Broumas' poetry makes use of many fairy tale motifs in this collection.

The Sun, the Moon and the Stars, by Steven Brust

A contemporary novel mixing ruminations on art and creation with a lively Hungarian fairy tale.

Possession, by A. S. Byatt

A Booker Prize winning novel that makes wonderful use of the Fairy Melusine legend.

Sleeping in Flame, by Jonathan Carroll

Excellent, quirky dark fantasy using the Rumplestiltskin tale.

The Bloody Chamber, by Angela Carter

A stunning collection of dark, sensual fairy tale retellings.

The Sleeping Beauty, by Hayden Carruth

A poetry sequence using the Sleeping Beauty legend.

Beyond the Looking Glass, edited by Jonathan Cott
A collection of Victorian fairy tale prose and poetry.

The Nightingale, by Kara Dalkey
An evocative Oriental historical novel based on the Hans Christian Andersen story.

Provencal Tales, by Michael de Larrabeiti
Rich, subtle, adult fairy tales based on French legends.

Jack the Giant-Killer and *Drink Down the Moon,* by Charles de Lint
Wonderful urban fantasy novels bringing "Jack" and magic to the streets of modern Canada.

Tam Lin, by Pamela Dean
A lyrical novel setting the old Scottish fairy story (and folk ballad) Tam Lin among theater majors on a midwestern college campus.

The King's Indian, by John Gardner
A collection of peculiar and entertaining stories using fairy tale motifs.

Blood Pressure, by Sandra M. Gilbert
A number of the poems in this powerful collection make use of fairy tale motifs.

The Seventh Swan, by Nicholas Stuart Gray
An engaging Scottish novel that starts off where the "Seven Swans" fairy tale ends.

Fire and Hemlock, by Diana Wynne Jones
A beautifully written, haunting novel that brings the Thomas the Rhymer and Tam Lin tales into modern-day England.

Thomas the Rhymer, by Ellen Kushner
A sensuous and musical rendition of this old Scottish story and folk ballad.

Red as Blood, Or Tales from the Sisters Grimmer, by Tanith Lee

A striking and versatile collection of adult fairy tale retellings.

Beauty, by Robin McKinley

Masterfully written, gentle and magical, this novel retells the story of Beauty and the Beast.

The Door in the Hedge, by Robin McKinley

The Twelve Dancing Princesses and The Frog Prince retold in McKinley's gorgeous, clear prose, along with two original tales.

Disenchantments, edited by Wolfgang Mieder

An excellent compilation of adult fairy tale poetry.

Kindergarten, by Peter Rushford

A contemporary British story beautifully wrapped around the Hansel and Gretel tale, highly recommended.

Transformations, by Anne Sexton

Sexton's brilliant collection of modern fairy tale poetry.

Trail of Stones, by Gwenn Strauss

Evocative fairy tale poems, beautifully illustrated by Anthony Browne.

Swan's Wing, by Ursula Synge

A lovely, magical fantasy novel using the Seven Swans fairy tale.

Beauty, by Sheri S. Tepper

Dark fantasy incorporating several fairy tales from an original and iconoclastic writer.

The Coachman Rat, by David Henry Wilson

Excellent dark fantasy retelling the story of Cinderella from the coachman's point of view.

Snow White and Rose Red, by Patricia C. Wrede
A charming Elizabethan historical novel retelling this romantic Grimm's fairy tale.
Briar Rose, by Jane Yolen
An unforgettable short novel setting the Briar Rose/Sleeping Beauty story against the background of World War II.
Don't Bet on the Prince, edited by Jack Zipes
A collection of contemporary feminist fairy tales compiled by a leading fairy tale scholar, containing prose and poetry by Angela Carter, Joanna Russ, Jane Yolen, Tanith Lee, Margaret Atwood, Olga Broumas and others.

Modern-day fairy tale creators

The Faber Book of Modern Fairy Tales, edited by Sara and Stephen Corrin
Gudgekin the Thistle Girl and Other Tales, by John Gardner
Mainly by Moonlight, by Nicholas Stuart Gray
Collected Stories, by Richard Kennedy
Heart of Wood, by William Kotzwinkle
Fairy Tales, by Alison Uttley
Tales of Wonder, by Jane Yolen

Non-fiction

The Power of Myth, by Joseph Campbell
The Erotic World of Fairy, by Maureen Duffy
"Womenfolk and Fairy Tales," by Susan Cooper
Essay in The New York Times Book Review, April 13, 1975

Beauty and the Beast: Visions and Revisions of an Old Tale, by Betsy Hearne
Once Upon a Time, collected essays by Alison Lurie
What the Bee Knows, collected essays by P. L. Travers
Problems of the Feminine in Fairy Tales, by Marie-Louise von Franz
Collected lectures originally presented at the C. G. Jung Institute
Touch Magic, collected essays by Jane Yolen
Fantasists on Fantasy, edited by Robert H. Boyer and Kenneth J. Zahorski
Includes Tolkien's "On Fairy Stories," G. K. Chesterton's "Fairy Tales," and other essays.

Fairy tale source collections

Old Wives' Fairy Tale Book, edited by Angela Carter
The Tales of Charles Perrault, translated by Angela Carter
Italian Folktales, translated by Italo Calvino
The Complete Hans Christian Andersen, edited by Lily Owens
The Maid of the North: Feminist Folk Tales from Around the World, edited by Ethel Johnston Phelps
Favorite Folk Tales from Around the World, edited by Jane Yolen
The Complete Brothers Grimm, edited by Jack Zipes
(For volumes of fairy tales from individual countries—Russian fairy tales, French, African, Japanese, etc.—see the excellent Pantheon Books Fairy Tale and Folklore Library.)